# Lies After Death

## K.J. Dando

Cahill Davis
Publishing

CAHILL DAVIS PUBLISHING

First published in Great Britain in 2023 by Cahill Davis Publishing Limited.

First published in paperback in Great Britain in 2023 by Cahill Davis Publishing Limited.

Printed and bound in Great Britain by Clays Ltd, Elcograf S.p.A

ISBN 978-1-915307-06-4 (eBook)

ISBN 978-1-915307-05-7 (Paperback)

Cahill Davis Publishing Limited

www.cahilldavispublishing.co.uk

For my wife Jo and daughters, Holly and Summer.

# Prologue

It was a few minutes after eight and almost four hours since the sun had set, on a cold and wet mid-November evening in South Wales. Beth Crane selected the phone symbol on the car's touch screen. She was driving through a narrow but well-lit street with cars parked on both sides of the road. Her recent call list appeared on the screen, and she selected the third option from the top labelled "Hubby". The music stopped playing and was replaced with the unmistakable long dial tone when making a call overseas.

As the second ring began, Beth's car approached the entrance of a country lane. Even though most of the leaves had fallen off the trees, the thick tangle of branches that extended over the road created a dense canopy. This, combined with the lack of any lighting in the lane, made it look as if she were heading towards a dark tunnel. Beth eased off the accelerator and slowed slightly. She even subconsciously ducked her head a little as the car passed beneath the branches and into the blackness. She flicked the stalk next to the steering wheel to activate her main beam headlights, illuminating the road in front of her. The ground was wet from earlier rain, with only a few small patches of black asphalt visible amongst the sodden mush of dead leaves.

Her husband's voice came through the speakers at the end of the fourth ring. "Hello, you."

"Hi, honey," Beth replied, relieved to hear his voice.

"Is everything okay?" Tom asked, his tone laced with concern.

"Oh no, sorry. I've woken you, haven't I?" She could just imagine Tom now, sat up in a four-poster bed in a fancy hotel room, or maybe even his own suite. He was currently away on a close protection detail for some wealthy business owners visiting Abu Dhabi. "I keep forgetting the time difference. What time is it there now?"

Tom chuckled. "Don't worry, it's fine. It's a little after midnight. Anyway, it's always good to hear your voice. Are you okay?"

"Yeah, I'm just on my way home, and I wanted to tell you how much I love you. You mean so much to me." Her voice broke slightly, and she blinked away the tears that sprang to her eyes. "I don't deserve you," she added, hoping that Tom wouldn't notice how emotional she was.

"That's sweet, and you, baby. It's just a couple more days and then I'll be back home with you."

"I really can't wait," she choked.

"Me neither. Where have you been tonight?"

Beth cleared her throat in an attempt to keep her emotions in check. "Oh, just out for dinner with a friend from work."

"A *friend* from work? Do I need to be jealous?"

Beth forced a laugh. "Yeah, right. I was with Ella."

"Now I'm definitely starting to get jealous," Tom joked. "You two have been inseparable these last few months."

Beth noticed a pair of headlights appear in her rear-view mirror, around a hundred yards or so behind. "Stop it. She's lovely, and we get on really well. You should be happy she's looking after me while you're away."

Tom chuckled. "I am, you know I'm just messing with you."

The headlights in the rear-view mirror became bigger a lot quicker than Beth had anticipated. Her heart rate quickened, and she felt an instant hit of adrenalin enter her system. She tried to focus on the winding road ahead but struggled to keep her eyes away from the golden globes growing in the mirror.

"Oh no," she uttered, her grip tightening on the steering wheel. "I think he's following me."

"Who's following you?" Concern was creeping into Tom's voice.

Beth was busy watching the headlights in the mirror. They weren't showing any signs of slowing, and she braced herself for impact. Thankfully, it didn't materialise. The driver applied the brakes at the last second and slowed.

"Beth, who's following you?"

The headlights quickly closed the gap again so that they appeared to be just a few inches from her rear window. She could hear the roar of the vehicle's engine. It was some kind of large SUV, and it dwarfed her little hatchback.

"Oh, nobody," she replied. "Just some guy with a bit of road rage. I think I may have cut in front of him on the roundabout earlier."

"Is he getting close to you?"

Beth was temporarily blinded when the SUV flashed its headlights just as she was looking directly into the rear-view mirror at them. She squinted and strained her eyes to look ahead and concentrate on the road. The headlights continued to flash behind her, filling her little hatchback with blinding light each time.

She grunted in frustration. "Yes, and now he's flashing me. I can't see properly."

"What an arsehole," Tom fumed over the speakers. "Listen, whatever you do, don't speed up and obviously don't stop. It sounds like he's trying to intimidate you. Just concentrate on the road and keep moving slowly. Is he still flashing?"

"Yes. What is he doing? He's an absolute psycho." Fear was beginning to seep into Beth's angry tone.

"Can you see the number plate? Or at least make out what make, model, or colour it is?"

"No. Nothing. It's pitch black. I think it's some kind of SUV. It looks big."

"Just try and stay calm. He can't do anything if you keep moving. He's not going to hit you and risk damaging his car. He's just trying to scare you. Don't let him. Just stay calm."

Another set of headlights appeared around two hundred yards in front, heading towards them. The flashing behind stopped. The country lane was extremely narrow; there was only enough space for one vehicle to pass at a time. Every fifty yards or so, it would widen on one side so that one of the cars could pull in to allow others to pass.

"A car's coming towards me. I might have to stop."

"Don't panic," Tom instructed. "Even if you do, it'll just be for a few seconds and then you'll be back on the move. He won't be able to do anything."

Beth watched as the SUV backed off slightly behind her. An area to her left opened up, and she pulled in as the headlights in front approached them. The SUV followed suit and stopped a few feet behind. In her peripheral vision, she noticed the car in front flash their headlights as a "thank you" when they passed by, and she naturally raised a hand to say "you're welcome", her eyes still fixed on the SUV behind.

The driver's door opened as soon as the car passed it, and the dark silhouette of a man got out, framed by the red glow coming from the taillights of the car that had just passed them as it continued down the lane. She immediately hit the accelerator and, after a few spins on the greasy surface, the tyres finally found some traction, and her small hatchback took off. The man was shouting, but she couldn't make out any words.

"What's happening?" Tom asked fervently.

Beth was too busy concentrating on the road ahead to answer. She just wanted to gain as much distance as possible.

"Beth, talk to me. What's happening?"

"He got out and started shouting at me," she blurted. The country lane curved to the right, and the SUV's headlights disappeared from view. "I'm just trying to get away from him."

"Is he still behind you?"

Beth was about to answer but stopped herself when the two globes reappeared in the rear-view mirror and sped towards her, even quicker than they had before. They started flashing from dipped to the main beam over and over again. Then, when he got to within a few feet of her rear bumper, the horn started blasting in short bursts.

"Is that him beeping his horn?"

"Yes." Beth's voice was shaky. "I'm scared, Tom."

"Listen to me carefully, Beth. Just keep driving slowly, don't speed up. Get through the lane and obviously don't turn into our house. Just keep driving and head to the police station. When you reach a main road with streetlights, try to take in as many details about the car as possible. If you get a view of the plate, try to memorise it. If he follows you to the station, great, the police can sort him out. If he doesn't, hopefully you'll have enough details so they can find him. Or better still, I can find him when I get back."

Beth could hear Tom's voice, but none of the words were going in. Her heart was pumping so hard it felt as if it were going to burst out of her chest. Her breaths were quick and shallow. The SUV was so close, she couldn't understand how it could get so close without actually hitting her. The sound of both engines racing, combined with the blasting horn, was beginning to reach deafening levels. Consciously, she knew that speeding up was the wrong thing to do, but subconsciously her foot applied more pressure onto the accelerator. She desperately wanted to get away, but the SUV wasn't letting up. Not even an inch. It stayed right on her rear bumper, lights still flashing, horn still blaring.

"*Beth*," Tom shouted. "Speak to me. What's going on?"

But Beth was completely oblivious to his voice. She was peering through the windscreen, trying not to be distracted by the flashing lights and the roaring noise. She focused solely on the road ahead, applying even more pressure onto the accelerator.

"*Beth*." There was desperation in Tom's voice. "*Please*. Tell me what's happening."

Suddenly, the flashing seemed to stop for a few seconds. Beth risked a glance in the mirror and then her eyes were hit with the full force of the main beams. It felt as if the light had scorched holes in the back of her eyes. She blinked frantically, trying to regain her vision, but all she could see was a big black circle ahead. She could just about make out the tree trunks rushing past on either side of the car in her peripheral vision, but there was a dark empty hole straight ahead. She had no idea that the lane was starting to curve to the left.

By the time she realised the hatchback was travelling off the road and up the embankment, it was too late. She stamped on the brake pedal, but the front wheels were already airborne and the rear tyres were on a mixture of dead, rotting leaves and wet grass. There was no traction to slow the momentum down. A drop on the other side of the embankment meant that the whole car eventually became airborne. Beth screamed as she sensed the weightlessness. The car twisted and began to turn on its side. Time itself seemed to almost stand still. She closed her eyes, tensed, and braced herself for impact.

They say in moments like this your whole life flashes before your eyes. But that wasn't the case for Beth. She didn't have time to think, she just felt a combination of regret and pure dread fill her entire being.

The hatchback was completely upside down when it struck the base of a giant beech tree. It was the classic case of the un-stoppable force versus the immovable object. Unfortunately, in this scenario, the immovable object won effortlessly. The beech tree stood strong and gallantly as the small hatchback crumpled into its trunk like an aluminium can being crushed against a wall. An eruption of exploding airbags, shattering glass, and the excruciating sound of metal being torn apart resonated around the woods. It was abruptly followed by a chilling silence.

The engine was no longer running; in fact, it was no longer in the engine bay. The impact had forced it back into the cabin. The wheels were no longer spinning, and all the electrics were ruined, leaving the wreckage in total darkness. If someone were to drive past, they would have no idea it was even there. No one would know the absolute carnage that had just taken place.

But one person knew.

That person stopped his SUV and stepped out onto the road. He ran back to where he'd seen the hatchback leave the road and scrambled up the embankment, slipping on the slimy surface. He looked down but could only see black. His eyes strained to adjust to the darkness, but their efforts were futile. No light reached the forest floor.

He took out a bunch of keys from his pocket. There was a small LED torch keyring attached to the bunch. He switched it on and used the small yet powerful beam of light to guide him as he clambered down the other side of the embankment. He could faintly smell petrol in the damp, cold air. It was getting stronger with each step closer. He focused the light on the wreckage and took a sharp intake of breath. It was difficult to imagine that this distorted lump of broken glass and metal had been a nice little hatchback driving on the road just a few moments ago.

He stepped around the left side. Now that the car was upside down, this was the driver's side. He crouched down and aimed the beam from the torch into the car, then immediately turned away, clamping his eyes shut and sucking in a breath through gritted teeth. With just a glance, it was obvious the driver had sustained catastrophic injuries that no human could have possibly survived. The man rubbed his eyes, trying to erase the grotesque image.

"I'm so sorry," he whispered.

He stood and moved to step away when something caught his eye. It was a glimmer of light obscured by a couple of leaves a few yards away, just past the beech tree. He stepped towards it and started to hear a strange noise. It sounded faint and tinny. A little like a man's voice shouting from the bottom of a well. As he stepped closer and bent down, he realised it was a phone.

He brushed the leaves off and picked it up. Now he could clearly hear a man's voice shouting.

"*Beth*." There was absolute despair in the man's voice. "*Beth*."

Remarkably, the phone had survived the crash and seemed to be fully functional. Somehow, it must have been thrown from the car during the impact and landed on the sodden dead leaves that carpeted the forest floor.

The man tapped the red icon on the screen to end the call. He proceeded to depress and hold down the power button on the side to switch the phone off, then shoved it into his pocket. He hastily made his way back up the embankment and sprinted to his SUV. He jumped in and, before his door was even fully closed, the chunky tyres bit through the layer of dead leaves and down into the asphalt. The SUV sped away up the lane with one final roar of its powerful engine.

Beth's heart had stopped beating the moment her hatchback struck the tree. The other smaller heart inside her continued to beat a little longer. A tiny heart that fought valiantly for its own survival but unfortunately faced a losing battle. Without its mother's support, the little heartbeat weakened until it eventually faded away.

# Chapter One

## Almost five years later...

Tom Crane hardly took notice of the impressive properties lining both sides of the road as he drove his dark grey pickup truck through one of the most affluent areas of Cardiff. He was only paying attention to the property numbers. Some were on the front doors, and others, typically where the house was set further back from the road, were displayed on plaques on the front wall. And even though the street was well-lit, most of the plaques were further illuminated with LEDs.

Crane was peering out of the driver's window at the even numbers, ignoring the odds ones on the left. He slowed the truck and flicked the stalk to indicate before turning into the driveway of number sixty-two. The home of the Welsh first minister. The first minister of Wales was the elected leader of the Welsh Government. Not that this meant or changed anything; a client was a client. Nothing more, nothing less.

He drove through two red brick pillars, the black iron gates with gold spears at the top left wide open behind him. The surface of the driveway appeared to have been recently finished with a resin compound, meaning the pickup's all-weather tyres rolled silently over the smooth surface. Well-manicured lawns lay on either side. The driveway opened up wide for parking as it got closer to the large double-bay fronted home. Two cars were already parked up facing the house—a red Range Rover Evoque on the left and a black BMW saloon on the right. Crane came to a stop behind the Evoque.

It had been a warm and sunny mid-august day, but at almost 10 p.m. and a little over an hour since the sun had set, the temperature had dropped a few degrees. It wasn't cold; there was only a slight chill beginning to creep into the night air. Crane stepped out of the truck and closed the door behind him. Standing at six feet two, he was tall but not too tall that he would stand out in a crowd. He was athletic and trim like a cruiserweight in boxing. Again, nothing that would stand out too much in a crowd. Not underweight, not overweight, and not bulky like a bodybuilder. He was handsome, in a rugged way, with neatly trimmed dark hair. He wore grey denim trousers, dark walking boots, and a burgundy T-shirt. Comfortable, practical, and easy to blend in. Nothing too memorable. His only standout feature was his piercing ice-blue eyes.

He walked towards the house and noticed a large dent on the bonnet of the Evoque, highlighted by the security lights shining down on it. As he reached the couple of steps leading up to the front door, it opened. A slim man around five feet ten dressed in a navy suit and a red tie stood before him. He looked to be in his mid to late twenties, blonde hair gelled in a side parting.

"Are you the fixer?" he asked.

Crane hesitated before nodding. After four years of freelancing as a fixer, the term "Fixer" still seemed a little funny to him. He often referred to himself as a consultant, but essentially clients would come to him with a problem and he would help make their problem go away for a considerable fee. So, admittedly, "Fixer" probably was a more accurate title for the work that he did.

"I'm Adrian," the man said, offering his hand. "I'm the first minister's personal assistant."

"Crane." He took Adrian's hand and gave it a firm squeeze. "What needs fixing?"

"You'd better come in." Adrian moved aside to let him past.

Crane stepped in and waited for Adrian to close the door before following him into the living room. The decor inside the house was old-fashioned, with lots of colours, and even more patterns. There was a well-dressed lady standing in the bay window, in front of some very busy red and gold curtains. She had a large glass of red wine in her hand. The bottle, with half its contents gone, stood alone on an enormous mahogany coffee table in the centre of the room. It was difficult for Crane to put an age on the woman. She was wearing a lot of makeup and he suspected she took regular trips to a cosmetic clinic for botox injections to help drag back the years. She could have been in her late forties, but he wouldn't have been surprised if she was actually a decade or so older. A young man, probably early twenties, with brown scruffy hair sat on the sofa. He was bent forward with his head in his hands, wearing skinny jeans and a black hoodie. Crane could instantly feel the tension when he entered the room.

"Patricia and Lloyd, this is Mr Crane. The fixer," Adrian announced.

"Thank you for coming at such short notice," Patricia said. Her voice was controlled, but her eyes were showing the strain.

Crane nodded. "How can I help?"

She took a gulp of red wine before replying. "Well, my son has had an accident. You see, he borrowed my car earlier today to go and see one of his friends. Then, when he was on his way back, he..." She looked at her son and shook her head. "I can't even say it, Lloyd. You tell him."

Lloyd lifted his head. His eyes were puffy and bloodshot, as though he'd either been crying or rubbing them. "I was driving back from my friend's house, who lives on the other side of Cardiff, near the Principality Sta—"

Tom's get-to-it glare had the desired effect of cutting Lloyd off and pushing him to the point.

"Anyway, on the way back, I mostly stuck to all the main roads, but to save a little time, I cut through the quiet road that goes behind the school grounds. There's a part of it where it opens up a bit so that you have the woods on the one side and the school playing fields on the other. The sun was going down by the fields and it was really, really low and shining right in my eyes. I mean, I couldn't see a thing. Seriously, it blinded me. I slowed down but..." His voice trailed off and he started to fidget. "It wasn't my fault."

"*Shut up*," Patricia spat. "Of course it was your fault. *All* of this is *your* fault."

"What was she even doing there?" Lloyd retorted, crossing his arms like a sulky child. "There's no pavement for pedestrians. She must have been walking right in the middle of the road. Who does that? How was I meant to know she'd be there?"

"That's your defence?" Patricia asked, raising an arm in exasperation. "*She* shouldn't have been walking there. It was all *her* fault, was it?" She turned her attention to Crane. "In case you haven't put two and two together, he hit a young girl with my car."

"That explains the dent on the bonnet," Crane replied matter-of-factly. "What happened after you hit her?"

Lloyd rubbed his face vigorously before continuing. "I stopped, obviously. I didn't know what I'd hit. I thought maybe it was a fox or maybe a sheep that had escaped from a local farm or something. I mean, I knew it was something big, but..." He lowered his gaze to the floor and took a deep breath. "But I never thought it would be a person. She was just lying there, in the middle of the road. All twisted and not moving. I was going to call an ambulance, but she was already..." He put his face in his hands.

"Dead," Patricia finished for him, saying the word as if it left a bitter taste in her mouth. "She's dead, Mr Crane. Lloyd killed her."

"Where is she?" Crane asked.

"In the boot of my car," she replied, turning away and taking another mouthful of red wine.

Crane turned to Adrian. "Show me."

He followed Adrian out to the Evoque. Apart from the open gate for the entrance to the driveway, tall Leylandii hedging surrounded the entire perimeter of the property, providing complete privacy from potential nosy neighbours. Adrian pressed a button on the key, and the lights flashed on the red Evoque, the tailgate clicked, and it raised open electronically. There she was, illuminated by the artificial light from inside the boot. She looked young—Crane guessed she was around sixteen, but she could have been younger. He had planned to check for a pulse, just in case, but as soon as he laid eyes on her, he knew that it would be futile. He'd seen a lot of dead bodies in his time, and unfortunately this poor young girl was another one to add to the list.

Her eyes were open wide and looked as though they were made of glass. She had a ghastly, pained expression frozen on her face and her skin already had a pale grey hue. Thin trails of dark, dried blood came from both of her nostrils and another came out of one corner of her mouth. She was wearing a yellow summer dress with a blue floral pattern, one white sandal remained on her left foot, and the other sandal seemed to have been thrown haphazardly into the back of the luggage compartment with her. Her long auburn hair had been tied up in a high ponytail, but it was now loose and limp, caused either by the impact of the accident or from being thrown into the boot of the car. Which was exactly how she looked—like she'd just been tossed into the boot of the car without any care, without any respect, without an ounce of remorse.

Crane took his phone out of his pocket and took a photograph.

"What are you doing?" Adrian asked warily. "Why are you taking pictures?"

"I'll explain when we get back inside," Crane replied. "Close the boot."

Adrian did as he was told. The lights flashed again before the electric motor hummed and the tailgate lowered until it locked shut. Crane walked around the car and took another picture of the front, then he took one of the dent on the bonnet and another one of a crack he found in the headlight on the driver's side. Adrian watched him dubiously the whole time. Judging by the damage on the car, Crane guessed he must have been travelling at over forty miles per hour when he struck the girl. Possibly even closer to fifty. A lot faster than he should have been driving for a cut-through road. Certainly too fast if you're blinded by the sun. Reckless.

"Open the driver's door for me."

Adrian once again did as he was told. Crane, without touching the car, leaned in and had a quick look around. Apart from a packet of chewing gum inside the centre console cup holder and a can of deodorant on the floor of the passenger footwell, it was relatively clean and tidy.

"Okay." He nodded. "Let's go back inside."

Adrian locked the Evoque, and they both went back into the house and back into the living room. Patricia was still standing in the window bay; Lloyd was still on the sofa with his head in his hands. Crane noticed that Patricia's wine glass had been refilled. The bottle was still in the same place on the coffee table, but it was now down to its final quarter.

Crane walked up to Lloyd. "Stand up."

Lloyd looked up at him. "What?"

"You heard me. Stand up."

Lloyd pushed himself up off the sofa. Once fully standing, he swayed slightly, a little unsteady on his feet. He looked down at the floor like a child being scolded by a teacher.

"Look at me," Crane instructed.

Lloyd was a few inches shorter than Crane. He raised his head and looked up until they made eye contact.

"Okay. Sit back down."

Crane stepped back as Lloyd flopped back down on the sofa. He turned his attention to Patricia.

"I can't help you."

"What?" Patricia's brow furrowed "What do you mean you can't help us?"

"Sorry." Crane held his hands up. "I'll rephrase that. I don't *want* to help you."

"What are you talking about? You're a fixer. This is a problem, and *you*"—she jabbed her index finger in his direction—"need to fix it."

"Let me explain," Crane said coldly, glaring at Patricia's finger. "I get the impression that your version of fixing this problem is by making that young girl's body disappear, fixing up your car, and then you all carry on with your lives like nothing happened."

"That's exactly how we want you to fix it," Lloyd chipped in.

"Look." Patricia raised her hand to Lloyd as a signal for him to be quiet. "I get it. This is a big job; you want big money. How much are we talking? What's your price?"

Crane shook his head. "It has nothing to do with money. It's simply down to morals and principles."

Patricia snorted. "Yeah, right. You're a fixer with morals and principles? Come on, Mr Crane, stop playing games and tell me how much you want." She bent down, placed her wine glass on the coffee table, and dragged a large burgundy leather handbag out from underneath. Conveniently, a chequebook and pen were at the top and within easy reach. She stood up straight, opened the chequebook, and looked at Crane with an arched brow. "Forty thousand? Fifty? We have very deep pockets."

"It's not about the money, Patricia. You can keep it," Crane said, keeping his eyes away from the chequebook to make his lack of interest clear. "In fact, I think you'll probably find that your money is part of the problem. It's one of the main reasons you've ended up with an entitled brat of a son who thinks he can go around getting high on drugs, kill an innocent young girl, and get away with it without any repercussions. Which it seems he can because he knows Mummy will come along with her big chequebook and make it all go away."

"*Hey*," Lloyd cried out, turning to Patricia and shaking his head. "I haven't been taking drugs. Don't listen to him, Mum."

"She isn't stupid, Lloyd. You might think you fooled her by spraying yourself with deodorant and chewing a piece of gum before you came back in the house, but whatever you've been smoking is radiating from you. You stink, and so does the car." Crane looked down at Lloyd disdainfully, as if he were nothing more than a skid mark on the seat of the sofa. "Just take a look at yourself in the mirror; your pupils are so dilated I've got no idea what colour your eyes are even meant to be."

Lloyd jumped up from the sofa. "This is bull—"

"*Shut up*," Patricia yelled, "and sit down." She took a breath to steady herself before continuing. "He's right, Lloyd. You're not fooling anybody. You do stink and your pupils are the size of dinner plates, for Christ's sake." She took another sip of wine. "Look, I'll admit Lloyd has some issues, and yes, it probably would be good for him to take responsibility for his actions a bit more. But at the end of the day, he's my boy. I can't let him go to prison."

"No, you can't," replied Crane. "But let's not pretend you want to keep him out of prison for his benefit. It's because you don't want this to affect your and your husband's reputations. It wouldn't look good for the first minister to have a son go to prison for killing a young girl under the influence of drugs, would it?" Crane paused, but only for a second. He wasn't going to give her an opportunity to respond. Not yet anyway. "The papers would have a field day. It would certainly be an embarrassing topic of conversation for you at your posh dinner parties. I can see it now, all of your so-called friends at your private members' club and your fancy health club and your husband's golf club. They'll love it. I'm sure they'll all have a good laugh and gossip at your expense."

"How dare you." Patricia's face reddened to a deep shade of crimson. "Throwing accusations around and judging me. Judging my family. How dare you. I love my son, and I'm doing this for him. He means the world to me."

"I'm sure the poor girl that has been dumped in the back of your car is loved. She's someone's daughter, someone's granddaughter. She's someone's world too. But that doesn't matter to you, does it? It doesn't matter to you that a young girl has lost her life tonight, lost her entire future. All because your drugged-up son decided to get behind the wheel of a car and drive like a lunatic." It was Crane's turn to jab his index finger towards Patricia. "You don't care that her family will have no idea what happened to her. That they will spend the rest of their lives desperately searching for her. Desperate to know what happened. Desperate for some kind of closure. As long as you and *your* family are okay, and as long as your privileged lifestyle doesn't have to change at all. To hell with everyone else."

The veins in Patricia's neck and temples protruded as if they were about to burst. "Get the *fuck* out of my house."

Crane bowed slightly and tipped an invisible hat. "With pleasure."

Lloyd turned and looked up at his mother like a scared little boy. "What are we going to do now, Mum? I can't go to prison."

"Don't worry," she said, "we'll find a real fixer who can help us."

"Unfortunately not," Crane said, pulling his phone out of his pocket. "I took the liberty of taking a few pictures of your car. I got some decent snaps of the body, clearly showing your number plate too. I even have a few close-ups of the damage on the bonnet and the headlight."

Patricia looked at Adrian, contempt burning in her eyes. "Is this true? Did you let him take pictures?"

Adrian nodded timidly. "He said he would explain why later."

"Idiot." Patricia scowled and turned away from him.

"I've also recorded this conversation." Crane turned the phone so that they could all see the voice recorder was active. "So this is what's going to happen next—I'm going to leave and you're going to call the police. When they arrive, you're going to tell them exactly what happened. Every little detail."

"What if we don't?" Lloyd challenged.

"Put it this way, if you're not in a police station confessing in an interview room within the hour, I'm going to start preparing an anonymous package for them. It will include pictures and an audio file that will clearly show not only what you did, but also how you and your mum tried to cover it all up. I think a few media companies would appreciate a copy of it too. I could be wrong, but I suspect you're all bright enough to know which scenario will cause the least amount of damage."

He went to walk out of the room, but Adrian stepped in front of the doorway and placed a firm hand on his chest. Crane looked down at the hand, then back up and into Adrian's eyes.

"Really?"

Adrian quickly removed his hand and stepped aside.

"Say hello to the first minister for me."

"He isn't here," Adrian said. "he's in London, getting prepared for meetings tomorrow."

Crane raised a brow. "Really? Does he often go to London for meetings without his personal assistant?"

"I'm meeting him there tomorrow."

"Of course you are," was what Crane said; *plausible deniability* was what he thought.

As he walked out through the hallway, Patricia called out, "You'll regret this, Mr Crane."

"I doubt that very much," Crane called back, closing the front door firmly behind himself.

# Chapter Two

The pickup's tyres crunched over the loose gravel as Crane turned into the driveway leading to Ricky Burr's barn. He had met Ricky over seven years ago on a close protection detail for an electronics-based technology company. Ricky had been the "computer genius" of the four-man team sent to Beijing to pitch a new app they had created to a number of Chinese tech firms, with Crane hired to protect them throughout their trip. Ricky's full background check on Crane within an hour of them meeting each other had both impressed and intrigued Crane.

At the end of those sixty minutes, Ricky knew what schools Crane had attended, he knew his father had died in a motorcycle accident when he was two, and he knew his mother had died after an arduous battle with cancer when he was twenty-six. He knew that he'd joined the army as an engineer at sixteen straight from school, and although it was classified, he even knew that Crane had later served in the Special Reconnaissance Regiment before leaving to pursue a career in close protection. Not only did he know what Crane's bank details were, he told him exactly how much money was in his current account, right down to the penny. He had even put a tracking app on Crane's mobile phone without him knowing, which Crane thought was impressive, but it also scared the hell out of him.

During that trip to Beijing, they'd struck up a close friendship, and in recent years their relationship had inadvertently evolved into a joint business venture too.

Crane parked just a few yards from the front door, his pickup the only vehicle on the driveway. The barn had been completely restored and renovated around three and a half years ago, just before Ricky moved in. It was now a fresh and modern-looking property.

As Crane approached the front door, there was an audible clunk as the electric motorised multipoint locks on the door disengaged—Ricky took the security of the barn very seriously due to the abundance of valuable computer equipment inside. Crane pushed down on the chunky steel handle to enter.

Inside, the barn was very spacious and all open plan. There was a kitchen and dining area to the left and a work area at the back, where the rear wall was practically filled with computer monitors and other electrical items Crane couldn't identify, let alone work out what they were for. A spiral staircase was dead centre, which led up to what looked like a balcony but was actually the sleeping quarters. Again, it was all open plan up there amongst the huge wooden beams. To Crane's right was a sitting area, with big leather sofas surrounding a TV the size of a billboard, and that was where all five-eight of Ricky stood with a big grin that was barely visible inside his bushy brown beard and his arms open wide in a greeting. What appeared to be some kind of shoot-em-up video game was paused on the enormous screen behind him. Ricky was slightly overweight, mostly due to the lack of any kind of physical exercise more than his diet. Although his diet wasn't the healthiest either. Crane had tried to entice Ricky on walks many times, but it was clear to everyone except Ricky and his denial that he was suffering from a very real case of agoraphobia.

"How did it go with the first minister?"

"Good question," Crane replied. "When they called, did you ask them what their problem was?"

"No, it was the first minister's personal assistant. I just assumed it was some kind of political issue. Why? What happened?"

"And why shouldn't you assume?"

Ricky rolled his eyes. "I make an *ass* out of *you* and *me*."

Crane cracked a smile and dropped himself down on one of the sofas. "I'm just busting your balls, I would have thought the same, but it ended up being a job that I had to turn down."

"Really? Why?" Ricky asked, seating himself on the sofa opposite. "Morals and principles?"

"Morals and principles," Crane agreed before explaining exactly what had happened with the first minister's wife, son, and personal assistant.

"That's horrendous," Ricky exclaimed after Crane had finished talking, scrunching his face up in disgust. "What a bunch of scumbags. Where was the first minister when all this was happening? Wasn't he there?"

"Oh, he was definitely there, but I didn't see him. I think he was hiding upstairs. His assistant told me that he was in London getting ready for meetings tomorrow."

Ricky raised a cynical brow. "Surely his assistant would be with him?"

"Exactly."

"Plausible deniability?"

Crane nodded. "That's what I was thinking."

"I'm sorry." Ricky sighed. "I should have asked more questions when they called."

"Maybe not," Crane said, with a single-shoulder shrug. "It all worked out for the best in the end. The girl's family will now get some closure, which I know doesn't sound like much, but it's certainly better than not knowing what happened to her. On top of that, if the British judicial system works, Lloyd will be made to pay for what he did. If you'd asked them more questions over the phone and then turned the job down, they may have found someone else willing to cover it all up for them."

"That's true."

Crane yawned and stretched. "I'm going to take a long weekend off. So, unless someone calls you with a problem that could result in the world coming to an end, I'm on radio silence until Tuesday."

"I'm hearing you loud and clear." Ricky gave a thumbs up.

Crane pushed himself with effort off the sofa, ready to leave. "How about we go to the pub for a pint tomorrow night?" He already knew what the answer would be, but he felt a need to still try his luck, hoping for some sort of miracle.

Ricky visibly squirmed. "I can't, sorry. I've got a few things to sort out."

It was Crane's turn to raise a cynical brow. "Really?" He looked around the almost obsessively clean and tidy barn. They didn't have any work on and Ricky hadn't mentioned any new clients getting in touch, hence the long weekend off. He didn't have a girlfriend and hobbies didn't count as "sorting things out", so what could he possibly mean? "Like what?"

"Don't look at me like that. You don't know what I get up to when you're not here."

"Maybe not, but I have a good idea."

"Go on, then," Ricky said. "What do you think I get up to when you're not here?"

"I think you spend all your time alternating between playing video games and masturbating vigorously to hardcore porn."

They both burst out laughing.

"You know me too well," said Ricky, struggling to breathe from laughing so hard.

He was still laughing when Crane left the barn and the door closed behind him.

Standing at 271 metres above sea level, some geographers would argue that Caerphilly Mountain technically wasn't a mountain, being twenty-nine metres short of their 300-metre requirement, but those who ventured around the popular walking routes of the summit considered the title to be appropriate and well deserved. Around the peak, people were treated to spectacular views of South Wales. The one side looked down onto the valley and town of Caerphilly, which boasted the largest castle in Wales and the second largest in the UK; the other side displayed stunning views across the city of Cardiff, all the way down to the Severn Estuary.

As Crane turned off the main mountain road near the summit of Caerphilly Mountain, he pressed a button on his key fob. The electric front gates parted as he approached the entrance of his home and were open wide enough for him to drive his truck straight through by the time he reached them. He'd done it so many times it had now become a habit that was timed to perfection. His driveway led to a double garage, which was already occupied by two other vehicles, so the pickup was always left outside. It was the workhorse, albeit a workhorse that was less than a year old.

Crane's home had only been built a little over six years ago. He had bought the land with Beth just as he was leaving the forces and starting his career in close protection. It had taken the best part of three stressful years to plan, design, and build the large four-bedroom property. All worth it. Contemporary in style, it had striking, clean lines, with light grey stone complemented by sections of dark grey wood siding and lots of glass.

They had planned for it to be their forever home, the home they were going to start and raise a family in together. Unfortunately, they'd only got to spend a little over a year enjoying it together before those plans were stolen from them. Losing Beth was heartbreaking enough, but finding out after the post-mortem that she'd been pregnant at the time truly broke him. He kept thinking back to the emotion she'd been trying to hold back on the phone that night. She would have been desperate to tell him, but she wouldn't have wanted to tell him over the phone—not something of that magnitude. She may have even been a little nervous to tell him. They'd discussed starting a family but hadn't officially agreed to start trying; they were waiting for "the perfect time". *Does the perfect time even exist?*

Over the last couple of years, Crane had considered selling up and maybe downsizing; after all, the house was far too big for him on his own. But he just couldn't bring himself to do it. Too much had gone into creating and building it and he also felt as if he would be betraying Beth's memory. Technically it was only bricks and mortar, but it was their bricks and mortar. And even if you took all those reasons away, the truth was he loved it. It was his dream home that he'd built from scratch, and he couldn't imagine himself living anywhere else.

Crane unlocked the front door and then held his alarm fob against the unit to deactivate it as he stepped in. He locked the door behind him and then reactivated the alarm. In his line of work, he'd learned a long time ago that you could never be too cautious.

The foyer of the house contained a wide elegant staircase leading up to the first floor, but Crane went left and into a spacious open-plan kitchen-diner. The whole house was decorated in a clean almost clinical style using mostly whites and greys, with the odd splash of colour from the cushions on the sofa and several landscape paintings on the walls. The kitchen had large white floor tiles, light grey cupboards, and solid white marble worktops.

Crane checked the time on his watch—five minutes to midnight. He shrugged. It was almost Friday and the start of his long weekend off, so why not treat himself to a nightcap? He walked around the island in the middle of the kitchen and grabbed a large tumbler out of a cupboard. Next, he stepped sideways to the large American-style fridge freezer and added two large ice cubes to the glass before heading to his whisky cupboard, which was the furthest cupboard from the double oven and its heat. A number of bottles stared out at him. He took a minute viewing all the bottles before finally settling on one of his favourites, a single malt Welsh whisky, matured in bourbon barrels and finished in ex-Madeira casks. He poured three fingers and then took out a bottle of ginger wine from the fridge and added three fingers to the whisky. Equal measures. The perfect whisky Mac. He took a sip and savoured the heat and the sweetness.

He took his drink upstairs and into the master bedroom, placing it on the bedside table so he could undress. An involuntary sigh escaped him as he sat on the bed, the situation from today taking him back to the past, back to losing Beth, and even though he knew it wasn't a good idea before bed, he opened an album on his phone that he had filled with pictures of Beth. He flicked through the pictures slowly, taking each one in. A picture of her on a beach in Spain, wearing sunglasses and holding a colourful cocktail, her long brunette hair flowing to one side in the warm breeze, smiling without a care in the world. Another one of them together at the top of Mount Snowdon, wrapped up warm in woolly hats and scarfs, surrounded by ice and snow. He remembered climbing it with her like it were yesterday. Enough time had passed that he was now able to look at the pictures without tears, but he still felt the familiar lump in his throat coming back.

He drained the whisky, closed the album, and headed into the ensuite to shower and brush his teeth. Afterwards, he turned out the lights and slid into bed. He connected his phone to the bedroom's Bluetooth speaker and started to play a relaxing guided meditation. He had been struggling with sleeping for a few years now; his mind seemed to constantly be on the go. Whenever he stopped, there was a faint hum or buzz inside his head. He joked sometimes that he was so highly strung he was a knot and he needed some help to unwind. Tonight, he had the warmth from the whisky and a soothing voice playing over the speaker. They both helped him to drift off in just a few minutes.

# Chapter Three

Crane's body clock woke him up at six, but he forced himself to stay in bed and doze until a little after eight. The first thing he did was check the news headlines on his phone. The top headline read, "First Minister's Son Involved in a Traffic Accident". It went on to explain that there were reports of a young girl losing her life in the incident. The police were in the very early stages of their investigation, and the first minister's son was cooperating fully with the police. *Of course he is*, thought Crane.

He put on a pair of shorts and a running T-shirt, then went downstairs and fixed himself a bowl of muesli and a coffee. He didn't want to exercise on an empty stomach, although he didn't want to exercise too soon after eating either, so he waited around twenty minutes before starting some dynamic stretches. Once he'd got a bit of blood flowing and loosened his muscles a little, he set off for a quick jog around the mountain trails. It was a route he knew well, just under five miles in total, with a good mix of inclines and declines. It took him just under thirty minutes—not too shabby for a warmup.

It was a radiant summer morning with clear blue skies in every direction. The sun was warm, but the fresh mountain air made it comfortable and cool, which was perfect for some high-intensity training. Crane ran around to the back of the house and unlocked a set of bifold doors that opened into the gym room. He went inside to fetch a pair of dumbbells. Today, he was going to make the most of the weather and the fresh air.

He took the weights around to the side of the house where he'd built a frame out of scaffolding bars. The frame consisted of two horizontal bars, one of which was overhead and the other around waist height. He used it for two of his favourite exercises—chin-ups and inverted rows. A lot of people spent too much time doing pushing exercises and neglected the pulling movement for their backs. Not Crane. He knew the importance of creating balance throughout the whole body.

He preferred using bodyweight exercises whenever possible, and this workout was no different. He used a combination of bodyweight exercises and a couple of exercises that required the dumbbells, completing five different exercises that incorporated every body part and utilised every range of motion. After five rounds, he grabbed a bottle of water from the kitchen, then repeated another five rounds. To finish, he went into the gym room and went six rounds with the heavy bag, which hung from a reinforced section of the ceiling in the centre of the room. It was a brutal workout, but Crane relished the feeling of the endorphins flooding his system.

He walked around the garden with his hands on his head to open up his chest and inhaled deeply to cool down and recover. Drenched in sweat, he closed his eyes and tilted his head up towards the sun, enjoying its warming rays on his face.

Before heading inside, he grabbed his keys out of the bifold doors and walked around to the front of the house and down the driveway, pressing a button on his fob. The electric gates silently parted towards him. Built into the stone wall just outside the gate was a mailbox. He used a small key to unlock it and grabbed everything inside. He hadn't emptied it for a few days, so there was more inside than he'd expected. He was only just about able to grab all the letters and leaflets inside with one hand and then he locked it back up and headed up the driveway. The gates closed smoothly and soundlessly behind him; they were timed to automatically close after thirty seconds.

Once inside, he dropped the mail on the island in the kitchen and grabbed another water, this time in a glass and the water coming from the filter that was built into the fridge. He leaned against the island to sort through the mail, putting his drink down next to him. First was a menu from a local takeaway, which he filed into the recycling. Next was a charity bag collecting clothes to raise money for cancer research, which he toyed with for a minute before finally putting it to the side; despite being pretty sure he didn't have any clothes to donate, he always felt disrespectful throwing charity bags straight into the recycling. Meaning it would most likely still end up in the recycling, just not today. The next envelope was addressed to "The Occupier", with the logo of a broadband company. He didn't need any time to consider what to do with that one—into the recycling it went. As he went to grab the next envelope, he stopped, his hand hovering just above it. It was a white envelope, standard letter size, but it had no postage stamp and no address. Normally, hand-delivered letters weren't that unusual, but glued to the front and centre of this envelope were five small square pieces of glossy paper, most likely cut from magazines. All the letters were different, either in size, font, or colour. The five letters spelled out his name.

Crane tore it open and pulled out a letter. As he did, something dropped onto the worktop. It was a cardboard drink coaster, the kind you would find on tables in every single bar, club, and cafe up and down the country. This one was jet black. One word—*"Corkers"*—was written across it in a white fancy font. Maybe it was a drink brand, or maybe it was the name of the bar it had come from. He unfolded the single sheet of white A4 paper from the envelope. On it were six rectangular pieces of glossy paper, similar to the ones on the envelope, neatly cut and glued to it. Six words, each a different size, font, or colour. *"I know who was following her"*.

As he stared at the words, it was as though the world around him dissolved away. It was just him, the letter, and a wave of adrenalin. So many questions raced through his mind. His immediate thought was to check the security camera footage to see if he could find out who had posted the letter. There were seven CCTV cameras around the house, which all had the ability to record up to thirty days of rolling footage, but not one of them recorded anything outside the property grounds, particularly at the front. The engineer who'd fitted the security system had advised him that because it was a public road, it could cause him some legal issues if he had cameras out there recording. Apparently, some people get very sensitive about their privacy and don't like to be recorded. Which Crane empathised with, but it didn't help him in his current predicament. There was one camera outside the grounds, built into the intercom system, but it was only activated when someone pressed the button on the intercom, and even then, it didn't have the ability to record.

He grabbed his phone and typed "Corkers" into the search engine. The first page of results came up with a number of different businesses, which were mostly based in England. He typed in "Corkers Wales" and hit the search button again. This time, several different businesses came up in the results, all based in Wales, but nothing that seemed to fit. He tried again with "Corkers Wales Bar". The top result was a business listing with an address in Cardiff City centre. It listed the business activities as bar, food, and dancing. There was a phone number but no website. Unusual in this day and age to have a business, let alone a bar, without a website. He closed down the browser and dialled Ricky.

Ricky answered after two rings. "I thought you were on radio silence?"

"Me too," Crane replied, "but I've just received a letter."

He described the letter and the coaster to Ricky as he played with the corners of the A4 page.

"Is it worth seeing if it's got any fingerprints on it?"

Crane considered it for a second and then huffed dejectedly. "I could be wrong, but I would assume someone who goes to the effort of cutting and gluing bits of a magazine on a letter is being quite conscious about not leaving any fingerprints."

Ricky laughed. "What happens when you assume?"

"Touché, Mr Burr. Touché," said Crane, nodding with a wry grin.

"You're probably right though. I doubt there's anything there."

"Can you look into Corkers Bar for me?" Crane placed the letter facedown on the kitchen island and picked up the drink coaster. He turned it over in his hand, inspecting it closely as he spoke. "There's no website, and I can't see much about it online. Just try and find out whatever you can, no rush."

"Leave it to me."

# Chapter Four

Crane had been staring at the anonymous letter for so long that his vision was starting to become unfocused. *Who posted it? Do they really know who was following her? Why wait until now to make contact?* He'd managed a hot shower and some breakfast, but he hadn't been able to get the letter out of his mind, so here he was again, back sitting at the kitchen island.

A buzz sounded loudly in the foyer, and he jumped in his seat, the numbness in his backside now becoming a herd of tingles. The buzz from the intercom for the front gates was a sound he rarely heard. He stood from the stool and made his way out of the kitchen and to the wall next to the front door. The intercom's seven-inch screen was built into the wall, with a brushed chrome surround and a row of control buttons along the bottom. Crane's eyes immediately narrowed and he scowled as he recognised the man's face looking out of the digital display. It was a face he hadn't seen since Beth's funeral. A face he didn't want to see again. His hands involuntarily clenched into fists.

Crane jabbed a button on the intercom, his mouth set in a thin line. "I told you to stay away from me," he said slowly, punctuating each word with sternness.

"Come on, bro."

Crane's back teeth ground together at the word "bro".

The man pleaded with his eyes as well as his tone. "I need your help."

"Don't call me bro," Crane replied coldly. "I told you after the last time I helped you, I never want to see you again."

Despite actually being twins, Crane couldn't stand the word "bro" coming out of Dylan's mouth. And it wasn't as if he'd have trouble hiding the fact they were related—they looked nothing alike. For a start, Dylan had light hair to Crane's dark hair and brown eyes to Crane's blue eyes. And the differences between them were not just physical. Dylan was a troubled individual. Over the years, he'd had issues with alcohol dependence and recreational drug use, not to mention a gambling habit that had got him into debt on more than a few occasions.

Dylan hadn't been the most supportive of brothers when Beth died, only calling once a couple of days after the accident to say he was sorry to hear the news. He came up with some cock and bull story about breaking his phone as to why he hadn't called sooner, really shocking Crane. Even though they had their differences, they'd always been quite close, but it was as if he weren't interested in supporting his brother during his darkest time.

Then the funeral. Dylan had turned up evidently hungover and reeking of stale booze. He'd quickly got drunk at the wake and had a big argument with his wife, Sarah, in front of all the mourners. She tried to get him to go home or at least slow down, but he was having none of it. She ended up leaving with their daughter, understandably embarrassed by his behaviour. He stayed and continued knocking them back until he eventually passed out at the bar.

Crane ended up taking him back to his and let him sleep it off in one of the spare rooms. The following morning, Crane woke up to find Dylan in his and Beth's walk-in wardrobe with his hand inside Beth's jewellery box. It took all of his willpower not to hurt him there and then. He gave Dylan an opportunity to explain himself, and Dylan broke down in tears. He pleaded with Crane and told him that he was desperate for money, he'd been living above his means for a long time and had gotten himself into a lot of debt. He couldn't keep up with all the repayments on his cards, bills, or his mortgage. He feared that his home was going to be repossessed any day and his family would be homeless.

If it weren't for the fact Dylan had a family to care for, Crane would have kicked him out and told him to sort his life out; after all, it wasn't the first time he'd given Dylan money to help him out of a spot of bother. But he couldn't see his sister-in-law and niece out on the street. He asked Dylan how much he needed. Dylan said twenty-three thousand would get him back on track. Crane gave him thirty but made it clear that it was the last time he would ever get another penny from him. No more handouts. He wasn't going to be Dylan's safety blanket anymore. It was time for him to grow up.

The fact he'd just been about to steal from him was bad enough, but to steal sentimental possessions, Beth's possessions, on the day after her funeral was unforgivable. He hoped that Dylan would do right by his family and take good care of his wife and daughter, for their sake's, not his. But as far as he was concerned, he never wanted to see Dylan's face ever again.

Yet there he was. At his front gate. Asking for help once again.

"I know, I know," Dylan begged. "But, please, I really need your help."

"Goodbye, Dylan." Crane turned and walked away, shaking his head.

"It's Chloe."

*Chloe.* Crane stopped abruptly at the sound of his niece's name, and a cold shiver ran down his spine. His hand felt blindly for the intercom, one foot still impatiently in front of the other. "What?"

"Can I come in and explain?" Dylan asked. "I don't want to do it over this thing."

"Is Chloe in trouble?" The answer to the question was very important to Crane's next decision of hearing Dylan out or walking away again. And the next time he stepped away from the intercom, he wouldn't be walking back to it irrelevant of how long Dylan waited around or what came out of his mouth.

"I think she might be."

Crane's finger hovered over a different button on the intercom for a second, his neck muscles tense, but his desire to help his niece surpassed his desire to never see his brother again. Hoping he wouldn't regret it later, he pressed the button on the intercom that opened the front gates.

The last time he'd seen Chloe was at Beth's funeral when she was nine, which made her fourteen now. Apart from sending her birthday and Christmas cards, he hadn't been involved in her life at all. He felt more than a twinge of guilt about that. Crane remembered Chloe as a sweet little girl who loved Disney princesses and unicorns. She was a teenager now. No doubt she would have changed a lot. He wondered whether he would even recognise her.

Crane opened the front door and came face to face with his brother. Dylan was an inch shorter than him, a very slim build, although Crane did notice he had the beginnings of a pot belly forming. He had light brown scruffy hair and about three days' worth of stubble. He was dressed in jogging bottoms and a Cardiff City football jersey.

Dylan held out his hand for a shake, but Crane just looked down at it and then looked back up, making no effort to hold his own hand out. Dylan hesitantly and awkwardly lowered his.

"What's happened to Chloe?" Crane didn't care for small talk. Chloe was all that mattered in this situation. Straight to the point.

"Where do I start?" It was more of a statement than a question. Dylan sighed and rubbed his stubbled chin. "I'm not sure if you've heard, but me and Sarah separated."

Crane hadn't heard, but he wasn't surprised. "Good for her."

"I probably deserve that." Dylan bit his lip, taking the jab. "It's actually been almost two years, and to be fair, she seems a lot happier now than when we were together." He gave a one-shoulder shrug, but then his eyebrows pinched together. "Chloe, on the other hand, seems to be going off the rails a little. I mean, I've tried to do my best since I moved out, but she's a teenager. She'd rather be out with her friends than spending time with her old man. I haven't seen much of her at all this past year, but Sarah has agreed to let me take her away to West Wales next week. I've booked us a caravan in Tenby, and we're due to set off on Sunday afternoon, just the two of us, to have some quality father-and-daughter time together.

"Anyway, I picked her up this morning to go shopping for some summer clothes ready for the holiday, and she did a runner on me." Dylan shook his head, seeming genuinely perturbed. "I only turned my back for two seconds, and she was gone. I've tried ringing her phone about a hundred times, but she just keeps declining my calls and sending me to voicemail. The thing is, it's taken a while for me to get Sarah to agree for me to take Chloe away, and if I don't get her back home safe and sound this afternoon, she'll kill me. She'll probably make me cancel the holiday."

"She ran away from you?" Crane snorted, beginning to regret opening his gates for Dylan. "It sounds like she doesn't want to go on holiday with you anyway."

"She's a teenager," Dylan said, rolling his eyes. "She just wants to be out with her friends or on those social media things all the time. When she's there, by the seaside and in the fresh sea air, she'll love it."

Crane waited for more, still not understanding how he could help. "It still sounds like a Dylan problem rather than a Chloe problem. And it *definitely* doesn't sound like a me problem." He started to shut the door. He'd open the gates via the intercom system to let Dylan out.

"She's got in with the wrong crowd," Dylan said, placing a firm palm against the door to stop Crane from closing it any further. "That's the real reason Sarah has finally agreed to let me take her on holiday. To get her away for a while. Away from them."

Crane's brow furrowed as he dropped his hand from the door handle before folding his arms. "What do you mean by *the wrong crowd*?"

"From what Sarah has told me, she's become friends with a couple of older girls in school. She says they're a real bad influence on her, and one of them has an older boyfriend who apparently sells drugs to some of the kids in the school. Sarah's obviously scared about where it could lead. I am too. She's a good kid, and I don't want her going anywhere near drugs." His voice turned to nearly a whisper. "I've been there, and it's not a good place."

"So, you think she ran off to see these girls?"

Dylan held his arms out, palms up. "Honestly, I don't know. I think so, but I don't even know who these girls are, never mind where they are, and I obviously can't ask Sarah. That's why I'm here. I've heard through the grapevine that you're good at finding people." Dylan raised his hands and placed his palms together in a begging motion. "Please, Tom. I just want to get her away from these girls and hopefully talk some sense into her."

"Come in," Crane relented, leading him to the kitchen. He grabbed his phone and handed it to Dylan, wondering who exactly had been feeding back about his work to his brother. "Put her number in there."

"Thank you."

"Don't thank me," replied Crane sharply, one side of his top lip curling upwards involuntarily. "I'm not doing this for you, I'm doing it for her."

Dylan handed the phone back once he'd tapped Chloe's number in. "I didn't think you were the type to go to Corkers," he said, noticing the drinks coaster on the kitchen island.

Crane gave Dylan a sideways glance. "You've been there?"

Dylan sniggered. "No, but a few of the lads in work have been."

"What kind of place is it?"

"It's a twenty-four-hour strip club, amongst other things."

Crane tilted his head slightly and frowned. "Other things?"

Dylan smirked. "Apparently you can pay extra for... extra services, and I don't just mean a private dance."

Crane nodded in understanding despite the stark contrast of his thoughts. *What the hell could a seedy strip-club-cum-brothel have to do with Beth's death?*

"Why have you got a coaster from Corkers if you've never been and don't even know what the place is?"

"Someone posted it in my mailbox."

"What? With this?" Dylan asked, picking up the letter and turning it over, which had been facedown beneath the coaster. "*Holy shit.*" He stared down at the words, his eyes open wide. Eventually, he tore his eyes away and looked back up at Crane. "Do you think it's genuine?"

"I've no idea." The corners of Crane's mouth downturned. "Maybe, or maybe it could be someone messing with me. Either way, I intend to find out."

Dylan screwed his face up in confusion and raised the letter in his hand. "But who would do something like *this* to mess with you?"

Crane didn't answer straight away. It was one of the questions he'd been asking himself since he opened the letter. When he did answer, he spoke more for his own benefit than Dylan's. "I've made a lot of friends in my line of work, but I've also made a *lot* of enemies. If there's one thing I've learned, it's to not take everything at face value." In an effort to end the conversation, Crane abruptly changed the subject. "Do you still have the same phone number?"

"Yep."

"I'll call you when I find her."

"Wait, I can come with you." Dylan straightened up. "We could find her together."

Crane took the letter out of Dylan's hand and placed it back on the island. "Don't try and turn this into a family reunion. Now, get out of my house."

# Chapter Five

Crane sent a message to Ricky of Chloe's number, asking him to trace her phone. In less than six minutes, a location marker popped up on his screen. It was followed by a message reading, "So much for a long weekend off!"

Crane recognised the name of the street immediately—it was not in a pleasant area of East Cardiff. It was an area that was renowned for its high crime rate, drugs, and gangs. Not the kind of place he wanted his niece to be. He knew all this because it was where he'd grown up, only a few streets from where Chloe's location marker was currently flashing.

He locked up the house and jumped into the pickup. It took him just under thirty minutes to reach Llanrumney.

Not much had changed since he'd left and joined the army when he was sixteen. The standard group of suspicious-looking young men were loitering around outside the shops, with nothing better to do and nowhere better to be, intimidating the local residents. An old silver hatchback full of boys in their late teens drove past on the opposite side of the road, the bass from the stereo rattling its windows. The big bore exhaust desperately tried and failed to roar like a high-performance supercar.

When he reached the road where Chloe's location marker was flashing, he slowed the truck down. The road was exactly how he remembered. Semi-detached houses lined both sides of the street. Around one out of every three had made some kind of effort to maintain their front garden, but the majority were completely neglected and overgrown. He drove past two boarded-up houses, one with plywood for windows and doors, the other with steel sheets. One house seemed to be collecting old derelict cars on the driveway, one of which didn't even have wheels and was precariously defying gravity balancing on stacks of bricks. Another of the cars had some kind of moss growing on the rubber surrounding the windows and even had bits of foliage peeking out from beneath the bonnet.

He parked the pickup on the opposite side of the road from where the marker was flashing. It appeared to be coming from a red-brick semi that looked just like all the other houses on the street. The front garden was overgrown, but not quite as bad as some of the others. All the curtains were drawn, in the middle of the day, although that wasn't unusual in this part of Llanrumney. The driveway was empty.

As he approached the front door, he could hear faint music and some voices coming from inside. There was no doorbell, so he knocked, his knocks sounding like dull thuds on the solid black composite door. After a few seconds, he heard the door unlock from inside and then it opened, revealing a young man. The big lump of a lad looked to be in his early twenties, around six-three, maybe even six-four, built like a rugby player, probably a second row. He completely filled the doorway, although he failed to block the stench of marijuana that emanated from inside the house. He also failed to block the sound of young girls giggling over the loud music.

"What?" the lad asked. His whole demeanour oozed arrogance.

"Is Chloe in there?" asked Crane calmly.

"Who the fuck are you?"

Crane's jaw clenched and his blood began to boil, but he maintained his composure. "Speak to me like that again and I'll be the man who teaches you some manners."

The lad snorted. "Yeah, right. How about you fuck off before you get cut," he threatened as he slammed the door shut.

Crane stepped forward and knocked again, more firmly this time, before quickly retreating six steps. When he heard the door lock unlatching again, he launched himself forward, the six steps becoming three huge strides and a front kick to the door. He hit the door with well over two-hundred pounds of weight and the dynamic force of a charging bull. The door swung open, barely slowing from the impact of hitting the lad behind it. He was unconscious before he hit the floor, his nose unnaturally bent to the right. Blood was already gushing from his nostrils and a little dripped from where the cartilage had split the skin.

Crane stepped over him and into the house, following the smell of marijuana through a doorway to his right. He ended up in the lounge, the air grey and hazy with smoke. The only sources of light were two tall lamps, one at each end of the room. There was no natural light getting through or around the closed curtains. Two young men and three young girls were sitting on black leather sofas and armchairs around a coffee table, which had a couple of well-used ashtrays on it. One of the girls pressed a button on her phone, and the music stopped playing. The room fell completely silent and then the two men stood up. One was around six feet and rotund, the other was five-eight and scrawny.

"Sit down before I put you down," Crane ordered, unfazed by the prospect of having to floor two more lads. It may have been his tone or maybe the look in his eyes, maybe even their mate unconscious in the hallway, but they both obeyed and sat back down immediately.

"Uncle Tom?" the smallest of the three girls said, her voice high-pitched and quiet.

He focused on the young lady, who was not the little girl he remembered anymore. She looked older... all grown up, but her big brown eyes were unmistakable. They were her father's eyes.

"Hi, Chlo-Chlo," Crane blurted before he could stop himself. He hadn't used his nickname for her for almost five years. "Long time, no see."

She stood up quickly, rapidly blinking and holding her hands out questioningly. "Wh-what are you doing here?"

"Come with me and I'll tell you."

Chloe hesitated and looked at her friends for reassurance or permission, failing to even receive any eye contact, let alone words. She made one more sweep with her eyes around the room before shuffling past them to get around the coffee table.

Crane stepped aside to let her pass. "You might want to check that your friend's airways are clear," he said to nobody in particular, then he turned and left with Chloe.

Chloe was a petite fourteen-year-old. She was wearing a little bit of makeup, not too much, and even with the makeup she still looked fourteen. Which Crane thought was a good thing, but he was sure Chloe wouldn't agree. She had long black hair, which she wore in a high ponytail. Crane watched her out of the corner of his eye as they sat silently side by side in the truck, and it was only then that he noticed the diamond nose stud.

Chloe lifted her feet onto the seat and hugged her knees. "Do you know what you've just done?" she asked as Crane pulled the truck out into the road and started to drive aimlessly.

"What do you mean?"

"You just knocked out Billy Ford. That's John Ford's son. As in *the* John Ford." Chloe turned and glared at Crane, waiting for his "oh shit" reaction.

"Okay," Crane said, turning to look at Chloe with a raised brow. "Are those names meant to mean something to me?"

Chloe's eyes nearly popped out of her head. "They're like, the biggest drug dealers in this part of Cardiff." She said it as if this information was as widely known as the sky being blue. Then her voice suddenly took a more serious tone. "They're gonna come after you."

Crane laughed. "Firstly, I'm really not worried about some two-bob wannabe-gangster drug dealers, let them come after me. Secondly, and more importantly, what are you doing in a place like that? With people like that?"

Chloe dropped her feet off the seat and folded her arms defensively. "They're my friends."

"They're grown men," Crane pushed on, "smoking weed with fourteen-year-old girls in the middle of the day. They're not your friends, they're scumbags."

"No, the *boys* are not my friends," Chloe protested, "but the girls are, and they're only sixteen." She unfolded her arms abruptly. "Anyway, what is this? I haven't seen or heard from you in years and then all of a sudden you burst in and attack my friend's boyfriend, and now you're lecturing me about what friends I should have. You haven't bothered with me for the last five years, why should I bother listening to you now?"

Crane remained composed, but her words had cut him. And the truth was, he deserved it. He shouldn't have let his brother come between his relationship with his niece, especially after knowing what it had felt like when Dylan wasn't there for him.

He spotted a space at the side of the road and pulled the truck over. He shut off the engine and turned to Chloe. Her face was red and tears were welling in her eyes. She was upset, but there was definitely fire in her eyes. She was a fighter—Crane could see it straight away.

"Good point well made." What was the point in making excuses? She was right. He continued in his softest voice, but even to his ears it sounded a little awkward and more matter-of-factly. Comforting fourteen-year-old girls certainly wasn't one of his expertise. "You're right. I've been a useless uncle. I fell out with your dad, and I let that affect my relationship with you. I never should have allowed that to happen. I buried my head in the sand and missed five years of your life. I'm sorry."

Chloe was quiet for a moment, gathering her thoughts. She sniffed and wiped her eyes. "I know I was young at the time, but I understood you went through a lot when we lost Auntie Beth. I miss her, and I've really missed you too. I also know what my dad's like." Chloe wrinkled her nose in distaste. "Dad can be a real arsehole when he wants to be, but what did he do to make you stay away for so long? It must have been something really bad."

"It's not something I think I should go into with you; he's your dad, and whatever happened between me and him shouldn't have affected your relationship with him. Just like it shouldn't have affected my relationship with you." Crane smiled apologetically and was relieved to see Chloe's eyes brighten a little and a grin appear on her face. "Your dad said you're meant to be going away with him on Sunday. Why did you run away from him today?"

"Run away?" Chloe asked, flinching backwards. "Is that what he told you?"

"He said you were out buying summer clothes ready for your holiday, and you disappeared when he turned his back for a minute."

Chloe shook her head and rolled her eyes.

"What really happened, then?"

"We were meant to be shopping for some holiday clothes, but he said he wanted to pop into the bookies on the way into town and put a little bet on. I stood outside waiting for him for over an hour. I tried waving to him and even knocked on the window to get his attention, but he was too busy cheering on the horses and making more bets. I think he forgot I was even there. I'd had enough of waiting, so I text my friends and met up with them at Billy's." She let out an exasperated sigh. "My dad's a compulsive liar. He doesn't care about me."

Crane had a strong urge to agree with her; Dylan was a compulsive liar and always had been, and he was definitely not shocked that Dylan was still gambling. But for Chloe's sake, he put on his responsible uncle hat. "I'm not one for defending your dad, but he definitely cares about you. He's still your dad at the end of the day."

"He cares more about himself," Chloe retorted.

"Now, that may be true," Crane said, cracking a grin, "but he does still care about you, and your mum cares about you, and I care about you. We don't want you going anywhere near the likes of Billy Bob and Johnny Boy the drug dealers."

Chloe giggled. "It's Billy Ford and John Ford."

"I don't care what their names are, they're bad news. You really need to stay away from them, and if your friend is seeing the one with the wonky nose, you should stay away from her too."

Before Chloe could respond, Crane's phone started ringing in his pocket. He pulled it out and checked the screen.

"I need to take this," Crane said, opening the door to get out. "Do me a favour and call your dad to let him know you're safe. I'll drop you off at his place after this call."

Chloe nodded and pulled her phone out. Crane closed the door and walked to the back of the pickup truck to take Ricky's call.

"What have you got for me?" Crane asked.

"I'm still digging, but I thought I would give you an update on what I've found so far."

Ricky informed him that Corkers was indeed a twenty-four-hour strip club. He'd also found posts and messages from customers on social media platforms that hinted at a lot more happening on the premises than just stripping and drinking. It sounded exactly like Dylan had described to him.

It was owned by a man named Luke Maddocks. He was Cardiff born and bred, now in his mid-forties, with a lengthy history of violence including convictions for assault, GBH, affray, and sexual assault to name but a few. Most of the convictions were back when he was in his twenties and early thirties. He had been arrested on numerous occasions since, but all charges were miraculously dropped. Apparently, over the last seven years or so, there always seemed to be insufficient evidence to press charges or witnesses seemed to be unwilling to testify against him.

Luke was the managing director, and a man called Paul Jenkins was listed on Companies House as the operations director. It turned out that they'd been best friends since school. Paul had a similarly colourful past as Luke, full of violent convictions, some of which crossed over.

"But apart from that, they seem lovely," Ricky finished sarcastically.

"Have you found anything that could link them to us or any jobs we've done in the past?"

"Like I said, I'm still digging at the moment. I'll keep you posted."

"Okay," Crane said. "Cheers, Ricky." He ended the call and got back into the truck.

"Did you speak to your dad?" he asked Chloe, who just shook her head in response.

Crane frowned. "Why?"

"He didn't answer. I tried three times." She said it in a way that gave Crane the impression this was the norm.

Phone still in hand from his call with Ricky, Crane searched his contacts and dialled Dylan. Sure enough, it rang six times before going to voicemail. "Why is he not picking up?" Crane huffed, not expecting an answer.

"It's the afternoon, so he's probably drunk by now."

Crane gave up and pocketed his phone. "I told him I would call once I found you. I don't even know where he's living nowadays."

"I do," Chloe said. "I'll direct you."

# Chapter Six

Chloe guided Crane back to North Cardiff, to not far from Ricky's barn. Dylan was living in a three-storey block of apartments on a quiet road. It was a big red-brick building with small white balconies, one for each apartment. Apparently, he had been renting it from a friend for the last six months. Crane drove around the back and into the car park. It had enough parking spaces for over a dozen cars, but only three were currently taken.

"There's his car," Chloe said, pointing to a dark blue Ford Focus.

Crane parked next to it, and they both got out and walked around to the main entrance. The door needed to be opened either with a key or electronically by a resident from inside their apartment. There was a panel next to the door with numbered buttons from one to six. Chloe pressed the button for number four, and a faint ringing sound came from a small speaker above the buttons. The sound stopped as soon as she removed her finger. They waited. Nothing happened. She went to press it again, but Crane beat her to the panel of buttons. He used both hands to press all six buttons in quick succession.

Chloe looked at him through narrowed eyes. "He lives in number four."

"I know."

A muffled sound came out of the speaker, followed by, "Hel-lo." It was a female voice, so definitely not Dylan.

Chloe's mouth dropped, her brain seemingly reaching a blank. "Umm, I—"

"Have a delivery," Crane finished in an unusually cheery voice.

It was a gamble, but it paid off. With the popularity of online shopping nowadays, it was inevitable that someone would be expecting a delivery of some sort, and even if they weren't expecting anything, curiosity would likely prevail. A loud buzzing sound came from the door as it was electronically unlocked by the female resident. Crane opened it for Chloe to lead the way. She headed up the stairs and took a right, a beige-coloured fire door with a chrome number four just above the peephole and a matching chrome handle now right in front of them.

Chloe knocked, but Crane didn't have the patience to wait. He tried the handle, and the door opened. The faint noise of a television could be heard inside.

"Stay here," Crane instructed.

"He's probably just drunk," Chloe said quietly.

He paused in the doorway. "Please, just indulge me and wait here."

Chloe didn't look too pleased, but she nodded, leaned against the wall, and folded her arms.

Crane stepped into a short hallway with five doorways, two on each side and one dead ahead. Three were closed, two were open. The first open door was a kitchen on the right. Dirty plates and bowls were piled next to the sink, and a couple of used saucepans filled the bowl in the sink, soaking in water that looked as if it was at least a couple of days old. The bin was overflowing with empty beer cans and a couple of cereal boxes. A small table and two chairs sat in the corner, an empty pizza box left open on the table, with two crushed beer cans next to it.

He moved on to the next open door, again on the right, and entered the room where the sound of the television was coming from. Crane immediately noticed Dylan on the sofa, his arms flailing over his head and back down in front of him. He rushed forward, panic rising in him at the belief Dylan could be having a seizure. Then he stopped, the beginning of a growl in his throat as he realised Dylan just had earphones in and was enthusiastically playing the air drums, his eyes closed, oblivious to Crane's presence.

There was a bottle of vodka on the table in front of Dylan, with only a few measures left inside. A highball glass was sitting next to the bottle, half full of what appeared to be neat vodka. Crane could smell it as he got closer. Some daytime quiz show was playing unwatched on the television.

It appeared as if Dylan hit some sort of a crescendo to the song, then he reached forward and grabbed the glass. He almost jumped out of his skin when he saw Crane standing in the room. Somehow, he kept hold of the glass but spilled a lot of the contents over himself. He pulled the earphones out of his ears, and his iPod clattered to the floor in the process.

"Christ," Dylan exclaimed. "You almost scared me to death."

"What are you playing at?" Crane fumed. "We've been trying to call you."

"Have you?" Dylan looked around for his phone. He found it down the side of the sofa and checked the screen. "Oh yeah, sorry. The sound was off for some reason."

Crane shook his head in a mixture of disapproval and disbelief. "I really don't understand why you are the way you are."

"What's that supposed to mean?" Dylan slurred. He tried to stand up, but he was clearly unsteady on his feet and fell back down onto the sofa.

"You came to me this morning supposedly worried about your daughter, then came back here and got yourself smashed on vodka while I was out trying to find her." Crane glanced at his watch and then looked Dylan up and down. "Look at the state of you, and it's only four in the afternoon."

"I just needed a drink to calm my nerves. I was worried about her."

"Bollocks," Crane retorted. "You didn't look worried when you were doing your Phil Collins impression when I walked in.

A worried father would be checking their phone every thirty seconds; they certainly wouldn't have it stuffed down the side of the sofa with the sound switched off."

Dylan said nothing. He had no defence.

"You need to step up to the plate and be a dad," Crane continued. "She's a great kid, but she is hanging around with some really bad people. We need to get her away from them." Crane walked over to a window and looked down at the street below. He took a couple of deep breaths, trying to hold in his frustration at doing Dylan a favour and for what, but then he noticed a little girl skipping along the pavement, holding her mother's hand, and it reminded him of who he was really doing this for.

"Look, I'll take her back to her mum's now," Crane finally said. "You get yourself sobered up and get ready to take her away on Sunday. Don't mess this up; she needs you."

"Okay," Dylan said, actually sounding as if he was choking up a little. Crane wasn't sure whether his emotion was real or an act, but he chose to give him the benefit of the doubt. "I'm sorry. Thank you, bro."

"Don't call me bro," Crane said through gritted teeth. There was still no relationship between them to make him feel okay with that word, but he was doing what he knew was right for Chloe.

He took the glass from Dylan and the bottle from the table and then he went into the kitchen and emptied the remnants into the sink. Chloe was waiting for him at the top of the stairs when he left the apartment.

"He was drunk, wasn't he?"

"Ask me no questions, I'll tell you no lies."

Chloe rolled her eyes. "I knew it."

"Come on. I'll take you back to your mum's."

They headed back to East Cardiff once more. Chloe, now she was fully comfortable in Crane's company, turned into a bit of a chatterbox during the journey. She spent most of it talking at him, telling him all about her favourite school subjects and her least favourite teachers.

Chloe and her mum, Sarah, still lived in the family home Sarah and Dylan had bought together before Chloe was born. It was in one of the more pleasant areas of East Cardiff. A nice three-bed semi in a quiet cul-de-sac.

As Crane pulled up outside, the front door opened, and Sarah stepped out smiling and waving. She hadn't changed a bit. She was slender, with dark curly hair that she always wore tied back. Her black-framed glasses glinted in the sunshine.

"I texted her and told her we were on our way," Chloe said, smiling. "I knew she'd be excited to see you."

Crane stopped the engine and stepped out of the truck to greet Sarah. They hugged briefly and exchanged hellos. There were no comments about his disappearance, no made to feel bad, no signs of awkwardness or a grudge.

"It's so good to see you," Sarah exclaimed.

"And you," said Crane. "Sorry I haven't stayed in touch."

Sarah waved off the apology. "I'm just glad you're good. You're looking really well." She stepped back and jokingly inspected him from head to toe while nodding her approval.

Crane couldn't help but chuckle. Sarah had always been a bit of a joker and seemed to relish trying to make people feel a little uncomfortable.

"So, you're back on speaking terms with your brother now?"

Crane gave a harsh shake of his head. "I definitely wouldn't say that. Only when it's completely unavoidable."

"Guess what, Mum," Chloe interrupted.

"What?"

"Uncle Tom said I could stay over at his house tonight for a sleepover. He said it's been such a long time since he saw me last, he wants to have a good catch-up."

Crane's eyes immediately widened. To say he hadn't been expecting her to say that was a huge understatement. He was so used to his own company and hadn't hosted anyone in his home for so long that he felt a little uneasy at the prospect of a "sleepover".

Sarah looked at Crane, her eyes almost as wide as his. "Is that right?"

Chloe gave a cheeky wink and a thumbs up to him behind her mum's back. He didn't answer straight away, so she put both hands together in a prayer position and mouthed "please" to him eagerly.

"Apparently so," Crane replied.

"I'll go get my overnight bag." She rushed off into the house before Crane could change his mind, leaving him and Sarah alone.

"You know you could have said no," Sarah said, giggling.

"Really? You could have told me that before I agreed to it," he joked. "I'm just messing. It'll be good to spend some time with her. I've missed five years of her life; it's the least I can do."

"Just don't let her walk all over you. She likes to push boundaries."

"Isn't that the same with all teenagers?" His mind flashed back to the moment he'd found out about Beth being pregnant. His child would still be young now, nowhere near a teenager, but the fact he'd never got the opportunity to experience having a child and would never get to watch it grow, guide it through its teenage years and adult life still sent a pang to his heart. He pushed the thought away, not wanting Sarah to see any vulnerability in him.

"That's true." Sarah laughed, then her expression quickly changed to a look of deep concern. "I don't know if Dylan told you, but she's just made some new friends that are a bad influence on her."

"He did." Crane nodded. "I think getting her away next week is a good idea. I'll see if I can have a good talk with her tonight too." And there was another good deed done for Dylan. He'd dropped it in, but he wouldn't push the matter any further. He frowned, reminding himself it was for Chloe, not Dylan.

"Thank you."

"Changing the subject slightly, what happened between you and Dylan for you to finally call it a day?" He had a good idea of many potential reasons, but he wasn't sure Dylan would have given the actual reason. He seemed to be in denial about a lot of his mistakes, past and present. Nothing had changed.

Sarah gave Crane a lopsided smile. "Do you mean how did I eventually come to my senses?"

"I suppose you could put it like that." Crane smirked.

"Well, he uh... he was having an affair with the local barmaid." She said it quietly, as if she didn't want Chloe to potentially overhear and have to relive one of her dad's many wrongdoings. "He took himself to bed hungover one day and left his phone downstairs. It beeped with a message and I happened to see the preview." Her expression darkened. "I wouldn't want to repeat what it said, I'd need to wash my mouth out."

Crane shook his head. "Idiot." There was no "I can't believe Dylan would do that" because, quite honestly, nothing Dylan did surprised him.

She gave a look that told him there was more to come. "I was prepared to forgive him. Can you believe how naïve I was? Even after years of putting up with his drinking and drug use and getting us into serious debt. But when I confronted him, he didn't show any remorse; he didn't even apologise. He told me, and I quote, 'She's not the first.' To be honest, I'm glad he said what he said. I couldn't stay with him after that. I'm happier now than I ever was when I was with him." She smiled and nodded, as if confirming this to herself, but Crane could still see a flicker of pain behind her eyes. He doubted it was because she missed Dylan. It was more likely to be lingering pain from how badly he had treated her.

"I'm glad to hear you're doing well," Crane said. "You deserve to be happy."

Chloe burst out of the front door and bounded down the path to them. "I'm ready," she announced.

"Okay. Well, have fun, you two," Sarah said, giving Crane a wry, knowing grin.

Back in the truck, Crane pulled away from the pavement and turned around at the end of the cul-de-sac. They waved goodbye to Sarah as they drove past, then he glanced at Chloe.

"I don't know about you, but I'm starving. What kind of food do you like?"

Chloe considered the question for a moment before answering. "Pizza, pasta, chips."

"Sounds good to me," said Crane. "Let's go find an Italian restaurant."

# Chapter Seven

Crane and Chloe arrived at Luigi's just before five—a small fam-ily-run Italian restaurant just on the outskirts of the city centre, with great food and an authentic feel. Solid oak tables and chairs, light-coloured stone flooring with white walls, and pictures of Italy adorning every wall. There was not a great deal of natural light coming in through the windows, so Tiffany-style uplighters were used to create dim but homely lighting. The whole vibe of the place was warm and friendly, none more so than Luigi himself, who welcomed every customer who entered like an old friend.

Being just before five, they were way ahead of the dinner rush. They almost had the whole restaurant to themselves; the only other customers were an elderly couple sitting in the front win-dow, tucking into their starters. Luigi was a short and portly man with a dark goatee and a beaming smile that never seemed to leave his face. He let them choose their own table, as it was so quiet. Crane chose a table for two in the rear corner and took the seat with a wall behind it and a clear view of the entrance. Old habits die hard.

Chloe ordered a Coke, while Crane ordered water because he was driving and he wasn't a fan of fizzy soft drinks. Chloe went for dough balls to start and carbonara for her main. Crane went for the bruschetta followed by a meat feast calzone. As they were finishing their starters, Crane ordered another Coke for Chloe and another water for himself.

"So, going back to your so-called friends that I had the pleasure of meeting earlier," Crane said, "what draws you to them? Why would you want to be friends with people like that?"

Chloe looked down at her last remaining dough ball and shrugged.

"There must be something you like about them to want to spend time with them," Crane persisted.

Chloe nibbled on her lower lip while she considered her response. "The truth is, I've struggled to make friends in secondary school. The girls you saw earlier are two years above me, but they're the first girls in school that have seemed to take any interest in me." Chloe lowered her gaze again to her empty plate to avoid eye contact. "I don't expect you to understand; you've probably got loads of friends."

"I get it," Crane said. "It's been a long, long time since I was your age, but I can tell you making friends didn't come easy for me either." Crane wasn't just paying her lip service, he had struggled to make friends, and not just when he was at school. He was never the life and soul of the party and struggled in large group situations; in fact, the larger the group, the more alone he would feel. He preferred to connect with people one-on-one or in small groups.

Chloe raised a cynical brow. "Really?"

"Really. But your dad, on the other hand, was always the class clown and never struggled to make friends. Kids flocked to be around him."

Chloe's face scrunched up in thought. "If that's true, why has he ended up the way he is? Like, why does he drink so much?"

It was Crane's turn to shrug. It was an impossible question to answer. Why was Dylan so... damaged? Technically they shared the same genes and had the same upbringing, but they were polar opposites, and they always had been. "Maybe it came too easy to him as a kid, and when things changed as he became an adult, he found it difficult to deal with. Maybe your challenge of finding friendships in secondary school will build up your resilience and character so that you become a better and stronger person when you grow up. You've experienced hardship at a young age and coped, so if it happens again when you're older, you'll know how to deal with it."

He could almost see the cogs turning in Chloe's head.

"I never really thought of it like that," she said.

"You'll end up gaining lots of friends and acquaintances throughout your lifetime, trust me. Although, you'll probably only have a handful of true friends." Crane knew from experience that there was a big difference between a friend and an acquaintance. Sometimes people appeared to be popular with lots of friends but were really surrounded by acquaintances. Crane was now wise enough to realise that one true friend, a friend like Ricky, was worth a hundred acquaintances. "A true friend is someone you would trust with your life, someone who selflessly wants the best for you, someone who makes you a better person. Would you put the two girls you were with today in that category?"

Chloe scoffed and shook her head. "No."

"That's the point I want to make. Don't get me wrong, there's nothing wrong with being friendly with those girls—you certainly don't want to make enemies of them. What I'm trying to say is be careful who you invest your time in, who you spend time with. Who your friends are will have a huge impact on who *you* become, especially at your age. If you spend your time with good people, you're more likely to end up good. If you spend time with bad people..."

"I will end up bad."

"Potentially," Crane said. "Hopefully not, but just choose who you invest your time in wisely. Try to be around people who possess the qualities that you value."

"So, not people who smoke weed?" Chloe grinned.

Crane laughed. "I can't say that's considered a good quality."

Luigi came over with their mains, and they tucked straight in. Crane finished his calzone before Chloe was even halfway through her carbonara. As he pushed his plate to the side and sat back, his phone started vibrating and ringing in his pocket. He pulled it out and looked, but the incoming call was displayed on the screen as "Private Number", so he declined it.

"Why didn't you answer it?" Chloe asked. "Is it because I'm with you? It might be something important."

"I never answer private numbers. If it's important, they'll leave a voicemail and I'll call them back."

Within moments, the table vibrated with a buzzing sound, and their eyes flashed to Chloe's phone—which was faceup on the table—just as a quiet but audible ringtone started. They could both clearly see the words "Private Number" displayed on the screen.

Chloe's eyes moved between the phone and Crane, clearly stuck between her wondering of the call's importance with Crane's own voicemail views. "Should I answer it?"

"It's your phone," he replied. "It's your call. Literally."

She tentatively swiped to answer and held the phone to her ear. "Hello."

Her eyes widened and the colour seemed to instantly drain from her face. Crane had witnessed the symptoms of shock enough times to know that whatever she could hear on the phone was terrifying her.

She held the phone out for Crane. "It's for you."

Crane took the phone and silently held it to his ear.

"I know who was following her," an unnaturally deep and robotic voice said. Whoever was speaking at the other end of the phone was using an electronic voice changer.

Crane leaned forward and felt the muscles in his neck and shoulders tense up. "Who is this?"

"Luke Maddocks was following her."

"How do you know? Who is this?" Crane snapped, trying but failing to keep his voice down.

"I know lots of things," the voice said. "For now, enjoy your Italian food with your niece."

The line went dead.

The words sent a chill down his spine. They were being watched. He looked around the restaurant. A few more tables were now taken, mostly couples, but nobody had a phone out. Nobody was paying them any attention. He peered out through the two small windows either side of the door, searching for a face, for movement. Just an empty pavement and parked cars outside. But he knew that didn't mean they hadn't been looking through a window at some point.

He handed Chloe her phone back. "Stay here," he instructed. "I'll be right back."

Crane got up, his chair complaining noisily as it was quickly scraped back against the stone floor. The sound was loud enough to gain the attention of every customer in the restaurant. Crane didn't care. He rushed outside, almost knocking Luigi over on his way. The restaurant was situated in the middle of a residential street. Terraced houses lined both sides and cars were parked tightly on either side of the road. Only a single pedestrian was out—a middle-aged lady walking her dog on the opposite pavement to Crane. He turned his attention to the cars. He walked up and down the street, glancing into every car, hoping to find the caller. He crossed the road and repeated the process with the parked cars on that side too. Nothing. There was nobody in any of the cars parked near the restaurant.

Next door to Luigi's was a small craft beer house. Crane looked in through the window and could see two men sitting at the bar. They were sitting too far apart to be together. Between the door and the bar were three evenly spaced wooden picnic benches, all stained to match the bar and stools. If it hadn't been for the bare brickwork on show behind the bar, it could have been mistaken for the inside of a giant shed. He entered, and a bell above the door announced his arrival. The barman and two customers looked up at him. The one on Crane's left was an older man in his sixties. Probably retired and out for a swift one before dinner. The one on his right was in his thirties and looked to be a painter and decorator judging by the splatters of paint on his clothes and the spots of white emulsion on his forearms. He was probably having a leisurely one to unwind after a hard day's work before going home to his family. The barman was early forties, completely bald, clean-shaven, with a welcoming smile on his face. He was evidently pleased to see a new customer. He was wearing a black T-shirt with the bar's name across it in yellow writing, and he had the standard bar towel draped over one shoulder.

"What can I get you?" the barman asked.

Crane was too busy looking at all their reactions to answer. He was looking for a glimmer of recognition, a hint of anxiety, something that would implicate the caller. But there was nothing. The painter and decorator had already turned back to his beer, disinterested.

"What can I get you?" the barman asked again.

"Sorry," Crane said. "I was just looking for someone."

Back on the street, Crane felt a little uneasy. Humans have five basic senses—touch, sight, hearing, smell, and taste—but there are variations; for instance, touch can be broken down to pressure, temperature, vibration, pain, and more. There are also additional senses, like balance and proprioception: the perception or awareness of the position and movement of the body.

Although it isn't a sense as such, Crane had carried out surveillance and been the target of surveillance enough times to be a firm believer in scopaesthesia: the feeling of being watched. The strange thing was, he didn't feel as though he was being watched now and he hadn't felt it all day, which meant either the caller was good, possibly a professional, or Crane was slacking. Or even worse, maybe it was both. Crane was frustrated with himself, but he didn't have time for hindsight. He just needed to focus.

# Chapter Eight

Chloe had eaten all but two spaghetti strands of her carbonara, and the colour had just about returned to her cheeks. She was slightly hunched over her plate and her mouth formed a thin line as she watched Crane walk back to their table.

"What was that all about?" Her voice was shaky, and Crane couldn't tell if it was the uneasiness she was clearly feeling causing it to shake or the fact she was bouncing her legs. Either way, it stemmed from apprehension.

"I don't know," Crane replied, sitting down, "but I intend to find out. What did he say to you?"

"Nothing really. He just said, 'I want to speak to Tom Crane.' It was just the sound of the voice. It really freaked me out."

"It's nothing for you to worry about. I promise. He was just using an electronic voice changer. If anything, it shows he's scared. Scared enough to disguise his real identity."

"You think he was watching us, don't you? That's why you rushed outside and looked in the cars." Chloe leaned in closer, her forehead crinkled with worry lines. "Do you think it was the Fords? Am I in danger, Uncle Tom?"

Crane shook his head and smiled dismissively in an effort to calm and comfort her. "It wasn't the Fords. Whoever it was and whatever it's about, it's nothing to do with you, it's about me."

She didn't look convinced. "He called *my* phone."

Crane couldn't argue with that point, and it was something that bothered him too. He reached out and gently placed a reassuring hand on top of hers. She was trembling slightly, but at least her legs had stopped bouncing now. He looked directly into her eyes. "He called your phone because I didn't answer mine. Trust me, I won't let anything bad happen to you." Still, the fact they had Chloe's number was unnerving him. That was the part that didn't make sense if they only wanted to reach him.

Crane offered to buy her a dessert, but she said she didn't feel like it. He wasn't surprised. He settled the bill with Luigi and gave a generous tip, then they left. The sun was getting lower in the sky, but it was still warm and bright. There were still a couple of hours until sunset.

Crane unlocked the truck and told Chloe to get in. He walked to stand behind it and dialled Ricky, who picked up within the first ring.

"Hey, what a coincidence," Ricky said, "I was just about to call you."

"Why? What have you got?"

"I've been looking into the company finances for this Corkers place, and I noticed something that I think is quite interesting—Luke Maddocks isn't the real owner."

Crane tilted his head to the side. "What do you mean? You told me he was the owner earlier."

"Well, his name is on the deeds, so technically he is, but there's someone above him who really owns it." Ricky paused, then after a couple of clicks of what sounded like a computer mouse, he began to explain. "About seven years ago, he came out of prison after a three-year stretch for GBH. He didn't have a penny to his name, then all of a sudden, a transfer for the exact amount of money required to purchase the club that is now Corkers landed into his bank account."

Crane's eyes narrowed at this. He stepped onto the pavement and looked into the wing mirror. He could see Chloe's reflection—her head was down and she was busy on her phone.

"I've done a preliminary trace, and the money was bounced around from different shell companies before finally reaching his account. I'll keep trying to find out where it came from, but it looks like a lot of effort has been made to hide the origin, and as seven years have passed, it may be impossible to trace it all the way back."

"That is interesting."

"And that's not all I found," Ricky continued. "Judging by the amount of cash that they run through their books, I think it's being used to launder money. I've got a suspicion that whoever gave Luke the money for the club uses it to clean their ill-gotten gains. You should see how the profit from the club is transferred every month from the main company account to a different bank in the name 'Corkers Group' before being split down and transferred out again to different shell corporations. It's a big accounting operation; there's money flying around all over the place. Don't get me wrong, their tax returns look spot on, but the quantity of cash going through the place should be ringing alarm bells at HMRC." Ricky scoffed into the phone, "Although, I suppose they turn a blind eye when it's bringing in so much money for them too."

It was all compelling information, but Crane couldn't see how any of it could possibly relate to him or Beth. "Have you found any links to us at all? Are there any links with any of our previous clients?"

"Nope. Nothing."

Crane sighed and massaged the tension out of the back of his neck. "Something doesn't feel right. I don't know what it is, but something is really not sitting right with me."

He went on to tell Ricky all about the call to Chloe's phone and the electronic voice implicating Luke Maddocks. He asked Ricky if he could look into tracing the call, but he knew it may be difficult or even impossible with the number being blocked.

"I'm not surprised it's not sitting right with you. Being followed and a weird call on your niece's phone wouldn't sit right with anyone."

Crane didn't say anything; he was lost in his thoughts. Questions swirled around inside his head. There was something else bothering him, but he just couldn't pin it down.

"There is one thing that..." Ricky started to say, but then he trailed off.

"What?"

"I mean, it could be something, but it could be nothing. In fact, it's probably nothing."

"What is it?"

"Well, on the night of Beth's accident, you said she was being followed by a big car, like an SUV?"

"That's right."

"Well, five years ago, Luke Maddocks had a Range Rover Sport registered in his name. But look, that really doesn't prove anything. Lots of people drive big cars."

Crane froze, his eyes fixed on his reflection in the tinted rear window of his truck, his mind processing and reasoning. Ricky was right; it could be nothing, it could just be a coincidence. But... it could be something. "Can you do me a small favour?"

"Of course. What do you need?"

"I need you to look after Chloe for me. Just for an hour or two."

"I, I don't know," Ricky stuttered. "I'm not really sure if—"

"Thanks," Crane said, cutting him off. "You're a star. I'll drop her round now." He ended the call and got into the truck.

"You wouldn't happen to like video games, would you?" he asked Chloe as he started driving towards Ricky's.

Twenty minutes of Crane being talked at later, they arrived at Ricky's barn. Chloe had spent the entire journey enthusiastically telling him that she was playing some sort of shooting game called Eradicate. Apparently, it was a really popular online game where people all over the world entered different worlds, or "rooms" as she called them, and killed each other until there was only one person left standing. She explained that the more kills you made, the more tokens you earned and then you could use those tokens to purchase better weapons and equipment. Apparently, she was really good and had achieved a huge kill count and a big stash of tokens—her avatar was "fully kitted out". Crane did his best to come across as if he were interested, not that he wasn't, it was just that his mind was a little preoccupied.

The electric motorised locks disengaged with the usual metallic clunk. Crane opened the door and introduced Ricky and Chloe to each other. Ricky awkwardly shook Chloe's hand and stood back rigidly. He was sweating a little. His social anxiety was getting the better of him.

Crane broke the silence. "Do you play a game called Eradicate?"

Ricky snorted. "Of course. Who doesn't?"

*Me for one*, thought Crane, but instead he said, "This young lady said she's the world champion of Eradicate. She said she can kick your butt."

"I did not say that." Chloe laughed. "Although, the first part isn't far off the truth."

"What rank are you?" Ricky asked, eyeing her suspiciously.

"I just ranked up yesterday. I became an Ace," Chloe answered, a smug grin on her face.

Ricky gave a cursory head tilt with pursed lips, looking impressed but not threatened. "That's pretty good. You've got some skills."

"What rank are you?"

"Grand Master."

"*No way*," exclaimed Chloe. Her eyebrows raised so high that Crane thought they were going to pop off the top of her head. "I thought that was impossible."

"It's definitely possible." Ricky laughed, and his tension seemed to dissipate. "Want me to show you?"

"Yes, please." Chloe pretty much skipped with excitement as she followed him to his sofas. Judging from the popping eyes and slack jaw, she was in awe of his enormous screen and gaming setup. To Crane, it was as if they were speaking a foreign language as Ricky set up the game and discussed it with Chloe. Crane could just about make out that they were going to team up in the rooms to make kills and earn tokens. He waited around ten minutes until he was confident that they were engrossed in the game and having fun before getting up to leave.

"I'm just going to pop out," he called to them over the sound of gunshots. "I won't be long."

Ricky looked over and gave him a thumbs up, but Chloe was concentrating too hard to acknowledge him properly, giving just a quick nod.

He closed the door just as Chloe started shouting.

"*Oh no*, that guy just shot me in the face."

# Chapter Nine

Most of the roads in the city centre were either pedestrianised or only accessible to buses and taxis, so Crane parked on a street just a few minutes away on the outskirts of the city centre. He walked across Cardiff Bridge, which extended over the River Taff. The colossal Principality Stadium loomed a few hundred yards away on his right, dwarfing the smaller Cardiff Arms Park in front of it. Cardiff Castle was up ahead to the left. Crane waited for a bendy bus to pass before crossing the road and turning right onto Westgate Street. It was a street enriched with history, full of elegant buildings that had been mostly built during the eighteenth and nineteenth centuries. The majority of the businesses seemed to honour the architecture; however, some shops, restaurants, bars, and particularly the fast-food takeaways spoiled the perspective by plastering the ground floors of the buildings with garish signage.

The pavement was busy with couples on their way to an evening meal together and small groups of youngsters excited about the start of their Friday night of drinking and debauchery. He passed a bar with a giant front window, where there was a stag party inside cheering on the stag as he downed a pint of lager. The stag was dressed as Snow White and his friends were dressed as the seven dwarfs, complete with brightly coloured waistcoats, fake beards, and big pointy hats. One of them was even holding a small plastic axe. Crane couldn't help but crack a smile. They were going to have fun tonight. Although he certainly didn't envy the hangover that they would all wake up with in the morning.

An orange glow was starting to surround the sun as it dipped even lower in the sky. It was about one hour away from finally setting for the day. Crane approached the place where he was expecting to find Corkers, and he almost walked straight past it. It was just a large plain black door with a bulbous brass handle in the middle, and it was sandwiched tightly between a small bar on the left and an Indian restaurant on the right. The door was surrounded by an ornate stone architrave with a small matte black plaque a foot or so above the door. The word 'Corkers' had been laser cut out of it, in a swirly flamboyant font. There was no doubt that it would illuminate from the back when it got dark.

Crane twisted the brass knob and pushed the door open inward. It was solid and heavy, with a hydraulic door closer overhead that smoothly shut the door behind him. He stood in a short dimly lit hallway. Pink light strips ran along the tops of the skirting boards like a runway. They led to a long dark staircase heading underground. The light strips followed the stairs all the way to the bottom, illuminating each step on the way. The ceiling of the stairway was arched like a tunnel. It looked a little bit brighter at the bottom of the stairs. Still pink, but there definitely seemed to be more light at the end of the tunnel.

Crane headed down. Twenty-four steps in total. The bottom opened up to a reception room of sorts. Straight ahead were black double doors with vertical chrome bars for pull handles, and to the left was a white reception counter with a doorman sitting on a stool behind it. The doorman stood up as Crane entered. He was a good six inches shorter than Crane, but he was as wide as he was tall. He was dressed in a black suit and an open-collared white shirt—at least, Crane guessed it to be white, but it actually looked pink under the lighting.

"Good evening, sir," the doorman greeted him politely.

As Crane moved closer, he noticed a scar just to the side of the doorman's left eye, almost like an extension of his eyebrow. His round head and square jawline were both cleanly shaved. He had the look of a man who had experienced more than his fair share of barroom brawls, and he only looked to be in his mid-twenties.

"Evening," Crane replied, stepping over to the counter.

"Are you a member, sir?"

Crane shook his head. "I'm not. To be honest, I've only popped in to see Luke. Is he here?"

The doorman smiled as if it were a silly question. "Luke's always here. Are you a friend of his?"

Crane almost laughed. "Not exactly. I just need a quick word with him."

The doorman's eyes narrowed. "What about?"

"It's a private matter."

"What's your name?"

"What's with the third degree?" Crane asked, beginning to lose patience. "I only want a quick two-minute chat."

The doorman visibly tensed and stood a little straighter, trying to make himself as wide as possible. "Put it this way, if I go to Luke and tell him there's a bloke here to see him but he won't tell me what it's about or what his name is, he's gonna tell me to piss off."

"Fair enough," Crane said, with a one-shoulder shrug. "It's Mike."

"Mike what?" the doorman asked impatiently.

"Rotch," Crane said straight-faced, looking the doorman straight in the eye. "R-O-T-C-H."

"Okay, Mr Rotch." The doorman had clearly missed the innuendo. "Grab yourself a drink inside, and I'll see if he's available to speak to you."

Crane gave a quick nod and stepped towards the double doors.

"Wait," said the doorman. "I almost forgot. The entry fee is ten pounds for non-members."

Crane looked over his shoulder and raised an eyebrow. "Really?"

The doorman shrugged dismissively. "I don't make the rules, I just enforce them. If you get to speak to Luke, you can take it up with him."

Crane hesitated. *Pick your battles*. He pulled out his wallet and dropped a ten pound note on the counter, then he turned and pulled open the double doors. He was surprised at how well the doors had muted the music from the reception area. It was incredibly loud inside, and the bass seemed to thump right through his entire body.

The inside of the club was truly cavernous, much bigger than he'd anticipated. Comfy armchairs and sofas surrounded large circular glass-topped tables in front of him. Further out to the left and right were a number of private alcoves with U-shaped seating areas and curtains that could be drawn if the occupants wanted privacy. One of the alcoves had a group of four men drinking bottles of beer and watching a dancer wearing only tall black stilettos and a minuscule black thong gyrating in front of them. They all gawped at her with wide eyes and slack jaws like four dogs staring at a treat that was just out of reach. One of the alcoves on the right had the curtains shut the whole way across.

Further ahead, six or seven steps led down to another seating area that surrounded the main stage. The main stage was circular with a narrow catwalk leading to it from the back of the club. The stage was on the same level as the outer seating area Crane was currently standing on, which meant everyone in the club had a view of the naked dancer currently twirling around the chrome pole that stretched from the centre of the stage all the way up to the ceiling.

The pink lighting continued inside, with just a few purple wall uplighters for a slight contrast. It wasn't busy, but there were certainly more customers than Crane would have expected to see so early of an evening. Behind him, just over his right shoulder, was the bar. Three attractive young ladies were lined up along it, all dressed in seductive lingerie, just like the ones who were either chatting to the customers in the seating areas or floating around serving drinks. All three of them smiled at Crane, but only the one in front approached him. It was obviously her turn to speak to a punter.

She was a petite blonde with long wavy hair, big sparkling eyes, and a bright smile. Her hips swayed excessively from side to side as she made her way to him. She was dressed in high heels, suspenders, and a low-cut silk vest, all in black, just like the others. Black seemed to be the uniform colour. Crane thought she couldn't have been more than nineteen years old.

"Good evening, sir," she said in heavily accented English. Eastern European. Slovakia was Crane's guess.

"Evening," Crane replied.

"What can I get you to drink?"

"Nothing, thank you. I'm just waiting to speak with Luke."

She recoiled slightly and furrowed her brow. "Please, sir. I need to get you a drink."

"Honestly," Crane insisted, raising a hand to decline the offer, "I'm just here to speak with Luke, nothing else."

The sparkle in her eyes faded and was replaced with something different. Worry. Maybe even fear. "But, sir," she pleaded, "you don't understand. I *need* to get you a drink."

Crane looked around to see if anyone could overhear them, but there didn't seem to be anyone close enough to hear a single word over the booming music. He leaned in a little closer to her. "Why?" he asked curiously.

She glanced over her shoulder briefly. Crane followed her stare and noticed a camera above the bar. It wasn't easy to spot in the dark corner where the wall met the ceiling, but he quickly spotted another three overlooking this quadrant of the club.

"Please," she said again, this time quieter, looking at the floor.

"What will happen if I don't buy a drink?" His hand was already in his pocket, fiddling with his wallet.

She shook her head. "I've already said too much."

Crane nodded and pulled out his wallet for the second time in almost as many minutes. He handed her a twenty and told her to get him a bottle of beer, which he had no intention of drinking. He also told her to get a drink for herself. He was going to want to know a bit more about the situation here when she came back.

He walked over to an empty seating area and sat down in one of the armchairs. He had a good look around and spotted a few more cameras dotted all over the club. Understandable really—they were a lot more discreet and customer-friendly than having security guards standing around. There would still be security guards, but they would be sitting in a surveillance room somewhere, watching an enormous cluster of monitors, ready to pounce at the first sign of trouble. Probably behind one of the doors labelled "Staff Only". So far, he'd spotted three of them.

The petite blonde came back with a bottle of beer and what looked like a gin and tonic. She handed him the beer and went to sit on his lap, but then she seemed to think better of it and chose the arm of the chair instead. She clinked the neck of his beer bottle with her glass and took a sip. Crane rested his beer bottle on his leg, untouched. He noted there was no change from his twenty, not that he'd really expected any.

"What would have happened if I didn't buy a drink? Who would have punished you?" Crane tried again.

"Forgive me," she said, flicking her hair over her shoulder and producing a fake smile. "I should not have said that. You're here to see Luke. You are friends, no?"

"No, we're not friends," he stated firmly. "Is it Luke who punishes you?"

She shook her head and clamped her lips shut tight. Obvious contrasts in body language being exhibited—she wanted to say something, but she was stopping herself.

"Trust me," Crane said, leaning closer to her and fixing his gaze on hers. "I'm not friends with Luke. I've never even met the guy. To be honest, from what I've heard of him, I already don't like him."

She tilted her head back and giggled, eyes flashing to one of the cameras. "He is not a nice man."

"In what way does he punish you?" Crane persisted.

"It is not just him," she said. "Paul is just as bad. Paul is his friend, his second in command. Also, sometimes the security guys join in too." She took another sip of her drink.

"What kind of punishments are you talking about?"

She looked down at her glass and traced her index finger around the rim as she spoke. "There are a lot of things. It depends on what we do wrong. It can be taking money from us. Or worse, they can increase our rent. They own where we live, and our rent comes out of our wages. It then affects the other girls we share an apartment with, that way the other girls get angry with you too."

Crane consciously kept his expression impassive while she talked. He didn't want the cameras picking up any negative body language that could get the girl into trouble. "And they would do that because someone comes in and doesn't have a drink with you?" Crane asked, raising his beer bottle and clinking the neck on her glass again—for the cameras.

"No. That would usually be a different kind of punishment."

"Like what?"

"How do you say? Physical?"

"They hit you?" Crane asked, struggling not to frown.

"Sometimes," she said, "if they are drunk or they have had too much coke, but they try not to. A stripper with bruises can't work, and a hooker with bruises is worth less. They more do... sexual punishments."

This time, Crane was unable to stop himself from frowning. "They rape you?"

She paused for a moment and then her lips curled into a smile, but the smile didn't reach her eyes. "I do not think they call it rape when it happens to a sex worker."

Crane stared deep into her eyes, and she stared back, holding his gaze. "I do."

"Thank you," she said. "You have kind eyes. I can tell you are not like them."

"Why are you thanking me?"

She shrugged. "For treating me like a human."

"You are a human. You're a young lady. Why don't you just quit and leave?"

She laughed. A real laugh, but a "you have no idea" kind of laugh. "Where else can I go? I'm not meant to be here. In this country." She frowned. "Believe it or not, this life is actually better than the one I escaped from."

Crane felt sorry for this poor young girl and the dreadful life she had experienced so far, but he was also full of admiration for her. She was evidently a very strong and resilient young lady. He didn't want to change the subject abruptly, but he wasn't sure how much time he had left with her, and he needed to know more about the club layout. Luckily for him, she answered all the questions he fired at her without hesitation. Clearly, his "kind" eyes and treating her like a human had led to her trust. He found it sad how little it had taken for him to gain it. He worried that she could potentially confide in others too easily, but he couldn't let that rule his thoughts right now.

She told him the door behind the bar led to another four doors. One was the stockroom for the bar, another was the surveillance room, which always had at least two doormen on camera duty at any one time. Another doorman would be at the front desk, and they would usually rotate every hour or two, meaning there were always at least three doormen on duty. The other two doors were staff toilets and a changing room for the girls.

The door at the rear left of the club led to another four doors, four doors for four rooms, which were used by the girls to perform "extra services". These rooms were meant to be used for pre-booked and "trusted" clients only, but it wasn't unusual for a fresh unknown customer to request and be permitted the services that were provided back there, as long as they had enough money.

The door at the rear right of the club led to Luke's office. She said he practically lived there. Apparently, he spent more time at the club than anyone else. She also explained that both of the doorways at the rear of the club had stairs leading up to fire exits; however, the one on the rear left was usually chained shut unless a health and safety inspection was due.

As she talked, he noticed the doorman from the front desk walk into the club and through the door behind the bar. He emerged a minute later with another doorman, wearing the same black suit and white shirt. He was taller than the first doorman, but he was slim, almost skinny. The taller doorman headed to the reception area, and the doorman with the scar headed towards Crane with a scowl on his face.

"It looks like that's all the time I have," Crane said. "You don't have to answer this, but is scarface one of the guards who often get involved in your punishments?"

She followed his gaze, then looked back at him and said, "Yes."

Scarface stopped a few feet from them and puffed out his chest, trying to make himself look as big as possible. He glared down at Crane. "Mike Rotch?" he spat. "Think you're a funny fucker, do ya?"

"Are you trying to say I've got a funny name?" Crane replied with a wry grin.

"Just get up and come with me; Luke wants to see you."

Crane looked at the girl. "What's your name?"

She slid off the arm of the chair, ready to make her way back to the bar. "Ivanka."

"Well, it's been a pleasure talking to you, Ivanka." He stood up, placed his untouched bottle of beer on the table, and pulled out his wallet once more. He handed her all the cash he had left, probably around a hundred and twenty pounds. She took it, and the sparkle returned to her eyes as she smiled and thanked him.

"Look after yourself," he said.

# Chapter Ten

Crane followed the doorman through the club, weaving around and in between seating areas all the way to the back of the club and towards the rear right door labelled "Staff Only". The doorman went through first and held it open briefly for Crane, although he didn't look behind to check that Crane had reached the door before letting it go. It was a half-hearted attempt at door etiquette, which amused Crane as he caught the door just before it closed on him. He had obviously gotten under the doorman's skin.

They stepped into a bright hallway. Black tiled floor, white walls, two uncovered fluorescent tubes running along the ceiling one after the other. Around ten yards ahead, the black tiles ended and bare concrete steps started rising into darkness. He couldn't see the top, but he knew that they led up to the fire exit, just like Ivanka had described to him. There was a plain black fire door with a well-worn stainless-steel handle on the left. The doorman knocked twice and waited.

"Come in," a muffled voice called from inside.

The doorman pulled down on the chrome handle and pushed the door open to enter. Crane followed him inside. The so-called office was huge and looked more like a youth recreation centre than a workplace. To the left was a blue-topped pool table, and to the right was an ivory-coloured leather sofa and two armchairs surrounding a small glass-topped coffee table and a wall-mounted TV. Two game console controllers were sitting on the coffee table. At the back was a large old-fashioned mahogany desk and a black executive chair. Mounted on the wall behind the chair were four huge screens, each screen split into four quarters, each quarter showing live footage from different cameras within the club. The other walls were covered with sporting memorabilia—signed boxing gloves, signed football and rugby jerseys—there was even a signed Formula One helmet on top of a drinks cabinet, which was situated in the rear left corner of the room. There was a door on the right-hand side of the rear wall. *Probably an ensuite*, Crane figured.

There were two men inside. One of them was throwing darts at a dartboard that was on the left wall in the space between the pool table and the desk. He was in a throwing stance at the end of a rubber oche mat. Seven feet, nine and a quarter inches from the dartboard. He threw his third and final dart and then turned to look at the new arrivals. He was around five-ten and stocky, like a prop in a rugby team. His head was shaved, apart from a wide but short Mohican. He was wearing black shoes, black trousers, and a black short-sleeved shirt. Black was definitely the uniform colour. His left arm was tattooed, a full black and white sleeve, a mix of smoke and skulls. He smiled a big, exaggerated smile that bared his teeth. Something yellow glinted in his mouth—a gold tooth, his top left incisor. He seemed to have an air of authority about him.

"Here he is, Boss," the doorman announced. He directed his words to the man who had just finished throwing his darts. Luke Maddocks, Crane presumed.

This meant that the other man who was part sitting, part leaning against the mahogany desk and waiting for his turn to throw the darts must be Paul Jenkins. He was an absolute behemoth of a man. At least six and a half feet tall and built like a proverbial brick outhouse. He was clearly a bodybuilder who was no stranger to steroids and growth hormones. His silhouette looked part man, part mountain gorilla. His head was shaved, but in contrast he had a huge, bushy black beard. A thick tribal tattoo started on the outside of his left bicep and ended with a spike up the side of his neck, just beneath his earlobe. He wore flip-flops, a training vest, and long baggy shorts. He was dressed as if he'd just finished a workout. Crane noted that shorts were a bad choice of attire for him, as like with a lot of bodybuilders, it highlighted that he often skipped "legs day".

"Ahh, the comedian," said Luke. "I wouldn't normally agree to an impromptu meeting, but I had to meet the man who got young Leon here to ask if I wanted to speak to his crotch."

Crane sensed the doorman tense next to him as both Luke and Paul laughed at his expense.

"Thankfully, I'm not as naïve," Luke continued. "So, what is your real name?"

"At this point, it's irrelevant," replied Crane. "I've only come here to ask you one question."

Luke narrowed his eyes and pursed his lips as he seemed to ponder this for a second. "You've got me intrigued, but I do think it's good etiquette to introduce ourselves. I'm Luke, this is Paul, and I've already told you Leon is the young man you've embarrassed this evening."

"I'm not here to make friends," Crane said nonchalantly. "Like I said, I've only come here to ask *you* one question."

Luke's expression darkened. He wasn't accustomed to being spoken to so abruptly.

"Tell him to fuck off, Luke," Paul chimed in.

"Excuse me, princess," Crane said, directing his words to Paul, "the grown-ups are talking."

"What did you just say?" Paul growled.

He jumped up from the desk and stomped towards Crane. Leon took a step to the side to get out of the way. Paul looked like the Incredible Hulk about to start a rampage. Crane had seen it all before. He'd witnessed big bullies relying on their size to intimidate people many times. Paul would be expecting him to run away, take a step back, or at least flinch. Crane did none of those things. He stared him straight in the eyes and took a step forward. A step towards the oncoming mass. Paul tried not to show it, but it definitely threw him off guard. He wasn't expecting that response, and it made him think twice. He stopped a yard away from Crane and stared him down, arms out wide, as if he were carrying a rolled-up carpet under each one. His fists were clenched, but he didn't attempt to throw a punch.

Crane wasn't bluffing. He may have been a few inches shorter and a few stone lighter, but he more than fancied his chances against Paul. In his experience, bodybuilders were never great fighters. They were big and heavy but sloth-like slow. Most of them struggled with the range of motion to throw a decent punch; in fact, most of them struggled with the range of motion to wipe their own arse properly.

"Leave it, Paul," Luke ordered.

Paul turned back to Luke, fists still clenched. "Seriously."

Luke nodded. "Just take a seat and chill out. Let's all calm down, shall we?"

Paul turned back to Crane. He scowled at him and then did as he was told and sat down in the armchair that faced Crane. He leaned forward, legs wide apart, elbows resting on the inside of his knees, ready to jump up at any moment like an American football player braced and ready for the whistle.

"So, what's this question you want to ask me?" Luke smiled, intending for it to look at least somewhat inviting, but it reeked of fakery.

Crane focused all his attention on Luke. This was the moment he had come for. He wanted to see his reaction clearly. He wanted to see if there was any glimmer of recognition. "What were you doing on the fifteenth of November almost five years ago?"

Nothing. Absolutely nothing. No reaction, no glimmer of recognition in his eyes, nothing at all. Then, a second later, he burst out laughing, a rapturous bout of laughter that both Paul and Leon joined in with.

"I can't remember what I did five days ago, never mind five years ago," Luke exclaimed. "What the hell is this? Wait, are you a copper?"

Crane shook his head. "No, but I am doing an investigation of sorts. I just need to know what you were doing on that date so that I can rule you out." Although deflated, he wasn't ready to give up on the lead yet. With Luke's background, he couldn't exactly expect him to remember one bad incident of many. Although the day had been beyond devastating for him, and the devastation was still much a part of his everyday life, it would have been just a moment in Luke's.

"Rule me out of what?"

"If you weren't involved, you don't need to know." Crane sealed his lips into a thin, tight line, feeling more hopeless by the second.

Luke smirked. "This is all very cryptic, but I must admit, I'm kinda curious to know what I was doing. Let me have a look." He pulled out his phone and started swiping, tapping, and scrolling. "Fifteenth of November five years ago?"

"That's right," Crane confirmed.

Luke stopped scrolling and tapped the screen. "I was in the Canary Islands, Gran Canaria to be precise. On holiday with my ex. I've even got the pictures to prove it."

Crane knew how easy it was to make a lie up on the spot, especially for a hardened criminal such as Luke. He knew he probably had a list of lies he went between, which probably came out of his mouth as easily as the truth. "Can I see them?"

"Of course you can," Luke replied, putting his phone back in his pocket. "Just come back with a warrant, and I'll happily show them to you."

"I told you, I'm not the police."

Luke smiled broadly and held his arms out wide. "Well, if you're not the police, then I think you'll agree that I've been very accommodating with you so far."

Crane considered pushing it, but he was confident Ricky would be able to confirm if his alibi was genuine, and the truth was, he trusted Ricky more than he trusted some pictures on Luke's phone.

"That's fine," Crane said. "I've got ways of checking."

Luke tilted his head slightly and gave Crane a steely stare. "If you're not the police, who the hell are you?"

"Someone you don't want to see again," replied Crane. "I'll see myself out. Do you mind if I use your fire exit?"

"Be my guest, officer."

Crane turned and walked out of the office and headed up the bare concrete steps. At the top was a standard fire exit door with a push-bar to open. He did just that and came out onto Womanby Street, which was more of a narrow lane than a street. It was pedestrianised and ran almost parallel to Westgate Street at the front of the club. The sun had finally set, and only a few lights illuminated the dark street. There were lots of blind spots in the nooks and crannies, making it appear quite eerie, like something out of an old serial killer movie. Crane made a mental note of where the fire exit was and then headed back to his truck.

\*\*\*

Luke waited until he heard the fire door close, then he walked over to the doorway and looked up the stairs just to check that the man had definitely gone.

"Who the *hell* was that?" he exclaimed. "And what the *hell* was that all about?"

"Why did you stop me from beating the shit out of him?" argued Paul, Luke assumed due to feeling as if he'd had his manhood compromised.

Luke tutted. "I know you're loving the steroids at the moment, but I think it's messing with your head and your judgement. Did you see the look in his eyes when you went for him? He didn't even flinch. It was as if he wanted you to take a swing for him. You mark my words, he's definitely some kind of law enforcement, maybe not strictly police, maybe a three-letter abbreviation of some sort."

Paul nodded thoughtfully, his irritation seemingly already weakened by the reason for keeping his fists to himself one he deemed good enough. "He did seem over-confident."

"He did," Luke agreed. "And why else would he be so confident? We know he wasn't armed because Leon would have put the metal-detecting wand over him. It's part of our club protocols. Every single customer gets checked with the wand before they're allowed in. And even if he forgot to put the wand over him, which I'm sure he didn't, Leon definitely would've patted him down before bringing him back here. Isn't that right, Leon?"

Luke knew full well Leon hadn't done any of those things. For all they knew, their mystery guest could have been carrying a weapon.

Leon looked like a schoolboy who had been caught smoking behind the bike shed by the headmaster. He tentatively nodded.

"Are you sure about that, Leon?" Luke asked. "Did you check he was unarmed?"

After a short pause, he said, "Sorry, Boss. I forgot." He actively avoided any kind of eye contact with Luke.

Luke tutted a few times while shaking his head. "That's not good enough, Leon."

"Sorry, Boss. I promise it won't happen again."

"Which fucking part?" Luke yelled. His face turned bright red with rage, and the veins in his neck protruded like cables running up into his jaw. The outburst made Leon jump, it even made Paul flinch. He continued his rant with the same vigour. "Is it the part where you thought his name was Mike fucking Rotch? Or the part where you didn't put the wand over him when you let him into the club? Maybe even the part where you let him back here without even patting him down? Or was it the part where you just fucking lied to me?"

Leon stared at the floor, and his legs began to tremble uncontrollably.

Luke turned his back on Leon and sauntered over to the dart-board. He pulled out his three darts and stepped back to the end of the oche. He quietly and calmly said, "You need to be punished, Leon. Put your hand on the dartboard."

"B-Boss?" Leon's voice caught in his throat.

"I said, put your hand on the *fucking* dartboard."

Leon glanced over his shoulder at the door, but he slowly and grudgingly walked to the dartboard, away from the point of exit.

Paul stood up and made his way back to the desk, back to part sitting, part leaning on the edge of it. A sinister smile spread across his face, and there was a gleam of excitement in his eyes. He was a true sadist.

Leon haltingly raised his visibly trembling right hand to the board. He placed it flat, palm to the board, dead centre, right on top of the bullseye. His back was to Luke, chest against the wall, head turned to the left. Luke could tell he did not want to see what was coming.

"The way I see it," Luke said, "you made three big mistakes, and I've got three darts. Now, whatever you do, do not move your hand. If you take your hand off the board, I've got another punishment lined up for you, and trust me, this punishment pales in comparison." Luke lined his right foot along the throw line of the oche mat and raised a dart in the air as if he were making a toast. "This first dart is for your naivety." He paused for effect before baring his teeth and growling the name, "Mike Rotch."

Leon tensed and held his breath in anticipation.

Luke lined up the first dart and then released for the throw. A standard throw, not too hard, but certainly not soft. It sailed through the air and hit the nail of Leon's middle finger. Due to the curvature of the nail, the point slid to the right and dug into the flesh on the side of Leon's fingernail. By this point, the dart was at an angle and had lost a lot of its forward momentum. The tip continued on its travel, hit one of the metal number dividers, and then dropped to the floor. It tore a small flap of skin out of the side of Leon's nail, which began dripping with blood immediately.

Leon exhaled slowly and noiselessly. It was painful, but it wasn't as bad as it could have been.

"You lucky bastard," Luke muttered, irritated by the poor shot. He swiftly raised another dart. "Now, this second dart is for not checking if our mystery guest was armed."

Leon held his breath once again.

Luke took aim and threw the second dart with a lot more venom than the first. The dart zipped through the air before the point penetrated the web of skin between Leon's index and middle finger, close to the space between the knuckles. It passed straight through the skin and lodged itself deep into the sisal fibres of the board. The barrel of the dart pinned and trapped the web of skin on Leon's hand tight to the board. A short guttural grunt escaped his throat, but he didn't move his hand.

"Nice shot." Paul laughed.

Luke held up the third and final dart. "Now, this one is for your worst transgression—you lied to me. I need to make this one count. You need to understand that you *never, ever* lie to me."

Luke silently took a step closer, which seemed to delight Paul, who was grinning like an evil clown. He was enjoying the show, probably a bit too much. This time, Luke didn't line the dart up; instead, he raised his left knee like a baseball pitcher and then ferociously hurled it at the board. It slammed into the centre of Leon's hand with a jarring thud.

Leon howled. A chilling howl of genuine agony.

Paul howled too, but with laughter instead of agony, and slapped his knee in delight. A sinister, twisted laugh from a sinister, twisted man.

Luke took purposeful footsteps towards Leon and then breathily whispered into his ear, "Don't you ever lie to me again. Now, go and clean yourself up, and clean my darts while you're at it." He meant for it to feel more threatening than yelling.

Luke walked over to the drinks cabinet and fixed himself a brandy, neat, while Leon pulled the dart from the web of skin between his index and middle finger. He did it quickly, as if he were ripping off a plaster. It was the only dart that was attaching his hand to the board. Once he was free from it, he picked up the first dart from the floor and then left the office, cradling his injured hand, the final dart still stuck deep into the back of it.

"Leon," Luke called out after him, "which one of the sluts was talking to the mystery man earlier?"

The response was immediate. "Ivanka, Boss."

"Tell her to come and see me. I want to know exactly what they were talking about."

"Yes, Boss."

"Oh, and, Leon. It might be worth showing her what happens to people who try lying to me."

# Chapter Eleven

Ricky and Chloe were exactly how Crane had left them—on the sofas, frantically pressing buttons on their controllers. Gunshots resonated around the barn. He wasn't surprised he'd had to let himself in.

Crane walked up to the seating area, but he didn't sit down. "You guys almost finished?"

"Almost, just three left to kill," Chloe replied through gritted teeth. Her eyes were squinted at the screen in concentration and her lips were clamped shut. "Wait, who's—" Her eyes popped open from a squint to full circles and her hand came up to cover her mouth. "*Nooooo*. Someone just snuck up behind me and slit my throat."

Ricky laughed at Chloe's reaction. "Don't worry, I'll get him for you."

They watched the screen as Ricky's character went on a rampage around what looked like an abandoned factory and killed the three remaining players in less than a minute. The screen immediately changed colour after the last one was killed, and a list of names filled the screen. Two names were in bold—Chloe had come fifth and Ricky was declared the winner at the top.

"You're like, insanely good at this game," Chloe exclaimed.

Ricky's cheeks reddened slightly from the praise. "Thanks."

"Come on, then," Crane said. "I'd better get you back before it gets too late."

Chloe stood up, leaving her controller on the sofa. "Thank you, Ricky. That was awesome." She held her hand up for a high five. Ricky looked at it for a second before awkwardly giving it a soft tap with the palm of his hand. Chloe giggled and headed to the front door.

"Jump in the truck, I'll be there in two minutes," Crane said. He watched her skip outside and then he turned to Ricky. "Thank you for looking after her for me."

"There's no need to thank me," said Ricky, waving a dismissive hand. "She's a great kid and, to be honest, I've had a great time."

"It looked like it." Crane laughed.

Ricky's expression suddenly turned serious, his smile disappearing and his brow furrowing. "How did it go with Luke Maddocks?"

Crane gave him a lopsided grin. He hadn't actually told Ricky where he was going or what he was doing, but Ricky knew. He always knew. "I just went there to ask him what he was doing on the day Beth died. I wanted to see his reaction. I wanted to see the whites of his eyes when I said the date to him. I wanted to see if there was any kind of recognition."

"And...?" Ricky gestured with his hands for him to continue, eager to know what had happened.

"There was nothing," Crane said. "The date didn't seem to mean anything to him at all."

"What does that tell you?"

Crane folded his arms and took a thoughtful breath before answering. "Not much, to be honest. On the one hand, it makes me think it wasn't him because most people would remember the date they caused someone's death. But on the other hand, he seems like the kind of scumbag who really wouldn't give a toss." He looked at the floor, lost in his thoughts for a second, then looked back up and fixed his gaze on Ricky. "I do need you to look into something for me though, if you would?"

"Of course, what is it?"

"When I asked him what he was doing on the date, he checked his phone and said he was in Gran Canaria. He said he had pictures to prove it. Is there any way you could check it out?"

"I've already tried looking him up on social media, but he doesn't have any kind of online presence. He certainly doesn't seem the type to go posting his holiday pictures online." Ricky paused for thought, then said, "Do you know which holiday provider or airline he would have used?"

Crane shook his head.

"Any idea what airport he flew from?"

Crane shook his head again.

"Any idea what date he was meant to have flown out?"

Another shake of the head.

"I'll need to do some searching and digging." Ricky was speaking to himself rather than to Crane, putting together an action plan. "It's not gonna be easy. I'll start with historical flight data from Cardiff Airport. Although he could have flown from Bristol or even one of the London airports. In fact, it might be better if I try and hack the destination airport and their arrivals data." He turned slightly, as if he was eager to head over to his workstation at the back of the barn. "I'll see what I can find in Gran Canaria Airport, although I'm not sure how good their data capture would be or how long they keep records for."

"There's no rush," Crane said. "It doesn't completely prove his guilt if he's lying, but it would completely rule him out if he's telling the truth."

"If he was in Gran Canaria that day, it would mean your mystery caller is trying to set you up."

"Exactly. But if Luke is lying and he wasn't in Gran Canaria, we'll have more digging to do."

"Leave it with me."

Crane left and closed the door behind him. He didn't bother waving to Ricky before jumping into his truck, knowing he'd already be at the back of the barn getting to work. He started his engine and swung his pickup around in the gravel driveway.

Chloe put her seatbelt on as Crane pulled away. "What's going on?"

Crane glanced at Chloe, who was staring at him attentively. "What do you mean?"

"First we had that weird phone call at dinner and then you left me with Ricky and disappeared for two hours."

"You seemed to have fun," Crane said in a half-hearted attempt to digress the conversation away from what had been going on, but as he'd anticipated, it failed miserably.

"I did, but that's not the point. I can tell something's going on." She crossed her arms and glared at him.

"You're right, something is going on," Crane conceded, with a sigh, "but to be honest, I'm not sure exactly what's going on myself."

"Should I be worried?"

Crane stopped the truck to look at Chloe just before turning out of Ricky's driveway, hoping she could see the trust in his eyes. "You have absolutely nothing to worry about, I promise."

"Has it got something to do with the Fords?"

"Who?" Crane asked. "The drug dealers?"

She nodded.

"Not at all," Crane assured her. "Look, to put your mind at rest, it's to do with Beth. It's about her accident. I'm still trying to find out exactly what happened on that night." He saw her eyes soften slightly, but she still looked tense and full of worry. "You don't need to know any more details than that. I just want you to know that you're safe, and I promise you have nothing to worry about."

She seemed to be reassured by this and eased back in her seat.

Crane pulled out and headed towards Caerphilly Mountain. It took a little less than the usual ten minutes to get home due to the lack of traffic on the roads at this time of an evening.

Crane pressed the button on his key fob to open the gate before it was even in sight. He eased on the brake to slow down more than he normally would've if he was on his own and turned into the driveway.

"*What?*" Chloe exclaimed, leaning forward and peering up at the house. It looked particularly impressive at night—illuminated by several LED uplighters and with the night sky as its backdrop. "You live here?"

"You know you've been here before, right?"

"When I was like eight." She snorted. "It was a long time ago, and I didn't have the same sort of ability to be impressed. I mean, I knew you had a nice big house on the mountain, but *this*... this is something else."

"Thank you," Crane said. "A lot of blood, sweat, and tears went into building it." He cringed at his own choice of words, but Chloe was too busy staring out the window and up at the house to notice.

He parked in front of the double garage as usual and shut off the engine.

"Why don't you park in the garage?" asked Chloe.

"It's full."

She stared at the garage intensely. "Of what?"

Crane didn't want to get into it, but he also didn't want to lie. "Stuff."

"What kind of stuff?"

"What's with the interrogation?" He hoped the poke at the fact she was pushing the same question would get her to drop the intrigue, but Chloe seemed pretty fixated on finding out exactly what was in there.

She smiled. "Because judging by the house, I think you've got a nice car in there."

He couldn't help but laugh. "You're a very perceptive young lady."

Crane got out of the truck without answering and pressed another button on his key fob. Chloe jumped out and stood next to him. The left garage door began to open electronically, and the light inside automatically switched on, activated by the movement of the door. Bright white light seeped out onto the driveway in front of them. The door continued to rise and revealed a Maserati GranTurismo Centennial Edition in magna red.

Chloe raised her hands and partially covered her mouth. "Oh. My. God. That is like, sicker than sick."

She walked into the garage and around the side of the Maserati, then she saw what was in the other bay, and her jaw dropped to the floor. She was looking at a Ferrari F8 Spider finished in Argento Nurburgring Silver with yellow brake callipers.

"Wow," she whispered. "Just... wow." It was the first time today Crane had seen her speechless.

She walked around them both slowly, stepping over the electrical cables that trailed across the floor for the trickle chargers. They were always connected to the batteries when they were parked up in the garage to prevent them from going flat. He didn't drive either of them very often.

"I've never been this close to a Ferrari before," she said. "Why don't you drive these instead of the pickup truck?"

"They're not the most practical, especially for work."

"How much did they..." She seemed to catch herself during the question. "Sorry, it's rude to ask."

Crane laughed, then pointed at the Maserati, knowing full well what question she'd begun to ask. "This one was actually a gift from a client. He noticed me admiring it from his vast car collection while I was doing some work for him, and he gave it to me after I helped him."

Chloe stood unblinking, seemingly trying to process what she'd just been told for a few seconds. "Really? What did you do for him?"

Crane had hoped she wouldn't ask that. He thought quickly and gave a vague answer. "I did some consultancy work for him and saved him some money."

Chloe brushed her fingertips across the bonnet of the Maserati. "You must have saved him *a lot* of money."

Crane nodded. He had. Four and a half million pounds to be precise. At least, that was how much the painting he'd recovered was worth now after it had been stolen from one of his client's homes in London.

"What about this one?" she asked, referring to the Ferrari.

"That one I bought myself. As a treat."

"A very, very nice treat."

"It is," he agreed, "but if I can give you some life advice, the satisfaction you get from buying material items is short-lived. It's amazing how quickly you can get used to having something before you're then looking for the next thing"—he looked at the Maserati—"and then the next thing"—his eyes flicked across to the Ferrari—"and then the thing after that." He pictured a Lamborghini Urus in his head, a car he'd done well to avoid buying so far. After a while, he'd realised getting nice vehicles only filled temporary voids.

She looked at him blankly.

"You're not getting it, are you?"

She shook her head. "I would never get used to having a Ferrari."

Crane chuckled to himself, knowing he would have had that exact thought once upon a time. "I tell you what, I'll do you a deal. If you stay away from those girls from earlier today, knuckle down with your schoolwork, *and* get good results in all of your exams, it's yours when you pass your driving test."

Her eyes popped and she took a sharp intake of breath. "Really?"

"No." Crane grinned. "It would cost too much for your insurance and it would be too dangerous, being over seven hundred horsepower."

Chloe laughed half-heartedly and gave him a playful push.

"But I will pay for your driving lessons and buy your first car. Something small and not too powerful."

She looked at him through narrow eyes. "Really?" Her response wasn't as high-pitched with excitement this time.

"Really." He nodded. "But only if you do well in school. That's your incentive."

"Deal." She held out her hand to shake on it, and Crane immediately shook it.

"Come on, let's go in. It's getting late."

Crane pressed the fob to close the garage door and walked around to the front door of the house and opened it. He disarmed the alarm, re-locked the door once they were both inside, and then re-armed the alarm.

"You take your security very seriously," Chloe commented.

He told her about the seven cameras that recorded all the grounds around the property. He also told her that the alarm was set so that she could go anywhere inside the house, but she shouldn't open any external doors or windows. If she did, she would wake up half of Cardiff and half of Caerphilly. He didn't tell her that behind a canvas picture next to the front door was a hidden compartment built into the wall that held a loaded Heckler & Koch VP9 Match 9mm pistol with two spare seventeen-round magazines. He also didn't tell her about the shotgun he had hidden under his bed.

He gave her a full tour of the house, all twelve rooms of it. They finished in the spare room she was going to be staying in. It was quite a plain but cosy room. Plush grey carpet, just like the rest of the first floor, white walls, and a king-size bed covered in a light grey duvet set. A touch of colour came from a canvas picture of a coastal sunset on the wall above the bed and a few throw pillows. They had been Beth's touches. Chloe looked around and nodded in approval. She dropped her overnight bag onto the bed.

"Where does that go?" she asked, pointing at a second door in the room, this one closed.

"It's the ensuite," Crane said plainly—having ensuites was another thing in his life he'd learned to take for granted.

"What?" The thin line of her brow jumped in surprise. "I have my own bathroom?"

"Yep, it's all yours."

She ran to the door and opened it, a big grin on her face as she turned back to Crane. "This is awesome."

"I'm glad you approve," Crane said, chuckling. "I'm going downstairs to get a drink. Do you want anything?"

"No, thanks, I'm good." She plonked herself on the end of the bed, looking all around the room. Crane wondered if she was trying to spot any other doors.

"OK. If you do want anything during the night, just go down and help yourself." He pointed to the TV, which was mounted on the wall opposite the bottom of the bed. "The control for that should be in the bedside drawer. If you need anything else, just give me a shout or a knock."

"Okay." She lay on her back and smiled up at the ceiling, seemingly content. "Goodnight, Uncle Tom."

"Goodnight, Chloe." His hand reached for the light switch as he started to pull the door to, and he quickly moved his hand away, hoping Chloe hadn't noticed. A small seed of sadness floated down and landed at the bottom of his heart as it hit him, as it often did, that he didn't and most likely wouldn't ever have a child now after Beth's death.

"Uncle Tom?"

He glanced at Chloe.

"I just want to say thank you, you know, for letting me stay over." If she'd seen his near touch of the light switch and immediate sadness after, she didn't show it.

"You're welcome."

"I've really enjoyed spending time with you today."

Her words meant a lot to Crane, but he'd spent so long trying to swim away from his emotions for fear of them drowning him completely that he didn't now know how to completely express what he was feeling. "Me too," he said. "I'm sorry it's been so long. Goodnight."

"Goodnight."

He headed down to the kitchen and fixed himself a whisky Mac, same as the night before, but this time using a twelve-year-old scotch—it was Friday night after all. He took a sip and savoured it before heading back upstairs, drink in hand. The door to the spare room was closed, and he could hear the shower in the ensuite running as he walked past on his way to the master bedroom.

Once there, he followed Chloe's lead and took a long hot shower in his own ensuite. Afterwards, he drained his whisky Mac and got into bed. He went to play a guided meditation to help him fall asleep, but he was conscious that Chloe might hear if she came out of the spare room. He got out of bed and went into the walk-in wardrobe. After a few minutes of searching, he found what he was looking for towards the back of a drawer. It was an old set of big, padded headphones, the ones that cover the whole of your ears. Not ideal, but certainly more comfortable than earphones. He popped them on, got himself comfortable in bed, and pressed play.

# Chapter Twelve

Crane's body clock woke him up. He knew what the time would be even before he raised his head and glanced at his watch on the bedside table—six on the dot. He didn't even attempt to stay in bed. Too many thoughts and too many questions had been and still were swirling around inside his head, leaving him restless. Could Luke Maddocks have been the man in the SUV following Beth? Could he be the man who'd caused her to crash? Who was the mystery caller? A disgruntled employee? If it was a disgruntled employee, how would they have linked Luke Maddocks to Beth's accident? Had Luke Maddocks confided in someone who now wanted to clear their conscience? Or maybe they wanted to get back at Luke for some reason? Or what if he was just being set up? Could the mystery caller be using Beth's accident to create a conflict with Luke Maddocks? They were all plausible theories, but for now he just needed to be patient. He would know more once Ricky confirmed whether or not Luke had been in Gran Canaria at the time of the accident.

He got dressed in shorts and a training T-shirt and headed downstairs, making sure he was extra quiet as he tiptoed past the spare room. He didn't want to disturb Chloe this early on a Saturday morning. He went into the gym room, but he had no plans for a brutal workout today. He ignored the cable machines, the free weights, and the heavy bag and went to the back of the room, where there was a wall-mounted TV. He picked up the remote control and then got himself comfortable on a yoga mat just in front of it. He spent a few minutes searching before eventually selecting a sixty-minute Yin Yoga routine by one of his favourite instructors. The practice of holding poses and stretches for between three to five minutes ensured that the stretches went deep, all the way to the connective tissues. Crane always found Yin Yoga did him the world of good, both physically and mentally. It was a great way to release tight muscles and an effective way to calm a turbulent mind. The session ended in the usual Savasana pose, and he felt calm and loose, the choppy waters of his mind now serene and still.

Crane made his way into the kitchen, his footsteps heavier than they'd been upstairs, yet still somehow light from relaxation. He stepped through the open doorway of the kitchen-diner and stopped, squinting slightly as he double-checked he was seeing things right. Yep, despite his generalising of teenagers, Chloe was definitely sitting on a stool at the island, phone in hand at just after seven on a Saturday morning.

"I wasn't expecting to see you up so early."

Chloe looked up from her phone and smiled. "I never really sleep in late."

"A teenage girl who doesn't sleep in late? I'm no expert in the matter, but I'm pretty sure that would make you one of a kind."

Chloe giggled. "I don't sleep very well, to be honest. I haven't for a while."

"Why? What you got going on in that mind of yours?" asked Crane as he approached the island.

She shrugged and put her phone facedown on the island. She began twisting and fidgeting with the metal finger grip on the back of the glittery lilac phone case. "I don't know, just stuff. Do you ever get anxious?"

"Of course I do. Everyone does."

Chloe's head snapped up to look at him. "Really?"

"Yeah." Crane smiled. "It's a form of fear, the oldest, most natural feeling known to all living creatures, not just humans, and certainly not just you."

Chloe's brow was furrowed, trying to take it all in. "How do I stop it?"

"Stop anxiety?"

Chloe nodded.

"You can't stop it. It's your brain's way of telling you to get your game face on because something important is happening." Crane pulled out another stool and sat down at the opposite side of the island. "Back in caveman days, it was something that helped keep them alive. That uncomfortable feeling would have told them to stay safe back in the cave, to not go out in the dark, to not cuddle that sabre-tooth tiger."

Chloe giggled, reminding Crane of her actual age and not that wannabe young adult hanging around with older teens who smoke weed he'd met just yesterday.

Crane leaned forward and rested his elbows on the cool marble worktop of the island. "The difference nowadays is we're relatively safe from the kinds of threats we would have faced back then, but our brains don't understand this." He tapped his temple with his index finger. "Thousands of years of evolution have got our brains wired to be constantly looking for dangers, and in this day and age, the dangers it finds are usually small and mundane, nowhere near the life-threatening dangers humanity faced back in those days, but the brain still creates the same feeling for us."

Chloe's shoulders sagged slightly. "So, you're saying there's no way of getting rid of the feeling at all? Not even for a little bit?"

"Yes and no. In the short term, you can do things that can temporarily ease the feeling, like breathing techniques and visualisation exercises, which are all great tools to use. But in the long term, the best advice I can give you is to accept it."

Chloe chewed the inside of one cheek as she looked at the worktop, deflated. Crane knew he wasn't giving her the answer she wanted to hear, but he didn't want to say something just to comfort her; he wanted to give her the truth. He also knew that although she was only fourteen, she was switched-on enough to tell if he tried to bullshit her.

"It's just a feeling," he continued. "Just accept that you're feeling it. You could even thank your brain for looking out for you, for protecting you."

Chloe scrunched up her nose and looked at him as though he smelled of spoiled milk. "Thank my brain?"

Crane smirked. "I know it sounds funny, but it works. Trust me. It helps you to detach yourself from the feeling itself. The main point I'm making is don't fight it, don't try to stop the feeling, you'll just make it snowball and it becomes bigger and stronger. Just accept it and then do what that Disney Princess told you to do, you know, the one in the snow and ice. You wouldn't stop singing her song when you were younger."

"Elsa." Chloe laughed. "'Let it go'."

"That's it," he said, laughing with her. "Accept it and then let it go. One of the main reasons they make the training in the military so challenging—not just physically, but mentally too—is to grow your comfort zone. It's to make sure that even under times of high stress and anxiety, you can still perform your job. You still feel the feeling, but it doesn't stop you from doing what needs to be done."

Chloe nibbled on her bottom lip thoughtfully.

"This is a very deep conversation for a Saturday morning," Crane said. "Come on, what do you want for breakfast?"

Chloe grinned. "What you got?"

Crane went through the different options he had to offer. She settled on porridge topped with sliced banana, honey, and a sprinkle of chia seeds. She washed it down with orange juice. Crane had the same, but he washed his down with coffee.

"Uncle Tom?" Chloe's head was turned down slightly and she was looking up at him with puppy-dog eyes.

Crane looked up suspiciously.

"I was wondering, is there any chance we could go for a drive in your Ferrari?" She beamed an infectious smile that made him chuckle.

"Go and get dressed," he said, with a sideways nod of the head.

Chloe was strapped in next to him, the retractable roof was open, and so was the garage door in front of them. The morning sun beamed down onto the driveway, and clear blue skies stretched as far as the eye could see. Invisible birds could be heard singing cheerfully in the trees. Unfortunately, Crane disturbed them by pushing the start button. The three-point-nine-litre V8 engine roared to life. The sound was truly thunderous in the enclosed space of the garage. Chloe let out an excited squeal next to him. He pressed the key fob to open the front gate, waited for it to fully open, and then they took off. The giddy smile never left Chloe's face the whole time they were out.

Afterwards, he pulled back into the driveway, turned the Ferrari around, and reversed it back into its space in the garage. He allowed the engine to idle and gradually cool a bit before shutting it down.

"That was epic," exclaimed Chloe.

Crane turned to look at her and couldn't stop himself from bursting out laughing. Chloe had worn her hair down for the drive, but not much of it was down anymore—it was puffed up all over the place. She looked as if she'd travelled in time and come back from an eighties music video.

"What are you laughing at?"

Crane turned the rear-view mirror so that she could take a look at herself.

Chloe screeched with laughter. "Look at the state of me."

Crane was pleased she had the ability to laugh at herself.

They went back inside the house for Chloe to tidy herself up, or at least put a brush through her hair. She came back downstairs carrying her overnight bag, with her hair up in a high ponytail, just like she'd had it the day before. Crane locked up the house and then they jumped into the pickup truck. This time, when he started the two-point-eight-litre diesel engine of the Hilux, Chloe didn't squeal; instead, she performed an exaggerated sigh and pouted her bottom lip. She told him it was no Ferrari.

On the way to dropping Chloe back home, he stopped at a fuel station to get some cash out of the cashpoint to replenish what he'd spent the night before. He always liked to carry cash on him—it was useful, especially if you needed to loosen lips and gain information. He also popped inside the shop and grabbed himself a large coffee in a takeout cup and a strawberry milk-shake, as requested by Chloe.

"Thank you for last night," Chloe said as they pulled up outside her home. "And this morning."

"You're more than welcome."

"Can we do it again soon?" She looked at him hopefully as she undid her seatbelt.

"What? The sleepover or the joyride in the Ferrari?" Crane joked.

"Both." She giggled. "Maybe we could go out in the Maserati next time?"

Crane chuckled. "Definitely. You enjoy your holiday this week, and we'll catch up when you get back."

There was a slightly awkward moment where it looked as if she wanted to hug him. She seemed to consider all her options before eventually settling on holding her fist out for a fist bump.

Crane obliged by bumping her fist.

"See ya," she said, jumping out of the truck.

Crane lowered his window, and as she walked around the bonnet and reached his side of the truck, he said, "Remember, be good and work hard in school. You've got a big incentive now."

She beamed, her eyes shining with excitement. She gave an enthusiastic nod and then headed up the path to the front door. It opened just as she reached it, and Sarah stepped out. He couldn't hear exactly what was said, but Chloe's body language appeared to be very excitable. He managed to catch the words "amazing" and "Ferrari".

Sarah seemed to tell Chloe to head inside and then she walked down the path towards Crane.

"It sounds like she had a blast with you," she said, smiling at him.

"We both did," Crane replied, grinning. "She really is a great kid."

Sarah nodded in agreement, but the corners of her lips were downturned. "She is. I just hope she finds some decent friends and stays away from *those* girls."

"Well, I've given her an incentive to do just that," said Crane. "Well, that and she needs to work hard in school and get good results in her exams."

Sarah arched an inquisitive brow. "An incentive?"

Crane nodded. "I told her I would pay for her driving lessons when she's old enough and buy her a car when she passes her test."

Sarah's mouth dropped into an "O" shape. "You'll pay for lessons *and* buy her a car?"

"Only if she's good and does well in school. I'm sure you'll have to keep reminding her of that part."

"I will, don't you worry about that," said Sarah, "but buy her a car? That's way too much." She took a step closer and lowered her voice to make her next point, even though there was no way Chloe would be able to hear her from inside the house. "Also, it might be wise to only offer to pay for a block of lessons. We don't know how many she'll need; it could get expensive. Maybe as a birthday or Christmas present."

"It's too late," Crane said, chuckling. "We already shook on it and I gave her my word."

"You can't," Sarah replied, grimacing. "It's way too much money."

Crane shook his head. "Not if it helps to keep her on the straight and narrow. It'll be worth every penny."

Sarah hesitated, as if she was still unsure about being able to accept such generosity, but she eventually seemed to accept that it wasn't really up to her. "Thank you," she said. "You're a good man, Tom." She placed her hand on top of his forearm, which was resting across the lower ledge of the open window.

Crane waved off the compliment, partly because he wasn't good at accepting compliments and partly because she left her hand on his arm a little longer than he felt comfortable with.

"And what's this about a Ferrari?" she asked. "I knew you'd done well for yourself, but wow. Business must be booming."

This was exactly the reason he had been reluctant to show Chloe what was in his garage. It was the only extravagant purchase he had made that truly advertised his level of wealth, and it made him cringe. He hated the idea of being flashy or showy with money. He wore decent clothes, but they were unbranded. He wore a nice watch, but nothing too flashy. Admittedly, his home was impressive, but Chloe was the first person he had invited inside in years.

"Yeah, it's been going well," he admitted, "but I probably shouldn't have splashed out on it; it was a bit frivolous of me."

Sarah tutted and swatted his comment away with her hand. "Don't be daft. If you can do it, why not? If anyone deserves to treat themselves, it's you. You've been through so much."

Crane forced a smile and tried to change the subject. "I hope you don't mind, but I agreed that Chloe could stay over again soon. I didn't say when, I just said that I'd speak to her after the holiday and we'd book something in."

Sarah snorted. "Of course I don't mind. I think it's great for her to have a positive and responsible male role model in her life."

Crane just gave a lopsided grin at the half compliment to him and half dig at his brother.

"Sorry," said Sarah, tapping his forearm and rolling her eyes. "I'm babbling on at you, and I'm sure you've got places to go and people to see."

He did, but not until later. He was due to meet a friend for lunch. A friend that wasn't Ricky. Instead of saying that, he said, "Don't apologise; it's always good to catch up with you."

She thanked him for having Chloe and then they said their goodbyes. He turned the truck around in the cul-de-sac and waved as he drove past. Sarah stood on the doorstep and waved back before closing the front door.

He turned right out of the cul-de-sac, and as he drove away from the junction, a black Audi pulled out directly behind him. When he reached the next junction, he took a left. A little later, the Audi also took a left. He reached a set of traffic lights that were fortunately showing green for the filter to turn right. He turned right. A little later, the black Audi turned right. That was when Crane really started to take notice of it.

# Chapter Thirteen

Crane continued to drive normally—he didn't speed up, he didn't slow down—but he did take the next four consecutive left turns, effectively doing a big square. The Audi made every turn that he did and continued to sit twenty to thirty yards behind him. Crane then slowed down slightly in an effort to make the Audi catch up with him, just so that he could try and make out who was driving it or at least find out how many there were in the car, but the Audi slowed with him to keep its distance. He could just about make out two men in the front, but the rear windows were heavily tinted and the interior was dark, so he couldn't tell whether or not there were others in the back.

He led them further east, just to get away from the built-up residential area. He took a main road that would have taken them to Newport, but he didn't stay on it for long, turning left into a country lane after a couple of minutes. The Audi turned off a few seconds later but still held its distance. Crane had ridden his bicycle through the country lane plenty of times as a kid, so he knew the lane well. About half a mile down, there was a nine-hole pitch and putt golf course on the left, which he drove straight past. Crane and Dylan had cycled to the pitch and putt course during the summers when they were teenagers, usually to use the driving range. They'd share a bucket of balls and see who could hit the furthest shot.

A little further on, there was a turn-off to the right, which he slowed and turned into. It opened into a rectangular gravel patch of wasteland about the size of a five-a-side football pitch. He chose it because it was always deserted and it was surrounded by empty farmland. There was no risk of any collateral damage with whatever happened next. It also had another exit, just in case the Audi blocked the entrance that he had just pulled into and he needed to get away.

He drove around to the left and stopped towards the end of the rectangle, in front of where the goalmouth would have been if it actually were a football pitch. The other exit back onto the lane was directly to his left. All he would need to do in order to make a quick escape would be to full-lock the steering wheel to the left and hit the accelerator. He could then pull back into the lane and choose whether to go left, back the way he'd come, or take a right.

The Audi slowly rolled into the gravel yard and then turned left and stopped so that it was directly facing the back of his pickup truck, around thirty yards behind him. It was in front of where the opposite goalmouth would've been.

Crane leant across and opened the glove compartment, reaching inside and pressing up firmly. There was an audible click and then a hidden compartment slowly and silently lowered. Sitting snug inside the hidden compartment was a black plastic case, of which Crane could only see the handle. He grabbed it and pulled the case out. It was made from thick, textured, hard plastic. It certainly weighed a lot more than it looked, and not just because of its contents. He placed it flat on the passenger seat, unclipped the two catches either side of the handle, and lifted the lid open. Neatly stored inside was a loaded Heckler & Koch VP9 Match 9mm pistol and two spare magazines, identical to the one he had next to his front door at home. He took it out of its cut-out in the foam and held it firmly in his right hand. It fitted perfectly. Cold and hard.

He watched the rear-view mirror intently. Thirty seconds passed, and nothing happened. The Audi sat there idling, the two men in the front unmoving, staring at the back of the pick-up. Crane didn't recognise either of them.

A few seconds later, all four doors opened simultaneously and four men got out. The driver was tall and chunky, like a retired rugby player. Big and broad, but a little soft around the edges. He had a full dark beard that joined with the hair going around the sides and back of his head. Textbook male pattern baldness was on display. In his right hand, he was holding what appeared to be the metal bar from a dumbbell set. It looked to be about a foot and a half long, shiny stainless steel, and it glinted brightly in the sunshine.

The passenger was a couple of inches shorter than the driver and wiry. He was holding the other dumbbell bar.

The guy getting out rear right was short and stocky. He had the biggest, but the weakest, weapon—a wooden baseball bat. It looked like an American-Louisville-Slugger-style bat. Long, heavy, and cumbersome, but completely useless when the person you're trying to hurt steps in close. Very poor choice.

Crane recognised the man getting out of the rear left immediately; however, he did look a little different to when he'd first met him the day before. His nose and cheeks were heavily taped and bandaged, and his eyes were swollen and black. A front door to the face would do that to you. He was gripping a claw hammer in his right hand.

It was the Fords and a couple of their cronies out for retribution.

Crane put the Heckler and Koch back in the case, locked the catches, and slid it back into the hidden compartment. He pushed the hidden compartment up until there was another audible click and it was secure again, then he closed the glove compartment back up. Instead of taking his gun, he grabbed his take-out cup of coffee from the centre console, which now only had around a third of its contents remaining, and those contents were now curdled and cold. He opened the door and stepped out of the truck.

He walked casually up to the four men, as if he had just popped out for a nice stroll in the sunshine. The driver, who Crane assumed was John Ford, was front and centre, the wiry one was on Crane's left, and the stocky one with the bat was on his right. It was completely the wrong place for him to be with a baseball bat—judging by which hand he was holding the bat in, he was right-handed, so he would need to swing it to the right in order to hit Crane, but that would put John Ford directly in the firing line.

*Amateurs*, thought Crane.

Billy, the son, was behind them, being protected by the three older men.

Crane stopped a few yards in front of them and raised his coffee cup in a "cheers" gesture. "Good morning, gentlemen," he said, with a friendly smile.

Now he was closer, he was even more sure the man front and centre was John Ford. There was a strong family resemblance. He looked like an older, uglier, and less bandaged version of Billy. There were more than a few grey specks in his beard and sideburns. Crane pegged him to be in his mid-forties, same as his two cronies by the look of it.

"I take it you know what we're here for?" asked John, striking the palm of his left hand with the dumbbell bar menacingly.

"Well, I'm assuming you're here to thank me for teaching your boy some manners," replied Crane.

John looked either side of him, at both of his cronies in turn. "It looks like we've got ourselves a comedian, lads." He sneered, then put his focus back on Crane. "We're here to make an example outta you. No one breaks into my house and hurts my boy."

Crane feigned a confused look. "I did."

The wiry one snickered, but he stopped himself almost immediately.

John glared at him, then he looked back at Crane and smiled. "And that's why we're gonna break you."

"Okay," said Crane, "but can I just clear up some rules before we get started? I'm guessing by the fact that you've brought some tools with you... and they've brought some weapons too, this is going to be a no holds barred, anything goes type of thing. But just so we're crystal clear from the start, this ends today." He tipped the coffee cup towards John. "If you win, I won't seek revenge." Then tipping the cup back to himself, he said, "If I win, you don't go anywhere near me or my niece ever again. Whatever happens, we all go our separate ways and hope to never cross each other's paths again. Deal?"

"If *you* win?" John asked, with an overly arched eyebrow and a sinister grin. "There's four of us, with weapons, and one of you, with a cup of coffee."

"That's true." Crane nodded. "But what do you guys do for a living? Drive around selling drugs all day? Do you want to know what one of the main parts of what I do for a living is?"

They looked at him blankly.

"I *hurt* people."

"Nice speech," said John, and they all sniggered.

"It's true. Just ask your son over there."

Billy scowled.

"Enough talking," said John. "Let's do this."

He went to step forward, but Crane raised his right hand, palm out, as a signal for him to stop. "Wait."

John hesitated and sneered, as if he was expecting Crane to beg for mercy.

"Is there any chance one of you wimps could hold my coffee?"

As he said it, he tossed the take-out coffee cup high into the air above them. Two natural and inevitable things happened—all four pairs of eyes watched the cup as it sailed above them and all of their chins raised slightly. Distraction and positioning. In the time that the cup was in flight and they were distracted, Crane stepped forward and hit John with a vicious roundhouse punch that struck the sweet spot on his raised chin. His jaw instantly shattered with a sickening snap and his lights went out while he

was still on his feet. Crane wasted no time. He had thrown the
punch with his right hand, so he was now naturally facing the
wiry one as he finished the movement.

The wiry one raised the dumbbell bar, but he was far too
late. Crane was already vaulting upwards from his semi-crouched
position, driving his legs up like pistons, and at the same time, he
whipped his elbow up. The point of his elbow connected with
the underside of the wiry one's chin. It was a ferocious blow that
almost took his head off. His entire body lifted off the ground a
few inches and he went completely stiff. He fell backwards like
a surfboard at the beach being blown over by a strong gust of
wind. Crane thought the shot may have even connected a little
too well.

Crane spun around to find the stocky one raising the bat up
and over his right shoulder. It was now cocked and ready to
take a swing. Crane feinted an attack, flinching his upper body
forward towards him. The stocky one reacted exactly how Crane
had hoped—he pushed back with his leading left leg, leaned his
upper body backwards, and made a wild swing with the bat. It
sailed harmlessly in front of Crane's face. The stocky one's left
leg was now fully locked straight out in front of him. Crane
pushed off his back foot and raised his front right knee, then he
drove his leading foot forward and down in a half front kick,
half stamping motion. His heel landed squarely on the stocky
guy's patella. Crane's foot barely slowed its downward motion
as his weight and the force behind it folded the guy's knee back
on itself. It felt and sounded like snapping the branch of a tree in
half. Ligaments, tendons, and cartilage all gave way at once with
a resounding crack.

The guy dropped the bat immediately and collapsed to the
ground. He grabbed his destroyed knee with both hands—it was
a natural reaction, according to biologists, it apparently helped
to reduce pain—unfortunately, it didn't seem to be working too
well for the stocky guy. He released an eardrum-shredding scream
that would have been heard for miles around. Crane swiftly

kicked him in the head, rendering him unconscious, only to quieten him.

That left the heavily bandaged son, Billy. But Billy hadn't moved an inch. He was frozen to the spot, the realisation of being the last man standing seemingly dawning on him as his whole body began to visibly tremble. In less than five seconds, he'd just witnessed his dad and both of his dad's cronies getting seriously hurt by one man. A man who appeared to be extremely competent at hurting people.

Crane looked him in the eye and could tell straight away that he didn't want any of it. "Can you drive?"

Billy blinked. "Wh-what?"

"Can you drive?"

Billy nodded.

"Good. Because it looks like you're going to be the designated driver to get this lot to the hospital. Now, drop the hammer."

Billy hesitated, Crane assumed out of fear of being weaponless, but then he shakily let the hammer slip from his grasp. It landed with a thud.

Crane bent down and firmly pushed two fingers into the front of the wiry one's neck, searching for his carotid artery. He had a strong pulse, but his breathing was extremely laboured. He was sucking in shallow breaths through a gaping mouth, and a mixture of blood and saliva oozed out of one side, where his head was tilted. Most of the teeth on view to Crane were either snapped or missing. Crane couldn't be sure if all the missing teeth were due to him or from previous fights, but he was pretty sure his teeth hadn't looked like that a few minutes ago. Crane rolled him onto his side, into a half-hearted attempt at the recovery position, before doing the same with the other two.

He stood up and fixed his gaze on Billy, who still hadn't moved a muscle. "Can I trust you to remind your dad that this is over?"

Billy stared back at him with wide eyes that were full of fear. It seemed to take a couple of seconds for him to realise that Crane had been speaking to him. Eventually, he blinked and stuttered, "Wh-what?"

"Am I seriously going to have to repeat everything to you?" Crane's expression and voice remained stern, but in truth, he was actually finding Billy's state of shock quite amusing.

Billy shook his head with small, quick movements. "Sorry, no, I'll remind him."

Crane's eyes narrowed. "Seriously, Billy, if you, your dad, or anyone even close to being linked to either of you goes anywhere near my niece, I'll kill you. And I mean that in the literal sense." Crane paused, as though a thought had crossed his mind. "You do know what I mean by the literal sense, don't you, Billy?"

Billy hesitated, but then nodded, short and sharp.

"Good."

Crane turned and walked back to his pickup truck, no fear within him that Billy would follow or attempt to jump him while his back was turned. He knew himself to be a good judge of character and good at sensing people's emotions and intentions, and it was glaringly obvious that Billy was incapable right now.

He jumped into his pickup, started it up, and turned the wheel full lock to the left. He gave a quick glance in his rear-view mirror. Billy was standing gormlessly, unmoving, staring at the back of the pickup. His dad and two cronies were still motionless on the ground in front of him. He looked like a six-foot-three lost little boy.

Crane accelerated and then pulled out of the patch of waste ground. He turned left and headed back up the lane. Back the way he had come. He left the Fords and their cronies where they belonged: in the past.

# Chapter Fourteen

Just as Crane was about to make the turn into Ricky's driveway, his phone started to ring through the speakers of the truck. The name of the caller was displayed on the touch screen in the centre of the dashboard. Crane chuckled and shook his head at the coincidence before tapping the green phone icon on the screen to answer the call.

"You got something for me?" he asked.

"Uh... yeah, I have," replied Ricky hesitantly.

"That's good timing. Open your front door; I'm just pulling up outside."

As Crane cut the engine and stepped out of his pickup, Ricky opened the door and hovered in the doorway as he waited, biting his lip. Crane stepped inside and then made himself comfortable on a sofa while Ricky made them both a coffee and then seated himself on the sofa diagonal to Crane.

"Come on, then," said Crane, resting his coffee on the arm of the sofa. "Spit it out. What have you got for me?"

Crane could already sense a nervous energy; Ricky wouldn't normally make them a coffee before telling him about something he'd just discovered. He was normally too excited to share his findings to even think about coffee. He was stalling for some reason.

Ricky shifted uncomfortably in his seat. "Before I tell you what I've found out, I need you to promise me that you're not going to do anything hasty or reckless."

Now Crane was really intrigued. He leaned forward. "What have you found out, Ricky?" His tone came out sharper than he'd intended, and he knew immediately that it hadn't been in line with someone ready to promise not "to do anything hasty or reckless".

"I mean it, Crane." Ricky tilted his head down and looked up at him through his eyebrows like a referee instructing a football player that he was on his final warning before getting cautioned. "I wouldn't normally need to say this, because you're always methodical and cautious with everything you do, but this is personal to you. It carries a lot of emotion for you."

"I understand what you're saying," said Crane, "but I'm fine, honestly." He hoped Ricky hadn't noticed his inability to promise yet again.

"I'm just making the point that we can't go jumping to any conclusions." He sat forward, resting his elbows on his knees, and hugged his coffee mug in both hands. "What I've found out doesn't prove that Luke Maddocks was in the car following Beth, it doesn't prove that he was anywhere near her."

"Okay," said Crane, starting to become impatient, but trying his best not to show it. "So, what does it prove?"

"Well, after a ridiculous amount of time searching through flight manifest after flight manifest after flight manifest, I eventually found out that Luke Maddocks flew business class from Bristol Airport. He boarded a direct flight from Bristol to Gran Canaria. The flight left at its scheduled time, on the fifteenth of November. But... the flight wasn't until eleven at night. So, technically, Luke Maddocks was *not* in Gran Canaria at the time of the accident."

Crane pursed his lips. *Luke lied.*

"But just because he wasn't in Spain at the time of the accident doesn't mean he was in the car behind Beth."

"No, it doesn't," said Crane, "however, if his flight was at eleven o'clock from Bristol Airport—which is just over an hour away from here, and usually passengers need to be at the airport two hours before a flight—if he was in the car behind Beth at eight o'clock, it would explain why he was driving so erratically, like he was in a rush to get somewhere." Crane gripped the handle of the mug tighter, the seed of potential growing in his mind. Irrelevant of the Gran Canaria holiday not being a lie, Luke Maddocks hadn't technically been there when Beth was killed, which made him even more of a suspect than before in Crane's mind.

"It does, but that's not enough."

"And he had a Range Rover Sport at the time," Crane dropped in, adding to the evidence.

"He did." Ricky nodded. "And it was booked into the Silver Zone car park at Bristol Airport while he was in Gran Canaria. But that's still not enough. It's all circumstantial; it doesn't place him or the car at the scene of the accident."

"You're right," agreed Crane, "It's not damning evidence, but it is starting to build a very compelling picture. There's a few too many coincidences for my liking." He was glad he hadn't promised Ricky anything. "I think I should pay Luke Maddocks another visit."

Ricky flashed his teeth in a grimace. "Before you go doing anything rash, there is something else we could check out first. The name of his ex-girlfriend was obviously on the flight manifest too. Her name's Sophie Davies. Maybe you could speak to her and find out if she was with him during the day before they went to the airport, find out if she was with him during the time of the accident that night."

"That's a good call," said Crane. "Where can I find her?" He was contemplating downing the rest of his coffee, ready to jump back into his pickup. He needed to collect all the puzzle pieces as quickly as possible for his own mind, needed to work out if they all completed the picture or if he was still stuck staring at an empty table, the pieces of Beth's puzzle elsewhere.

"I haven't got that far yet, that's the next thing on my to-do list." Ricky took a sip of coffee before continuing. "Do you remember I told you that Luke has been arrested on a number of occasions, but the charges have always been dropped due to insufficient evidence or a lack of witnesses willing to testify against him?"

Crane nodded.

"Well, on one of those occasions, an ex-girlfriend and her family had him arrested during a disturbance at their home, but then they dropped all charges and claimed it was a misunderstanding."

Crane raised a brow. "Sophie Davies?"

"That's right."

Crane sat up a little straighter. "What if she's the mystery caller? What if she was with him when he caused the accident and now she wants to clear her conscience?"

"That's a lot of what ifs," said Ricky. "If that is the case, why would she do it in such a cryptic way? If she wanted to clear her conscience, why wouldn't she just call you directly and tell you what happened? Or better still, why wouldn't she just call the police and tell them?"

Crane took an ample swig of coffee while he considered the points Ricky had raised, then he slowly lowered his mug and rested it on his knee. "Maybe because she's scared of implicating herself. If she was there, she was part of what happened. Whether she was driving the car or she was the passenger, she left Beth to die too. She would be guilty by association."

"Okay," said Ricky, "but playing devil's advocate, what if she wasn't there? What if Luke Maddocks wasn't there either?"

Crane couldn't deny that even though things were beginning to point to Luke Maddocks, there was still something niggling at him. Like a little bug crawling around in the back of his brain. Something that just didn't feel right. Although the truth was that none of it was feeling right. The weird letter. The mystery caller. He couldn't pinpoint it, but he couldn't stop feeling as if he was being set up in some way. But if he was being set up, who was setting him up? And why? What was the motive? What was the end goal?

"I agree," said Crane. "There's nothing so far that definitively puts Luke Maddocks in the car behind Beth, but there's also nothing that puts him anywhere else. I need to keep looking into it, but you're right, something else could be going on and we need to be careful." He took his final sip of coffee and placed the empty mug down on the table in front of him. "Can you find Sophie Davies for me? I'll speak to her before I do anything else."

Ricky placed his own mug on the table and jumped up from the sofa. "I'm on it."

Crane checked his watch. "Great, can I leave that with you, and I'll give you a call in a bit?"

"You got somewhere better to be?"

"I'm meeting Ella for lunch."

Ricky's brows shot up and he pursed his lips. "Oh yeah. Meeting Ella for lunch, are we?" He said it in a mocking "ooh la la" voice followed by some kissing noises.

"Don't." Crane smiled and shook his head. "You know it's not like that. She was Beth's best friend, for Christ's sake."

# Chapter Fifteen

Crane didn't have far to drive, as he was meeting Ella in a vegan cafe in an area of North Cardiff just over five minutes from Ricky's barn. It was a peaceful and affluent area of Cardiff, where the high street had a real village feel to it.

It was full of independent businesses—an organic bakery, a florist's, a post office, a local butcher's that had been there since the beginning of time, a hairdresser's with an adjoining barber shop for men, and a couple of quaint boutique shops, to name but a few. Only a handful of national franchises slightly ruined the village look and feel, like the fast-food sandwich bar and the betting shop. They were the proverbial sore thumbs of the village.

Crane drove down the high street, but as usual there was nowhere to park. He turned off the high street and into a side road that was predominantly residential but with a couple of businesses near the main high street, almost as if they were trying to create their own little extension of the high street. Fortunately, he found a spot just in front of a small off-licence. It was the last business property before the road ahead became fully residential and permits were required for parking. In Crane's experience, people who lived in those sorts of areas took parking very seriously indeed.

Just as he was about to shut off the engine, his phone began to ring through the speakers of the truck. He looked at the touch screen, expecting to see Ricky's name on the display, but it read "Private Number".

His finger hovered over the green icon to answer, but why should he? He never normally answered private or withheld numbers. Admittedly, he was curious to know if it was the mystery caller, and he was also interested to find out what they had to say. Maybe they would even answer some questions this time. But why give them the satisfaction of answering their anonymous call? No. He wouldn't answer. If they wanted to speak to him, they could do it on his terms. No more playing games. No more anonymity.

The phone rang off after six rings, and Crane knew the voicemail would have kicked in for the caller. He shut off the engine and checked the road. There was a car coming up behind, which he watched in the wing mirror and waited for it to pass, then opened the door to get out. As he stepped down and out of the truck, his phone beeped in his pocket. He had a new notification. He closed the door and pulled his phone out. The display on his phone informed him that he had a new voicemail.

He tapped the notification, and it automatically dialled his voicemail account. The automated system reconfirmed that he had one new voicemail, and it instructed him to press the number one if he wanted to listen to it. Crane tapped the number one.

A deep robotic voice, the same voice that he had heard on Chloe's phone in Luigi's said, "I'm surprised to see Luke Maddocks is still alive and kicking." Then it abruptly cut off, and the automated system asked him if he wanted to save, delete, or listen to the message again. He deleted the message and hung up. It was eleven words, eleven useless words; he didn't need to hear them again.

He walked back to the high street and found the vegan cafe, where he was meeting Ella. It sat between the florist's and the organic bakery. The signage above the storefront was made up of small planks of wood that had been stained in light, medium, and dark shades of brown. The planks were arranged in a random order, which gave it an interesting texture. The cafe name, Nourish, was emblazoned across it in black and gold lettering.

Ella wasn't strictly vegan or vegetarian, but she did like vegan and vegetarian food and would generally choose it over any of the meat options on a menu. The polar opposite of Crane. She had mentioned this place to him the last time they had met up for lunch, and he had promised he would give it a try the next time they were to get together, which was today.

After Beth's accident, Ella had really helped and supported Crane, and she'd played a big part in the funeral arrangements. Crane had been in a very dark place at the time, and her support helped him through. He didn't know how well he would have coped with it all without her. She'd called and visited him regularly after the funeral until eventually they got into a habit of meeting for lunch once a month for a catch-up.

Ella had worked with Beth at the University Hospital of Wales. They were both paediatric nurses and had become close friends before the accident. Ella technically still was a paediatric nurse, but she now worked for a charity that supported families with sick and often terminally ill children. Crane admired her for what she did, as he had Beth. To have the strength and courage to help families in their time of such desperate need was truly commendable.

He pushed the door open and entered the pleasant little cafe. It was bright and airy inside. Light hardwood flooring and square tables that were made of driftwood, or at least designed to look like they were made of driftwood. Each table was surrounded by four whitewashed wooden chairs, and there was a cardboard menu standing at the centre of every table, alongside a small wooden box containing all the condiments. Around halfway in, on the left side, was a long deli-style counter that ran all the way to the back of the cafe. The young waitress behind the counter glanced up and gave Crane a welcoming smile, then she continued preparing something for the elderly lady standing in front of her at the counter.

Crane scanned the rest of the cafe. There was an elderly couple sitting together at the table at the front and two middle-aged women sharing a table halfway down on the right, huddled and engrossed in a deep conversation that seemed to warrant an array of facial expressions and hand gestures but also hushed voices.

There was no Ella yet. Although he was five minutes early, as always. From the age of sixteen, the army had ingrained into him that he should always set his watch five minutes ahead, that way, he would never be late. Although his watch was no longer set five minutes fast, he still aimed to arrive at all his appointments five minutes early.

He weaved between the tables and headed towards the back corner—his favourite spot wherever he ate or drank. He took a seat, a seat that gave him a view of the whole cafe, with only bricks and mortar behind him.

The waitress handed the elderly lady a brown paper bag, which she placed in her shopping trolley and zipped up. The waitress then made her way around the counter and opened the front door for the lady, who gingerly walked out rolling her shopping trolley behind her. After saying goodbye and closing the door, the waitress pulled out a small notepad and pen and made her way towards Crane. She was small, slight, and young—early twenties was Crane's guess. She had a pale complexion, with light brown hair in a dreadlock style that was loosely tied back. There were at least six different piercings around the outer edge of each of her ears. She wore bright white trainers, black leggings, a black T-shirt, and a white half apron with "Nourish" printed across the front in black writing.

She stopped in front of Crane and smiled. "Can I get you anything?"

"Could I get a coffee, please? And do you do any herbal teas?"

"Of course, which one would you like? We have about ten different flavours and combinations."

"There's ten different flavours?" queried Crane. He could only name two off the top of his head, maybe three at a push. "In that case, I think we should wait till my friend gets here to decide for herself."

The waitress giggled. "No worries, I'll just get the coffee for now."

She turned and walked back to the counter to make a start on his coffee. Just as she grabbed a white mug from the shelf beneath the coffee machine, the front door of the cafe opened. Ella stepped inside looking radiant in a white floral summer dress and white sandals. Ella was around five-six, with long blonde hair that she often curled slightly at the ends. She was an avid yogi, and it showed in her lithe physique. As the door closed behind her, she pushed her sunglasses up, revealing her luminous green eyes, and rested them on the top of her head before giving Crane a smile and a little wave to let him know she'd spotted him. He got up to greet her as she weaved her way to him. They gave each other a friendly hug and a peck on the cheek.

"I was going to order you a herbal tea, but the waitress said they have ten different flavours, so I took the safe option and said I'd wait for you to decide."

Ella laughed as she took the seat opposite Crane. "They do some lovely ones here. You should try one."

"I'm not sure," he said. "I tend to find herbal teas smell delicious, but they end up tasting like dishwater."

"Well, these ones are lovely," said Ella in a light-hearted "so there" kind of way. "You can try some of mine and see if I can convert you."

The waitress came over with his coffee, and Ella ordered a nettle and cherry tea. They perused the menu while the waitress was preparing the tea, and they gave her their lunch order when she brought the tea to the table. Crane went for a beefless beef burger and triple-cooked chips. The burger was apparently homemade using beetroot, red onion, cashew nuts, and red lentils. Ella went for a Nourish bowl, which was effectively a stir fry with lots of vegetables, crispy tofu, and tofu rice marinated in peanut butter.

"Come on, then," said Ella. "Try some of my tea." She pushed the mug towards him.

He picked it up and inhaled the vapours. "It smells good," he said, then took a little sip. He exaggerated savouring it, his face then scrunching as he forced himself to swallow the disgusting liquid. "Yep, it tastes like dishwater."

They laughed together and then had a catch-up while they waited for their food. Ella told him all about a breathwork course she was currently doing with her yoga instructor. She passionately told him about how different breathing techniques could improve your physical and mental wellbeing and how certain slow breathing techniques stimulated the vagus nerve to help reduce stress and activate the parasympathetic nervous system. Crane listened with genuine interest.

When she asked what had been going on with him, he told her about Chloe staying over and that it was the first time he'd seen her in years. He told her she was a funny and bright kid, he had enjoyed spending time with her, and that he felt bad he hadn't stayed in touch. But he didn't tell her the reason why he'd fallen out with his brother. He also didn't tell her about the Fords or Luke Maddocks or the mystery caller.

Their food came, and they ate in relative silence. Crane had to admit that the food was pretty good, although he would reserve full judgement until later, as he wanted to see how well it sustained him compared to a big slab of real beef. Ella's food looked good too, and she commented on more than a couple of occasions at how tasty it was. Overall, Crane was impressed. Once they'd both finished, the waitress took their plates away. They both ordered another drink but politely declined to look at the dessert menu. Ella had another tea, but a Matcha green tea this time. Crane just had water.

"So, have you got another one for me?" asked Crane, tapping the side of his glass. Another one meaning another case within the charity Ella worked at where financial support was needed. It had started just over a year ago. Ella would tell him about some of the children and families she was supporting, and Crane would try and get the families' details out of her, just names and the areas they lived, as Ricky was usually able to do the rest. A day or two later, they'd receive an anonymous payment into their bank account or an envelope containing a gift of sorts. It had actually taken Ella a little while to realise what was happening.

"Surely you can't keep doing this?" Ella said, giving him a sideways glance. "You'll end up bankrupting yourself."

"If I couldn't afford it, I wouldn't do it." Truth be told, Crane *needed* to do it. It gave him purpose; a reason to wake up in the morning and do what he did. He didn't have money growing up and had spent most of his life chasing financial security. Now that he'd achieved that, he was no longer motivated by money—he was driven to help others. And who deserved help more than sick, innocent children?

Ella smiled shyly and sensitively. "It's just so kind."

Crane shook his head. "To be honest, it isn't a completely selfless act. It makes me feel good to help them."

"You can play it down as much as you like, but you've given a crazy amount of money to these poor children and their families over the last year or so, and you do it all anonymously. Even the people you help have no idea where the money has come from. Most people doing what you do would be making a big song and dance about it, calling the newspapers to tell them what they're doing and wanting to get press and praise for it." Ella reached out and put her hand on top of his. "You do it because you're a good man."

Crane would have been lying to himself if he said he didn't feel anything when she touched him. He did. He received a big hit of oxytocin. Some people describe it as electricity, which is an accurate description. Unfortunately, the feeling was quickly extinguished by a wave of guilt. He thought that he shouldn't be having those kind of feelings for another woman. He felt as if he was being unfaithful to Beth. As if he was being disloyal. And having those feelings towards her friend of all people...

He pulled his hand back. "Sorry," he muttered.

Ella flinched and quickly withdrew her hand. He saw the sparkle in her eyes dim for a split second. She was hurt by his reaction, but she quickly recovered. "No, I'm sorry," she said, waving it off as if it were nothing.

"No, really, I am sorry," said Crane. "I shouldn't have, it's just..."

He tried to find the words to say that would make her understand, but the right words were just out of his grasp. A few awkward moments of silence passed before Ella rescued him.

"You don't have to explain; I understand," she said softly, shifting in her seat and straightening her back to sit more upright.

Crane was unsure whether he was relieved or disappointed that she was now further away from him.

"Anyway, swiftly changing the subject, I do have one for you. There's the sweetest eight-year-old boy I'm supporting at the moment. He's recently been diagnosed with a very rare and extremely aggressive blood disorder, one that I still can't even pronounce properly. They've tried a number of different treatments over the last couple of months but, so far, it's not looking good for him. They're anticipating he's got four to six months left, bless him." Her eyes glistened as she forced herself to hold back tears. "The family are lovely, and they've already been through so much. They lost their eldest daughter two years ago to an inoperable brain tumour, and now they've been hit with this. Some people just seem to have all the bad luck. It's really not fair."

Ella took a second. She seemed to have a thought that was threatening to push all of her emotions to the surface, but she was trying her best to remain composed. Crane didn't say anything, not wanting to interrupt the rest of what she had to say.

"Get this," she continued shakily. "I was with him yesterday morning, and we were talking. I was just asking him if he was okay and making sure he understood what was happening, and do you know what he said? He said, 'I feel bad for Mummy and Daddy because they're sad that I'm dying. I'm sad too, but I am looking forward to seeing my big sister again.' Honestly, it breaks my heart." Her voice faded at the end, and a tear rolled down her cheek.

Crane handed her one of the unused napkins from the table.

"Thank you," she said, taking the napkin from him and dabbing her tears away. "Sorry, look at the state of me."

"What are you apologising for?" asked Crane. "The pain and grief this family has experienced and is experiencing is unfathomable, and you're in it with them. I really don't know how you do what you do. You're by far the strongest person I know."

"That's nice of you to say," she said, then she gave him a cheeky grin. "But it isn't a completely selfless act; it makes me feel good to help them."

They laughed together, a laugh that released a lot of tension.

"Are you making fun of me?" he asked, smiling.

"Not at all," Ella replied, still giggling slightly. "It's actually the truth. As hard as my job is sometimes, it can be so rewarding."

"I can understand that," said Crane. "So, how can we help this little boy?"

"There's a special clinic in America that's starting to run trials on a new treatment that may help him. It's a long shot, but at least it's a shot, which is more than they have right now. I told the parents about it, but they're really struggling financially. It's hard for them to stay optimistic with everything that they've been through. You can see that they want to fight, but you can also see that they're broken." Ella took a sip of her green tea before continuing. "I'm going to help them with fundraising this week to see if we can get them to America as soon as possible. We need to be quick because he's got such an aggressive illness. Literally, every minute counts at this stage." Her gaze lowered to her mug on the table and her voice began to quaver once again. "To be honest, it may already be too late, but I can't just give up on him."

"How much do you need?" Irrelevant of the cost, he was ready to help. The satisfaction he got from helping these families lasted a lot longer than the thrill of a new car.

"Because it's a trial, they only ask for a contribution to their costs, just to cover things like routine tests, treatments, and procedures that would already be required as part of his standard treatment plan. But there's also the cost of getting him and his parents out there, and his parents are going to need somewhere to stay while he's going through the treatment." Ella upturned her hands and shrugged. "It's really difficult to put an exact figure on it."

"OK," said Crane. "How much do you *think* they'll need? What's your estimate?"

She chewed the inside of her cheek, as if she'd already decided the figure in mind was unachievable. "I've set a fundraising goal of fifty thousand, but they may end up needing more depending on how long he needs to be treated for—if the treatment works, of course."

Crane nodded. "I'll transfer fifty thousand to you this afternoon, and you can transfer it on to them. If the treatment works and they need more to stay out there longer, just let me know."

She swallowed, her breath catching. "N-no way. That's too much, Tom."

He shook his head. "I wouldn't do it if I couldn't afford it."

"It's still too much," she murmured, picking at the hem of her dress. "We're going to do some fundraising and set up a donation webpage this week, which will hopefully raise a big chunk of it." She smiled meekly, and it seemed to Crane she was trying to show confidence in her raising money efforts despite knowing it was a huge number to somehow gain, with a good chance of not being reached.

"But you said every minute counts," Crane pressed on. "This way, you can book their tickets today and hopefully start treatment in a few days."

Her eyes glistened again, but she kept her composure. "I don't think you realise how kind you are, Tom."

# Chapter Sixteen

Crane tapped his debit card on the machine being held by the waitress, and it chirped to confirm payment. The machine churned out a receipt, which she handed to Crane with a smile and a "thank you" before returning behind the counter. Crane and Ella stood up to leave, but before Crane slipped his wallet back into his pocket and followed Ella, he dropped a generous tip onto the table. As they stepped outside, they were hit by the contrasting brightness of the glorious sunshine and had to squint.

Ella turned to look up at Crane, her emerald eyes sparkling in the sunlight. "Thank you for lunch."

"You're welcome."

She clasped her hands together in front of her heart. "And thank you so much for your massively generous donation."

"Honestly," Crane said, waving a dismissive hand, "there's no need to thank me."

"Of course there is," Ella said, lowering her sunglasses from the top of her head to cover her eyes. "You've given us all hope. You deserve some credit."

Crane shook his head. "I'm just glad I can help."

They gave each other a friendly hug and a peck on the cheek goodbye. It was the standard friendly hug and kiss, the same as when they'd greeted each other earlier.

Crane's eyes lingered on Ella for a few seconds as she walked away, his feet glued to the pavement. He had so much more he wanted to say to her, and yet no matter how much he searched himself, he wasn't sure exactly what those words were. Maybe it was just purely the need to spend more time with her. As she pulled her key fob from her bag and her car lights flashed as she unlocked her small white hatchback, he turned and headed in the opposite direction, back to his truck, before she could catch him watching her. He sighed as he pulled out his phone from his pocket and dialled Ricky as he walked.

"How was your lunch date with Ella?"

Crane would have rolled his eyes if he hadn't been expecting the question. "It wasn't a date," he answered, giving the same reply he always did.

"Okay," said Ricky, in a tone that really said, "if you say so".

"Can you set up a transfer to her?"

"Of course, how much?"

"Fifty thousand."

Ricky gasped and then slowly exhaled. "Sorry. I think I misheard you." There was a long pause on the other end of the line. "Would you repeat that? I needed to quickly clean my ears out. I thought you said fifty thousand."

Crane knew he had heard him fine. "You heard me correctly. Fifty thousand."

He gave Ricky a brief run-down of the little boy Ella was supporting and told him that the money was going to be used to get him to America for a trial treatment. It was the final ray of hope for the little boy and his family.

"Well, it definitely sounds like a worthy cause," admitted Ricky. "I'll make the transfer now in a minute."

Crane sniggered. "Now in a minute? You're starting to sound like a Welshman, and you've only lived here a few years."

Ricky laughed. "That's from spending too much time with you."

Now the money transfer was being sorted, he was back to pure focus on the original issue that had been on his mind. "Have you found Sophie Davies?"

"I think so."

"You... *think*... so?" He stretched the pause between each word out, as if getting Ricky to retake a look at his terrible response and give an appropriate yes or no.

"Yeah, kind of."

Crane frowned—the "yeah" was definitely more what he'd been looking for, but the "kind of" once again had thrown him off.

"There's not a lot to go on, to be honest. It looks like she split up with Luke Maddocks about two years ago and then she practically disappeared. I mean, before they split up, her social media presence was excessive to say the least. She was posting things constantly across all the usual platforms—photos, videos, you name it—and most of the pictures she uploaded were of the two of them together. But then about two years ago, her status changed to single and she completely dropped off the radar. She's not been seen across any of the platforms ever since." Ricky paused to let that sink in, and Crane had to admit it did seem unusual. It begged the question "what happened?", but before Crane could ask, Ricky added, "What's even more strange is that she started working for a recruitment agency in Cardiff a few months before they split, and then around the time of them splitting, she stopped working completely. It says she resigned. Then there's no record of her working anywhere else since. I just find that a little strange because most people throw themselves into their work after a breakup, yet she did the opposite."

Crane wasn't so sure he found it strange. He'd imagine dating a guy like Luke Maddocks could really mess a person up. He wouldn't be shocked if she had agoraphobia or was in pure fear for her life. He guessed Luke Maddocks would have a lot of enemies.

Crane walked past the betting shop, then turned off the high street and onto the road where he'd parked his truck. "Is she registered to an address?"

"Yes, she's registered to the same address she's been registered to her whole life, with her parents."

"She still lives with her parents?"

"She's still only twenty-six; it's not that unusual."

"I didn't say it was," said Crane, pushing back at Ricky's defensiveness from not leaving home until he hit thirty. "I'm surprised because that means she was only twenty-one when she went to Gran Canaria with Luke. He's what? Mid-forties?"

"Forty-six."

Crane whistled, surprised but not shocked. "Twenty years—that's some age gap. So, what's her parents' address, then?"

"Before I tell you where that is, remember it doesn't prove anything; don't jump to any conclusions."

"Where is it, Ricky?" Crane asked impatiently.

"It's an address in Caerphilly."

Crane stopped walking, and not just because he'd reached his truck. The puzzle pieces in his head were slotting further into place. "If she was living at her parents' house in Caerphilly, Luke Maddocks could have been driving through the lanes on his way to pick her up before heading to the airport."

Ricky groaned. "I knew you'd say that."

Crane leaned against the side of the hardtop canopy on his truck. "Because you know it's a plausible explanation of what happened."

"That may be true," said Ricky, "but we don't have any evidence that that was what happened, and there could be hundreds of plausible explanations."

Crane took a breath, then said definitively, "I need to speak to Sophie Davies."

"I'll text the address to you now... in a minute."

"Thank you."

Crane ended the call, returned his phone to his pocket, and walked around the front of his truck to get in when something big and white on his windscreen caught his eye. His immediate thought was that it was just a sales leaflet of sorts, but no, it was a plain white A4-size envelope tucked beneath his windscreen wiper.

Crane glanced up the road, and seeing no cars coming, he pulled the envelope out from under his wiper and then jumped into the driver's seat of his truck. The envelope looked fresh and new—a blank canvas. Crane used his finger to tear the top of it open. Inside was a single sheet of paper. He pulled it out, and a picture of a man's face laughing stared back at him. A photograph of a laughing face printed on a standard piece of white printer paper. The quality of the print was poor, as if someone had cut, pasted, and cropped his face out of another photo and then enlarged it onto the page. The definition of the photo was just beginning to pixelate where it had been enlarged a little too much, but even so, it was clearly Luke Maddocks. Just beneath the photo of Luke Maddocks' laughing face were four printed words in a bold black font, with an exclamation point at the end: "*He's laughing at you!*"

Crane turned over the page, but nothing was printed or written on the back. He felt as if he was being played, and he didn't like it, not one little bit. His skin suddenly felt hot as the rage inside him threatened to bubble to the surface. He threw the picture onto the passenger seat, shoved the door open, and jumped out of the truck, directly into the path of a car coming up from behind. The driver, an elderly man wearing a flat cap, swerved out of the way and gave an angry beep of the horn. He appeared to shout something at Crane, but his windows were up, so Crane couldn't hear what was said. Judging from the scowl on the man's face, whatever it was certainly wasn't complimentary. But Crane had to admit, whatever the man had said, he fully deserved it. He raised a hand to wave an apology and cursed at himself. *Idiot.* He wasn't thinking straight. He was allowing his emotions to get the better of him. Shaking his head, he walked around the front of his truck and back onto the pavement. That was when the questions returned—How did they know he was there? Had someone been following him the whole time? Was someone watching him right now?

He scanned the area. There was a man jogging across the road on the opposite pavement. He looked to be in his fifties, with grey hair, and an experienced runner's physique. His blue vest had the name of a previous race he had run emblazoned across the front. He was paying no attention to Crane, or anything else for that matter, in the zone, breathing rhythmically, with a sheen of sweat covering his face and arms.

A mother and daughter were walking towards him on the pavement. The mum was mid-to-late thirties, with mousy brown hair, and glasses. Her daughter looked about five, maybe six, dressed in a pretty yellow dress and silver sandals. She held her mum's hand and talked the whole time as they walked past. He couldn't make out exactly what she was saying, but it sounded as if she was making a list of things she wanted to buy from the shops. The mum looked at Crane and smiled at him between the occasional "oh yeah?" and "really?". He returned the smile before continuing to eagerly search for a pair of eyes on him.

He walked up the road, glancing into the windows of all the parked cars. After a hundred yards, he crossed to the other side of the road and repeated the same process back towards his truck. Nothing. They were all empty. He couldn't see anyone watching him. He couldn't feel anyone watching him. Whoever had left the envelope was probably long gone.

And then, as he stepped onto the road to cross over to get back to his truck, something caught his eye. The off-licence he was parked outside of had a CCTV camera. It was above the black and red signage on the left-hand side and it was pointing down at an angle towards the front door, which was central. On either side of the door were two large windows covered with posters of different offers and promotions they were currently running. Buy one get one free on certain spirits. A ten-pack of lager for twelve pounds. Two bottles of a particular brand of wine for a tenner.

He continued crossing the road and stood at the front of his truck, looking up at the camera, trying to judge the angle and its field of view. It looked as if the back and the left side of his truck would likely be in the camera's shot, possibly the front left wing and part of the bonnet. But the right side of the bonnet, where the person who had put the envelope on the windscreen would have stood, was likely to be too far over to be captured by the camera's field of view.

Even if he got lucky and it was in the footage, the person who had left the envelope could have ducked slightly and stayed out of view behind the roof of the pickup truck; however, they may have walked along the pavement first and then stepped in front of the truck. If they had, they would be on camera for sure.

He knew it was a long shot. It was more likely that they would have spotted the camera and crossed from the other side of the road, left the envelope, turned around, and crossed back the way they had come. That would have kept them out of the camera's view the entire time. It also crossed his mind that the camera might not even be recording. For all he knew, it could be broken, or it could even be a dummy camera, a fake, just there as a deterrent. Either way, with the slight bit of potential he had, he had to check it out.

# Chapter Seventeen

Crane pushed the door open and stepped into the off-licence. A small brass bell *ding-a-linged* above his head, announcing his arrival to seemingly nobody. It was relatively dull inside compared to the glorious summer's day outside. The posters that covered almost every square inch of the windows blocked most of the natural light from getting in. Added to that was the fact that out of the twelve spotlights fitted into the square ceiling tiles, only eight were actually working. The ceiling tiles themselves looked gloomy and tired. Where they had once been brilliant white, they were now starting to turn a shade of beige, and almost all of them were either cracked, stained, or had broken corners. The pale linoleum floor had so many marks and scuffs on it, it was difficult to imagine what it would have looked like when it had been originally laid.

The left side of the shop had floor-to-ceiling shelves filled with wine bottles—white, red, and rosé. The right side of the shop had matching floor-to-ceiling shelves filled with cans and bottles. Directly in front of Crane were two shelving units, one on the left, one on the right. They created a walkway through the middle of the shop, leading to the checkout counter at the back. The left was filled with soft drinks and mixers, the right was filled with crisps and other savoury snacks.

Crane walked through the middle and stopped at the checkout counter. The standard array of chocolate bars and packets of sweets adorned the top. The till was on the right, and next to the till was a stand showcasing various brands and flavours of chewing gum. Sitting on a stool behind the counter was a young man who appeared to be of Middle Eastern descent. Dressed in blue jeans and a grey T-shirt, which was a little snug around his abdominal region, he had his head down, engrossed in his smartphone, his thumbs rapidly tapping the screen. He must have sensed Crane standing at the counter, as he looked up. He had short black hair and a neatly trimmed black beard.

"Sorry. How can I help you?" he said in a strong Cardiff accent, pocketing his phone but remaining seated.

"Does your security camera above the front door work?"

He looked at Crane as though he'd just asked him if there were a green unicorn outside. It was obviously the first time anyone had ever asked him about the security camera. "Umm, yeah it works."

"Great," said Crane, placing both hands on the checkout counter. "Any chance I can take a look at the footage from the last hour?"

The cashier almost scrunched up his entire face. "Why?"

"Because someone left something on my truck, and I want to see if they're on camera," Crane said calmly, as if this were the most obvious, potentially only answer.

The cashier seemed to mull this over for a few seconds before asking, "What did they leave on your truck?"

"Why does that matter?"

"I'm just curious. Was it a turd?"

It was Crane's turn to look at the cashier as if it was the first time he'd ever been asked a certain question. Which it was. "No. Fortunately, my truck is still turd free. It was just an envelope."

The cashier ever so slightly pushed his bottom lip out, seemingly disappointed, not that Crane could work out why. "Are you a policeman?"

*Would he ask to see my ID if I lied? Probably.* "No."

"Sorry," said the cashier, "it's company policy to only show the camera footage to the police."

"Why?"

The cashier shrugged. "To protect people's privacy and personal data and stuff like that, I suppose."

"Okay," said Crane. "In that case, I am a policeman."

The cashier peered at him through dubious eyes and stretched one corner of his mouth to the side. "Can I see some ID?"

Crane took out his wallet, removed a twenty, and placed it on the counter.

The cashier smiled. "Follow me, officer."

He got up from the stool and pocketed the twenty. He then walked from the right side of the counter to the left and lifted a section of the countertop. The section had hinges on the left side, so once it was fully raised, it could be rested against the wall. The wall was scuffed and indented where the section of counter had been opened against it so many times over the years. A waist-height wooden door was underneath. The cashier pulled it open to allow Crane through.

Crane followed him behind the counter and then through a door that opened into a storeroom. The storeroom also doubled as an office, judging by the presence of a desk and chair pushed against the back wall. It was quite cramped. Floor-to-ceiling industrial-looking shelves covered every wall apart from the one section the desk was slotted into. The shelves were filled with stock for the shop, most of which was still boxed up, but some of the boxes had been partially torn open. Crates of beer and cider were stacked haphazardly around on the floor, some of the stacks reaching up as high as their chests. One of the tall stacks wobbled precariously as the cashier squeezed past to get to the desk. Crane followed him through, being careful not to knock anything over.

The desk was wooden-topped with grey steel drawers on either side for the legs. It was an old battle-hardened desk that would have looked right at home on the set of a war movie. There was a tower of four plastic trays on the left that were stuffed full of paperwork and a heap of what looked like receipts and invoices on the right. In the middle was a fairly new laptop. At least, it looked new compared to the desk and the other fixtures and fittings in the shop.

When the cashier reached the desk, he turned to Crane and held his hand out to shake. "I'm Ali, by the way."

Crane gave it a brief shake to be polite but really wanted to crack on with looking at the camera footage. "Nice to meet you, Ali. Most people call me Crane."

The corners of Ali's mouth downturned slightly and he frowned. "Crane? Is that your surname?"

Crane nodded.

"How come you use your surname?"

"I used to be in the forces, and it just kind of stuck," replied Crane, making a point of looking at the blank screen on the laptop rather than Ali, hoping he would get the hint.

"Do you all use your surnames in the forces?"

Crane shook his head and struggled to suppress a sigh. "No, not everyone."

Ali looked at him as though he were waiting for Crane to add some more detail. When he didn't offer any, Ali just shrugged and nodded as if to say, "fair enough". Crane wasn't trying to be rude, but he was short on time and wasn't really in the mood for small talk.

Ali bent down and tapped the space bar on the laptop. The screen came to life. It was glaringly bright in the dark and dingy storeroom. He dragged his finger over the touchpad and tapped on a blue icon with a white outline of a camera inside it. A small window popped up requesting for a password to be entered. Ali manoeuvred his body to block Crane's view of the keyboard and tapped quickly away at the keys. He really didn't need to; Crane had no interest in knowing what the password was.

The screen split into quadrants. Three of them showed the inside of the shop and the bottom right quadrant showed the view from the camera out front. Ali dragged the cursor and tapped on the bottom right quadrant. It expanded to fill the entire screen. He then moved the cursor to the top of the screen, where there were two tabs. The left side, which was currently highlighted in red, had the word "live" on it. Ali tapped the right side, which had the word "recorded" on it. It changed to red and then a white bar appeared across the bottom of the screen.

"You said the last hour, right?" asked Ali.

"Maybe a bit more than that. Can you play it from five-to-twelve?"

Ali nodded and used the touchpad to drag a red line that was running through the white bar across to the left. He then tapped the play button. The camera's field of view was exactly as Crane had predicted. The pavement was obviously the focus point, but the right-hand side of the shot had the back and the left side of his pickup truck. The top right of the shot showed the front left wing and a bit of the road in front. He just had to hope that whoever had left the envelope had walked along the pavement before heading to the front of the truck.

The picture definition wasn't great, but it was certainly better than he'd expected and it was in colour, which was a big plus. Nothing happened for about thirty seconds, then an old lady walked slowly down the screen along the pavement, with a little Yorkshire terrier on a leash.

"Any chance you could speed it up?" Crane didn't want to stand and watch an hour's worth of tape in real time.

"Of course," said Ali. "Silly me." He clicked a button, and the time in the top left corner started moving twice as quickly as before. "Faster?"

"Please." Crane nodded. "Go as fast as you can. Just keep an eye out for someone carrying a big white envelope."

Ali tapped the touchpad three more times. The red line started to visibly move across the bottom of the screen, and the numbers representing the seconds in the top corner were changing so quickly, they were just small flashing blobs on the screen. A few people "walked" along the pavement, moving quicker than humanly possible, almost blurs flying up or down the screen.

Crane's head was moving frantically side to side to keep up with the walkers, eyes squinting to focus. "Maybe one click slower."

Ali obliged. The people were still moving quickly, but they could now at least see some detail. At this speed, they should be able to see if someone was holding a big white envelope. A large bald man went into the off-licence around thirty seconds later, which was probably around three minutes in real time. He stepped back out with a full carrier bag and walked away up the street. Crane focused his attention on the area in front of his truck, waiting and hoping to see someone with the envelope.

As the red line approached the right-hand side of the screen, Crane's hope was beginning to fade. They were approaching the time that he'd arrived back to the truck himself. Crane glanced at the top left corner of the screen to check the time of the footage. As he did, a flash of blue crossed the screen at the top right corner, exactly where he had been focusing his attention the whole time. He'd almost missed it.

"*Stop.*"

He made Ali jump with his outburst.

"Go back and slow it down. I think I saw something blue go across the top of the screen."

Ali had already hit the pause button. He dragged the red line back a little and then pressed play, but now in real time. They both watched closely. Nothing happened for a while, then all of a sudden a boy wearing a blue hoodie, black shorts, and white trainers ran into the shot from the top of the screen. He then immediately turned and ran across the front of the truck and out of shot. He was running the whole time in the footage, and he was quick, but he was clearly holding a big white envelope in his right hand.

"Can I see that again?" asked Crane.

"Of course. I'll slow it down to half speed."

A few more drags and taps and then they watched the same footage at half speed. Definitely a boy, judging by his height and size and mannerisms. He was heavy-footed; there was nothing delicate or graceful about the way he moved at all. Crane thought he only looked to be about twelve or thirteen. His blue hoodie was baggy on him, the hood up and partially covering his face from the camera the whole time, which had probably been the intention. His black shorts were also baggy, only the lower part of his pale, skinny legs showing. Crane looked at the time in the top left corner of the screen. He would've been saying goodbye to Ella at this time. He'd only just missed him by a couple of minutes.

On the one hand, Crane was glad they'd spotted the culprit, but on the other hand, he didn't know how much use it would be. The boy was probably long gone by now, and he had no doubt he had been paid to leave the envelope on his truck. The boy was obviously not the mystery caller; however, if he could identify and find him, he may be able to provide a description of the mystery caller.

"Thank you, Ali," said Crane. "Your help is much appreciated."

"No problem. So, what was in the envelope?"

Crane almost laughed at his forwardness. "Now, that information is on a need-to-know basis, and you don't need to know."

Ali drooped his head for a second before slowly raising it, and a mischievous grin started to spread across his face. "Is it a picture of a turd?"

Crane smiled and shook his head. "What is it with you and turds?"

Ali shrugged. "Shit happens." Then he laughed heartily at his own joke.

# Chapter Eighteen

Once outside, Crane spent a few minutes inspecting his pickup truck. It had crossed his mind that maybe a tracker had been fitted to it. He was frustrated that he hadn't spotted anyone following him, yet the mystery caller always seemed to know where he was. He had a good look up in the wheel arches and got down on the ground to scan the underside and behind the bumpers. He received a couple of curious looks from people walking past while he was in the process, but he found no signs of a tracker or any tampering.

Crane gave up the search and jumped in, the thought that the mystery caller hadn't needed a tracker so far right at the forefront of his mind. He double-checked no cars were coming up from behind, indicated, and pulled out into the road. He wasn't holding out much hope, just like with the CCTV, but he thought it was worth driving around the immediate area for ten minutes just in case he got lucky and spotted the boy in the blue hoodie. The last time he'd held out hope, after all, he had found somewhat of a lead.

He drove up the street and took the first turn that came up, which was on the right. It was just another residential street, similar to the one he'd just been parked on, except there were no business properties at all on this one. He followed it to the end and took another right, heading back towards the high street.

When he reached the high street, he took another right and then turned right again, back onto the road where he'd just been parked outside the off-licence. One big square. No sign of a boy in a blue hoodie. He drove past the off-licence and then past the right turn he had taken last time. Fifty yards further up the road, there was a left turn. He took it.

It was another residential street, almost identical to the others he'd just been driving through. Terraced houses with minuscule front gardens—it was literally two steps for the homeowners to get from their front door to their garden gate. A man was walking a German Shepherd on the pavement to the left and a lady was outside the front of her home, tending to her potted plants on the right, but there was no boy in a blue hoodie.

At the end of the street, he took another left, planning on completing another square. Then, just as he completed the left turn to head back to the high street, a tiny flash of blue in the far distance caught his eye as he glanced in his rear-view mirror. He slammed on the brakes and stopped the truck, already knowing there were no cars behind him from his glance. He stared into the rear-view mirror. Nothing. He did the same in the wing mirror. Nothing. No blue, no movement, nothing. Just cars and houses. He'd probably imagined it... but what if he hadn't imagined it?

He shifted the transmission into reverse and went back into the road he had just pulled out of. A car was coming down the road about forty yards back, so he quickly shoved the gear lever back into drive, accelerated, and turned right out of the junction. The street was just like all the others—terraced houses, cars parked on both sides of the road. Then up ahead, he noticed there appeared to be a large break in the houses on the left. As he approached, he could see a metal guard railing and then he saw grass. When he got even closer, he could see children and parents and dogs. It was a park. A very busy park—it was a warm and sunny Saturday afternoon after all. It crossed his mind that the boy might not even be wearing the hoodie anymore because it was so warm, but if he had taken it off, maybe it would be wrapped around his waist. He gazed through the passenger window intently as he drove past as slowly as he dared, trying not to attract too much attention to himself.

There was a play area for smaller children on the right and a compact skatepark towards the rear left corner. There were people everywhere and lots of colours too. Crane was scanning for the colour blue, but there was too much going on. It was like walking past a *Where's Wally?* poster and trying to spot the main man wearing his red and white striped jumper and bobble hat without stopping. Impossible.

He found a space to park a little further on and then walked back to the park. He stood at the guard rail and started searching. A few families with young children had picnic blankets set up on the grass, making the most of the nice weather. Two teenage girls were throwing a frisbee back and forth near the play area, and two young boys were riding their bikes around the perimeter. Four boys were playing a two-on-two football match with jumpers for goalposts.

Most of the bigger kids seemed to be congregating in and around the skatepark. He started to focus on that area, and that was when he spotted the colour blue that he was looking for. It was on an oversized hoodie being worn by a boy wearing black shorts and white trainers. He was standing at the top of one of the ramps, talking to another boy who was holding a skateboard.

Crane kept his eyes on him and entered the park through the gate. The boy with the blue hoodie gave the boy with the skateboard a high five and then jumped down from the ramp and sat down on the grass to watch the skaters. Crane knew that he needed to be tactical in his approach, as there were a lot of people around. The boy could easily cause a scene if he screamed or shouted, and if he ran away, it would look wholly inappropriate for Crane to chase him down.

Crane walked up the centre of the park, past a couple of families having a picnic, past the girls playing frisbee and the little ones' play area. He stopped when he was level but still a good twenty yards away to the boy's right. It was definitely the same boy. The same blue hoodie, the same black shorts, and white trainers, except now his hood was down. Just as Crane had guessed, he did look about twelve. He had short dark hair and a smooth, pale baby face. No signs of acne or facial hair coming any time soon.

Crane took another twenty out of his wallet and casually strolled towards the boy without looking at him. He pretended to be watching the skaters, all the while keeping the boy in his peripheral vision. He was surprised at how loud the hard plastic wheels of the scooters and skateboards rolling over the concrete were. That and the talking, shouting, and laughing. This was definitely the noisy and boisterous part of the park.

He stopped when he was a couple of yards away. The boy didn't run or even really pay him much attention at all. Crane could sense the boy glance up and look at him, but then he went straight back to watching his friends skating. He obviously didn't sense any danger.

Crane took another half step closer and then sat down on the grass just over an arm's length away. The boy looked at him again. This time, Crane returned the look and held out the twenty pound note lengthways between his index and middle finger.

"Here you go," said Crane, offering it to him.

The boy stared at the twenty pound note and scrunched up his nose in confusion. He looked at Crane, then back at the note, then back to Crane. Eventually, he said, "What's that for?"

"It's a payment for some information."

The boy recoiled slightly and his frown deepened. "What information?" His voice was still a boy's voice, but it was on the verge of breaking. It was just beginning to get a little deeper and rough around the edges.

"I want you to describe the person who told you to put the envelope on my pickup truck." Crane gently flapped the note, keeping the boy's attention on it.

There it was. His eyes widened. The look of realisation. He knew exactly who Crane was and exactly what he wanted. The boy looked around, over each shoulder in turn, but his gaze returned to the twenty in Crane's hand each time.

"There's no need to run; I'm not annoyed," Crane said reassuringly. "I just want to know what he or she looks like."

The boy gave a quick one-shoulder shrug and snatched the twenty. "It was a he."

"And what did he look like?"

"I dunno. Just normal-looking I suppose."

Crane figured getting a description out of a twelve-year-old boy was not going to be straightforward. "Was he tall or short?"

The boy thought for a second. "He was tall, like you."

"Okay, good. Was he fat? Skinny? What colour skin did he have? And how old do you think he was?"

"I think he was quite skinny... he definitely wasn't fat. He was white, and I dunno." The boy nibbled his bottom lip while he considered. "About your age, I think."

"What was he wearing?"

"A suit. Like he was going to a funeral or something. A black suit and a white shirt."

"Was he wearing a tie?"

The boy shook his head. "Nope."

"What about hair? Long? Short? Light? Dark?"

"Dark brown. Not short, but not really long. It was really wet though, like it had just been gelled and combed back." The boy used his hands to gesture pulling his hair back. "Like, slicked back."

"Beard?"

"Nope."

"Any distinguishing features?"

The boy looked back at Crane blankly, as if he'd just spoken in a foreign language.

He quickly rephrased the question. "Was there anything different about him? Anything that stood out to you?"

The boy looked at the ground, his eyes squinting, as though he was trying to picture the man in his head. Ten seconds or so passed, although it felt more like a minute to Crane. He was about to tell the boy not to worry, but then the boy's head popped up. There was a spark in his eyes; he'd thought of something.

"He was wearing glasses."

"Glasses?"

"Yeah, just plain ones with a black frame. Although he spent most of the time looking over the top of them, which I thought was a bit weird." The boy snorted. "Like, why bother wearing them?"

"Did he have an accent?"

The boy frowned, then shook his head.

"What did he say?" asked Crane, becoming impatient. He was running out of questions and was yet to hear anything that clicked in his mind, anything to make this guy stand out. "Tell me exactly what happened."

"I was walking to the park, and he was standing on the corner with the envelope in his—"

"Which corner?" Crane interrupted.

"Just up the road from where your truck was parked."

Crane nodded.

"He asked me if I wanted to earn a tenner. I thought he was some sort of weirdo or something. Then he showed me the money and told me that all I had to do was leave an envelope on the windscreen of a truck."

"That's it?" Crane raised a brow. "That's all he said?"

"Well, he pointed to the truck. We could just about see it from where we were standing. He told me to put it under the wiper so it wouldn't get blown away by the wind, and then he said that he would wait there for me. He said he'd give me the tenner once I'd done it. So, I ran down the road, did it, and ran back as quick as I could. He gave me the tenner and then he walked away, and I came here. Job done." The boy pulled a ten pound note from one of the pockets of his shorts, as if to present his evidence, then he shoved it back into his pocket along with the twenty Crane had given him.

"Anything else you remember?" asked Crane.

"Like what?"

"Anything else that stood out to you? Anything else he may have said that you haven't told me?"

The boy pulled up a daisy from the grass and started tearing off the white petals one by one. "No, I think that's everything."

Crane got back up to his feet, stretched, and twisted to loosen up his back.

"Thanks for the twenty pounds," said the boy, with a cheeky grin. "I would have told you all that for free."

"No problem," said Crane. "I would've paid you a hundred."

The grin fell from the boy's face, and Crane walked away.

# Chapter Nineteen

Crane checked his phone when he got back into his truck. As expected, there was a text message from Ricky waiting for him; in fact, the message had been waiting there for some time. It was the address for Sophie Davies. He had a good idea of where the address was in Caerphilly, but he still programmed it into the satnav to be sure.

While he was driving, he went over the description the boy had given him. The mystery man was about the same height as Crane, so around six-two, slim, slicked-back brown hair, and glasses. No accent, so he was presumably a local guy. The black suit and white shirt were exactly what the doormen in Corkers wore, but that could have been the intention.

Crane remembered seeing a tall, slim doorman in Corkers. He had switched places with Leon to cover the front desk when Leon had escorted him to the back office. That doorman almost fitted the description perfectly, apart from two features. He wasn't wearing glasses when Crane had seen him, although that didn't mean much, as he could wear contacts for work. Also, from what the boy had said about the glasses—"he spent most of the time looking over the top of them"—it sounded like the guy didn't normally wear glasses; like maybe he was wearing them as somewhat of a disguise or decoy. But the part of the description that ruled him out was the slicked-back hair. The doorman he'd briefly seen had a shaved head, not quite to the scalp, but very short. Definitely too short to be slicked back.

Could the mystery man be another one of the doormen he hadn't seen yet? Possibly. Could the mystery man purposely be dressing like the doormen in Corkers to keep pointing him in that direction? Also possible. Crane now had a decent description, but he still didn't feel as if he was any further forward.

Less than fifteen minutes after setting off, the female voice on the satnav informed him that he'd reached his destination. The house was in a small cul-de-sac at the top end of Caerphilly, close to St Martin's Church. The house itself was a neat three-bed semi with an adjoining garage. The front lawn looked as if it had recently been trimmed and a large concrete bird bath took pride of place in the centre. A six-year-old silver Nissan Pulsar was parked on the driveway, hopefully indicating that someone was home.

Crane parked on the road in front of the house and made his way down the slight decline of the driveway. The front door was white UPVC with a frosted glass panel on the top half. Next to the door was a small white doorbell. Crane pushed it and heard a faint ring coming from inside. Ten seconds later, a blurred shadow approached the frosted glass, followed by the sound of a key being turned inside the lock.

The door opened inwards and revealed a man wearing a friendly smile. He was short, around five-six. He had thinning grey hair with a slight combover. He wore cream shorts with a brown belt, a pastel blue short-sleeved shirt, and slip-on tartan slippers.

"Hello," said the man, in a welcoming tone.

"Mr Davies?" asked Crane.

"That's right."

"I'm looking for your daughter, Sophie. Is she home?" Crane peered behind the man, but all he could see was an empty hallway and staircase. He couldn't see anyone else, not that that meant the man was home alone.

The welcoming smile left Mr Davies' face and was replaced with a more serious expression. "Sorry, who are you?"

"My name's Crane."

"And why do you want to speak to Sophie?"

"I need to speak to her about one of her ex-boyfriends. Luke Maddocks."

The welcoming smile was now history as Mr Davies' expression took on a look of pure contempt. "That man and anyone associated with that man are not welcome anywhere near our home. I suggest you leave immediately before I call the police." He moved to close the door.

"Wait, Mr Davies," Crane said, raising a hand. "Please, just give me a second to explain."

The door was almost closed, but Mr Davies stopped and glared through the remaining gap.

"Thank you," said Crane. "I'm not a friend of his in any way, shape, or form, if that's what you're thinking."

Mr Davies said nothing. The door didn't reopen, but it didn't close any further either.

"Look, I have reason to believe Luke Maddocks may have been involved in my wife's death. It was around five years ago, while he was in a relationship with Sophie. I just need to ask her a few questions. She may have some useful information."

Mr Davies' expression softened as he appeared to mull this over for a few seconds before finally deciding to open the door fully. "You'd better come in."

Crane followed him into a pristine living room with a cream-coloured carpet that looked as if the vacuum cleaner had very recently been put around it. An elegant dark brown Chesterfield-style sofa was pushed tight against one wall, with a matching armchair in one of the opposite corners. A large TV was sat on an oak stand in the other corner of the room, right next to a window that looked out onto the front garden. All the walls were painted white apart from the chimney breast, which had been covered in wallpaper as a feature wall. The wallpaper was brown with an intricate cream-coloured swirling pattern running through it that matched the carpet.

Mr Davies offered Crane a drink, which Crane declined at first, but Mr Davies insisted he was making one anyway and that Crane might as well join him and have one too.

Mr Davies went to the kitchen to make them both a coffee. Crane remained in the living room, looking at the framed photographs sitting on top of the fireplace. The first one was of an attractive young redhead who looked to be around nineteen or twenty years old when the picture had been taken. He assumed it was Sophie. She was sitting on one of those mechanical rodeo bulls they have at fairgrounds, the ones that spin and buck up and down in a bid to throw you off. She looked really happy.

The next picture was a family picture taken in a photographer's studio with a plain white backdrop. Sophie was front and centre, Mr Davies on her right shoulder, and an older lady with short auburn hair on her left shoulder. Sophie's mother, he presumed. The picture looked a lot more recent. For a start, Mr Davies looked exactly like he still did in the flesh, and Sophie looked older, more mature than in the first picture. Crane also noticed something else. It was as if in the recent picture Sophie had lost a bit of sparkle in her eyes. She was smiling, just like her mum and dad, but there was a darkness behind her eyes.

As Crane looked at the pictures, he suddenly became aware of how quiet it was in the house. He could hear the kettle boiling and Mr Davies making the coffees in the kitchen, but apart from that, there was complete silence, complete stillness. Any hope he'd had of Sophie being upstairs and Mr Davies fetching her once the coffees were made disappeared. They were alone in the house. He had no doubt. Maybe Mrs Davies and Sophie had gone out together somewhere.

The final photograph on the fireplace was of Mrs Davies on her own. It was a headshot somewhere sunny. She had a beaming smile, as though she'd just been laughing, and appeared to be holding on to her straw summer hat to stop it from being blown away in the wind.

"That's my wife, Janet," said Mr Davies, walking in with the coffees. "Sophie's mum. We lost her at the start of the year."

"I'm sorry," said Crane, instinctively lowering his head solemnly.

"The big C." Mr Davies remained composed, but Crane could see the sadness in his eyes. "Breast cancer. She fought like an absolute trooper, all the way to the end."

Just the mention of his loss was enough for thoughts and visions of Beth to flood back to Crane. He understood better than anyone the pain and anguish Mr Davies was going through. The act of putting a brave face on for public appearances but battling to try and hold yourself together just underneath. He wanted to tell him that it got easier, which it did, but it still hurt. The pain was always there, lurking in the background, ready to pounce at certain thoughts, at the sound of a certain song, or even certain smells. Thankfully, over time, it had started losing some of its power.

"Here you go," said Mr Davies, handing Crane a mug of hot coffee.

"Thank you," said Crane, taking it from him.

Mr Davies sat down on the armchair, and Crane took a seat on the sofa.

"You've probably figured out that Sophie isn't here."

Crane nodded. "I did. Where can I find her?"

"Unfortunately, it's not quite as simple as that," said Mr Davies. "She's currently in a special rehab clinic, thanks to Luke Maddocks doing a number on her. That man broke her. That's why I was so..."—his eyes flitted around the room as though searching for the right words etched somewhere on his white walls—"reluctant to speak to you."

Crane puffed his cheeks out. "I'm so sorry to hear that. I can't even begin to imagine how you're coping with everything." His disappointment at Sophie not being here was completely over-shadowed by sympathy. "How did... how did he break her to that point?"

Mr Davies sighed, having to think back to that point in his life seeming to overwhelm him. "I guess it would be easier to start at the beginning. Sophie was the sweetest, most kind-hearted daughter we could have ever wished for. She was always smiling and laughing. She was a very confident young lady and truly a positive force of nature." He smiled to himself, as if swiping through memories of her in his mind.

"Then around five years ago, she met Luke Maddocks." Just saying the name seemed to produce a slight venom in his tone. "At first, everything seemed good. He was never mine or Janet's cup of tea, what with the age gap for a start, but he was always polite to us and seemed to make Sophie happy, and that was all that really mattered to us.

"Anyway, around a year into their relationship, we started noticing some changes in Sophie. Nothing major at first, but she just seemed to lose a bit of confidence in herself, almost like she was becoming a little shy. A few more months passed, and we started noticing that she was wearing more mature and reserved clothing, you know, covering herself up a bit more. We thought she was just growing up and maybe settling down a bit. Little did we know she was actually covering up the bruises." He lowered his head, his gaze falling to the carpet. The thought of his daughter covering up her injuries from abuse was certainly and understandably a sore subject for him to recall. "We had no idea at the time. She hid it all from us. She hid it from everybody."

"That's awful," said Crane, shaking his head.

"That's just the tip of the iceberg. By the time this was happening, we were barely seeing her. She was living with him and only seemed to find time to visit us once a month if we were lucky. When we did see her, it was like she had lost a little bit more of herself each time. By the third year that they were together, she was a shell of her former self. The confident, happy girl we had brought up." His voice broke off.

Crane didn't say anything, not wanting to interrupt or push him. The last thing Crane wanted was for him to clam up. Selfishly, this man could have information he needed. And as much as Crane didn't want to admit it, the loss of this man's wife had sparked a lot of empathy in him. For some reason, he was invested in this man's story, invested in this man's emotions, and invested in allowing this man to speak his hurt.

"She was gone. He'd beaten everything out of her, and I don't just mean physically. The psychological torment he put her through... he destroyed her." His eyes glistened, as if tears were close, but he quickly blinked them away and took a sip of coffee to give himself a second. As with most men who grew up in a certain era, it had been ingrained into him that he shouldn't allow himself to cry. Especially not in front of another man. He cleared his throat before continuing.

"Like I said, she hid it all from us at the time, but she opened up to us afterwards and told us how controlling and nasty that evil man was to her. He encouraged her to drink and take drugs from the start of their relationship and then, because her life with him was so bad, she became dependent on the stuff. She told us she was drinking and taking drugs just to get through the days. He encouraged her to do it; it was just another way of him controlling her."

"I hope you don't mind me asking, how did the relationship finally end?"

"She just turned up one day. No bags, no clothes, nothing. She didn't say a word... she didn't have to. I just knew; I could see it in her eyes. She was broken." Mr Davies shook his head, reminiscing.

"Did he ever come back for her?"

Mr Davies nodded. "That night. Him and his giant friend, Paul. I answered the door and told him she wasn't here. He obviously didn't take my word for it and burst in. I fell back and caught my head on the radiator." Mr Davies used a finger to push some hair out of the way and pointed to a two-inch pale scar on the top of his head. Probably the reason he opted for a combover. "Luke went up to her room, and they argued for a little while," he continued. "I was a little concussed at this point, but I do remember hearing her screaming at him to get out and to leave her alone. Then he started to come back down the stairs dragging Sophie by her feet. It was awful. She was clawing at the banister and screaming, but he was too strong for her. I went to stop him, but his friend held me against the wall by my throat. I couldn't breathe, and I almost blacked out." Mr Davies' face was twisted in anguish. He was evidently angry and projected hatred when he was describing what Luke and Paul had done, but there was something else too—an underlying edge of shame or embarrassment that he hadn't been able to protect his family. "Luckily, Janet had already called the police. They arrived just as he was dragging Sophie across the lawn to his car."

Crane already had a good idea of the answer to his next question, but he was interested to find out *exactly* what had happened. He knew Luke Maddocks had the influence and power to get his charges dropped, but how? Was it purely him intimidating his victims, getting other people to intimidate them, or did he have some sort of influence within the police force? "Did you press charges against him?"

Mr Davies looked down as if he felt shame or disappointment. "When the police pulled up, Paul was still with me and Jan in the hallway. He told us we needed to say it was just a misunderstanding and that I had accidentally fallen and cut my head. He said if we didn't, they would come back and burn down our house with us in it."

"And I guess you felt you had no choice but to listen?" Crane hoped he projected understanding in his voice and not judgement.

Mr Davies sat up a little straighter and jabbed a thumb towards his own chest. "I wasn't going to succumb to the threat, but Sophie came back in while the police were arresting them and begged me. She was petrified of them and what they would do."

"Did they come back?" Crane took a gulp of coffee, watching Mr Davies over the rim of the mug.

"No, they didn't. Apparently, he met someone else a few days later and moved on. It just proved that he didn't really love her, he just loved controlling her. Thankfully, we haven't seen him since." Mr Davies stared at his own coffee resting on his knee and chewed gently on his bottom lip. "I must admit, I do feel sorry for whoever he met, and I do feel a huge amount of guilt for not pursuing charges against him. I know that this is wrong and really selfish of me, but I'm just so glad and relieved that he's left us alone. That he's left my baby girl alone."

Crane gave an understanding nod. "How's Sophie doing now?"

"She's had ups and downs." Mr Davies sighed and his shoulders sagged slightly. "That man truly destroyed her. He stole all her confidence. She has been suffering from severe depression and anxiety ever since. We've been doing our best over the last couple of years to get her back, but I don't think she'll ever be the Sophie she was before she met him. She's battled with her addictions on and off, which leads me to where she is now. She was doing really well towards the end of last year, she was even talking about going back to work. But then her mum passed away in January, and it knocked her for six. Me too, to be honest. But Sophie relapsed again. She turned back to the drink and drugs. It's her coping mechanism. We tried a lot of the public services, but she needed more help. She's gone to a special rehab clinic. I've paid for a six-week package, and they guarantee results. They say she'll be back to her old self and clean for life. It wasn't cheap, but if it works and I get my Sophie back, it'll be worth every penny."

Crane saw a glimmer of hope in his eyes and allowed the thought to linger for a moment before asking, "Do you know how she's getting on so far?"

Mr Davies shook his head. "She only went on Monday, so it's not even been a full week yet. Plus, I'm not allowed to contact her for the whole six weeks. Apparently, it's a full mind and body detox."

"Is there someone at the clinic you can speak to?"

"They did give me a number, but I'm only meant to use it for emergencies. They don't want any interruptions in her treatment."

"Where is the clinic?" asked Crane.

Mr Davies went to answer, but then he stopped himself abruptly. It was as if it had just dawned on him that Crane was still effectively a stranger. He had been very open when it came to offloading his experience of Luke Maddocks and had even seemed to find it therapeutic to share his story with someone willing to listen. But being asked directly for Sophie's whereabouts understandably clammed him up, and Crane couldn't blame him. He feared that he'd pushed the questions a bit too hard and a bit too fast.

"I'm sorry," said Crane, raising an apologetic hand. "I didn't mean to be so direct. It's just... I really need to speak to her as soon as possible."

Mr Davies took another sip of his coffee and rested the mug back on his knee. "Why exactly do you need to speak to her?" His brow furrowed. "And why so urgently?"

Crane gave Mr Davies a brief overview of the accident. He told him that he'd been on the phone to Beth at the time and that she was being followed by an erratic driver. He told him that he'd received an anonymous tip telling him the man driving erratically was Luke Maddocks, and he'd since found out that on the evening of the accident, Luke flew out to Gran Canaria for a holiday with Sophie. He just wanted to know if she was with him at the time of the accident. She may have been a witness to what happened, or she may even have been his alibi. Either way, he needed to speak to her to find out if he could rule Luke Maddocks out.

Mr Davies listened intently, and when Crane finished, he said, "I'm sorry you lost your wife in that way. At least with Janet I had an opportunity to say goodbye."

Crane smiled thinly; after all these years, he was still uncomfortable being the recipient of sympathy.

Mr Davies picked up on it and swiftly offered a change of subject. "I remember her going to Gran Canaria with him. It was in the early days when they'd just started dating. Sophie was still living at home with us then. I remember he was going to pick her up and then they were going to drive to the airport together—Bristol, I think—she was really excited."

"Can you remember what time he picked her up?"

Mr Davies shook his head. "Sorry, I was working nights back then. I remember saying goodbye to her before leaving for my shift at the factory, which would have been around half five. I was on the six-to-six shift. Sophie was just finishing packing her case." A sadness came over him again. "Janet would have known what time she was picked up. She had a great memory. She was here with Sophie, helping her iron a few clothes before packing them. Anyway, sorry I'm blabbering on."

Crane knew he was being selfish, but he really wanted to speak to Sophie and he sensed an opportunity. He leaned forward and rested his elbows on his knees. "I know this is a big ask," said Crane, fixing his gaze on Mr Davies, "but do you think you could ask the clinic to let me speak to her? Just for ten minutes."

Mr Davies puffed out his cheeks and looked away. "I'm sorry... I really don't think it's a good idea to interrupt her treatment. Especially to ask her questions about the man who put her there. Maybe we can arrange to meet up when she comes out in five weeks?"

Crane felt his jaw tighten at this and hoped Mr Davies hadn't noticed. "Don't you think it would be better for me to speak to her at the start of her treatment rather than at the end?" Crane countered, and hated himself for saying it, but he was desperate, and to be fair, it did kind of make sense. But then he hated himself even more by adding, "I mean, I wouldn't want to set her backwards *after* the treatment."

Mr Davies was looking down at the carpet with his mouth clamped shut. It didn't look like he was convinced. He looked more like a man trying to figure out a polite way of letting someone down.

"What if I were to pay for her treatment?" Crane offered.

Mr Davies' head popped up with one eyebrow raised. "You'd pay for her treatment?"

Crane nodded.

"But you don't even know how much it costs."

"I don't care," replied Crane, holding Mr Davies' gaze. "Whatever it cost you. If you get me an opportunity to speak to her today, you have my word, I'll transfer the money to you later today."

Mr Davies stared back at Crane wordlessly. His mind was working overdrive considering Crane's proposal. He was also debating whether or not he trusted Crane's "word".

Crane could sense he had him on the ropes, but he still felt as if his decision could go either way. He decided to have one last throw of the dice. "Mr Davies, I need to know if Luke Maddocks caused my wife's death. If he did, I'm going to bring him to justice."

Mr Davies blinked and then gave a single, defiant nod. "I'll give them a call and see if they'll let you speak to her on the phone."

"To be honest," said Crane with a slight wince, "I would prefer to speak to her face to face."

"You would rather drive an hour there and an hour back just to speak to her for ten minutes?"

Crane smiled and said, "I'm a bit old-fashioned like that." The truth was he didn't want to risk the call being recorded.

Mr Davies nodded, stood up, and left the room. A few moments later, Crane could hear his voice coming from the kitchen at the back of the house, but it was too muffled for him to hear any specific words. It wasn't long before Mr Davies walked back into the living room with a cordless house phone in one hand and a yellow Post-it note in the other.

"You're in luck," he announced. "They said if you can get there before half five, they'll let you have ten minutes with her."

"Why half five?"

"That's when they have their evening meal and start their night-time routine. I'm not sure what it consists of, but apparently it can't be interrupted under *any* circumstances."

"Fair enough," said Crane, looking at his watch. It was a little after four. "In that case, I'd better get a move on."

He got up from the sofa, and Mr Davies walked him to the front door. He handed Crane the yellow Post-it note—which had the clinic's address scribbled on it, plus his phone number—and told him where exactly to turn off the main road to reach it. Apparently, it wasn't well signposted and the satnav would only guide him so far.

Crane flipped over the Post-it note and noticed that Mr Davies had written his bank details on the back but not the cost. "You haven't put down the amount I need to transfer?"

"I know." Mr Davies nodded and then slowly shook his head. "I can't expect you to cover the full cost; it's too much."

"But I gave you my word," Crane insisted.

"Well, once you've spoken to her, give me a call and we'll discuss it."

Crane didn't push the matter any further, knowing full well that he would somehow find out the total cost and transfer it to him. He bowed his head to demonstrate his gratitude and said, "Thank you for your help and hospitality, Mr Davies."

"Please, call me Derek."

"Thank you, Derek. You're a true gentleman."

They shook hands, and Crane turned to head back to his truck.

"Crane," Derek called after him.

He stopped and turned back.

"If you do find out it was Luke, I hope you will bring him to justice."

"Don't worry," said Crane, "I will." Then he muttered under his breath, "One way or another."

# Chapter Twenty

Almost an hour later, Crane was in the Brecon Beacons, and the satnav announced that he had reached his destination. He ignored it and continued for another half a mile, just as Derek had advised him to do. The turn-off he was looking out for came up on the left. There were no road markings and no signposts. If Derek hadn't pre-warned him, he would have driven straight past it.

Crane slowed the truck almost to a complete stop in order to make the tight left turn. The truck dropped slightly from the lip of asphalt road and down onto a narrow dirt track. It obviously wasn't used enough for the authorities to warrant surfacing it. The pickup truck rocked from side to side and rose and dipped as he slowly made his way over the uneven surface. Luckily, he was in the right vehicle for the job. The chunky tyres of the pickup didn't lose any traction even in the deepest of the countless pot-holes.

The track was lined with trees on either side, although it seemed like the woodland was denser on the right compared to the left. Every so often, he started to catch a glimpse of water between the trees on his left. *A pond or a lake or maybe one of the many reservoirs up here*, Crane thought. The truck continued bouncing and rocking as it made its way along the track. Crane was rattling around in the cab by the dips and bumps. He wondered how Derek had driven up here in his hatchback.

The track curved a little to the left for a while and then suddenly seemed to curve more sharply to the right and up a slight incline. A pair of wooden gates appeared up ahead. They were light brown. Scandinavian redwood. Over nine feet tall and probably twelve feet wide. They stood between two even taller stone pillars. The pillar on the right had a small sign made from a single sheet of slate with one word engraved across it. It was the name of the rehab clinic: Serenity.

Beneath the sign was a small black and chrome intercom unit. Crane brought the truck to a stop just a few yards from the gates and jumped out onto the dirt track. It was hard and dry and dusty, as it hadn't rained for the best part of two weeks. A rare, prolonged heatwave for Wales. He stood tall in the warm afternoon sun and twisted around a couple of times to loosen his back. After feeling a couple of satisfying pops in his lumbar spine, he walked towards the intercom unit, but just before reaching it, he heard footsteps on the other side of the gate followed by metal sliding against metal. The sliding sound ended with a solid clunk and then the left-hand gate opened inwards.

A man stepped out. He was five-eight, slim, and lean, with long but receding blonde hair tied up in a man bun. He had a neatly trimmed beard and was wearing scrubs like the ones doctors and nurses wear in hospitals, although his were black. He wore plain black running shoes with clean white midsoles. They looked brand new, straight out of the box. He appeared to be in his mid-thirties and had a friendly face with a welcoming smile.

"Mr Crane?" he asked.

"Don't worry about the 'Mr'; just Crane is fine."

"Nice to meet you, Crane. I'm Joe."

They shook hands.

"Follow me," instructed Joe. "You can leave your truck here. We're not expecting any other visitors today."

Joe walked through the gate, and Crane followed. Joe stopped briefly to close the gate. Crane wasn't sure what he'd expected to see on the other side of the gate, but whatever he'd expected wasn't what he saw. He looked down into a shallow bowl-shaped valley, and in the centre of the bowl was a substantial, ultra-modern building. It looked like two giant blocks stacked one on top of the other. The block at the bottom was painted black and protruded out towards them. The block on top was painted bright white and was wider than the bottom block, overhanging on either side of the black one beneath it by a good ten feet. But the most striking feature was the windows. Apart from the roof and the corners of the structures, every external wall was glass. They looked like giant glass boxes, one framed in black, one framed in white.

Joe started walking down the slight decline of the track, but when it veered to the right, he stepped onto a paved path that led all the way down to the front door of the building. The track was for vehicles and appeared to continue around to the side of the building. Crane guessed it must lead to a separate garage or yard for them to be parked around the back somewhere.

"We've got Sophie ready to have a quick chat with you, but I'm sorry, I have to stress that you need to leave before half five. I know that's not going to give you a lot of time, but we have to maintain the routine for our guests. It's really important for them."

Crane checked his watch and saw it was just after five. "That should be enough time; I only need to ask her a couple of questions. Thank you for allowing me to see her at such short notice. It's much appreciated. How is she getting on so far?"

"She's doing fantastic. She's really embracing everything that we do here, and she's making leaps and bounds. It's not even been a full week, but you'll see for yourself that her light is shining brighter already." Joe stopped and turned to Crane. "There is one thing I do need to check with you first. Mr Davies said you needed to speak to her about an urgent private matter. I just want to ask, is it something that is likely to upset her?"

Crane hesitated, knowing there was a good chance bringing up Luke Maddocks could upset Sophie, but he felt he had no other choice; he needed to know what happened that night. He decided on an answer that was both non-committal and honest. "I hope not, it's certainly not my intention to upset her."

Joe nodded as if he were satisfied with his response. He continued along the path with Crane in tow until they reached a black door with a chrome keypad next to it. Joe quickly tapped in four numbers, ensuring his body blocked Crane's view of the keypad. There was a faint click from the lock and then he pushed the door open.

The inside was mostly open plan, but there were a few doorways leading to rooms around the outer edges of the building. The floor was covered with spotless white tiles, and all the internal walls were painted white. The back of the building was also a huge panoramic window, and it looked out onto lush green lawns and wildflower beds. Crane could see a few giant teepees in the distance between some trees. In front of the glass at the back of the building was a long blue dining table surrounded by a dozen blue wooden chairs. Leaning over the table was another member of the clinic staff, also wearing black scrubs. She was laying out white placemats and cutlery on the dining table, preparing it for the evening meal. She looked up and gave Crane a friendly smile. She had shoulder-length ebony hair in a neat bob. She also looked fit and lean but seemed a few years younger than Joe.

Joe guided Crane around to the left and under a floating white staircase. The staircase led to the upper level, into the white block above them. Joe stopped in front of a plain white door and grabbed the handle. "She's in here. I'll give you a knock at twenty-five past to wrap it up."

Crane nodded, and Joe opened the door for him to go in. It was a small room. All the walls were painted brilliant white except for the rear wall, which was glass and looked out onto a small pond surrounded by more lush green lawns and wildflowers. It was a very tranquil view. In the centre of the room were two light blue bean bag chairs. They were facing each other, side-on to the view outside.

Sophie was sitting on the bean bag chair on the left. It looked as if she had been enjoying the view outside, and she turned to look at the door when she heard it open. She was wearing scrubs like Joe, but Sophie's were plain white and so were the running shoes she was wearing. Her bright red hair was tied back in a ponytail, and she wasn't wearing any makeup. Not that she needed to. She was naturally a very pretty young lady. The main thing Crane noticed was how happy and healthy she looked. Maybe it was because she exceeded his expectations. There was colour in her cheeks, and she seemed relaxed. Her smile was genuine.

"Hello," she said cheerfully.

"Hello, Sophie. It's nice to meet you. My name's Crane."

The door closed behind him, and they were left alone.

"It's nice to meet you too, Crane."

Crane plonked himself down on the opposite bean bag. "How are you doing?"

"Good," said Sophie, smiling and nodding. "Really good. I've not been here a full week yet, and I already feel better than I have for years. This place is amazing."

"That's good to hear," said Crane, holding her gaze. "I'm sorry to interrupt your afternoon, but I promise I won't take up too much of your time; in fact, I can't take up too much of your time, as Joe has already told me he's gonna kick me out before half five."

Sophie laughed, and he was pleased to see a slight sparkle in her eyes. "They're very strict with the routine," she said. "It's a good thing though. It makes everyone feel comfortable and it reduces stress when we all know what's happening and when it's happening."

"That makes sense," said Crane. "And I presume that the scrubs are so that everyone wears the same clothes and it alleviates the stress of choosing what to wear every day."

"Exactly," Sophie exclaimed. "They use the analogy of emptying our cup. Everyone here has experienced different kinds of traumas, and they teach us to accept what's happened to us in the past, then they train us and give us tools to be kinder to ourselves, to give ourselves a break, and to try to be our own best friends. We're all here because our cups were overflowing with anxieties and stresses and pains and what ifs, and now it's time for us to let go and try to empty our cups." She mimicked holding a cup in one hand and tipping it on its side to pour the contents out as she said it. "Obviously the cup will never be completely empty, but in less than a week, mine feels like it's stopped overflowing. I'm even starting to feel like I have a little space at the top, and it feels good. It feels really good. I was overflowing for so long I didn't think that it could ever change. I thought that that was it, that I would feel that way until the end." She got lost in her words, and for a split second her eyes glazed over, but then she blinked and gave her head the briefest of shakes to return herself to the moment. "Sorry, I'm blabbering on. They told me that my dad called and said he was sending someone to come and speak to me urgently?"

"Please don't apologise," said Crane, waving off her apology. "It's really interesting to hear what you've been doing, and I'm really glad that it's working for you. I do need to ask you a couple of questions, and I do need to apologise in advance. I have to bring up the person who caused your cup to overflow."

"Luke Maddocks," Sophie stated. There was no questioning tone or other options. Luke was the liquid in her cup, his abuse the ice cubes bobbing in her brokenness. "Don't worry, I've accepted who he is and what he did to me. I can no longer hide from it or fight it. I try to think of it like after I've watched a horrible scary movie—I can't change what happened in the movie, I can't change the actors or the director, and I certainly can't change the plot. The movie has been made, and I can't unsee the movie because I've already watched it, but now it's finished and it's in the past. I can talk about it because talking about it doesn't put me back in the movie. What happened during that part of my life doesn't determine who I am now or who I become in the future."

Crane had been apprehensive before meeting Sophie. He hadn't known if she would be well enough to speak to him, or even if she would be willing to speak to him, but the young lady sitting in front of him was exceeding all of his expectations. She articulated herself well and had a surprisingly calm demeanour considering he had asked her about a very sensitive subject. He was genuinely impressed and knew that it showed on his face. "That's an interesting way of looking at it."

"I find it's a really effective way to detach myself from the trauma. It may not work for everybody, but it really helps me." Sophie gently placed her right hand across her heart and smiled at Crane. It was a lips-closed smile, but it reached her eyes and made them sparkle. "Sorry, I feel like I'm talking your ears off. What do you want to know?"

Crane cleared his throat. "In the early days of your relationship, Luke took you on holiday to Gran Canaria. This is a long shot, but can you remember what time he picked you up from your parents' house to get to the airport?"

"About twenty past eight," Sophie said, without missing a beat.

Crane jerked his head forward slightly. "Are you sure?"

"One hundred percent. I remember because I was really stressing. Our flight was at eleven, and we needed to be at the airport for nine o'clock. He was meant to pick me up at seven, which would have given us plenty of time—two hours to do the one-hour drive to Bristol Airport and park the car—but he didn't show up." For the first time, a crinkle appeared between her brows as she concentrated to recall what had happened.

"I tried calling his phone, but it was switched off. When it started getting towards eight o'clock, I was really fretting. I started thinking that maybe he'd changed his mind about going on holiday with me. Then at eight o'clock, he called me, but when I answered the phone, the line went dead, as though he'd hung up. I tried calling him straight back, but his phone was switched off again.

"I was pacing up and down the front room at this point, panicking, staring out of the window, praying for him to pull up outside. Then all of a sudden, he did, at about twenty past eight." Sophie inhaled deeply through her nose and slowly exhaled between pursed lips. Crane had noticed that her pace of speech had increased as she told her story and relived the moment. Thankfully, the breath seemed to do the trick, and when she continued, her rhythm of speech returned to its original, natural pace. "I ran out with my bags, and he threw them in the back. We got to the airport car park at half nine, and then it was a mad rush to park the car, check-in, and get through security. We only just made it in time to board before they closed the gates."

"Did he say why he was late?"

"He said that he'd had a problem at the club he'd needed to sort out. He was really het up. When I asked him about the problem, he got really defensive and said he didn't want to talk about it. So, I left it. Even in the early days, I knew not to press him. He has really bad anger issues and a very, very short fuse. He can literally go from nought to a hundred with the flick of a switch. I've never seen anything like it." Sophie grimaced. "Anyway, whatever the problem was, it must have been something big. He didn't even have any luggage. He said he'd been so busy sorting out the issues at the club that he hadn't had a chance to go home and pack. I remember on the first day of the holiday we had to go shopping to buy a load of clothes for him."

"Did he say why he didn't call you to let you know he was running late?" asked Crane.

"He said his phone battery had died."

"Had it?"

Sophie paused, just for a second, and then she nodded. "I think so. I'm sure I remember him plugging it into the car and charging it as we drove to the airport."

Crane quickly glanced at his watch. He was almost out of time. "This may seem like a random question, but in your experience, if he was driving and someone were to cut him up, how would he generally react?"

Sophie snorted. "Like I said, he has terrible anger issues. I mean, even normal people get road rage, but Luke, he would explode. If someone annoyed him on the road, he would beep the horn and scream obscenities at them. In fact, I remember this one time we were coming back from a weekend in London and someone crossed into our lane on the motorway without indicating. He really went off on one, beeping and flashing his lights at them, shouting all sorts of names that I wouldn't want to repeat. He followed them and kept getting as close as he could without hitting them. He said he wanted to teach them a lesson." Sophie began to fidget with her hands and paused to look down at them. She made a conscious effort to stop before clasping them together and resting them back in her lap.

"We ended up missing our junction because he was so fixated on intimidating them. Luckily, by the time we reached the next junction, I was able to talk him down and convince him to turn around and head home. But it wasn't easy. He really loses it if he feels like he's been disrespected."

There was a soft knock on the door. Crane's time with Sophie was up.

"Look, I truly appreciate you taking the time to speak to me, and I'm really glad you're doing so well." He pushed himself up from the bean bag, realising there was no elegant way of doing so. "Thank you for being so open with me; it's been really insightful."

"So, that's it?" Sophie frowned. "That's all you wanted to know?"

Crane nodded.

"You haven't even told me what this is all about. Why are you asking about that night?" She pushed herself up from her bean bag.

The door opened, and Joe looked at them apologetically.

"Sorry, guys, but I must insist on you leaving now."

Crane gave Joe a thumbs up and then turned back to Sophie, knowing he couldn't leave without giving her something. He took a step closer and lowered his voice. "There was a traffic accident that night, just before Luke picked you up. I'm trying to figure out if he was involved. But, look, it's nothing that should concern you in any way. You just concentrate on emptying your cup and feeling better. You deserve it."

Crane followed Joe back through the building and out the front door. They walked up the path together, side by side.

"It's an impressive place you have here," said Crane, "and Sophie seems to be doing really well."

"She is," agreed Joe. "I have no doubt that by the end of her six weeks here, she'll feel like a completely new person."

Crane glanced over his shoulder for one final look at the remarkable complex. "Out of curiosity, how much does a six-week stint at the clinic cost?"

"Five thousand per week."

Crane whistled to emphasise that it was a lot of money, then said, "To be fair, I wasn't expecting it to be cheap."

"Our results are guaranteed too. If any of our guests relapse, they can come back for another six weeks free of charge. None of our previous guests have needed to come back. Touch wood." Joe tapped his head with his left hand.

"How many guests have you had?"

"This is our first group," Joe said with a smirk.

Crane sniggered. "Nice one."

"Since this place was fully completed just under seven years ago, we've had over five hundred guests stay with us; however, I must admit it isn't always plain sailing. If a guest fails to keep an open mind and doesn't embrace our treatments and tools, we will send them home. Especially if they disrupt the rest of the group. Thankfully, that's only ever happened a handful of times. Most people who come here want to get the most out of it."

# Chapter Twenty-One

Crane parked in the same spot as the night before. During the drive back to Cardiff, he'd called Derek to reassure him about the facility and Sophie's progress. Crane wasn't sure if it was because he was so relieved and grateful to hear that his daughter was doing well or if it were purely because he was such a humble and kind man, but he didn't mention the money to Crane at all, and Crane didn't mention it either. He didn't need to. He knew how much the clinic had cost and he would be transferring the full amount to him later. Now he needed to speak to Ricky. He locked up his truck and headed towards Corkers on foot, phone to his ear.

Ricky picked up immediately, as if he'd been waiting impatiently next to his phone for an update. "What have you found out?"

"Luke Maddocks picked up Sophie from her parents' home in Caerphilly at twenty minutes past eight, so the timeline fits. He was in the area at the time, he was driving a big SUV, he was in a rush, and according to Sophie, he has really intense road rage."

"Okay," Ricky said. "A lot of circumstantial fingers are pointing towards him. Not sure about the significance of the road rage. I mean, who doesn't get road rage?"

"I know, but you should have heard how Sophie described it. She said he tailgates as close as he can, beeps, flashes, and shouts. It's exactly how Beth described it right before she..." Crane let out a shaky breath, knowing he needed to keep his emotions in check, at least for now.

"So, you definitely think it's him?"

Crane paused. "I do, but..."

"But what?"

"I don't know," said Crane as he stopped halfway across Cardiff Bridge to look down at the glinting water of the River Taff, ignoring the procession of people walking across the bridge behind him. He watched a pair of mallard ducks casually floating side-by-side downstream. "The convenience of it all. The mystery letters and anonymous calls. The fact that this has all happened now, almost five years later. Who is the mystery caller who's tipping me off? And why now?" As the ducks disappeared beneath the bridge, Crane turned away from the water and continued on his way.

"They're good questions and they're also good reasons to hesitate."

"I don't know what it is, but something just doesn't feel right. Everything so far points to Luke Maddocks, but there's something in the back of my brain telling me that I'm missing something."

"So, what are you going to do?"

Crane suspected that Ricky already knew what he was going to do, but he answered anyway. "I'm going to go back to the club and speak to him. I'm going to give him one final opportunity to confess or convince me that it wasn't him. One last chance to provide me with a real alibi if he has one."

"And what if he confesses or doesn't convince you with an alibi?" asked Ricky.

"I think you know me well enough to answer that one for yourself."

"That's what scares me," Ricky replied, his words barely audible through the phone.

"I know you went through the company finances, but did you take a look into Luke Maddocks' personal finances at all?" asked Crane, stopping at a pelican crossing. The silhouette of the red man was illuminated, so he used his free hand to push the button on the crossing control panel and waited.

"It's funny you should ask that," said Ricky. "I had a look into it this afternoon, and I was surprised to see that he's a bit of a saver. He's got a savings account that he transfers the majority of his earnings into. It's as though he's saving up for retirement or something. He's built up quite a substantial nest egg over the last seven years."

The green silhouette illuminated and a loud beeping rang out from the control panel. Crane and four other pedestrians set off across the road. "What kind of savings account?"

"Just a standard one that's linked to his current account," replied Ricky.

"How much has he saved up?"

"A little shy of seven figures."

Crane whistled. "That's a lot of money to have just sitting in a savings account not doing anything. Maybe it's escaping money."

"What do you mean?"

"Well, if it were a retirement fund, why wouldn't he invest it? He could put it into property or maybe lock it away in some high-interest, long-term investments that would grow his portfolio; instead, he's got it earning next to nothing in a standard savings account. I can only think of one reason why he would do that—instant access. He needs to be able to access the funds immediately, like if he gets into trouble and needs to disappear."

"You mean if he gets into trouble with the police?"

"That or if the relationship he has with the person or people who backed and funded him to buy Corkers turns sour." Crane walked past the bar where the stag party had been celebrating the previous evening, but there was no Snow White or seven dwarfs in the window today. Instead, a group of men in normal civvies were drinking beer and watching a football match being played on a big screen.

"That would make sense," agreed Ricky.

"Is the money in a bank account that you can access?"

"Have you ever heard of a bank account that I haven't been able to access?"

Crane smirked at Ricky's cocky but justified response. "Point taken."

In the early days, Ricky had tried to explain how he was able to hack into secure databases, access and withdraw money from people's bank accounts, track phones and cars that were fitted with GPS, and a hundred other things that seemed impossible to the average computer user like Crane. He would listen to Ricky with genuine interest, but half the time it was as if he were speaking to him in Swahili. Eventually, Ricky must have noticed the glazed look on Crane's face, as he'd stopped trying to explain a while ago. Now, he just worked his magic and Crane said thank you. It suited them both that way.

"Can you start a drip at seven o'clock?" Crane asked.

"How much?"

"Ten thousand every five?"

"Consider it done," Ricky said before hanging up.

Crane twisted the bulbous brass handle to Corkers and pushed the cumbersome black door open with one hand, sliding his phone into his pocket with the other. He stepped inside and was immediately immersed in the familiar pink lighting of Corkers' entryway. The hydraulic door closer shut the door with a click behind him as he started down the stairs. At the bottom, basked in the slightly brighter pink lighting and sitting behind the reception desk was a familiar face.

"Good evening, Leon," Crane announced as he approached the desk, raising his arms out to the sides in greeting, an insincere smile on his face. "You're on the front desk again tonight?"

Leon looked up, and when he recognised who it was, he rolled his eyes. "Not you again."

Crane chuckled, amused by Leon's response. "They like having you out here meeting and greeting at the front desk, don't they? It must be because of your charming manner and warm personality."

Looking thoroughly unimpressed, Leon just sat and stared at Crane for a few moments before mumbling, "What do you want?"

"I want to see Luke."

"Well, he doesn't want to see you."

"How do you know?" asked Crane, raising a brow. "You haven't even asked him."

Leon shrugged. "I don't need to ask him. I know him. He won't want to see you."

"Just because you're blowing someone doesn't mean that you know them, Leon."

It took a second for the insult to register. When it did, Leon stood up and scowled, but that was all he did. He didn't take a single step forward. He obviously didn't feel confident enough to enter a physical confrontation. Why? Was it because Crane hadn't backed down to Paul last night, or because his tougher side was all for show, or because of the bandage on his right hand?

"What happened to your hand?" asked Crane.

Leon looked down at his bandaged hand. "Nothing," he said, then shoved it in his trouser pocket.

Crane laughed. "There's no point hiding it; I've already seen it."

"I'm not hiding it," insisted Leon, sounding like a sulky teenager.

"You seem a little sensitive tonight, Leon. Is everything okay? Do you want to talk about it?"

"Shut up."

Crane mockingly pushed his bottom lip out. "Do you need a cuddle?"

Leon just glowered at him.

"I'm bored of talking to you now. Why don't you be a good boy and use your strong hand to pick up the phone and call Luke? Ask him if he wants to see me."

It didn't really matter whether Luke wanted to meet with him or not; Crane was going to see him tonight one way or another.

He was currently opting for a diplomatic approach, but he was more than happy to change tact if the situation required it.

Leon grudgingly picked up a small cordless handset from behind the desk and pressed a single digit. Luke's office was obviously on speed dial. "Hi, Boss. I've got the guy from last night out here asking to see you again."

Leon was quiet while he listened to the response on the other end of the line, then he looked up at Crane. "Luke said he'll see you as long as you don't play any more games and you tell him who you are."

Crane shrugged. "I've got nothing to hide."

"He said okay, Boss." Leon was quiet again while he listened, then he said, "Yeah, okay. Will do, Boss."

He pressed a button on the phone that ended the connection with a beep, then he pressed another single digit and held the phone back up to his ear.

"You need to come and man the front desk. I've got to escort someone to the boss's office."

He ended that call with another beep and then returned the handset to its cradle. He reached under the desk and pulled out what looked like a stumpy black plastic bat. The word "Scanner" was printed across it in bold yellow writing. It was a metal-detecting wand.

"I need to scan and pat you down," said Leon.

"Go ahead," said Crane. "Like I said, I've got nothing to hide."

Crane stepped his feet wide and held his arms out straight. Leon waved the wand over him twice, then started to pat him down. He was very thorough—it was as if he really wanted to find something. When he was finally satisfied that Crane was unarmed, he placed the wand back behind the desk and gestured for Crane to follow him. They were both hit with a blast of bass from the music as Leon pulled open the door. The club looked a little quieter than it had the night before, but it was still very early.

Crane looked around for Ivanka as they weaved their way between and around the seating areas. She wasn't at the bar, she wasn't on stage, and she wasn't speaking to any of the punters, at least not from what he could see, but he may have missed her. He still hadn't spotted her by the time they reached the door at the back of the club. A couple of the private areas did have the curtains closed though, so maybe she was performing a private dance in one of those. Or maybe she had the night off. That last one was probably a bit of a stretch, as it was doubtful that she would have a Saturday night off.

Leon pushed through the door labelled "Staff Only", and they entered the bright hallway, leaving the gloomy pink club floor and deafening music behind them. Just like the night before, Leon knocked on the door and waited until he heard Luke's muffled voice instruct him to enter. Leon pulled down on the chrome handle, and they both stepped into Luke's office-cum-youth club.

Continuing the feeling of deja vu, the same two men were inside the office. Luke Maddocks and Paul Jenkins. There was only one thing that was different with the office compared to the night before—in the area where the oche for the dartboard had been laid out on the floor, a large poker table was now in its place. It had thick black padding around the edge, with a sunken green baize playing area. Built into the padded outer edge were ten stainless steel cup holders, but there were only six chairs. Black leather, straight back, no arms. There was an open case at the end of the table on the left filled with rows of different-coloured poker chips. Next to the case were three sealed packs of playing cards.

Luke was standing behind the poker table with his arms out wide, as if he were presenting a TV show and introducing his first guest. "Look, it's the man with no name," he announced.

Tonight, Luke was wearing black trousers and a white shirt, open collar, with the sleeves rolled up to his elbows, revealing his tattooed forearm. Paul was leaning his hulking mass against the office desk behind him. He wasn't dressed in gym clothes this evening. He wore dark blue chinos and a white polo T-shirt with a little blue logo. The T-shirt sleeves looked ready to burst from his enormous biceps. He had an amused expression plastered across his face. He was obviously entertained by Luke's brashness. Luke's manner was similar. It was as if they knew something Crane didn't.

Luke gestured for Crane to sit at the poker table. "Come take a seat."

Crane didn't move.

Luke pulled one of the chairs back and sat down without breaking eye contact with Crane. "Come on," he said. "You want to talk, so let's talk."

Crane approached the poker table, pulled the chair opposite Luke back, and sat down. Paul stayed where he was on the desk, and Leon stayed at the door behind him.

"You really are a curious man." Luke leaned forward and rested his forearms on the black padding of the poker table. "But I do know two things about you."

"Really? What two things do you know?"

"I know you're not a police officer, and I know you're unarmed."

"Okay," said Crane, smirking. He somehow refrained from clapping sarcastically. "Well done, Sherlock."

Luke laughed. Too much. It was forced and a little over the top. Leon and Paul joined in with their boss.

When his laughter finally subsided, Luke said, "I've got a question for you. If you're not a police officer and you're unarmed, what's stopping us from beating the shit out of you?" There was a big, malicious grin on his face.

Paul sniggered behind him.

"Nothing," said Crane, crossing his arms on the edge of the poker table. "You're more than welcome to try."

Luke raised his hand and slammed it down on the padding of the poker table, creating a loud slapping noise. He then used the same hand to point at Crane. "There it is, gentlemen. Look at that confidence. He looks very comfortable, doesn't he?" Luke looked around at Paul, and Paul nodded back, grinning smugly. "So, you're a fighter and you're very confident in your abilities. Maybe even a little *too* confident?"

Crane shrugged. "There's only one way to find out."

"That's true," said Luke. "But I have another question for you first."

Luke leaned forward and reached behind his back. He pulled something out from the waistband of his trousers and held it up so that Crane could see it clearly. It was black and metallic—a Glock 17. One of the most popular pistols in the world, and the most commonly issued firearm among all Home Office police forces. The Glock 17 was a good, durable, and reliable weapon in Crane's experience. He still preferred his Heckler and Koch, but the Glock was decent.

Luke rested the bottom of the grip on the edge of the poker table and aimed the barrel at Crane's face. "What's stopping me from putting a bullet in your head right now?" A cocky grin was spread across his face.

Surprisingly, it looked as if Luke was experienced at holding a firearm, although that experience could have just been from posing in front of a mirror, maybe performing re-enactments of Robert De Niro's famous scene in the film *Taxi Driver*. He certainly didn't have any military or law enforcement experience in his background.

Crane was only just over a metre away, so the Glock was within reach; however, Luke's finger was firmly on the trigger and there was no manual safety on the Glock. Even so, Crane was still tempted to go for it, but it was risky. Fortunately, he was in a position where he didn't need to take any risks.

"I've got a good insurance policy in place," answered Crane.

"What? Life insurance?" Luke laughed again, and his two cronies chimed in with him.

Crane shook his head. "Not quite. I know something about you that's quite interesting."

"What's that, then?"

"I know that you've been building a substantial nest egg for yourself. It's tucked away in a standard savings account that's linked to your current account."

The cocky grin instantly disappeared from Luke's face, and his expression darkened.

"If you want to check your balance, you'll find that it's now ten thousand pounds lighter than it was"—Crane looked down at his watch—"around three minutes ago."

Luke stared at Crane intensely for a few seconds, then he swapped the Glock from his right hand to his left, still keeping it trained on Crane the whole time. He used his right hand to retrieve his phone from his trouser pocket. He unlocked it with his thumbprint, then used the same thumb to tap away at the screen. He seemed to be tapping in a password, presumably to open his banking app and check his balance. His eyes suddenly narrowed at the screen.

"What the fuck?"

"Keep looking," said Crane, still looking at his watch. "You should see it drop by another ten thousand in three... two... one."

"What? How the fuck are you doing that?" Luke's face reddened, and the muscles of his jaw visibly tensed as he clenched and bared his teeth like a rabid dog. The veins at his temples protruded under his skin like cables. He stood up and shoved the Glock towards Crane's face. "Put it back, or I'll shoot you in the fucking face right now."

The Glock was now only a few inches from Crane's nose, in Luke's left hand. His weaker hand judging by the fact he'd originally held the gun in his right hand. It was an amateur move on Luke's part. Instinct kicked in for Crane. In a single movement, he tilted his head to the right, and his right hand snapped up, gripping the barrel of the Glock and rotating it to the left and then backwards towards Luke. At exactly the same time, his left hand came up and gripped Luke's wrist. He then wrenched the barrel upwards. In a fraction of a second, the Glock was now in his possession. It had happened so quickly Luke didn't get the opportunity to depress the trigger. The only disappointment was it had gone so smoothly that he hadn't broken Luke's finger or wrist in the process. Not so much as a chip of Luke's fingernail.

"I suggest you sit down," said Crane calmly.

Luke still looked angry, but his eyes were wide and a little fearful now that he was the one staring down the barrel of a Glock. Paul made a move to pull something out from behind him, but he'd spent too much time on the bench press. He was slow and he was struggling with the range of motion in his shoulder to reach behind his back with any trace of poise or ease.

Crane took aim at him. "Please give me a reason to pull the trigger."

Paul froze with his hand still behind him.

"You can get it out, but hold it with your index finger and thumb, then drop it on the floor and kick it towards me," Crane instructed. "Oh, and I suggest you move very slowly, otherwise I might flinch and pull the trigger."

Paul slowly pulled out another Glock 17, identical to the one Crane was currently aiming at his centre mass. He held it between his finger and thumb like he was holding a dirty handkerchief. Then he slowly bent down and dropped it to the floor before kicking it towards Crane. It made a sharp grinding sound as it slid across the black tiles. It caught on the leg of a chair to Crane's right and stopped a little short, but it was still close enough for Crane to reach it with his foot and drag it towards him, which he did. He left it on the floor, with his foot resting on top of it. He then returned his aim to Luke, who was still standing up. Luke slowly sat back down in his chair, having got the message without being told again.

Crane turned and looked at Leon, who was still standing by the door, mouth agape. His right hand raised in a half-hearted attempt to cover it. "Leon, are you armed?"

Leon shook his head.

"Okay. Come around and sit next to Paul on the desk."

He wanted the three of them where he could see them. As soon as Leon was next to Paul, he lowered the Glock under the table, out of sight. He noticed Luke was glancing down at his phone screen, checking his bank balance.

"You don't need to keep checking your phone; I can tell you exactly what's happening. Your balance is dropping by ten thousand pounds every five minutes, and it's going to keep dropping until I decide to stop it."

"How are you doing it?" growled Luke.

"You should be more concerned with why I'm doing it rather than how."

Luke just glared at Crane. If looks could kill, Crane would be six feet under by now.

"Let me put all of my cards on the table," said Crane. "On the fifteenth of November almost five years ago, the date I asked you about last night, my wife was driving through the country lanes near Fforest Fawr when a big SUV caught up with and started to aggressively tailgate her. The man driving the SUV flashed his lights, beeped his horn, and at one point jumped out and shouted at her. She was on her own, driving through dark lanes, and being pursued by a maniac." Crane paused briefly to allow the word "maniac" to linger in the air.

"She was understandably scared and sped up to try and get away, but the arsehole driving the SUV wouldn't let up. He continued to chase her down, and he eventually ran her off the road.

"Her car went up an embankment, overturned, and crashed into a tree. She died on impact, along with our unborn baby. The man driving the SUV left her there, in a cold, wet, dark ditch. He didn't even call the emergency services for her."

Crane watched Luke's reaction carefully, but he wasn't giving anything away. There wasn't even a hint of recollection.

"Look, I'm sorry for your loss, but I don't understand what any of that has got to do with me."

"You see, I've been receiving anonymous phone calls and letters from someone claiming they know who was driving the SUV at the time of the crash. Any idea who they're pointing the finger at?" Crane waited, tapping his fingers on the table.

Luke's eyes narrowed and then widened with realisation. "*What? Me?* No way, it's got nothing to do with me."

"The thing is, there's a lot of things that point to you, Luke. Let me run you through what I've found out so far." Crane held up a closed fist, ready to raise one finger for each thing he'd found out. "I know you weren't in Gran Canaria like you claimed you were, so you lied to me about that." Crane leaned forward and shot Luke a piercing gaze, raising his thumb. "I know that at the time of the crash, you were actually on your way to pick up your ex-girlfriend, Sophie, who lived in Caerphilly with her parents at the time." Finger one. "I know that the lanes near Fforest Fawr can be used to get to Caerphilly from Cardiff." Finger two. "I know that you didn't reach Sophie until twenty past eight, and the crash happened at around ten past eight, which fits snugly into the timeline." Finger three. "I know that you were in a rush to get to the airport to catch your flight." Crane had four fingers and thumb held up, and he closed his fist, dropping it, not prepared to move his other hand from the gun to carry on counting. "I know that you were driving a big SUV at the time. A Range Rover Sport to be precise. And I know that you like to tailgate, flash your lights, and beep your horn when someone pisses you off on the road."

Luke had shaken his head the whole time Crane had been speaking.

"No way, someone's trying to set me up. It wasn't me."

"So, convince me," said Crane. "This is your opportunity."

"It couldn't have been me," said Luke. "I was in police custody."

Of all the things Crane had envisioned Luke saying, he hadn't seen this one coming. He raised a brow. "What?"

"That's how I know you're not a police officer. You wouldn't have been asking me where I was on that day if you were. I'm sure it'll be on record somewhere that I was in Cardiff Central police station all day. I didn't get out until after eight. I was definitely nowhere near Caerphilly by ten past eight, I can promise you that. And on top of that, I don't even know what country lanes you're talking about. Where the hell is Fforest Fawr? I've only ever used the main roads to get to Caerphilly. A470 and then up Nantgarw Hill." Luke used his index finger to scratch out a big L shape on the green baize to emphasise his route. "Anyway, even if I did know about the lanes, there's no way I'd drive my Range Rover through them. I'm not gonna risk scratching the paintwork of an eighty-grand car through some country lanes. No chance."

"I'm going to need more details than that," said Crane, leaning further forward in his seat. "Why don't you try starting at the beginning."

"Okay." Luke nodded. "I was arrested at, like, four in the morning. Some slag had made a complaint that I'd touched her inappropriately or something, I can't remember exactly what she accused me of. Anyway, because I'd had a few drinks through the night, they said that they wouldn't interview me until they were sure I'd sobered up. Which was bullshit; I was sober enough." Luke rolled his eyes, and one side of his top lip curled upwards as he spoke. "I'd made the mistake of telling them that I was due to go on holiday and had a flight to catch that night. They purposely kept me in custody all day. They didn't even interview me until about half five. I remember because I was fuming and then the interview only lasted like ten minutes. As usual, they had nothing on me, and the slag who made the complaint in the first place had already changed her tune and retracted her statement." Luke sat back and folded his arms across his chest. "I knew what they were doing though, they were keeping me in custody just to piss me off. They were hoping to make me miss my flight. In the end, they released me without charge just after eight. Isn't that right, Paul?" Luke turned to look at Paul.

Paul nodded. "Yeah, it was about five past, maybe even ten past eight. I was waiting outside for you in your Range Rover all afternoon. When you got out, you didn't even have time to drop me back home. You dropped me off at that hotel on Coryton roundabout, and I had to get a taxi home from there."

"That's right," said Luke. "In fact, I didn't even have time to go home and pick up my bags. I had to go from the police station to get Sophie and then we went straight to the airport. It was a pain in the arse because I had to buy all new clothes when we got out to Gran Canaria." He unfolded his arms and held them out, palms up. "See, it couldn't have been me. I can't be in two places at once. I'm not your man."

Crane was quiet for a while. Externally, he was a man in complete control, contemplating his next move. Internally, he was in sheer turmoil. His head was spinning. He realised it was spinning because part of him had expected closure tonight. He wanted to have closure. It was still plausible that Luke was lying and it had been him who'd followed Beth that night, but it was also just as plausible that it hadn't been. There was no definitive proof either way. Part of him wanted it to be Luke Maddocks. He wanted to end Luke Maddocks' life and then move on with his own. But he couldn't. Not yet anyway. He couldn't because he believed him. He was frustrated with himself because he really didn't want to believe him. But he did.

Eventually, Crane said, "I hope for your sake you're telling the truth."

"I am. One hundred percent."

"I'm going to need to look into it. See if I can corroborate your story."

"Wait," yapped Luke. "What about my money?"

Crane stood up and dropped the magazine out of the Glock, then he pulled back the sliding mechanism so that the chambered round was ejected. It landed on the poker table and tumbled a few times before coming to a stop against the padding going around the table. By the time the round had come to a stop, he'd separated the sliding mechanism from the frame and popped out the spring and the barrel, dropping all four parts onto the table. He picked up the magazine and thumbed out all the rounds in quick succession. They tumbled onto the green baize and scattered.

Crane was surprised to find only sixteen rounds in the magazine. Another amateur move. It had the capacity for seventeen rounds. Anyone with an ounce of firearm experience would know to chamber a round, then replace the round in the magazine so you've got eighteen rounds ready and waiting. That one round could be the difference between life and death. Crane dropped the empty magazine onto the table and then picked up Paul's Glock from the floor and completed the same process. When he was done, he looked at Luke.

"The money will stop leaving your account within the next hour, but for now I'm going to keep what I've taken so far. If your alibi stacks up, I'll return most of it to you."

"Wait, what do you mean, most of it?" Luke asked, scrunching his whole face up.

Crane casually stepped back from the table and slid the chair he'd been sitting on back to its rightful place. His expression remained impassive and his tone was relaxed. "I mean thirty thousand pounds won't be going back to you even if your story holds up."

"What? Why?"

"Because after being in a relationship with you, Sophie is still so traumatised she needs to go to rehab. And I don't think it's fair that she or her father should have to pay for it. You're the catalyst of her trauma, so you should be the one who pays."

"That's bullshit," Luke spat venomously. "You can't do that."

"I think you'll find I can." Crane turned and started walking out.

"Who the fuck are you?" Luke called after him, still in his seat at the poker table. "You said you'd tell me who you are."

Crane stopped and turned back, then he shrugged. He had nothing to hide. "Tom Crane."

Luke, Paul, and Leon sat in silence. Even after they heard the fire exit door close, they didn't move, they didn't speak. Paul and Leon just watched Luke. Luke knew they were expecting him to explode into a rage. They were expecting the poker table to fly into the air and come crashing to the floor. They were expecting shouting and screaming and cursing. They both winced when Luke eventually pushed back his chair to stand up, but he surprisingly did it in a controlled manner. He turned to face them both. His face was still a shade of deep pink, and his eyes looked a little bloodshot. He looked like a man with a volcanic rage bubbling under the surface.

"This isn't over," he said quietly, in almost a whisper.

They said nothing, and Luke presumed it was because neither of them wanted to say or do anything that would tip him over the edge.

Then he said, "Can I have the room?"

Paul and Leon didn't need to be asked twice. They both swiftly walked out. Paul closed the door softly behind them.

Luke could feel his back teeth grinding together. He fought the urge to break something—it was difficult for him. *How dare that fucker come into my club, throw accusations at me, and steal my money! Who the fuck does he think he is?*

He picked up his phone and dialled a number. It rang four times before it was answered by a deep, mature man's voice. A voice with a slight cockney twang.

"Hello, Luke. Is everything okay?"

"I'm not sure, Chief," Luke replied. "Have you ever heard of the name Tom Crane?"

There was a long pause on the other end of the line, almost ten seconds of absolute silence until the man spoke again.

"I have," he said. "You need to stay away from him, Luke. He's an extremely dangerous man."

# Chapter Twenty-Two

Crane had immediately called Ricky after leaving Corkers to update him on the fact he didn't think Luke Maddocks was his man and to repeatedly convince him that Luke Maddocks was still alive. He'd asked Ricky to stop the drip—one hundred thousand pounds later—and transfer thirty thousand of it to Derek Davies. Now there was someone else he needed to call. He approached a red traffic light and came to a halt on the white line. While he was waiting for it to turn green, he used the infotainment system to enter his phone book and then selected a name he hadn't called in a while. Detective Sergeant Jon Carter.

A detective constable when they'd first met, DS Carter had been involved in the investigation into Beth's accident. He was a good guy and had shown Crane a lot of empathy during the investigation. Out of all the officers involved, he'd been the one who'd believed Crane about Beth being followed and subsequently ran off the road. The others had just looked at the physical evidence—no skid marks, no collision damage from another vehicle—and they'd just wanted to mark it down as an accident and move on to their next case. They'd tried to make out Beth was being paranoid, telling him that headlights can appear closer than they actually are in the dark, and that she'd panicked for no good reason. But not Carter.

DS Carter answered after the third ring. "Crane, how are you?" A television was quite loud in the background.

"Not too bad, Carter. How about you? Is your family good?" Crane could hear movement, followed by the soft click of a door closing, and then silence. "I'm so sorry to bother you, especially on a Saturday night."

"All good, and don't apologise; you've actually saved me from watching a Disney film for what must be the seven hundredth time," Carter replied, chuckling. Carter was married, with twin boys. The boys were about four now. "What can I do for you?"

"Do you know the name Luke Maddocks?" Crane asked as the light turned green and he pulled away.

Carter's tone immediately switched from jovial to serious. "Yeah, I do. The bloke's a nasty piece of work. What about him?"

"I just need to know if he was in custody on the day Beth died, and if he was, what time was he released?"

"Okay," Carter said hesitantly. "Do you think he might have been involved?"

"Maybe. I've been given a tip-off that he could be a person of interest." Crane flicked the indicator stalk down and crossed into the left-hand lane a little too quickly, the whole Luke Maddocks situation playing havoc with his mind. "I just want to be able to rule him in or out as a possibility. He says he was in Cardiff Central police station all day and that he wasn't released until after eight. Obviously if that's true, it completely rules him out as a suspect. I just need to know either way."

"Wait. You've already spoken to him?"

Crane classed Carter as a friend, but at the end of the day, he was still a policeman. He didn't want to say too much in case things did escalate—for Carter's sake as well as his own. "We've, uh, had a brief chat."

There was a short pause before Carter spoke again, and when he did, there was an edge of uneasiness in his voice. "Crane, you need to be careful. Trust me when I say he's not the kind of person you want to mess with."

"I know," said Crane. "And thank you for your concern. I'll be careful."

"Okay. I'm off this weekend, can I look into it and let you know on Monday?"

Crane was silent. He didn't want to wait until Monday, but he also didn't want to sound rude or ungrateful by saying "no". Although, technically, he knew his silence said it for him.

"I'll take that as a no, then," said Carter, thankfully in more of an understanding tone than anything else. "I've got a mate working the night shift tonight. I'll ask him to look into it for me, and I'll call you with an update in the morning."

"That would be great. Cheers, Carter."

After Crane ended the call with DS Carter, he turned off Northern Avenue and drove up a slip road and onto Coryton roundabout, one of the largest roundabouts in Europe—it was almost a mile all the way around. As he entered the roundabout, he had four lanes to choose from, and he chose number three. He was going to follow the lane around to take a right, to retrace Beth's final journey.

On his left was a big hotel with a busy car park. Huge signs on the front advertised that it wasn't just a hotel, it was also a bar, a grill, and a gym. It was the hotel where Paul claimed he'd been dropped off by Luke on his way to collect Sophie. After the hotel, there was a turn-off for a supermarket followed by a set of traffic lights, fortunately on green, so he was able to drive straight through. Next, he drove past a turn-off for the motorway to head west and then he went under a concrete bridge that went beneath the motorway above. Then came another set of traffic lights, unfortunately on red, so he stopped and waited. Directly after the lights was the turn-off to get back onto the A470—the quickest way to get to Caerphilly, at least when the roads were quiet. It was where Luke claimed to have turned off that night.

The lights turned green, and he followed the roundabout around to the right and beneath another concrete bridge, where the A470 passed over the roundabout. Another set of traffic lights appeared, these ones green, but they changed to amber as he approached. He made the decision to be an amber gambler and accelerated to get past them before they turned red. He continued to follow the roundabout around to the right and then it straightened out for a stretch. A filter lane came up on the left, heading towards Tongwynlais, a quiet little suburb with a village-like feel.

He took the filter lane. This was where he assumed Beth had cut in front of the SUV. He followed the road around, past another hotel and then through Tongwynlais. He drove past a primary school on his left followed by a couple of shops, a takeaway, and a pharmacy. He then took a right turn, which had a pub situated on the corner. This road was narrow due to cars being parked on both sides of the street. He was okay getting through in the truck, but if a car came in the opposite direction, he would need to find somewhere to tuck in and stop. Fortunately, the road was clear, and he continued up the slight incline.

He passed a left turn that headed up to Castell Coch—a nine-teenth-century gothic revival castle that translated to "red castle" from Welsh to English. It took its name from the red sandstone that was located in the area and from which it was built.

Up ahead was the entrance to the country lanes that ran through Fforest Fawr. He slowed the truck down subconsciously and checked the time. It was a few minutes after eight. The same time Beth had called him that night. He imagined her doing it, selecting his name on the infotainment system in her hatchback. It was the middle of August now, so there was still another half an hour of daylight left. In November, when Beth had been driving through here, it would have been dark.

The crowns of the trees on either side of the lane touched above it, almost creating a tunnel. Crane drove beneath the thick canopy of trees and into the shadow that they created. It would have been pitch black for Beth passing beneath here that night, he thought. He replayed the conversation in his head. He remembered how he'd desperately tried to calm her down, imploring her not to speed up.

Crane accelerated. He didn't consciously know why. He was reliving her final moments. He depressed the accelerator a little more and felt the torque from the diesel engine push him on. He focused ahead to make sure no vehicles were approaching as he carved around the bends. Left, right, left, right. He passed a number of sections where the lane widened on the left, knowing that one of them was the one Beth had pulled into that night to allow another car to pass. It was also where her pursuer had got out of his SUV and shouted at her. Crane's foot applied even more pressure onto the accelerator pedal. The truck rocked from one side to the other with each bend, the trees zipped past at an incredible rate, and he was starting to feel uncomfortable. This was too fast. On a road like this, it was crazy fast. It was extremely dangerous. But this is what Beth had done. In the pitch black of night. In the cold and wet. In a small hatchback. While being pursued by a stranger.

The lane straightened for a short stretch, and Crane floored the accelerator pedal. The engine roared and pushed him on even faster. He briefly glanced down at the speedometer as it hit the fifty miles per hour mark and kept rising. Then all of a sudden he released the accelerator and hit the brake hard. Not hard enough to break into a skid, but enough to bring the truck to a controlled, abrupt stop. Over fifty miles per hour. That was the speed the investigators estimated that Beth had been travelling when she'd left the road and hit the tree.

Crane pulled over to the left where the lane widened, activated the hazard lights, and jumped out of his truck. He couldn't see where the sun was, but he could tell it was getting really low. The sky was still blue, but the colour was deepening to the east, and there was a slight pink hue coming from the west. The forest surrounding the lane seemed to be getting darker by the minute. Crane walked across the asphalt and stepped up onto the embankment. He walked along it until it curved with the lane to the left and then he stepped down to the other side. The forest side. A few steps later, he was standing in the spot where Beth had died.

It was a small clearing that hardly seemed big enough to fit a car into it, but it had. The hatchback had flown through the air, overturned, and then smashed into the enormous beech tree Crane was currently standing in front of. The beech tree that barely had a scratch on its trunk after destroying Beth's hatchback and taking her life. Although not recently, he had visited this place hundreds of times since the crash. The first few weeks afterwards, he'd spent days on his hands and knees searching every square inch of the forest floor. He had been looking for Beth's phone, which was never recovered after the crash. There was no logical explanation for why it was never recovered. As far as Crane was concerned, the only conceivable explanation was the driver of the SUV had stopped and taken it.

He walked up to the beech tree and placed his hand against its trunk. It was cool and rough. Then he rested his forehead against it and closed his eyes. Crane didn't believe in an afterlife or heaven or hell or ghosts or souls, but even so, it didn't stop him from speaking to Beth. He knew she couldn't hear him, he knew she was gone, he knew she was never coming back. He knew first-hand the agonising finality of death. But it didn't stop him from talking to her anyway.

"I still miss you so much."

His voice was choked, but he forced the tears back.

"I'm still trying to find the man who caused this. I thought I was getting close, but now I'm not so sure."

He stayed there for a few minutes. Silent. His head and his hand resting against the trunk. Eyes closed. Breathing deeply and slowly. The next time he spoke, his voice didn't sound choked. It sounded strong and determined.

"I promise I will find him. Whoever it was, however long it takes, I will find him, and I'll end him. I promise."

# Chapter Twenty-Three

Crane didn't wake up until almost nine the next morning. A whisky Mac and a whole bottle of Argentinian Malbec had knocked him out last night, but it had also knocked his body clock out of kilter. He opened the bedroom curtains to another beautiful summer morning, bright sunlight and blue skies. Although the bright light made his head hurt even more than it had when he'd first opened his eyes. He cursed himself. *Why did I drink the full bottle of red?*

The first thing he did when he got downstairs was fill a pint glass with cold water and grab two paracetamols. He took the pills and downed the water, then refilled his glass. He made himself a bowl of muesli, ate it, and drank the second pint of water. As soon as the pills kicked in and his headache cleared, he headed to the gym room. He was going to punish himself this morning. He was going to sweat out every last drop of alcohol from his system and reclaim some control. A tough workout would force him to live in the present moment and refocus his energy.

He completed a five-minute warm-up of dynamic stretches and then he set up a circuit. He chose five exercises: press-ups, squats, inverted rows, Russian twists, and finally burpees where he would hold a twelve-kilogram dumbbell in each hand and incorporate a clean and press into the top portion of the movement. Forty-five seconds to complete as many repetitions of each exercise followed by a two-minute rest.

He completed six rounds, pushing himself to his limit, competing against himself with each round to try to complete more and more reps. By the end, he was dripping with sweat. His chest heaved, desperately trying to inhale enough oxygen for his overworked muscles. His whole body felt heavy and fatigued. But he wasn't finished.

Ten rounds on the heavy bag followed. Punches, kicks, and elbows. Two minutes per round with a one-minute rest between each round. After the tenth and final round, he was spent. Only his willpower prevented him from collapsing to the floor. He walked around the gym room with his hands on his head, sucking in deep breaths to recover. When his breathing finally normalised, he spent thirty minutes stretching. Strength and power were important assets, but suppleness and range of motion were important too. A tree that is too hard and stiff will snap and break. A tree that is too soft and weak will bend and be uprooted. Crane knew it was all about balance. He was flexible like a gymnast, yet he was as hard as granite.

Crane trudged into the kitchen and picked up his phone from the island where he'd left it. There was a missed call notification displayed on the screen, but no voicemail. It was DS Carter. He'd tried calling about twenty minutes ago. Crane grabbed a pint glass from one of the kitchen cupboards and filled it with water from the filter built into the fridge. He downed half of it in three big gulps before tapping the call back icon on his phone.

Carter answered quickly. "Hi, Crane." He didn't sound quite as jovial as he had the day before.

"Has your friend found anything?"

"He has," said Carter, "but it's as clear as mud."

Crane pulled out a stool and sat down at the kitchen island. "What do you mean?"

"So, there's a record of him being arrested just after four in the morning of the fifteenth, on suspicion of sexual assault. They held him in a cell, stating that he was uncooperative and under the influence of alcohol. They kept him there the whole day and didn't interview him until half five in the afternoon."

"Okay..." Crane bit his bottom lip, the conversation going as he'd had an inkling it would but had hoped it wouldn't.

"During the interview, his solicitor advised him not to answer any questions, and it only lasted thirteen minutes before it was interrupted. The interviewing officer received a note informing him that the complainant had recanted her statement and dropped the complaint. Apparently, she claimed that it was just a misunderstanding, she had been drunk when she'd made the complaint and hadn't fully understood what she was doing. They had no choice but to release him without charge."

Crane sat up, his interest peaking. If Luke had been released soon after the interview, it meant he would have been out of the police station well before the time of the accident. "So, is there a record of exactly what time he was released?"

"This is where it gets muddy," said Carter, sounding a little dejected. "Officially, or should I say according to the paperwork, he was released soon after the interview. Around six."

"It sounds like there's a *but* coming."

"Yep. The friend I asked to look into this was working in the station on that day, and he remembers that they kept Luke at the station a while longer. You need to understand Luke Maddocks is a popular man with the police in South Wales, and not in a good way."

It added a question mark to Crane's theory about Luke Maddocks knowing people within the police, although it didn't rule out the theory completely. A corrupt officer wouldn't want to be caught doing something corrupt, something like going against all the other officers and making themselves stand out.

"My friend said that the whole time he was in custody, he kept complaining that he needed to go because he was meant to be heading off on holiday that night. As usual, he was rude and obnoxious to all the officers on duty. So, when they ended the interview, the solicitor was taken to one side and informed that the complaint had been dropped and Luke was being released. But Luke wasn't told that, or at least not clearly.

"I'm not sure exactly how they did it, they probably just asked him to wait in a room for processing or something. Technically he wouldn't have been in custody, he wouldn't have been in a locked room, and he would have been free to leave. But they wouldn't have made that clear to him. He could have got up and walked out whenever he wanted, but they were winding him up and kept telling him to wait. Apparently, he was losing the plot, and they all took great satisfaction from it." Carter grunted. "To be honest, I don't blame them for wanting to piss him off. The bloke's an arsehole."

Crane drained the final mouthful of his pint of water and placed the empty glass down on the marble worktop of the island. "So, did your friend say what time Luke actually left the station."

"It was a long time ago, but he thinks it was around eight o'clock."

Crane stared at his empty glass and felt his jaw tighten.

"Sorry, I know that's about as useful as a knitted condom. He can't be ruled in or out with that."

Crane was quiet for a second, and then he eventually said, "Don't worry. It would have been ideal to have a confirmed time, but unfortunately we don't live in an ideal world."

"So, what are you going to do now?"

Crane sighed. "Honestly, I don't know."

"Okay. Well, if you need anything else, just give me a call."

"Will do. Thanks, Carter."

Crane ended the call. He placed his phone down next to his empty glass, rested his elbows on the worktop, and placed his head in his hands.

# Chapter Twenty-Four

Crane took a long, hot shower and then got himself dressed. He was going to take a walk around the mountain, as he wanted some fresh air and to clear his head. Before leaving, he picked up his phone from the kitchen island, but then he changed his mind and put it back down. He wanted peace and quiet. No distractions.

He locked up the house, opened the front gate with his key fob, and walked out. He turned left and strolled up the slight incline, heading towards the main road that travelled up and over Caerphilly Mountain. There was no pavement or pedestrian walkway of any kind, so he tucked in tight to the right edge and only veered into the lane to dodge the occasional overhanging tree branch. Although he had no direct neighbours as such, he did pass one other property on his way up, on the left. It belonged to the Greens—a lovely elderly couple who were both retired GPs. Apart from a small gap for their wrought iron gates, the lane was completely surrounded by thick undergrowth and trees.

When he reached the main road, he had to wait for a couple of cars to pass before crossing. Once he was across, there was a pavement that ran alongside the main road and led all the way to the car park near the summit.

The car park held enough spaces for around fifty cars, and it was always busy. The mountain was a very popular spot for hikers, dog walkers, and mountain bikers, especially on a nice day like today. In one corner of the car park was the Caerphilly

Mountain Snack Shack, which served the kind of burgers that would be described as heart-stoppers. Crane's stomach rumbled, knowing it was lunchtime. Maybe he would treat himself once he'd walked around the summit. He deserved it after his gruelling workout this morning; at least, that was how he would justify it to himself anyway. Crane maintained a high level of self-discipline in every aspect of his life, and his diet was no different. He ate healthily and naturally—a Mountain Snack Shack burger was neither. Occasionally, his rational side reminded his disciplined side that it was okay to let go sometimes.

Opposite the car park was a path that looped around and up to the summit. There were a few offshoots to mix up the route a little, and you could make your walk a bit longer or shorter depending on which paths you took. Crane stuck to the main loop. When he reached a part of the trail with a view that looked out over the city of Cardiff, he stopped for a minute or two. Most of the time when he came up here, he was jogging and didn't allow himself to take in and appreciate the stunning views that were on his doorstep.

The green of the trees and bushes of the lower part of the mountain gave way to the greys and browns of the city. The intricately woven web of man-made structures that stretched all the way to the water of the Severn Estuary. From this distance, Cardiff looked peaceful and still, but Crane knew all too well that down there, things were moving, and it wasn't all peaceful. One of the most prominent features that seemed to pop out of the landscape was the colossal Principality Stadium, which was only a stone's throw away from Corkers.

Crane continued to follow the path around, completing a clockwise loop and then up a steep incline to the summit. He walked past the tall stone marker at the peak and then stopped to take in the view on the other side of the mountain, looking down into the valley and onto the town of Caerphilly. He had to admit, it was an impressive sight. No wonder it was such a popular place for ramblers and dog walkers alike. Caerphilly Castle was the prominent feature of the town, surrounded by so much water it looked as if it were floating in the middle of its own mythical lake. It was magnificent.

Crane stood there for a few more minutes just taking the sight in, appreciating the landscape, breathing in the fresh air, feeling the warm sun on his face and arms, enjoying the moment, and clearing his mind. He could have stayed there all day, but his stomach had other ideas and started talking to him again. It was time to head to the Snack Shack.

The Snack Shack wasn't exactly a shack, although it had been many years ago when it first appeared on the mountain. It was now a large pagoda-style building with stone pillars, an over-hanging roof, and large glass windows. Although it looked big enough to, it didn't have any indoor seating. The serving counter looked out directly onto an area filled with picnic benches, some of which were under the overhanging roof. There was a small queue when Crane got there, but it gave him an opportunity to look at the menu and choose his poison. When he reached the counter, a young man in his early twenties was operating the till. He had spikey ginger hair and wore a white T-shirt and red apron with the Snack Shack logo embroidered on the front. Crane opted for the mountain monster, with a side of fries, and a bottle of water.

He paid and made his way to a wooden picnic bench near the counter, under the shade of the roof. As always, his back was facing the wall. He looked out at the people enjoying their food and drinks in the sunshine and was glad of the fact he didn't have his phone. It would have been so tempting to have pulled it out now to get lost in the screen while he waited. It actually felt quite refreshing to just sit and people-watch.

A group of mountain bikers were putting on helmets and getting ready to set off on a ride. An elderly couple was just coming off one of the trails, entering the car park hand-in-hand, with a black and white collie in tow. Soon, Crane became lost in his thoughts, paying no attention to anyone or anything around him. A lot had happened over the last forty-eight hours, and his mind began replaying and processing it for him.

A few minutes later, Crane was dragged back to the present when his number was called. He pushed himself up from the bench and walked to the counter to collect the humongous, greasy, meaty monstrosity. Three burgers with two rashers of bacon and a slice of cheese between each beef patty, topped with fried onions, and dripping with sauce. It was served with a generous portion of fries on a single sheet of greaseproof paper in a red plastic basket. His head was telling him that he shouldn't eat it, but his stomach was in charge now, and he took it back to the bench to tuck in.

He finished the lot and had to admit he felt satisfied. Or at least his stomach did. He used a small white napkin that felt as if it were made from tracing paper to wipe away any remnants of sauce or grease from his mouth, then scrunched it up and tossed it into his empty basket. That was when he heard someone call out his name. Crane started scanning the area, unsure where the voice had come from.

"Is there a Mr Crane here?" they repeated.

It was the ginger man leaning over the counter, holding a cordless landline telephone in his hand, looking around. Crane raised his hand to signal that it was him, then he picked up his basket, and made his way to the counter.

"It's a call for you," he said as Crane approached, looking even more surprised about the call than Crane.

"Who is it?"

The man shrugged and handed him the phone.

Crane raised it to his ear. "Hello."

"Hello, Crane," replied a raspy robotic voice. "It seems as though you don't mind that Luke Maddocks killed your wife after all."

Crane's neck and shoulders immediately tensed up. *How does he know I'm here?* "Who are you?"

"You'll find out in good time," said the voice. "Or maybe not. Maybe you'll never find out. Or maybe I'm waiting for you to kill Luke Maddocks before I reveal myself. I guess we'll have to wait and see."

Crane took a couple of steps away from the queue and lowered his voice. "You say it was him, but where's the evidence? You don't have any, do you?"

There was a slight pause before the scratchy voice answered. "I do, but there's still a lot you don't know yet."

"Like what?" asked Crane, his voice unintentionally increasing in volume. "What don't I know? Why don't you just stop with all your cryptic bullshit and tell me everything?"

The people in the queue were now looking at Crane, intrigued by the call or disgusted by his curse, he couldn't tell. He raised a hand and mouthed an apology when he noticed parents with a little girl at the back of the queue. They tutted and shook their heads.

"To help you out, I've just slipped an envelope under your front gate. It should make for very interesting reading."

*Shit.* Crane dropped the phone onto the Snack Shack counter and took off at a sprint, almost bumping into an elderly man taking his basket back to the counter. With a strong need to get home as quickly as possible, he shouted "sorry" over his shoulder, every second counting. His home was only a ten-minute brisk walk away, maybe half a mile. There was a chance the mystery man was still nearby, and he might just be able to catch him.

Crane's feet pounded the ground as he launched himself forward with each step. He glanced up and down the road, noticing a gap in the traffic, which was fortunate because he was already crossing and running too fast for a sharp stop. He strode across the asphalt and then bounded down the pavement, towards the turn for the lane where he lived. His heart was beginning to pound, and the lactic acid was building in his legs, making them burn. The last hundred yards or so were downhill, the gained momentum helping him make it to his front gate in just over two minutes. He shortened his stride and slowed his heavy legs as he approached the gate, eyes darting around, searching for a lone man or a vehicle.

*Shit, shit, shit.* The lane outside his home was deserted. He sucked in deep breaths to recover, holding the last breath at the top for a second or two so that he could listen. He was hoping to hear footsteps or maybe a car engine starting up somewhere nearby, but there was nothing. He walked down the lane a little further while he recovered from his mad dash. Still nothing. The mystery man was long gone. Even though he'd been half expecting this to be the case, it didn't make it any less disappointing. It still felt as if he'd missed a big opportunity to finally find out who the mystery man was. Crane made his way back to his front gate and pressed the button on his key fob. His front gates opened smoothly and silently, revealing a large white envelope on his driveway.

He bent down and picked it up. It was plain white, A4 size, exactly like the one that had been left on his windscreen outside the off-licence the day before. He tore it open and pulled out three pieces of A4 paper. As soon as he saw the top one, he felt as if he'd been kicked in the chest by a horse. It was a standard piece of A4 paper with a photograph printed on it. A photograph of Beth's phone.

He could tell that it was Beth's because the wallpaper displayed on the screen was a picture of the two of them. A picture taken in an Indian restaurant in Cardiff on one of their date nights just a few weeks before she died. They had been waiting for their starter to come when Beth tried to take a selfie of the two of them. When the waiter saw her struggling to hold the phone and take the picture, he kindly offered to take the picture for them. They were sitting at a small table for two, a pint of Guinness in front of Crane and a glass of prosecco in front of Beth. They were holding hands on the table and smiling naturally at the camera. Crane remembered the evening well. The food was good, but the company was better. He also knew the photo well. Beth had shared it with him after it was taken, and they had both set it as the background wallpaper on their phones. It was still the wallpaper on his.

Crane felt a chill run down his spine. This meant that the mystery man had Beth's phone. He pulled the top sheet away and placed it at the back of the three pages he was holding. The second page was another photograph of the phone, but this time it was displaying text messages. There was a name at the top of the display indicating who the message conversation was with. Crane's jaw tightened and his back teeth ground together when he saw the name—Luke. The messages were dated the nineteenth of July, only four months before Beth died.

Beth: "*What we did last night was so wrong.*" 11:13

Luke: "*But so right too?*" 11:14

Beth: "*Maybe...*" 11:16

Luke: "*I really want to do it again.*" 11:16

Luke: "*U can say no if u don't want to...*" 11:19

Beth: "*I do want to... xx*" 11:22

"These can't be real, they just can't..." Crane wiped at his wetting eyes with the back of one hand, shaking his head. "No, no, no."

He felt as if someone had shoved their hand into his chest, ripped out his heart, and started stamping all over it. Beth was stamping all over it. No, not his Beth. He *knew* his Beth. His Beth on a beach in Scotland, smiling despite the frosty air, the cloudy sky a beautiful backdrop as she danced across the sand, her brown golden-highlighted hair flying out behind her; Beth holding him to her outside Bristol Airport as he left for his first work trip abroad since meeting her, crying onto his shoulder, not wanting him to leave, his suitcase at his feet; Beth... His Beth wouldn't have done any of this... would she?

With shaking hands, he put the page at the back of the bunch to reveal the third and final page. It was a photograph of the phone showing text messages again, just like the second page, but these were dated October tenth. A little over a month before Beth died.

Beth: "*Have u booked the hotel for tomorrow night? Xx*" 19:43

Luke: "*Yep. And its got a big walk in shower room.*" 19:46

Beth: "*Great. Why do u care about the shower tho? Xx*" 19:47

Luke: "*Because I want to fuck u in it.*" 19:48

Beth: "*LOL! Can't wait... xx*" 19:49

Crane looked away from the pages and raised his fist to his mouth, trying to slow his breathing. He could feel the contents of his lunch rising up his throat, and he fought to keep them down. *No way. These can't be real. Beth didn't cheat. She wouldn't have looked twice at someone like Luke Maddocks. This must be some kind of sick, twisted joke.* He started to feel a little better, but then another voice in his head started to ask questions.

*Are you one hundred percent sure she wouldn't have cheated? How would you have known? You were away with work more than you were home. She could have got up to anything, and you would have never known. That is her phone in the pictures, isn't it? How well did you really know her?*

Crane rushed inside the house and into the kitchen. He picked up his phone and started searching back through his old work emails to check the dates. July nineteenth, he'd been in Egypt on a close protection detail and had been out there since the seventeenth. He didn't get back home until the twenty-third.

October tenth, home... ready to fly out to Lebanon in the early hours of the morning of the eleventh. Meaning he was in Lebanon on the day the messages suggested Beth was meeting Luke in a hotel to sleep with him. His mind was flip-flopping. Could the messages be real? Had she cheated on him? No. He didn't believe they were real. The way the messages were written, it didn't even sound like her. *But what if there was another side to her I didn't know?*

He grabbed the pictures and headed out. He needed a fresh pair of eyes and another perspective on this. He was doubting Beth. He was questioning their marriage. If she'd betrayed her vows. No. No, he wasn't. He trusted her implicitly. He knew her better than he'd known anyone his whole life. She never would have cheated on him. But what if she had? How could he be one hundred percent sure? Can anyone be one hundred percent sure they truly know someone?

He jumped in his truck and headed to Ricky's barn.

# Chapter Twenty-Five

Ricky kept shaking his head as he looked down at the three pages and read them one after the other. They were spread across his kitchen island. Crane sat on a stool on the other side of the island. He watched Ricky, not wanting to look down at the pictures again—he'd seen enough of them.

Once Ricky had looked carefully over each page twice, he looked up at Crane. "No chance," he said, still shaking his head. "They're fake."

"You're just saying that to appease me."

"I'm not. I'm just looking at it from the perspective of how easy it would be to fake this and put it together. I mean, what makes you even think that this is actually her phone?"

Crane pulled his phone out of his pocket and turned it around to show Ricky his background wallpaper. The picture of him and Beth in the restaurant.

"That's it?" asked Ricky. "You believe this is a picture of her phone just because it has that background wallpaper?"

Crane shrugged and held his arms out. "It was the wallpaper on her phone when she died."

Ricky snorted and then picked up his own phone from the kitchen counter. He started tapping and swiping away with his thumbs. "I recognise that picture, and not just because it's been the wallpaper on every one of your phones over the last five years. It was one of the last pictures ever taken of Beth. It was the last profile picture on most of her social media accounts. It was also the picture that was used by almost all of her friends and acquaintances on social media when they posted tributes to her online after the accident, although most of them did crop you out of the shot. But look, after just a quick internet search, you can do this."

Ricky turned his screen around to face Crane. The picture of Crane and Beth in the restaurant was now the wallpaper on Ricky's phone. His phone now looked exactly like Crane's and exactly like the one in the photographs.

"Okay, but what about the messages?" asked Crane.

"What about them?"

"They're date- and time-stamped."

Ricky snorted again. "That's elementary. You just get two phones and manually set the date and time to whenever you want the supposed conversation to have happened. Then you start texting back and forth between the two phones. The date and time-stamps for the messages come from the phone, not the network, so you can make it look like you had the text conversation whenever you want."

Crane gave Ricky a sideways glance. "Really?"

"There are other ways of doing it, but that's the easiest. Especially if you're not tech savvy."

Crane was starting to feel better already, although in another way, he also felt bad. He felt guilty. He had doubted Beth. He had questioned her fidelity. But he still had one more question.

"What's your thoughts on those particular dates? I was away working on both of them."

Ricky made a noise similar to the end of a horse's neigh, when the horse blows through their loose, flapping lips. "Are the dates really significant? This would have been back when you were working close protection. How many times have you told me that you spent more time away than you did at home? Personally, I really don't think the dates have any significance. I bet if we selected two random dates from back then, the chances are you would have been away with work. Shall we try it?" Ricky raised his phone almost as if he were making a toast with it. "Where were you on the third of May?"

Crane went back through his old work emails on his phone. A minute later, he said, "Dubai. I was in Dubai for three days. I flew out on the second."

"See," said Ricky. "How about the twentieth of June?"

A minute later, Crane said, "I was at home with Beth."

"Oh," Ricky said with a grimace, but he quickly shook it off. "But anyway, my point is it could easily be a coincidence and done with just a guess. If it wasn't a guess, then I'm sure there's a plethora of ways to find out when you were away."

"Maybe."

"There's no 'maybe' about it," insisted Ricky. "These are fake messages. Someone's screwing with you."

Crane nodded, but his expression remained impassive as he stared down at the pictures on the worktop. "Thanks, Ricky."

"There's no need to thank me. You were a loving, dedicated couple who worshipped each other. There's no way she cheated."

He genuinely did feel better. At least better than when he'd first read the messages. But the truth was, he still felt a little numb from the shock of it all. It had taken Ricky less than a minute to find the picture and set it as his wallpaper. Anyone could have done that. He didn't believe it was Beth's phone in the pictures. Beth was faithful; she never would have cheated. He was being played. The mystery man was setting him up. But, if he truly believed all that, why wasn't he feeling a wave of relief? Why wasn't he shaking Ricky's hand and thanking him for proving without a doubt that the messages were fake? Why was there still a great deal of tension in his neck and shoulders? And why did he have that uncomfortable itch right at the back of his brain again?

Crane stood up abruptly, almost tipping the stool over behind him. It teetered back and forth but remained upright as he strode purposefully towards the door.

"Where are you going?" Ricky called after him.

"To get one more perspective."

# Chapter Twenty-Six

Crane stood at the front door of a neat two-up, two-down semi-detached home in a quiet suburb in North Cardiff. There wasn't a doorbell, so he used the chrome knocker to announce his arrival. He'd called during the drive over to check if it was okay for him to pop round for a quick visit. A few seconds later, the chrome handle on the black composite door was pushed down from the inside, and the door swung open.

Ella stood in the doorway, dressed in tight purple leggings and a matching vest, a sliver of her exceptionally toned midriff revealed between the two. It was obviously her yoga outfit. The material hugged her impressive figure almost as though it were painted on. Her blonde hair was tied back in a loose ponytail, and she stood barefoot on her light-coloured laminate flooring. She smiled at him radiantly, and her green eyes glistened in the sunlight. Crane had to admit she looked good. Ridiculously good.

Rocko, her little beige pug cross, sat between her feet. He stared up at Crane with his permanently sad expression and kind eyes. Crane had met Rocko a few times before, and even though he generally wasn't a pet person, he had to admit Rocko was a cute little fur ball. He had a gentle and calm temperament and would literally watch and follow Ella wherever she went.

"Sorry to bother you on a Sunday," he said. "Did I interrupt your workout?"

"No, not at all," she said, waving him inside. "It was actually really good timing; I was just finishing a yoga flow when you called. Anyway, you know that you can interrupt me anytime you want."

Crane smiled and bent down to say hello to Rocko. He gave him a good scratch behind his ears, which Rocko seemed to like. He showed his appreciation by giving Crane's arm a lick.

"Do you want a drink?" Ella asked as they walked into the kitchen.

"A coffee would be great, thanks."

The kitchen was compact, clean, and very tidy. The same light laminate flooring from the hallway flowed into the kitchen and blended nicely with the cream cupboards and oak worktop. Crane noticed the dish drainer next to the sink contained a single plate, a knife, a fork, and a glass. They had drip dried but hadn't been put away yet. He couldn't understand why Ella was still single. She was smart, she was funny, she was attractive. No, she was stunning. Over the years that they'd got to know each other, she'd mentioned going out on a few dates, but nothing had ever seemed to turn into a serious relationship for her. She caught him looking at the drainer as she prepared the coffees.

"Yes, I'm still single," she declared. "Thirty-two and still eating meals for one."

"There's nothing wrong with taking your time to find your Mr Right," said Crane, leaning back against the worktop opposite her.

Ella handed Crane a mug of steaming coffee and held his eye contact as she said, "Or maybe I've already found him, but he just doesn't realise it yet."

Crane was more than a little rusty when it came to flirting, but even he recognised the vibes coming from Ella recently. The truth was, part of him wanted to reciprocate. But another part of him, a bigger part, wouldn't allow him to.

"You don't normally come and pay me a visit out of the blue. In fact, I think this is the first time ever. Is everything okay?"

"I need to ask you something," said Crane. "But I need you to promise that you'll be honest with me. Regardless of what the answer may be or how you think I'll take it."

"This conversation just took a serious turn." Ella was still smiling, but her eyes were filled with a mixture of intrigue and apprehension. "What is it? What do you want to ask me?"

"Did Beth ever cheat on me?"

Crane watched her reaction carefully. For a split second, it looked as if she was disappointed that that was the question, then she said, "Not that I know of."

Crane's eyes narrowed. "Not that you *know* of? So, you think she could have?"

Ella quickly shook her head. "No. I mean, I don't think so. She certainly never said anything to me if she did. She always spoke so highly of you and almost bragged about how amazing you two were together. Why are you asking? Do you think she did?"

"No," said Crane almost instinctively. "Or, at least, I didn't." He didn't know what to think anymore, and that was the reason he had come here and asked for her opinion—he wanted another perspective from someone he could trust. He was looking for reassurance. But Ella's reaction and response certainly didn't give him that. "You were her closest friend before she died, and when I just asked you, you didn't say a definitive no. The Beth that I knew never would have cheated on me. But it sounds like the Beth you knew could have?"

"No," she stated firmly. "It's not like that. I really don't think she did. Like you say, we were so close, I'm sure she would have told me if something was going on. It's just..." She trailed off, as if the next words evaded her.

He fixed his gaze on hers. "It's just what?"

"Nothing." Ella broke eye contact and looked down at the mug of coffee in her hand. "It's just I don't think she cheated on you," she finished quietly.

"That wasn't the thought," Crane pressed, taking a half step towards her. "You stopped yourself from saying something. It's just what?"

"Nothing."

"Please," Crane persisted, leaning down to try to catch her eye.

Ella paused and then slowly raised her gaze to meet his. "It's just sometimes I feel like you look back on her memory wearing rose-tinted glasses."

Crane flinched, his eyebrows pinching together. "What's that supposed to mean?"

"I'm sorry, I shouldn't have said anything. Please forget I ever said anything." She turned away from him and moved to put the coffee jar back in the cupboard.

Crane stepped forward and placed his free hand on the cupboard door, preventing her from opening it. "It's too late for that. Please, Ella, you need to explain what you mean."

Ella paused, her hand remaining on the handle of the cupboard, but she didn't attempt to pull it open. Eventually, she lowered her hand, placed the coffee jar back on the worktop, and turned to face Crane. "It's just, whenever you talk about her, you seem to describe this whiter than white, purer than pure, delicate little angel. Don't take this the wrong way, I loved Beth, I thought she was great, but that wasn't the Beth that I knew."

The words hit Crane like a shoulder charge from a loosehead prop. He dropped his hand from the cupboard and took a half step back. "Who was the Beth that you knew?"

Ella was quiet for a second. "I don't know. I don't know what I'm trying to say, please just forget it."

"Forget it?" Crane's voice raised a little. "You've just told me that my wife wasn't who I thought she was, and now you want me to forget it?"

"It's nothing, really. It's just... I always got the feeling there was more to Beth that I didn't get to see. You know how some people are open books? Well, Beth wasn't one of those people." Ella went to take a sip of her coffee but then seemed to change her mind and instead placed the mug on the worktop next to the sink. "Even though we were close, I never truly felt like I knew her. I always felt like she was a bit of a closed book and that she never fully opened up to me, or anyone else for that matter."

Crane was trying to hide his irritation, but he failed miserably. "What the hell is that supposed to mean?"

"It means that I can't tell you with any great degree of certainty that she didn't cheat on you, because I think there was another side of her that nobody knew. Not even you."

Crane remained silent, processing.

"It's been almost five years since the accident, and you still won't allow yourself to live. You won't allow yourself to be happy." Ella folded her arms across her chest. "I can almost guarantee that if it had been the other way around, Beth wouldn't have been like you. Yes, she would have grieved, but she would have moved on ages ago. She wouldn't have pined after you for five years. She wasn't the type."

Crane gulped down two mouthfuls of coffee, partly because his mouth had suddenly dried up, partly because he was trying to suppress some of the anger he could feel rising inside him. When he spoke, his voice was low and the words came through gritted teeth. "If you're just trying to muddy her memory so that we can be together, it's not going to work."

Ella's eyes glistened, as though tears were near. "It's not... I wouldn't... I'm... I'm just being honest with you."

Crane put his mug firmly down on the worktop. "I think I should go."

"I'm sorry, please don't go like this." Ella reached out to grab his hand but missed.

Crane ignored her and walked to the front door. Ella followed him with little Rocko trotting behind her, his claws clacking on the laminate flooring. Crane put his hand on the door handle to open it, but he found himself stopping, a little niggle in the back of his head refusing to subside, worming its way to the forefront.

He turned back to face Ella. Tears were in her eyes, but they were not yet running down her cheeks.

"I've never thought to mention this to you before," said Crane. "In fact, it's never even crossed my mind to question it until now. When I was speaking to Beth on the night she died, she told me that she'd been out for dinner. Out for dinner with you."

Ella slowly shook her head. "That's not true, Tom. I didn't have dinner with her that night. I briefly saw her on handover when we changed shifts on the ward, but I was working nights. She left the hospital just after six, but she didn't say she was meeting anyone for dinner. To be honest, she seemed a little preoccupied. She wasn't herself."

*She lied...* Never mind a shoulder barge, this revelation hit Crane like an uppercut to the solar plexus. It took every ounce of his willpower to hide his emotions from Ella, but it was nigh on impossible. He turned away from her, not wanting her to see his vulnerability. He reached for the handle but didn't open the door. Thoughts and questions were churning around in his mind, making him feel a little lightheaded and threatening to overwhelm him.

Beth had been working on the day of the crash. He remembered watching the home CCTV footage in the days after the crash. She returned home wearing her purple scrubs around half six, then she left about forty-five minutes later dressed as if she was going out for dinner. He remembered thinking at the time that they must've only had a quick bite to eat together, because she was already on her way back home when she called him just after eight. But if she wasn't with Ella, who did she meet? Where did she go? What exactly was she doing between quarter past seven and eight on that night? And why did she lie?

Without turning back to face Ella, he asked, "What do you mean she wasn't herself?"

"I'm not sure exactly." Ella placed her hand tenderly on his back. "She seemed worried about something. I asked her what was wrong, but she just laughed it off and changed the subject. I remember it vividly because... because it was the last time I saw her alive." She slid her hand up to Crane's shoulder and gave it a gentle pull, trying to get him to turn and face her, but he didn't budge. "Do you think she was meeting up with someone?"

"I don't know," replied Crane, "but I intend to find out."

He opened the front door and left Ella and Rocko standing in the hallway. He jumped in his truck, started the engine, and just sat there for a few moments. There was so much to process. So many questions hurting his head. So many answers he had no clue how to start finding. So many...

Crane huffed as his phone started to ring through the speakers of the truck via Bluetooth and he saw who was calling—Dylan. He immediately tapped the red icon to send it to voicemail. He wasn't in the mood to speak to Dylan. He was never in the mood to speak to Dylan. A few seconds later, the ringing started again, and Dylan's name reappeared on the infotainment system.

"Piss off," Crane growled, tapping the red icon once more.

Almost immediately, the ringing started up again. This time, Crane jabbed the green icon.

"*What*?" he answered, not even trying to disguise his irritation.

Dylan's panicked and hysterical voice blasted out of the speakers. "What the fuck have you done, bro?"

"What the fuck have *I* done?" Crane rolled his eyes. Everything was always someone else's fault. Never Dylan's.

"They've taken her," Dylan yelled. "They've taken Chloe."

# Chapter Twenty-Seven

Crane sped into the car park at the back of Dylan's apartment block. His dark blue Ford Focus was there with the boot wide open. It was packed with luggage, and Dylan was sitting on the lip of it, holding a big wad of bloodied tissue to his face. He stood up when he saw Crane's truck pull in. There were blood stains down the front of his mustard yellow T-shirt and over his hands. Crane came to an abrupt stop next to the Ford and jumped out.

"What happened?"

"Some guys broke my fucking nose and took her, that's what happened."

Dylan removed the tissue to show Crane the state of his nose. It was evidently broken, and the skin had split across the bridge. On the bright side, the bleeding did seem to be slowing down.

"Start at the beginning," Crane instructed.

Dylan unravelled a fresh wad of tissue from a toilet roll in the boot and blew his nose into it before starting. "Me and Chloe were here, packing up the car and getting everything ready to go, then a black Range Rover pulled up, and two blokes got out. One of them, you should have seen him, he was like a giant." He reached his free arm up as high as he could, giving Crane a massively exaggerated show of the giant's height. "He must have been close to seven feet and built like a brick shithouse. He just walked straight up to me without saying a word and sucker-punched me square on the conk. The other one grabbed Chloe and threw her into the back of the Range Rover. He was

smaller than the one that hit me, but he was still built like a tank."
He pulled the tissue away from his nose to check it and gave a sigh
of relief when he saw that it was still mostly white with only a
couple of red spots. He used his other hand to gently squeeze the
bridge, as if he was checking how straight it was, then the blood
started to come once again. He grunted and quickly replaced the
tissue over his nose.

"I was on the ground and I couldn't see properly because my
eyes were watering so much from my nose being popped, but I
could just about make out Chloe in the back. She was trying to
open the door from the inside and banging on the window, but
they must have had child locks on because it wouldn't open for
her. She looked so scared, bro." He sat back down heavily on the
lip of his open boot, the suspension groaning as it lowered under
his weight. "Then they drove off before I even had a chance to
get back on my feet. It all happened so quickly."

"Did they say anything?"

Dylan nodded. "The smaller one, the one driving, put his
window down just before they drove away and said, 'Tell your
brother nobody fucks with Luke Maddocks.'" Dylan looked into
Crane's eyes. "What have you done, bro? Why have they taken
her?"

Crane felt a rage building inside him. Luke Maddocks and
Paul Jenkins had made a grave mistake. "I'll get her back," he said
adamantly. "Does Chloe have her phone on her?"

Dylan shook his head. "She left it in the apartment."

"Shit." That was going to make things harder. "Go to the
hospital to get your nose looked at and then go to the caravan.
I'll bring her to you once I've got her."

"I don't need to go to the hospital."

"Then just clean yourself up and go to the caravan."

"No," said Dylan, shifting his weight forward to stand up.
"I'm coming with you."

Crane placed a firm hand on Dylan's shoulder to stop him
from getting up. "No, you're not. You can't be a part of what

happens next. Just go to the caravan, I'll call you once I've got her, and then I'll bring her to you."

Dylan frowned. "What happens next?"

"Use your imagination."

Crane jumped back in his truck, leaving Dylan standing next to his Ford, still dabbing away at his bloodied nose. Crane used the infotainment screen to call Ricky.

"Ricky, they've taken Chloe." Crane looked both sides of the road before zooming out, the cars far and few between.

Sounding both alarmed and confused, Ricky barked, "What? Who?"

"Luke and Paul."

"No way," exclaimed Ricky, sounding more angry than shocked. "Do you need me to trace her phone?"

"No, it's still in my brother's apartment. Can you trace Luke or Paul's phone?"

"Of course, I'll get on it straight away." The sound of footsteps came through the truck's speakers as Ricky made his way to his workstation.

"While you're at it, can you also drain Luke's bank accounts? Take every penny he's got."

"Consider it done. Where are you heading?"

"To the club for now, but call me if you find out where they are."

"Will do."

Crane ended the call and continued driving towards Cardiff City Centre. The inside of the truck fell quiet, leaving Crane alone with his thoughts. His mind immediately replayed the moment Ella told him she hadn't met up with Beth on the night she died. He pushed the vision away and suppressed his feelings about it. Beth's lie wasn't his priority right now—Chloe was. He needed to get Chloe back safe, and he needed to get her back now. That was the only thing he could allow himself to focus on, everything else could wait.

A few minutes later, the speakers in the truck started ringing, and Ricky's name appeared on the infotainment system. Crane tapped the green icon.

"How are you getting on?" asked Crane.

"Not good," said Ricky. "Both their phones are switched off, so I can't trace them by GPS or through the mobile towers. I can only tell you their last location before they turned their phones off."

Crane approached a set of traffic lights that were on red and had no choice but to join the back of a small queue. "Which was where?"

"Where you're currently heading. Corkers. Also, the money has gone. Luke's moved it all. I think I'll be able to trace it, but it's going to take time."

Crane frowned. "What? Their phones are off *and* the money has been moved? They obviously planned this."

"I would say so," agreed Ricky.

The lights up ahead turned green, and Crane eased off the brake. "Can you get me a list of potential addresses to search? Start with their home addresses, then work out to family and friends. Just text whatever you find to me. I'll head to the club for now. I doubt they're going to be there, but you never know. They may think that's their stronghold."

"Will do. But, Crane, please be careful."

"I'm always careful."

Ricky paused, just for a second. "You are, but this time there's emotion attached. They've got your niece."

"I know," said Crane, turning left onto the road he'd parked on the two previous evenings. "Don't worry, I won't let it cloud my judgement."

Crane didn't believe the words coming out of his mouth and knew Ricky wouldn't either. He was emotional. He was raging. They'd taken Chloe. He was going to get her back. And he was going to destroy them. Even if it meant destroying himself in the process. Things had escalated to a point where his judgement was already clouded.

"Just do what you do best," said Ricky before ending the call.

# Chapter Twenty-Eight

Crane parked in the same spot once again. He opened the glove compartment and removed the case from the hidden compartment inside. He unlatched the case and took out the Heckler and Koch before tucking it securely in the back of his waistband. He put the two spare magazines upside down in his left pocket, then he grabbed a black workman's gilet and a black baseball cap from the back seats and put them on. The gilet would cover the Heckler and Koch nicely. It would also add to disguise the rest of the items Crane wanted to take with him.

He got out of the Hilux and walked around to the back, then he opened it up and jumped inside. He had to stay on his knees and duck under the hardtop canopy. The inside was a contrast to everything Crane usually opted for. He liked things to be clean and tidy, he appreciated order and process, and he valued precision. The back of the truck looked a mess, but looks can be deceiving. The messy appearance was intentional. All the equipment inside was secured properly and had a purpose, either for genuine use or to add to the guise of being the truck of a handyman.

A thick pile of yellowish cotton twill dust sheets covered the truck bed haphazardly. They actually created a nicely padded area to sit or lay down, ideal during stakeouts. Gardening equipment, such as spades and a pickaxe, was strapped to the one side, which was handy for burying things. A set of small stepladders, three treads, was strapped securely to the other side above an array of cases containing different power tools. At the back was a big, heavy-duty, black plastic utility box that was bolted to the truck bed. Crane unlatched it and raised the lid. He pulled out a pre-filled tool bag that contained some essential items, then he unstrapped a thirty-six-inch titanium crowbar from the under-side of the utility box lid. Crane unzipped the tool bag and just about squeezed the crowbar in at an angle.

Next, he unstrapped the small stepladders, figuring they should be tall enough for what he needed. Finally, he grabbed a pair of black safety work gloves from the utility box. They were still wrapped in their original plastic packaging. He tore the pack open, put them on, and then backed out of the truck on his hands and knees. He placed the ladders and the tool bag on the pavement while he locked up the truck, then he picked them back up and set off on foot towards Corkers. He looked like a tradesman on his way to a job. Not a single person paid him the slightest bit of attention.

Rather than heading down Westgate Street, as he had done the previous two evenings, he walked a little further and turned into Womanby Street. The narrow road was quiet, with only a few pedestrians using it as a cut-through. During the two times he had used the fire exit to leave Corkers, he had taken the oppor-tunity to check what security was fitted to it. Surprisingly, there was no alarm, no contacts on the door or frame. The door was also old and tired, and there seemed to be a reasonable amount of play and movement within the frame. The only concern Crane had was a single camera positioned on the wall above the door. Fortunately, it was placed to the right side as you looked at the door and it pointed down to the left to cover the area in front of the door at an angle. It meant that Crane was able to walk up just underneath it and tuck in tight to the wall without getting into its field of vision.

Crane dropped the tool bag against the wall and then unfolded the set of steps directly beneath the camera. Pedestrians would assume he was just another maintenance man or engineer going about his business. The invisible man. The camera was around ten feet from the ground, so he climbed to the top of the three steps to reach it comfortably. As soon as he got up there and looked closely at the camera casing, he sighed in frustration. He could have saved himself the hassle of carrying the steps here. It was a dummy camera, and not a good one. The casing was cheap plastic and very poor build. No brand markings of any kind. There was a thin black cable leading from the back of the camera and down into the bracket that was bolted to the wall. The fact that the cable was visible and that it was so thin reinforced his theory that it was a fake camera. Crane gently pulled on the cable, and it popped out of the bracket without even putting up a fight. He couldn't understand it. Why would you have cameras over every square inch of the club, but not a single camera or any security measures on the rear door? The closest door to Luke's office. The most vulnerable point. It made no sense. It also made Crane feel a little uneasy. Was he missing something?

Crane folded the steps and left them leaning against the wall. He opened the tool bag and pulled out the crowbar. There was more than enough space between the edge of the door and the frame for him to force the chisel edge into. He did just that, getting the chisel edge right through to the other side around six inches above where he knew the push bar to be on the inside. He then swiftly and forcefully pulled the end of the crowbar to the side, away from the door. Both the frame and the door flexed with relative ease. The latch bolt slipped out of the lip in the frame, and the door popped open. He wasted no time shoving the crowbar back inside the tool bag, picking it up, and stepping inside. He removed the Heckler and Koch from his waistband and aimed it down the stairs as the door closed behind him with a click.

He stood at the top of the stairs for thirty seconds, listening and waiting. He didn't like it. It had been far too easy to get in. It didn't feel right. He waited another thirty seconds, expecting footsteps, shouting, maybe even bullets to start flying up the stairs, but there was nothing. Just silence. And then the faint sound of glass. It sounded like a glass bottle being dropped onto other glasses. He heard it again, and again. It was almost rhythmic. He stepped slowly and silently down the stairs one at a time, the Heckler and Koch aimed steadily at the bottom of the stairs. When he reached halfway, the sound stopped and so did he. He listened, feeling the pulse from the bass of the music coming from inside the club now.

He waited a few more seconds before continuing his descent. He could see the hallway now. It was empty. There was nobody waiting for him. Both doors were closed. He reached the bottom step and then crept silently to Luke's office door and listened. He could hear some movement, but no voices. Then the sound of glass hitting glass started again. Now that he was closer, it sounded like empty bottles being dropped into a bag of other empty bottles. He silently placed the tool bag next to the wall, then crouched down onto one knee in front of the right-hand edge of the door frame. When he opened the door, whoever was behind it would expect someone to be standing in the doorway. It would take them a split second to register that he was down low, and if they were aiming a weapon at the door, they would need to re-adjust. During that split second, Crane would already be in position ready to fire. He would also be in half cover behind the door frame, with the ability to get himself into full cover behind the wall in a split second if needed.

Crane took a deep breath, filling his lungs to the brim, then he exhaled slowly. He reached out, pulled down on the chrome handle, and shoved the door open aggressively. There was one person in the office, standing next to the poker table, with a large black refuse sack in their left hand and an empty beer bottle in the other. They visibly jumped in shock at the door opening so abruptly. Crane was aiming directly at their centre mass, but he released the pressure from the trigger almost immediately. He recognised the person standing in the office, although she did look a little different to the first time he had met her a couple of nights ago. It was Ivanka. She was wearing pink jogging bottoms and a matching hoodie, her blonde hair loosely tied back, but what stood out most to Crane was her cut and swollen bottom lip and badly bruised left cheek.

"Are you alone?" asked Crane.

She nodded.

Crane picked up his tool bag, stood up, and walked into the office. He closed the door behind him and tucked the Heckler and Koch back into his waistband. He couldn't help his hand reaching towards her face, but he quickly dropped it back down when she flinched. "What happened?"

"Luke happened."

"What? Why?"

Ivanka shrugged. "Because he can, and because he wanted to."

Crane generally didn't get satisfaction from ending a life, but he had a feeling that ending Luke's was going to be an exception to that rule.

Ivanka continued in her clear but heavily accented English, "I'm on cleaning duties until the swelling goes down."

"Are Luke and Paul here?"

Ivanka shook her head. "They went out a couple hours ago."

"Any idea where they went?"

"No, sorry. But Leon may know. He was talking with them before they left."

"Where is he?"

"In the room with the cameras."

Crane looked at the phone on the desk behind Ivanka. "Do you think you could call him and get him to come back here?"

Ivanka nodded readily and placed the bag of empties on the floor before turning to get the phone.

"Wait," said Crane, moving to stand in front of her. "For your safety, it might be better if we make it look like I got you to make the call against your will."

"What do you mean?"

Crane walked to the poker table. It was covered with empty bottles and glasses and there was also an ashtray full of cigarette butts and cigar stumps. The stench of stale alcohol and tobacco was pungent. He pulled one of the chairs into some space next to the table. "Take a seat," he instructed. "I'll restrain you to it to make it look like I've forced you to make the call."

Ivanka shook her head, backing away from the chair, closer to the phone. "No, no, I don't want to be tied up." She waved a hand to emphasise her point and then used the same hand to point to the phone. "I will call him anyway."

"I know you will, and I'm grateful for that, but if it looks like you were voluntarily helping me, it could cause you problems later on."

She looked around the room for a few seconds before finally giving in and walking nervously to the chair. Crane assumed she'd been punished over just about anything so many times that she knew being restrained was a much better prospect than another beating. At least, he hoped making her look like a victim would prevent that.

Crane opened his tool bag and grabbed a bunch of thick black cable ties and a roll of duct tape. He used the cable ties to loosely secure her ankles to the front legs of the chair and then used another cable tie to secure her wrists behind her back, as her arms weren't long enough to reach around the back of the chair. She was secure but comfortable.

He picked up the cordless phone from Luke's desk, which looked exactly like the one on the front desk. "What number for the surveillance room?"

"Two."

Crane pressed the number two, but nothing happened.

"Press green first, then two," instructed Ivanka.

Crane did, and then he heard a faint dial tone coming from the phone. He held it to Ivanka's ear. She looked to the floor as she waited for an answer.

One word sounded from the other end of the line: "What?"

Crane almost laughed; Leon knew it wasn't Paul or Luke calling, as there was no way he'd speak like that if it were.

"Leon, could you give me hand, please? I need to move poker table to clean floor properly."

She must have had a little resistance from him because a few seconds later she said, "I could, but if it scratch tiles, you know Luke will go mad."

She looked at Crane and gave a little nod to say he was on his way.

Crane pressed the red button to hang up the phone and replaced it back on the desk. Then he picked up the duct tape and tore a five-inch strip off. "I'm just going to cover your mouth with this so that it looks like you aren't able to warn him when he gets here." Ivanka's eyebrows pinched together; she was evidently unhappy about having her lips taped shut, but she didn't protest.

Crane gently covered her mouth, careful not to press down on her swollen lip, then he went and stood behind the door to wait. A minute or so later, he heard the door in the hallway open, then footsteps. The door to the office opened, and Leon walked in.

"What the...?" Leon froze as soon as he saw Ivanka gagged and cable-tied to the chair.

Crane pushed the door closed. "Good afternoon, Leon."

Leon spun around to face Crane. Crane smiled and then punched him, a straight right to the face, hard, but it wasn't intended to be a knockout blow, it was just meant to stun and disorientate him. Unfortunately, Leon apparently couldn't take a punch as well as his face implied. He stepped back, but his legs had turned to jelly. He fell and hit the back of his head on the unforgiving black tiles, his head making a sickening hollow thunk as it made impact and put him to sleep.

Crane walked over to the poker table and pulled another chair out into the space, then he bent down and grabbed Leon under his armpits from behind. He dragged him back and plonked him onto the chair, his dead weight heavy and awkward but manageable.

Crane turned to grab some cable ties and the duct tape, but as he was bending down, there was a loud, heavy thump behind him. He whipped his head around to see what had caused the noise and found Leon's limp body in a heap on the floor next to the chair. He was still out cold and had likely taken another knock to the head.

"For fuck's sake." Crane hoped it wouldn't be too difficult to get Leon conscious. He also hoped his short-term memory wouldn't be too badly affected.

He plonked Leon back onto the chair and secured him to it with a few loops of duct tape around his chest, under his arms, and around the back of the chair. Not too tight—he didn't want to restrict his breathing, at least not just yet. For now, he only wanted to prevent him from falling off the chair again. Crane then secured his ankles to the front legs of the chair with cable ties, as he had with Ivanka, but he certainly wasn't as gentle. Next, he used more cable ties to secure Leon's wrists together behind the back of the chair before tearing off a six-inch strip of duct tape to seal his mouth closed. The whole time, Leon remained unconscious.

Crane then went over to Ivanka and turned her chair around so that it was facing away from Leon. The legs of the chair scraped noisily on the black tiles. "You won't want to see this," he said to her quietly.

Crane went back to Leon and removed his shoes and socks, then he used more cable ties to go around his shins and just below his knees, locking them firmly to the legs of the chair. He tried to pull Leon's knees apart, but they didn't budge. Satisfied with his handiwork, Crane pulled a claw hammer and a bevel-edged chisel from his tool bag before walking to the dartboard on the wall and pulling two of the darts out. He placed everything on the floor in front of Leon's feet just as Leon began to stir.

"Wakey wakey, rise and shine." Crane lightly slapped Leon on the side of his face until his eyes focused.

Leon abruptly sat up straight, eyes wide as he looked around. Crane could see the chair wobbling with Leon's attempts to move. He tried to say something, but he could only make muffled nasal noises.

"Leon, are you with me? Do you understand where you are? And do you realise that you're securely restrained to the chair?"

Leon nodded, all nasal sounds stopping as he focused on Crane.

"Good. You may already know some of this, but just in case, I'll start with why I'm here, which will then lead me to why you're there." Crane jabbed him in the chest with an index finger, then stood upright and took a step back. "Luke and Paul have just kidnapped my fourteen-year-old niece. They went to my brother's home, attacked him, and took her. I need you to tell me where they are so that I can get her back safe."

Leon tried to say something, but again only muffled nasal sounds escaped.

Crane ignored him and continued, "Now, I do have a bit of experience in situations like this, and what usually happens is you'll try to tell me that you don't know where they are, then I'll threaten you with a bit of violence and torture. You'll think I'm bluffing, or you'll believe that you're braver than you actually are, or maybe even think that you have a higher pain threshold than you actually do." Crane began pacing, his hands animated as he spoke. "You'll continue to deny knowing anything. Then I'll hurt you, then you'll talk. I've found that if we skip all the preliminary bullshit and I jump straight to the part of hurting you, it tends to focus the mind and loosen the lips." He stopped pacing and turned to face Leon, a natural-looking smile on his face. A smile he'd perfected over the years that told people he was perfectly comfortable doing what he had to do.

"So, this is what's going to happen." Crane bent down and picked up the two darts. He began dragging the tip of one slowly and firmly down the side of the poker table, leaving a white scratch behind that gradually got longer and longer as he spoke.

"Firstly, I'm going to put the tip of these beneath your big toe-nails, one in each toe. Then I'm going to gently tap them under your nail with my hammer until both darts reach the cuticle." Scratch finished, he dropped the two darts back on the floor with his tools. "Once that's done, I'm going to use the hammer and this chisel to pop off your little toes. But don't worry, you don't really need them anyway. Once that's done, I'll allow you to speak. If you don't tell me where they are, it at least gives you the opportunity to say goodbye to your other little piggies."

Leon's eyes were filled with panic, and he seemed to be desperately trying to say something, his eyes flitting between Crane, the tools on the floor, and the scratch on the poker table.

"Now, let's get this party started."

Crane, now standing alongside Leon, stepped forward and stood across the top of Leon's right foot with his left so that Leon couldn't wiggle or move it. He then knelt on his right knee and used his left hand to push down and hold Leon's big toe tight to the floor so that it couldn't be moved. Crane was glad he was wearing gloves for this bit. He picked up one of the darts and pushed the sharp point underneath the nail plate, just enough so it was secure and ready to be hit with the hammer. He wasn't lying about gently tapping it—the pain from the nail plate being slowly separated from the nail bed far exceeded the pain of them being ripped off quickly. Crane picked up the hammer and touched the flight of the dart with the pane, just lining it up ready to strike. Crane looked over his shoulder at Leon, who was frantically shaking his head and desperately squealing through his nose to say something.

"There's no way you want to tell me where they are already?"

Leon nodded furiously.

"Let me just warn you, If I let you speak and I'm not happy or convinced with what you have to say, I'll put the tape back over your mouth and pop all your toes off before you get another chance to speak. Do you understand?"

Leon nodded.

"So, you definitely want to tell me where Luke and Paul are?"

Leon nodded again.

Crane released Leon's toe and foot, but he left the dart protruding out from under his toenail. He reached out and ripped the duct tape off Leon's mouth, but he left an inch or so stuck to his cheek so that it hung down limply.

Leon sucked in a deep breath and flexed his mouth open and closed a couple of times. "They're at Green Fields industrial estate in Rumney, but I swear to you, I know nothing about your niece."

"What exactly did they say to you before they left?"

"They just said that they were going out for a couple of hours to pick up a package. They said they weren't taking their phones with them, which I thought was weird. I asked them how I should contact them if there was an emergency, and Paul told me that I couldn't. He said that I would have to deal with everything on my own, but they would be back in a few hours. Then, as I was walking out of the office, I overheard Luke mention Green Fields. But I swear, I didn't hear them say anything about you or your niece."

Crane narrowed his eyes. "Why have you given them up so easily?"

"Because they're fucking arseholes," Leon exclaimed. "I'm not losing any of my toes for them." One side of his top lip curled up as he spoke about Luke and Paul. He then tried to shrug his right shoulder but couldn't because his arms were secured tight behind the chair. It turned into more of a flinching head tilt. "Anyway, they didn't tell me where they were going, I just happened to overhear them, so you didn't find out from me."

"Okay," said Crane. "One last question." He motioned with his hand around the room as he spoke. "Why are there cameras over every square inch of this club, but there's no cameras or security back here or on the fire exit?"

Leon snorted. "Because the cameras are to protect the girls and keep an eye on the punters. Luke doesn't need protection. The only person crazy enough to mess with Luke is apparently you."

Crane gave a half-shrug. "Fair enough."

He replaced the tape over Leon's mouth, and Leon immediately started making muffled sounds, trying to speak again.

"Oh, you don't seriously expect me to take your word for it, do you?" He patronisingly patted Leon's knee twice. "Sit tight here for a bit. If it turns out you're lying to me, I'll come straight back with my tool bag. If I don't come back, I was never here, do you understand?"

Leon nodded.

Crane picked up the hammer and chisel, then walked behind Leon to his tool bag, which was next to Ivanka. He put them inside and zipped it closed as Ivanka watched him closely. He mouthed "sorry" to her. She nodded back at him and winked. He picked up his tool bag and left, knowing that it wouldn't be long before one of the other doormen came to check on them anyway.

# Chapter Twenty-Nine

The drive to Green Fields industrial estate would normally take a little under twenty minutes. Crane did it in thirteen. It helped that it was a Sunday afternoon, so the traffic was quiet, and he did get fortunate with a few of the traffic lights, but he also drove like a man on a mission. Which he was.

Green Fields was one of four or five industrial estates in this part of East Cardiff. Having grown up in East Cardiff, Crane knew the area well, and he knew exactly where Green Fields was situated.

Crane had already driven past an industrial estate and a small business park, both of which were deserted, their main gates securely locked, as to be expected on a Sunday. A left turn was coming up that would pass across the front of Green Fields industrial estate and lead to a right turn into its entrance. Green Fields had nine units, four on each side, with the largest of the nine units running right across the back of the estate. The entrance opened onto a road that ran straight down the middle, with roads peeling off to each unit. All Crane could see at the moment was the corner unit, and he wound his window down to listen. So far, everything looked and sounded just as desolate as the other industrial estate and business park he had already driven past.

Crane slowed the truck right down to a crawl as he approached the entrance. The gates were unlocked and wide open. Someone was definitely here. He came to a stop directly opposite the entrance and looked down the centre road of the industrial estate. All the units looked the same. Red brick bottom half, grey corrugated steel cladding on the upper half.

Crane picked up his Heckler and Koch from the passenger seat where he'd put it while he drove. The spare magazines were still in his pocket. Ultimately, he was aware that he could be walking headfirst into a trap, but what else could he do? They had Chloe. If it was a trap, he would go down in a blaze of glory and take them with him. *They won't know what hit them. There will be no hesitation.* He held the Heckler and Koch in his right hand and rested it on the inside of the door, just out of sight.

He released the brake pedal, allowing the truck to crawl forward, and he used his left hand to steer, turning right until the front of the truck pointed directly down the centre road of the industrial estate. He straightened the wheels and let the truck idle forward, slowly and quietly, keeping his eyes peeled and leaning out the side window slightly to listen.

He passed between the open gates. They were tall and grey with vertical steel bars along their full length. The gate on the left had a thick galvanised steel chain wrapped around its handle and was locked in place with a heavy-duty sliding bar padlock. The truck drew level with the first two units. Still no sign of life. It was as if he were heading into an abandoned town in the Wild West to have a showdown with the outlaws. Crane glanced left and right as he gradually came to the end of the first units and reached the first gap to the next set of units. Nothing. The roads peeling off left and right between the units were empty.

He glanced in the rear-view mirror, half expecting someone to be closing the gate to lock him in, but they remained open and abandoned. Halfway down the second row of units, he thought he heard something and leaned a little further out of the side window, listening hard. Nothing. Maybe his ears and his mind were playing tricks on him. The truck crept forward at a brisk walking pace. Coming towards the end of the second row of units, Crane glanced left, right, left, right. Still nothing. Both roads leading between the second and third rows of units were empty.

But as he drew level with the next set of units, he definitely heard something. It was really faint, but he was sure he could hear voices, men talking. His entire head was almost fully out of the side window as he listened hard, trying to determine where the voices were coming from. There was another sound too. A low drumming. By the time he was halfway down the third row of units, he'd determined that the sounds were coming from the right, between the third and fourth rows. The voices were louder and the low drumming sounded like a big diesel, maybe a HGV engine. He pulled over to the left to increase his distance and angle, then continued to creep forward, his right foot hovering above the space between the accelerator and the brake. His eyes were fixed on the corner of the third unit on the right.

The rear end of a black Range Rover was the first thing that gradually came into view. The windows were tinted, but Crane could still make out Chloe's silhouette in the rear right passenger window. Next to the Range Rover were three men deep in conversation, two on the left, one on the right. The two on the left were Paul and Luke, the man on the right Crane hadn't seen before. He was around the same height as Luke, with grey hair and a large beach ball belly, wearing blue jeans and a green polo T-shirt. Behind the new man was a HGV facing out towards Crane. Luke and Paul had their backs to the Range Rover. They were side-on to Crane and engrossed in conversation. They hadn't spotted his truck yet. The dull thumping of the HGV engine masked the sound of his pickup, for now.

Crane turned to the right until he was pointing directly at the space between the Range Rover and the HGV, the three men directly in front, then he planted his foot firmly down on the accelerator. The pickup jumped forward, the sound of tyres biting into asphalt grabbing their attention. All three turned their heads to see Crane's dark grey pickup truck hurtling towards them and rapidly picking up speed. Naturally, it took a second for them to realise what they were looking at, and by this time, Crane was only around thirty feet away and closing the gap fast.

Both Paul and Luke made the same grave error, reaching behind to grab their Glocks, wasting another precious second that they could have been using to get out of the way. The new man was frozen to the spot, eyes wide, staring open-mouthed at the onrushing lump of steel. In the final moment before impact, all three moved to dive out of the way, but Paul and the new guy were heavy and far too slow. The pickup ploughed into them with bone-crunching force. They bounced off the front grill and bumper, then disappeared out of sight below the bonnet just as the corner of the truck's bumper caught both of Luke's lower legs right on the halfway point between his knees and ankles as he dived to the side. The tibias and fibulas in both of his legs either snapped or fractured. The impact caused his whole body to spin, and he dropped the Glock. It flew out of his hand and went scuttling across the asphalt behind the Range Rover. Crane's pickup truck raised as the chunky tyres drove up and over Paul and the new guy. The back tyres did the same and then dropped down with a heavy bump. Crane applied the brakes and brought the truck to a stop.

He jumped out and walked back to the carnage he had just created. The new guy lay motionless, facedown, in a twisted heap, either already dead or dying.

Paul was lying on his back, his hips twisted unnaturally to one side. He was heaving and wheezing where one or possibly both of his lungs had collapsed, likely punctured by his own broken ribs. His eyes were wide and filled with panic. He knew he was dying. A drop of blood escaped from the corner of his mouth and ran down the side of his face.

Luke was on his front, using his elbows to drag himself towards Paul. His feet and ankles seemed to wobble a little like jelly over the asphalt where the bones in his lower legs were broken and no longer supporting his feet properly. He made a painful grunt through gritted teeth with each heave forward, determined to reach Paul. But his eyes weren't on Paul and being there for his friend as he died, Crane could see they were actually focused on the Glock that was visibly protruding from Paul's waistband. Luke was almost there. He needed just one more drag forward using his left elbow. He reached out with his right hand, then yelped as Crane stamped on his forearm. Crane easily took the Glock from Paul's waistband, leaving Luke where he was. He walked to the back of the Range Rover to fetch the other Glock, feeling Luke's eyes watching him. He wondered if Luke had already figured out that all of his options had disappeared. Either way, he didn't care, his priority was getting Chloe. Once she was safely in his pickup truck, then he would deal with Luke.

Crane held both Glocks in his left hand and used his right to open the back door of the Range Rover. He was about to instruct Chloe to get out of the car, but there was a problem. The terrified girl sitting in the back looking up at him wasn't Chloe.

# Chapter Thirty

The girl was young but not quite as young as Chloe. She was maybe sixteen or seventeen. She had raven hair worn in a high ponytail, just like Chloe normally did. Her dark brown, almost black eyes were filled with fear, and she was muttering foreign words. Her hands were clasped together just below her chin as if praying, or maybe begging him not to hurt her. Eastern European. It sounded like Bulgarian to Crane. He closed the door and turned to Luke, who was now sitting with his back against the front wheel of the Range Rover.

"Where is she?"

Luke looked up, his skin pale and clammy. "What?"

"Where is she?" Crane repeated through gritted teeth. "My niece. Where is she?"

Luke scrunched up his face in confusion. "Your niece? What the hell are you talking about?"

"Don't play dumb with me. Where is she?"

"Seriously, I have no fucking idea what or who you're talking about."

Crane jabbed an accusatory finger at Luke. "You just broke my brother's nose and took my niece. So, where is she?"

Luke's brow was deeply furrowed, then all of a sudden his eyes went wide. "Wait, you're Dylan the Donk's brother?"

Crane frowned. "Dylan the Donk?"

Luke snickered. "Your brother's a terrible poker player. Hold on, did Dylan tell you we took your niece?"

Crane nodded slowly, wondering where this conversation could possibly be going.

Luke lowered his head solemnly. "Then it looks like he's set us both up."

"Explain," said Crane, folding his arms across his chest.

"Paul gave Dylan a smack and broke his nose, but we didn't touch the young girl with him."

"When I said explain, I meant start at the beginning. How do you even know Dylan?"

Luke shifted his position to sit more upright and seemed to immediately regret his decision. He sucked in a sharp breath through gritted teeth, and Crane could just imagine the excruciating pain shooting up his legs. He paused for a few seconds before speaking again. "Every Saturday night, I host a high-stakes poker game at the club. It's a closed group, invite only. Last weekend, one of our regular players vouched for your brother to come and join us. To be fair, he turned up with an envelope full of cash ready for the buy-in." Luke winced and took several shallow breaths.

"So, what happened?" Crane asked, gesturing with an impatient hand for him to keep talking.

"The first hand was dealt, and Dylan went all-in." Luke sniggered and shook his head. "With a two and seven offsuit—the worst possible hand. It was a real donk move to try and stamp his authority on the game, hence the nickname. It backfired big time though. One of the other guys had been dealt pocket kings and took him out."

Luke used his forearm to wipe the sweat from his brow and grunted like a powerlifter. The movement shifted his weight, and Crane watched his whole body tense from yet another tidal wave of excruciating pain from his broken legs. "Dylan asked to rebuy back into the game. He said he'd settle up afterwards if he lost. We don't normally allow rebuys, but against our better judgement, we all agreed."

"I take it he lost again?"

Luke gave a weak lopsided grin. "It got down to just me and him, and I took him out with a flush. After the game, I gave him my bank details to transfer the money for the rebuy, but he told me that he needed a few days to move some funds around. I could tell by the look on his face that he didn't have it. I gave him one week to pay up. That expired last night, hence us paying him a visit today."

Crane looked down at Luke, his forehead crinkled with frown lines. "He's a forklift driver going through a divorce. Why did you think he had the money to play high-stakes poker?"

"When someone walks in with twenty-five grand in cash, you kinda give 'em the benefit of the doubt that they've got money."

"Twenty-five thousand?" Crane asked, recoiling in disbelief. "He walked in with twenty-five thousand in cash?"

Luke nodded. "That's right, that's the buy-in. I can't let someone get away with not paying me back twenty-five grand. I've got a reputation to uphold."

Crane struggled to wrap his head around it all. It was Dylan all along. Dylan was the mystery man. He had set him up to kill Luke over twenty-five thousand pounds. He'd used Beth's death to manipulate him and lied about his daughter being kidnapped to push him to take Luke out. All to wipe his debt clean. The phone calls, the letters, the pictures. All for twenty-five grand. At least, that's what it looked like. But something just didn't add up to Crane. He still felt as if he was missing something. As if he was still a few chapters away from knowing the full story. Where had Dylan even got twenty-five grand from in the first place?

"So, who's that?" Crane asked, pointing at the back of the Range Rover.

Luke shrugged. "A new slag for the club."

Crane's jaw tightened. The way Luke talked about the scared young girl infuriated him, and knowing how she would be treated along with the other girls in the club sickened him. "She's an illegal immigrant that's been smuggled into the country by that guy?" Crane pointed at the dead man in the green polo T-shirt and at the same time noticed Paul was no longer heaving and wheezing. He was dead. His vacant eyes stared up at the sky.

Luke gave a single nod of his head in affirmation.

"You get them working in the club, and in return you give them a place to stay and a little bit of pocket money. Just enough for them to get by."

Luke smirked. "That's how it works."

"And you left your phone turned off so that the police couldn't track you here?"

"How do you know my phone is off?"

"Because I tried to trace it."

Luke snorted and shook his head. "Of course you did."

Crane moved one of the two Glocks from his left hand to his right and aimed it at Luke. Luke's eyes went wide and his arms began to raise. He was about to say something, probably going to plead for his life, but Crane didn't give him the opportunity. He depressed the trigger, and a bullet almost instantly entered Luke's skull through his right eye socket. His head snapped back in a shower of skull fragments, brain matter, and blood. Then his lifeless body leaned over to the left and dropped to the ground. The sound of the gunshot thundered and reverberated between the two industrial units, the surrounding silence making the shot sound incredibly loud.

Crane switched the Glock back into his left hand with the other one and then used his right hand to open the back door of the Range Rover again. The girl was no longer praying, she was cowering in the opposite footwell, curled up. Crane pulled out his phone and used a search engine to bring up an image of the Bulgarian flag—three horizontal stripes, red at the bottom, green in the middle, white at the top. He turned the screen to show the girl. She looked at the phone, then looked back at him and nodded—a small, quick, vertical movement that was barely visible. He started a translation app on his phone and spoke into the microphone.

"You are safe now. I am not going to hurt you."

A female voice came from the phone's speaker repeating what he had said in Bulgarian. She stayed cowering in the footwell, but he could sense her tension drop a level.

"The police will be here soon, and they will take care of you."

The female voice translated, and the girl nodded tentatively.

"For now, I need you to go back into the lorry."

This time when the female voice translated, the girl cowered back down slightly and shook her head.

Crane raised a hand, open palm. "It won't be for long. It's just so that when you tell the police that you didn't see anything, they will believe you."

The voice translated and then Crane added, "You didn't see any of this happen because you were in the back of the truck. Do you understand?"

This time, she looked at him, hesitated for a second, and then said, "Da."

Crane didn't know many Bulgarian words, but he did know that "da" meant "yes".

He made a hand gesture for her to get out and follow him. She obeyed. They walked to the back of the HGV, where the door was still wide open. The young girl was tiny, but she was strong and nimble like a gymnast. She climbed up and into the back with ease. Crane used the translation app one more time just to reassure her that she wouldn't be in there long, then he locked her inside.

Crane got to work. He dropped both Glocks into the back of the Range Rover, then he dragged Luke by the legs and pulled him up and into the rear footwell. He positioned him so that he was lying across the full length of the footwell, although he was a little tall to fit in neatly. Crane had to settle with bending Luke's knees and allowing his head to overhang out of the door sill.

Next, he went into the back of his Hilux and grabbed two large bottles of white spirit and a small box of matches. He headed back to the Range Rover and emptied half a bottle on Luke's body, then he dragged the truck driver's body closer before picking him up in a fireman's lift and dumping him on top of Luke. The remaining contents of the first bottle of white spirit went over him.

Crane turned and looked down at Paul's hefty bulk and shook his head. There was no need to put his back out.

He jumped in his pickup truck to reverse it away from the scene. The rear left wheel raised and bumped over Paul's body followed by the front left wheel.

He stopped the truck just before reaching the main road that ran up the middle of the industrial estate. There was a rattle coming from the front left of the truck where it had collided with Paul. Crane jumped out and gave it a brief inspection. Considering the force of the impact, the front of the truck was in pretty good condition, but Paul had caused a big crack across the headlight and snapped one of the brackets holding it in place, which was causing it to rattle between the bonnet and the bumper.

Crane made his way back to Paul's body and dragged him away from the HGV and into the open area in front, then he emptied the second bottle of white spirit over him, drenching him and his clothes. He jumped into the driver's seat of the Range Rover and pressed the start button. Luke must have had the key in his pocket because the engine fired up without hesitation. Crane manoeuvred the Range Rover and parked it so that it was directly above Paul's body.

He checked that the Range Rover was far enough away from the HGV and the buildings. He didn't want the fire spreading. Then, finally, he pulled out the small box of matches. He struck three matches at once and threw them under the Range Rover. Paul's body burst into flames with an audible whoosh. Crane did the same with another three matches into the back with Luke and the truck driver. Within just a few seconds, the Range Rover was completely engulfed. Crane turned away and walked back to his pickup truck.

# Chapter Thirty-One

Crane made an anonymous call to the emergency services and told them that he could see smoke coming from Green Fields industrial estate. He ended the call abruptly before they could ask him any questions. He hoped they would just send a unit to investigate and wouldn't try to trace his call. If they did try to trace his call, they would be asking how he could see the smoke from France or Germany or Belgium. Ricky had installed an app on his phone that when activated made his calls appear as if they were originating from a random destination. Typically, they bounced around from different cities across mainland Europe. After he hung up with the emergency services, he dialled Ricky.

"What's going on?" Ricky asked eagerly.

"It was Dylan," Crane revealed.

"What was? What do you mean?"

"The mystery man. The man behind the letters and the phone calls. It was Dylan all along, setting me up." Even though the words were coming out of his mouth and he knew them to be true, he was still struggling to process the fact that his own brother had set him up.

"What? Why?"

Crane hesitated, partly because he was concentrating on pulling out onto a roundabout and partly because he wasn't one hundred percent convinced with what he was about to tell Ricky. "He owed Luke Maddocks twenty-five grand. Luke was threatening him, so he set me up to take him out."

"What about Chloe? Have you got her back safe?"

"They didn't take her," huffed Crane. "Even that was a lie."

"So, where is she?"

"I'm assuming Dylan's taken her west, to the caravan. Can you do me a favour and trace her phone to check?"

"I'm on it." Footsteps could immediately be heard through the truck speakers. "I can't get my head around this, it's crazy. If he was that desperate for money, why didn't he just ask you?"

"Because he knows I wouldn't have given it to him. I told him before that as far as I was concerned, I didn't have a brother. I wouldn't have given him a single penny, especially now that he's getting a divorce and no longer supporting Chloe." Crane paused and then continued as if he were thinking out loud rather than talking to Ricky. "What I can't get my head around is, what does he expect to happen now? He used Beth's death to manipulate a conflict between me and Luke, and then as a last-ditch effort, he used Chloe to force me into killing him."

"Maybe he's thinking along the lines of it's easier to ask for forgiveness," Ricky suggested. "So, what *are* you gonna do?"

Crane gave the question some consideration before eventually saying, "Honestly, I have no idea. I think I'm going to confront him and see what he has to say for himself. I still feel like there's more to this, like I'm still missing something."

Crane could hear a mix of clicking sounds, like the keys on a keyboard and buttons on a computer mouse being pressed, then Ricky said, "I've got Chloe's phone on GPS, and judging by how fast she's moving, she must be in the car with Dylan. They've just passed Saundersfoot and turned left. They're now heading south towards Tenby."

"So, he did tell the truth about that." A big part of Crane was actually surprised by this.

"I'll ping this to your phone now so that you can track them yourself."

"Thanks," said Crane before ending the call.

Crane spent the rest of the journey in silence, replaying the last few days over in his head. The miles went by over the next hour and a half without him even registering them. He was somewhere else entirely. It was only when he saw a glimpse of the vast expanse of water in the distance that he realised he was getting close.

He snapped his attention back to the present and pulled into a lay-by. He grabbed his phone out of his pocket and pressed an app notification that Ricky had sent. A map immediately filled the screen, with an orange arrow representing Crane and a red dot representing Chloe. She was in a caravan park just behind Tenby South Beach. Crane knew it well. It was the same caravan park his mother used to take him and Dylan to when they were young boys. It was a stunning part of the world, particularly on a bright summer's day like today.

Crane placed the phone in the centre console so that he could keep an eye on it while he drove. The sun was getting low and beginning to get into his eyes, so he lowered the visor for some shade before pulling back onto the road. Judging by the sun's position in the sky, there was less than an hour of daylight remaining.

A few minutes later, Crane took a left into the caravan park. He drove past a big white sign with Twilight Holiday Park written across it in bold black letters, with a cartoon sun complete with a big toothy smile and sunglasses above it waving. He followed the road until he came to a junction. He could turn left or continue straight ahead. He glanced at his phone and saw Chloe's red dot in the top left corner of the screen. Crane drove straight ahead.

Coming up on his right was the holiday park's minimarket. Apart from new signs, it looked exactly like he remembered from when he was a kid. Big glass windows in the front with dinghies and other inflatables on display and hanging outside, a rack of body boards sat on one side of the front door, and a display stand filled with sunglasses on the other. Next door to the minimarket was a fish and chip shop. There was a small queue inside, waiting to give their orders.

The road gradually curved to the left, then straightened out. There was grass on either side of the road and caravans as far as the eye could see. Crane's orange arrow was closing in on Chloe's red dot. A minute later, just before the arrow and the dot were about to touch, a small car park came up on the right. Crane pulled into it. There were enough spaces for ten cars, and seven of the spaces were already taken. Two SUVs, three large estates, and two hatchbacks. One of the hatchbacks was a dark blue Ford Focus. Dylan's dark blue Ford Focus.

Crane reversed into the space opposite and turned off the engine, then, using his index finger and thumb, he zoomed in on the map. Chloe's signal appeared to be coming from a caravan a little further on from the car park and to the left. Crane leaned forward and looked back over his right shoulder to where he suspected the caravan to be. He could just about see the front corner and one of the doors through a gap in the trees surrounding the car park.

He reached for the handle to get out of the truck, but then he stopped when the caravan door swung open. Dylan stood in the doorway with a big grin on his face. Crane thought that maybe he'd spotted him for a second, but he dismissed it when Dylan's grin turned into a big yawn and a stretch. He'd changed into blue jeans and a blood-free pink polo T-shirt. His face had also been cleaned up, and he had a small white bandage taped over his broken nose. He was wearing aviator-style sunglasses, probably to hide his black eyes rather than to protect them from the sinking sun. He closed the caravan door behind him and started walking on the grass alongside the road, in the direction of the minimarket. He strolled past the entrance of the car park without even glancing in, seemingly relaxed and carefree.

Once Dylan was out of sight, Crane got out of the pickup and made his way to the caravan. He went up the two steps he had just watched Dylan descend and opened the door. Chloe was sitting on a cream L-shaped sofa, with her feet up on the coffee table.

She calmly looked up from her phone at the opening door, most likely believing her dad to have forgotten his wallet or something.

"Hey, Chlo Chlo."

"Uncle Tom." She beamed. "I didn't know you were coming."

"Me neither."

Crane stepped into the caravan and closed the door. It was smart and modern inside. Lots of whites and creams with turquoise cushions and curtains. The L-shaped sofa faced a small electric fireplace built into a unit that had a widescreen TV sitting on it. Next to the lounge area was a modern kitchen with dark grey worktops, and next to the kitchen was a rectangular dining table with four cream chairs. At the back was a door that led to the bedrooms and bathrooms. Crane sat down on the L-shaped sofa, next to Chloe.

"Did you find the men that broke my dad's nose?" asked Chloe.

"Tell me," said Crane, turning to face her, "what do you know about the whole situation?"

Chloe pinched her eyebrows together and tilted her head to the side slightly. "Just that Dad owes some bad people money, although he didn't tell me that. I heard them say it to him." She placed her phone facedown on the seat between them. "Every time I ask him about what happened, he just gets defensive and says it's nothing for me to worry about."

"What exactly happened?"

Chloe dropped her feet from the coffee table and twisted in her seat towards Crane. "Didn't Dad tell you?"

"He told me *his* version, but I want to hear *yours*."

"Okay." Chloe shrugged. "I was trying to squeeze a bag into the back seat when this big black car pulled into the car park really fast and stopped right behind Dad as he was putting something in the boot. Two men jumped out—they were both big, but one of them was huge"—she puffed her shoulders up and pushed her elbows out—"like the Hulk from the *Avengers* movies.

"Dad turned around, and when he saw them, he seemed to really panic. He started saying that he just needed one more day. The biggest one opened the back door of their car, and it looked like they were going to force him to get in, but when they saw me, they both stopped. The smaller one told the big one to 'give him a taste'. That's when he punched Dad and broke his nose. The smaller one then said something about Dad having twenty-four hours to get the money to him, no more chances. Then they got back in their car and drove off." She held both hands out, palms facing up. "I don't even know what money they're on about. What money could Dad possibly owe? I didn't think he had much."

Crane leaned forward and rested his elbows on his knees. He softened his expression. "It must have been scary for you."

"It was." Chloe nodded. "But I was more worried about Dad. The big guy really hit him hard. I tried to help him up and asked if he was okay, but he just told me to go back up to the apartment. He told me to stay up there and lock the door and not to come out under any circumstances until he came to get me." She paused, as though deep in thought, then she said, "He said it was for my safety, just in case they came back.

"I did as he told me to, but I did have a peek from behind the curtains when I heard someone pulling into the car park. I thought they'd come back, but they hadn't, it was you. I watched you pull up and speak to Dad, then rush off. I guessed that he was asking you to help him with the bad guys?"

Crane looked down at his clasped hands. "Yeah." He sighed. "Something like that."

Chloe was about to say something else but got distracted when they heard someone walking up the steps and opening the caravan door. Dylan stepped inside holding a six-pack of lager and a plain white carrier bag.

"They didn't have any chicken nuggets, so I got you a jumbo sausage."

Dylan closed the door, removed his sunglasses, and looked towards Chloe. He saw Crane and froze, his mouth dropping open slightly, but only for a split second. He quickly recovered and seemed to fake an act of normality in front of Chloe.

"Tom, I didn't know you were coming. I'd have got more chips if I'd known."

"I've lost my appetite anyway," replied Crane. "Maybe we could go for a little walk. See if it comes back."

An awkward silence fell over the caravan, but again, Dylan was quick to recover. "Sure." He smiled. "I'll just grab a jumper. It's starting to get a little nippy outside."

He dropped the bag of chips on the dining table and put the six-pack of lager in the fridge, then he went through the door to the bedrooms. The aroma of salt and vinegar from the chips had already filled the caravan.

"What has he done?" Chloe said quietly so that only Crane could hear.

"What do you mean?"

One of Chloe's brows arched upwards. "Come on, I've got eyes and ears. He's done something, I can tell. I could have cut the tension between you two with a spoon."

Crane couldn't help but smile at Chloe. "You're too switched on for your own good."

Chloe returned the smile, proud of herself. "So, what has he done?"

"It wouldn't be right for me to tell you, but I promise it's nothing for you to be concerned about."

Chloe rolled her eyes. "I wish you'd both stop treating me like a child."

"But you are a child," said Crane, "albeit a fourteen-year-old going on forty."

Chloe giggled as Dylan walked back through the door wearing a dark blue zip hoodie over his pink T-shirt, the zip left undone.

"Get tucked into your food before it gets cold," Dylan said to Chloe. "I'll reheat mine when we get back."

Chloe got up and went into the kitchen as Crane headed to the door with Dylan. He looked back at Chloe, who was blindly feeling for a plate inside one of the cupboards, watching them. A hint of worry was showing in her eyes.

Crane tried to give her a reassuring smile. "We won't be long," he said, not really knowing if that was the truth.

# Chapter Thirty-Two

There were too many people around to start the conversation Crane wanted to have, so they walked in silence towards the minimarket but then veered left towards the entrance of a coastal path. After thirty yards, the coastal path split in two, with one path leading down to the golden sands of Tenby South Beach and the other path curving to the right and continuing behind the full length of South Beach. Crane went right, and Dylan followed. The ground was hard and dry, with a thin layer of sand on top. The path was flanked on either side with long, dense tufts of marram grass. It was only just wide enough for them to walk side by side, although Dylan spent most of the time trailing behind Crane to allow other walkers to pass.

The sun was dipping really low in the sky now—it was just a small orange ball beginning to touch the horizon in the distance. With night-time closing in, everyone was walking in the opposite direction to them, heading back to their caravans and holiday homes before it got too dark. When it finally looked clear ahead for a stretch, Crane was the first to break the silence.

"So, you set me up to kill Luke Maddocks for twenty-five grand."

Dylan scoffed. "Is that what you think?"

"Don't try to deny the phone calls and the letters. I know it was you."

"I'm not denying it, it was me. I made the calls and the letters. I tracked you using an app on Chloe's phone when you took her to

Luigi's, and I also got lucky a couple of times too. Like yesterday, I'm in the bookies on one of the slot machines by the window, and guess who drives past? You. I mean, it was like the whole thing was written in the stars or something. I couldn't believe my luck when I watched you walk across the road to meet that blonde hottie for lunch." Dylan raised a hand to his chin in a show of feigned contemplation. "Hey, wasn't that blonde hottie one of Beth's friends?"

Crane was about to bite back, but an elderly couple with a small Yorkshire terrier was walking towards them. Crane and Dylan continued in silence. Dylan tucked in behind Crane to allow the couple and their little terrier to pass. They all politely nodded and smiled at each other. Crane wondered if the elderly couple could sense the tension like Chloe had. He certainly felt as if he had tension oozing out of his pores.

The path ahead was beginning to incline and curve to the left, leading them up towards Giltar Point. It was like a giant finger of land stretching out into the ocean. Rising fifty feet above the powerful waves that crashed into its rugged cliff face, it was extremely popular with walkers due to the panoramic clifftop views over the ocean and Caldey Island a mile or so away.

When the elderly couple was far enough behind them to be out of earshot, Crane went to break the silence once again, but a lone man appeared up ahead. He looked to be in his sixties, wearing a grey sun hat, and using two hiking poles. Once again, they nodded and smiled politely as they passed each other. This time, Crane and Dylan continued to walk in silence and waited until they were close to the furthest edge of Giltar Point. They stopped when they knew that they were all alone, where there would be no more interruptions, no more prying ears.

Dusk was truly setting in; it was getting darker by the minute. Under different circumstances, Crane would have enjoyed the walk up here, breathing in the fresh and salty ocean air, and taking in the sights. The constant roar of the waves crashing into the cliff face below seemed to rise up and surround them, giving them an even stronger sense that they were now all alone in the world.

"I'm all ears," said Crane, looking out to the ocean.

"I set you up, but my aim wasn't to get you to kill Luke Maddocks." Dylan was next to him, side-on, hands in his zip hoodie pockets.

"Now this should be interesting. Go on, then, give me another plausible explanation for pushing me into a conflict with Luke Maddocks and blaming him for Beth's death."

"You're right. I was trying to push you into a conflict with Luke Maddocks, but I wasn't expecting you to kill him."

Crane turned to look at Dylan, eyes narrowed. "What the hell did you expect to happen?" He could feel the rage building inside him. His skin felt hot all over. He tried to keep his voice down before continuing, but it was a struggle. "You were trying to make me think he was responsible for Beth's death, and when that didn't do the job, you tricked me into thinking he kidnapped Chloe."

Dylan nodded, calmer than Crane. "I did."

"So, how can you say you weren't expecting me to kill him?"

Dylan closed his eyes momentarily before turning to face Crane, their gazes now meeting. "Because I was expecting *him* to kill *you*."

Crane paused for a second, taking those eight words in and trying to process them. Eventually, he muttered, "What?"

"That's right," Dylan said, scornfully spitting the words at Crane. "He was meant to kill you."

The revelation brought so many different emotions to Crane—upset, hate, anger, irritation, confusion to name a few—that the emotional side of his brain shut off completely, bringing a momentary sense of numbness. Too many questions exploded like fireworks in Crane's mind at once. He could only bring himself to ask, "Why?"

"Really?" Dylan smirked. "Mister perfect. Mister smart arse. Mister always one step ahead doesn't understand?"

Crane said nothing. He was using every ounce of his willpower to stop himself from wrapping his hands around Dylan's throat, the strength of the anger starting to push all the other emotions aside.

"So, last week I was outside the gates of your lovely home, getting myself all geed up to press the buzzer on your intercom, trying to work out exactly how I was gonna ask you for money to get Luke Maddocks off my back. And I couldn't stop thinking about all the things you'd said to me during our last conversation five years ago. You made it perfectly clear we were no longer brothers, that we were no longer family, and how did you put it? You never wanted to see my face ever again. I was mulling all this over, and then boom, it just hit me: I'm your next of kin," Dylan exclaimed, a devilish grin stretching across his face. "Mum and Dad are dead, Beth's dead; I'm the only immediate family you have left. I'm your next of kin. Why come to you with my tail between my legs begging you for money when I could inherit it all? All of your money and your nice big house on the mountain. Oh, and I hear you've got some tasty motors hidden away in your garage too."

Crane was rooted to the ground in stunned silence. He'd always known Dylan was a nasty piece of work, a narcissist even, but this... this was too much. He'd spent years ignoring what he knew Dylan to be, but now Dylan had gone too far, and it was time to see him for what he truly was—a psychopath. He was frustrated with himself for allowing Dylan to catch him hook, line, and sinker. Even more frustrating was the fact that Dylan was right. After Beth's death, he hadn't even contemplated making a will. Technically, Dylan was his next of kin and would get everything. Everything that he'd worked so hard for.

Dylan, still smirking, raised his left hand and tapped his temple twice with his index finger. "It was a no-brainer. You made it clear that I didn't have a brother anymore, so I had nothing to lose... but everything to gain."

"I always knew you were an evil bastard," Crane growled, taking a step towards Dylan.

Dylan had anticipated it and quickly took a few steps back. He pulled a small snub-nosed revolver from his pocket. Crane could have kicked himself. Dylan had kept his hands in the pockets of his zip hoodie since he'd put it on, and Crane hadn't even questioned it.

"Not so fast, bro," said Dylan, with a brazen grin. "It looks like I'm the one that's been thinking one step ahead."

"I suppose there really is a first time for everything," replied Crane. "Have you ever killed anyone before?"

"Nope," said Dylan. "But like you say, there's a first time for everything."

"You really think you've got it in you to pull the trigger and kill me?"

"What other choice do I have?" said Dylan. "If I don't, you're gonna kill me."

"You've got that right," said Crane coldly. "But it's nothing less than you deserve after what you've done. You used your own daughter to get to me. You used Beth's death to push and taunt me. Christ, you even tried to make me think that Beth cheated on me."

Dylan laughed. "You really have no idea, do you?" He leaned forward slightly and looked Crane straight in the eyes. "Beth *was* having an affair. She was having an affair with *me*."

# Chapter Thirty-Three

## 15th November, almost five years earlier...

The hotel room was bland and plain but clean and tidy. It had a bed, which was all Dylan really cared about. He didn't have any use for the desk beneath the wall-mounted TV unless, of course, they got a little adventurous later. He certainly didn't have any use for the wardrobe—he wasn't planning on spending the night, so he hadn't brought any spare clothes with him. After all, he had a wife and daughter to go home to, and his wife asked enough questions when he went out for a few hours of an evening, so he would never get away with a whole night. Although, if he was honest, it suited him that way. He wasn't the type to enjoy a cuddle afterwards.

He was lying on the bed, wasting time playing an online poker game on his phone while he waited. He checked the time at the corner of the screen—just gone half seven. *She should be here by now.* Coincidentally, just as he finished that thought, there was a light knock on the door.

He jumped up from the bed like an excited teenage boy. She was here. He closed down the game on his phone and tossed it onto the bed as he made his way to the door. He pushed down the handle and pulled the door towards him. There she was, looking as gorgeous as ever. Five-six, brunette, deep brown eyes that you could get lost in, and a figure to die for. Which is exactly what would happen if his brother found out he was meeting his wife for another sordid rendezvous.

Beth smiled radiantly. She was dressed in knee-high black boots and a figure-hugging grey jumper dress. Her black overcoat was draped over her left forearm. A slice of her smooth thighs was visible between the top of her boots and the bottom of her dress, grabbing Dylan's attention as she stepped into the hotel room. He couldn't stop himself from reaching out and putting a hand around to the small of her back and pulling her towards him. She giggled as he closed the door with his other hand and nuzzled her neck before backing her up and pinning her against the wall. She smelled floral and sweet. Her skin was warm and silky. She sighed with pleasure in his ear, and it drove Dylan wild. His lips moved up her neck until they met hers, and they kissed, gently at first, and then passionately, hungrily even. Like two wild animals unable to resist their instincts. He pushed his hips forward, pressing into her, and she gave a satisfied moan.

Then, all of a sudden, Beth pulled back slightly and put her hand on Dylan's chest. She tried pushing him away gently, but Dylan didn't read the signal. There was too much testosterone coursing through his veins. Beth turned her head to the side to break away from the kiss.

"Wait," she whispered.

Dylan pulled back. "What? What's wrong?"

"We need to talk." She turned her head back to look at him. Her gaze had hardened, but Dylan was too drunk on lust to even notice.

"Can we talk afterwards?" Dylan went to kiss her again, but she kept her hand on his chest, keeping him at a distance.

"Please, Dylan, it's important." There was a serious edge to her tone, a sternness.

Dylan let out a disappointed sigh, but he stepped back to give Beth some space. She walked past him and sat down on the lone armchair in the corner of the room. Dylan stood where he was for a few seconds, wondering how the mood had gone from intoxicating lust to sober and serious in the flick of a switch.

His head and shoulders slumped slightly before he turned and followed her.

He sat down on the corner of the bed opposite her, within touching distance, close enough to still smell her perfume. He observed her perfectly formed legs, which were now crossed and revealing even more of her smooth and silky skin. He wanted her so badly. She was the forbidden fruit. And even though he'd already tasted the forbidden fruit plenty of times over the last few months, he couldn't stop himself from wanting more and more.

Beth took a steadying breath and then said, "I'm pregnant."

Of all the things she could have said, those two words hadn't even been close to being on Dylan's radar. They hit him like a freight train.

"H-how?" he stuttered.

Beth smirked. "Do you want me to draw you a picture?"

"I mean, I thought you were taking the pill?"

"No," said Beth, "you assumed I was taking the pill, but you never actually asked or checked with me. Anyway, I have been taking the pill, but I've obviously missed a couple at the wrong time."

Dylan was quiet for a second, then he said, "Do you think it's mine?"

Beth shrugged. "I don't know."

"But it could be mine?"

"Of course it could," Beth said, raising a brow. "Do you need me to explain the birds and the bees to you?"

Dylan slowly shook his head. It was such a shock; he didn't know how he should react. In fact, he didn't even know how he felt about it. Did a part of him hope that the baby was his? Maybe. A part of him definitely didn't want it to be his brother's. "What are we going to do?"

"We?" Beth almost choked with amusement as she said the word. "There can't be a *we* anymore. That's why I'm here. What we've been doing is wrong. Fun, but wrong. It needs to stop."

It wasn't what Dylan wanted to hear. "But what about the baby?"

"There won't be a baby by this time tomorrow; I'm booked in to have a termination in the morning. I can't risk having this baby not knowing if it's yours or your brother's."

"But I don't want this to stop," protested Dylan. "I don't want *us* to end." He almost blurted out the words "I love you" but stopped himself, afraid that he would look stupid if Beth didn't feel the same way about him.

"Awww." Beth stood up and tenderly placed her hand on Dylan's cheek. "It's been fun, but it has to end now. Let's not pretend like it was anything more than it was."

Dylan looked up to meet her gaze. "What was it?"

Beth shrugged. "Fucking."

Beth surprised herself at her own callousness, but she was doing what needed to be done. Dylan had to know definitively that things between them were over, and this was the only way she knew how to get the message through to him. She'd said what needed to be said, and now she needed to get out.

Beth bent down and kissed Dylan on the forehead, a parting gift, then she turned away and walked out of the hotel room. She made her way down the hall and decided to take the stairs. They were only on the second floor, so it would probably be quicker than waiting for the lift anyway. As she pushed the door leading to the stairs open, there was a loud bang behind her that made her flinch. It sounded like someone or something had hit a wall or a door. She didn't look back; instead, she trotted down the stairs and through another door into the foyer. People were loitering around, just like they do in hotel foyers the world over. A couple with matching compact suitcases on wheels were at the counter checking in, another couple were dressed up for dinner and walking hand in hand towards the entrance of the restaurant, two women dressed in gym clothes had just entered and started to head towards the stairs that led down to the gym. Beth walked around them and out the front door.

The air outside was damp and fresh. It must have only just stopped raining a few moments ago, as the ground was saturated. Beth threw her overcoat on and made her way down the steps and into the car park. She strategically walked to her small hatchback, dodging the many puddles that were dotted around. She felt as if there were eyes on her and almost looked back up to where she thought Dylan's room would be, but then she thought better of it and jumped straight into her little hatchback.

Beth reversed out of her space and followed the road markings to the car park exit, then she took a left and followed the road before entering Coryton roundabout. As she approached the first set of traffic lights on the roundabout, they turned amber and then red. Beth came to a stop on the line.

"For fuck's sake," Beth cursed, eyes flitting to the lane she should've been in. She hadn't been concentrating, her mind elsewhere, part of her back in the hotel room with Dylan, part of her thinking about what she was doing tomorrow. Out of the four lanes, she was now in number two. She needed to get into lane three to go right. If she stayed in lane two, she would be heading up the slip road and onto the motorway heading west. She looked to the right to see if she could pull into lane three.

"Well, this just gets better and better," she growled as a black Range Rover came to a stop alongside her. She watched as the driver appeared to lean over and start doing something with his hands on the passenger seat. She couldn't see what he was doing, she was too low in comparison to the big SUV, but she could see he wasn't paying any attention to the road or the traffic lights. She got herself ready to get off the mark quickly. If she were fast enough, she could easily nip in front of him when the lights changed from red to amber. No doubt he'd still be fiddling around and doing whatever it was he was doing.

*\*\**

Luke Maddocks was on his way to pick up his new girlfriend and take her on holiday to Gran Canaria, but, after being stuck in a police station all day, he was late, really late. The police had purposely kept him in custody to frustrate him and try to ruin his holiday; at least, that's what he thought. And when the police had eventually given him his phone back, the battery was completely dead. He'd plugged it into the car to charge after he'd left the station, and it was now showing a three-percent charge. He pressed the on button, and the phone went through its usual sequence of initialising. He kept glancing up at the lights, willing them to change. The phone displayed his home screen and informed him that his Bluetooth was now connected to the car. He quickly tapped the icons to call Sophie, who he knew would be panicking by now.

The speakers in the car vibrated with the sound of a dial tone, and the lights changed from red to red and amber. Luke shifted his foot from the brake pedal to the accelerator, but just as the Range Rover jumped off the mark, a little hatchback in the lane on his left cut across into his lane. He slammed his foot down onto the brake pedal to avoid smashing into the back of the little hatchback. The Range Rover forcefully rocked forward on the suspension as its forward momentum was brought to an abrupt end. Luke's phone slid off the passenger seat and dropped into the footwell, the charging cable popping out of the socket as it fell. The phone automatically switched itself off.

"*You fucking idiot*," Luke shouted, slapping his palm onto the steering wheel to sound the horn. He kept his hand on the horn, shouting further obscenities at the top of his voice even though his windows were up and the moron driver wouldn't be able to hear him.

The little hatchback just continued ahead as if nothing had happened, which infuriated him even more. Under normal circumstances, he would have gone after them, he would have chased them down, and if it were a bloke, he would have smacked him. But today was their lucky day. He had a plane to catch. He didn't have time for a detour.

*Damn, he was paying attention to the lights after all*. She raised an apologetic hand in front of her rear-view mirror, but his horn was still blaring, so she doubted he could even see it. She continued following the roundabout around to the right and could still hear his horn when he was well out of sight.

A filter lane came up on the left, which Beth took and followed the road around into Tongwynlais. She was shaking slightly, and not just because it was cold. A shot of adrenalin had entered her system during the near miss with the Range Rover, and now that it was gradually wearing off, a wave of emotion suddenly hit her. Thoughts of her husband came to her, followed by thoughts of Dylan, and then thoughts of the baby growing inside her. The baby that she was terminating in the morning because she couldn't be sure if it was her husband's or her brother-in-law's. *What have I done?* she thought, almost bursting into tears. She had the perfect home, the perfect husband, the perfect marriage, the perfect life, and she had risked it all. Why? Because when things in her life were going well, she tended to press the self-destruct button.

A little voice in her head kept asking questions that she couldn't answer. *What were you thinking? Why do you have to try to destroy everything?* And then it told her something she already knew to be true. *You don't deserve Tom*. He was a good man.

An overwhelming urge to speak to him hit her. She wasn't sure what she was going to say, but she knew despite all her flaws and bad decisions that she sure as hell loved him, and in that moment, she needed to hear his voice.

Dylan sat on the bed in the hotel room in stunned silence. He had watched Beth walk out and close the door behind her. He'd wanted to tell her to stop, to stay and talk, but he'd been frozen to the spot. She was pregnant. Possibly or even probably with his baby. He flopped back in frustration onto the bed and winced when something hard dug into his back. He reached behind and grabbed his phone. Seemingly out of nowhere, now that the numbness was subsiding, a rage exploded inside him. He launched his phone at the wall, immediately regretting it as it smashed into the plasterboard, leaving a sharp dent. The phone and small flakes of paint fell onto the floor. The phone itself appeared to be in one piece, but the screen had been shattered by the collision. He slid off the bed, leaving his phone on the floor, no clue whether it was still working or if its internal components had been damaged.

He stepped over to the window and opened the curtains. The car park below was busy as always. He watched a compact sports car pull into a tight parking space, and two middle-aged women wearing gym clothes got out. The driver said something, and they both laughed, or cackled from what it sounded like to Dylan through the glass. Then they walked towards the entrance and disappeared out of sight below him.

That was when Beth appeared from below, wearing her black overcoat. She elegantly walked down the steps and then made her way to her car, dodging the puddles of rainwater as she went. Dylan was expecting her to look back, to look up at him, maybe even have second thoughts and come back. She didn't. Even when she opened the door of her little hatchback and got in, she didn't so much as glance back up at the hotel. The brake lights on her hatchback illuminated brightly as she started the engine, then she reversed out of the space and followed the car park around to the exit.

A Range Rover pulled up at the hotel entrance below, and what could only be described as a giant jumped out of the passenger side. The bloke couldn't have been far off seven feet, and he was built like a Sherman tank. The giant raised a hand to wave goodbye to the driver and closed the door. The driver must have been in a hurry because the wheels spun on the wet tarmac for a second before finding traction and propelling the huge lump of steel forward. He roared out of the car park and took a left, just like Beth had.

Beth was on her way back home. On her way back to her fancy life with his twin brother Tom. Life. In the morning, she would be ending the life of her baby. Possibly his baby. No, he couldn't just give up that easily. Yes, it had started as a fling, but for him it had become something more. He needed to tell her. He needed to explain how he was feeling. Maybe she didn't need to terminate the baby. Maybe they could run away and be together, as a family. No, that was a crazy thought. Or was it?

He turned from the window to grab his phone to call her, then saw it among the paint chips on the floor and remembered what he'd just done.

"*Idiot,*" he cursed himself loudly. He frantically grabbed his wallet, keys, and broken phone and shoved them into his pockets before running out of the hotel room and to the stairs. He threw himself down them three or four at a time, not having a second to waste. He needed to catch up with Beth to speak to her before she got home. Tom had their home locked up like Fort Knox and had recently installed a new camera system that covered every square inch of the grounds outside. If he were spotted on the cameras, how would he explain visiting Beth at this time of night? On a night when he knew that his brother was away working. A night that he'd told his wife he was working overtime. He couldn't. He desperately needed to catch her before she got home.

Dylan hurried through the foyer at a fast-walking pace, every part of him wanting to run, but he was trying not to bring any attention to himself. As soon as he got outside, he bounded down the ten steps to the car park and sprinted to his car. He pressed the button on his key to unlock the doors and jumped inside his ten-year-old black Mitsubishi Shogun SUV. With a firm twist of the key in the ignition, the big three-point-two-litre diesel engine fired up, and he reversed out of the space with only a cursory glance behind to check nothing was coming. Without even coming to a full stop, he shoved the transmission into drive and took off out of the car park. He took a left and drove onto Coryton roundabout, with no attempt to slow down for the give way line, then accelerated down the straight towards the first set of traffic lights. He put his foot down, seeing they were green, and shot right through them, then followed the road around to the right. The next set of traffic lights were also green, but they changed to amber before he reached them. An impatient and determined growl erupted in his throat as he floored it, the lights changing from amber to red at the exact moment he roared over the stop line.

Dylan continued around the roundabout until a filter lane came up on the left, then he pulled into it. He followed the road around and into Tongwynlais, then he took a right heading towards Castell Coch and the lanes that ran through Fforest Fawr. He got through the tight residential area without running into any oncoming cars and drove past the turn that led up to Castell Coch. As soon as he entered the black hole that was the start of the country lane, he put his foot down. He was running out of time and beginning to worry that he may already be too late.

Dylan drove around the first couple of bends but only saw darkness up ahead. The branches overhead created a thick canopy that blocked any light from getting down to the road. It almost felt as if he were driving through a tunnel. The road curved around to the left and that was when he saw red taillights up ahead, glowing brightly. It was Beth, he was sure of it. His right foot pushed down on the accelerator pedal even harder to catch up to her. Which he did. Closing the gap really fast. Too fast. Almost driving straight into the back of her hatchback and having to brake hard to avoid contact. He dropped back slightly but then accelerated to close the gap again and started to flash his lights, hoping she would realise it was him and pull over, but she didn't. She drove on, seemingly oblivious to his pulsing headlights behind her.

Suddenly, a set of headlights appeared up ahead travelling towards them. He backed off slightly and stopped flashing. This could be his chance. The lane was too narrow for two cars to pass comfortably, so Dylan hoped Beth would pull over to allow the other car to go past. She did. As soon as the road widened, she pulled over to the left, and Dylan followed suit, tucking in behind her. The car approached them slowly.

Dylan had his hand on the door handle, ready to jump out. "Come on," he urged the other car as it haltingly drove past. If he opened his door now, the other vehicle would take it off.

As soon as it was clear, Dylan popped his door open and jumped out onto the wet and spongy ground. He'd landed in a large patch of dead sodden leaves. He took a step towards Beth, but she immediately took off, her tyres sliding and grinding for traction and her small turbocharged petrol engine screaming.

"Wait!" he called after her. "Beth, it's me."

With Beth's hatchback still zooming off and knowing he was probably just a shadowy figure to her at this point, he jumped back into the Mitsubishi and slammed his foot down on the accelerator before he had even closed the door, although he didn't need to, as the forward thrust closed it for him.

He lost sight of her around a right curve in the lane, so he pushed the accelerator pedal to the floor, and the big old diesel engine roared as it propelled the Shogun around the curve. There she was, not too far ahead. He closed the gap again even quicker than before. He flashed his lights again, hoping she would get the message. *It's me. Pull over.* But she wasn't getting the hint. He was running out of time.

In pure desperation, he pushed down on the centre of the steering wheel and started to beep his horn in short bursts. *Surely she'll know it's me now. Who else would be flashing and beeping at her?*

But Beth didn't stop and pull over; in fact, she started to speed up. Dylan stayed with her, about a car length behind, flashing and beeping more urgently. He couldn't let her get home without speaking to her.

The speedometer of the Shogun was creeping up to and then past the fifty-miles-per-hour marker, but Dylan was too busy trying to keep up with her to notice. Up ahead, the lane started to curve to the left, but Beth didn't appear to be adjusting her line. The little hatchback continued to go straight as an arrow, her brake lights only illuminating after she'd gone up the embankment. The little hatchback was launched into the air and began to rotate anti-clockwise.

Dylan watched on in pure horror, hearing a voice screaming Beth's name. It took him a while to realise the voice he could hear screaming was his own.

As he firmly applied the brakes to come to an abrupt but controlled stop, he heard and felt an explosion like a bomb going off. The sound of glass shattering, metal being crushed and torn, and airbags erupting reverberated around the forest. Then the noise disappeared, leaving only a dreadful silence in its wake.

# Chapter Thirty-Four

Crane was down on one knee, partly because he genuinely felt as if he was going to vomit, but mostly because it was tactically a useful position to be in when someone had a gun aimed at you. It was a non-threatening position that gave the aggressor a false sense of security. Being down on one knee appeared weak and submissive, but there was a big difference between being down on one knee compared to two. One knee meant that Crane could hold most of his body weight over his leading foot and still have the ability to use his trailing leg to push off and forward. In essence, he was poised and ready to strike if an opportunity arose.

Dylan was just a few yards ahead of him, with his back to one of the many cliff edges of Giltar Point. It was now fully dark, but a slim crescent moon cast an ominous dark grey blanket over the landscape surrounding them. The waves crashed relentlessly against the cliff face below. Dylan had the revolver trained on Crane and seemed to be relishing every second of his supposed position of power.

"You know," Dylan said, "on the morning after Beth's funeral when you caught me in the wardrobe going through her jewellery box, I was actually just trying to find something to remember her by. A little memento of some kind. I really had to think on my feet when you caught me, so I came up with that bullshit story about having money problems." Dylan snickered. "I was actually doing fine for money, but you fell for it big time and gave me *thirty grand*.

"It's funny because I didn't want Sarah to find out about it and I couldn't use it for anything flash like a car or a holiday because if you found out, you'd have realised that I lied. So, I hid it away. We had one of those small old-fashioned safes up in the attic the previous homeowners left behind. I locked the cash inside, but then I lost the fucking key." Dylan shook his head, recalling his frustration.

"When I moved out, I searched the house from top to bottom thinking that I was bound to come across it, but nope, it was gone." Dylan shrugged, his mouth beginning to curve into a smile, as if his story was about to take an unexpected twist. "I took the safe with me, not really sure what I was going to do with it, and then, a few weeks ago, I met this bloke down the pub that turned out to be a locksmith that specialised in opening safes. He came around to the flat, and in less than an hour, he had it open. I gave him a slice of what was inside for his troubles and then we went back to the pub to celebrate. We got chatting with this posh bloke standing at the bar in a fancy suit with a flash Rolex. He was bragging about how he makes a killing from playing high-stakes poker every week at Corkers. He told us that the buy-in was twenty-five grand and it was a winner-takes-all game. I thought to myself—well, *I've* got twenty-five grand."

Dylan continued, seemingly unfazed by Crane's silence. "Lucky at cards, unlucky in love. That's the famous saying, isn't it? Because the truth is, bro, I did love Beth. We had something special. I mean, yes, it started out as a fling; in fact, it started out as me trying to get one over on you. All our lives, *you*"—Dylan jabbed the barrel of the revolver at Crane—"were always the clever one, *you*"—another jab of the revolver—"were always the one that was good at sport, *you* were the successful one. *You* ended up joining the army and then went on to earn a fortune doing your bodyguarding stuff, and I just drive a forklift. *You* built a nice big house for yourself on the mountain, and I lived in an ex-council house. I was always the loser. The runt. But I've gotta tell you, when I was screwing your wife"—Dylan inhaled deeply, then exhaled with an exaggerated sigh—"I felt like a king."

Crane looked at the ground, desperately trying to process what Dylan had told him. "I don't believe you." His voice was barely audible over the sound of the crashing waves. "Beth wouldn't have gone anywhere near you." It hurt him to say the words out loud. It hurt because he didn't believe them. He wanted to. He'd never wanted to believe anything more in his life, but he knew Dylan wasn't lying. For once in his life, Dylan was telling the truth. *Beth was having an affair with my brother.*

Dylan laughed. "You don't believe me?" He pulled a mobile phone from his left pocket and tossed it onto the ground just in front of Crane. It landed with a dull thud. "There you go, that's her phone. Those text messages were real, and there's plenty more on there. Go ahead, take a look."

Even though he'd spent the best part of five years obsessing about the phone, Crane didn't make a move to pick it up. He knew what he would find on it, and it disgusted him. Instead, he looked up and glared at Dylan, his eyes filled with pure hatred.

Dylan laughed again, as if he'd just recalled a funny anecdote. "Do you remember around a month before Beth died? You were working abroad as usual. I think you were in Turkey. Or was it Morocco? Anyway, wherever you were, you phoned Beth, and she was all out of breath. She told you that she'd just finished a fitness class in the gym and asked you to call her back a little later so that she could get home and have a shower." An arrogant smirk spread across Dylan's lips. "I was actually taking her from behind the whole time you were on the phone to her. God, did we laugh about it after. You had no idea."

The red mist descended, and Crane was no longer in control of his actions. Any sense of caution, tactics, or even self-preservation was gone.

Crane launched himself towards Dylan, spreading his arms wide, and then closing them together violently, aiming for Dylan's hand and arm. His right palm smashed into the inside of Dylan's wrist and his left middle knuckles cracked the back of Dylan's hand. The revolver flew out of Dylan's grip before he even registered that Crane had moved. His arrogant smirk immediately disappeared, and he yelped in shock. Crane didn't stop. He pumped his legs and drove his shoulder upwards, directly into the centre of Dylan's chest. The impact lifted him off his feet. Dylan should have fallen back and landed with a bump on the ground behind him, but there was no ground behind him. He opened his mouth to scream, but no sound came out. All of the air had been knocked out of his lungs, winded from the impact with Crane's shoulder. Dylan dropped silently over the edge, his arms and legs flailing desperately to try to grab something, anything.

Crane took a sharp breath and circled his arms backwards, realising he'd created too much forward momentum, but the action was too late, the drop too close. Something deep in his subconscious, an automatic response, a raw instinct told him to jump, to push himself as far away from the cliff edge as he possibly could. His legs catapulted him out and into the open space away from the cliff edge.

Crane had never been afraid of heights, although, like all of humanity, he had an innate fear of falling; however, right now, as the feeling of weightlessness engulfed his body and the air began to rush around him as he dropped into the dark void below, he felt no fear. He felt no panic. He felt nothing.

As Crane fell, he heard a sickening wet slap and knew it was Dylan's body landing on an outcrop of rocks at the base of the cliff. Before he had time to process what was happening, process how he felt, process the cheating, the loss of his wife, the death of his brother, the outright betrayal from them both, he slammed into the surface of the ocean. Crane plummeted deep into the frigid dark water, and a small part of him wondered if maybe he'd suffered the same fate as his brother. It was cold, pitch black, and silent. Was this death?

No, he wasn't dead. He couldn't be. He'd always imagined death to be a nothingness, yet he could still hear his own voice in his mind. He expected to feel pain, but as he internally scanned himself, there was none; he wasn't physically hurt. He was fully conscious and knew exactly where he was and what was happening, but he remained completely motionless and allowed himself to sink into the abyss.

He knew that to live he needed to move, he needed to swim, he needed oxygen. But the question he found himself asking was—*do I want to live?*

He had been living in the shadow of Beth's death for so long, did he even know how to live anymore? Did he even want to try? The agony he'd experienced when he lost her and then the subsequent unfathomable ache of mourning her for all these years had all been a waste. He'd been mourning a stranger. Everything they'd had together, everything he'd thought they were was all a lie. A huge part of his life, a huge part of who he was had all been built on false pretences.

His lungs were beginning to burn, his body becoming ever more desperate for oxygen. Alarm bells were ringing inside his brain, starting to scream at him to rid himself of the carbon dioxide that was building in his lungs. But still, he remained motionless, suspended in the chilly obsidian waters of Carmarthen Bay.

# Chapter Thirty-Five

Chloe watched silently as her dad fell backwards over the edge of the cliff. Even in the darkness, she could see the panic on his face. She'd always known her dad was selfish, conniving, deceitful, and many other negative things, but people had always said, "He's still your dad." She knew her heart should've broken in this moment, her world should have felt as if it were falling apart, yet she felt nothing—no sadness, no remorse. Being treated like a child, especially when she didn't feel anything like one, had left her knowing the bare minimum about what had been going on the past couple of days. No one had taken into consideration that she'd *had* to grow up, had already seen many bad aspects of the world—addiction, cheating—all because of her dad. And despite everything she'd imagined he could be capable of, no part of her had imagined the ultimate betrayal she'd heard all about from her hiding place behind a rocky outcrop.

As Chloe continued to watch her father fall, she suddenly noticed something that caused almost every muscle fibre in her body to instantly contract. Uncle Tom had pushed too hard and too fast, he was teetering on the cliff edge. She sucked in a breath so forcefully it caused her to choke. Uncle Tom couldn't stop. He was going to go over. Then, as she looked on, urging desperately with her eyes for him not to fall, he did something she thought was crazy... he jumped.

Chloe screamed and sprinted to the cliff edge, dropping to her hands and knees. Her fingers curled over the edge of the cliff as she peered down into the darkness, afraid to stand too close to the edge, afraid to fall, afraid to... Her eyes landed on a silhouette of a body on an outcrop of rocks at the base of the cliff, but it was too dark and too far away to tell if it was her dad or Uncle Tom.

"I hope it's you, Dad, I hope you're dead," she shouted through tears. She put one hand over her mouth, balancing the front half of her weight on the other, surprise temporarily overtaking her other emotions, but it was too late to take the words back.

Chloe frantically scanned the water, her hand running through her hair before curling back over the cliff edge, yearning, praying to see Uncle Tom's head bob up. She was willing him to appear out of the frothy, inky water, willing him to swim to safety, but there was no sign of him.

She waited for over a minute, a minute that felt like a lifetime. She closed her eyes, a choked cry escaping her. He was gone. She knew it. She could feel it. Her vision blurred as tears flooded her eyes, and she began to tremble uncontrollably. Her legs wobbled as she crawled away from the edge and moved to a sitting position. She hugged her legs tightly and rested her forehead on her knees, sobbing into the night.

# Chapter Thirty-Six

The alarm bells inside Crane's head were screaming at him to swim to the surface, then they eventually reached a crescendo and began to dissipate and quieten. Crane knew it was almost over. The pain, the anguish, all of it would soon be gone forever. *He* would be gone forever.

But then he saw Ricky sitting on the sofa in his barn, laughing at something Crane had said; Ella holding little Rocko in her arms and giving him a good scratch behind the ear as Rocko, in turn, nuzzled into her neck and made her giggle; Chloe in the passenger seat of the Ferrari, her hair all windswept, beaming from ear to ear as her eyes sparkled.

Crane shook his head gently, a couple of bubbles floating up from the corners of his mouth. *I'm not ready to die.*

He kicked his legs and reached up with his arms. His body's natural buoyancy had already brought him near the surface. It took just two strong downward strokes with his arms before his head burst out of the water. He sucked in a few deep breaths while treading water. His burning lungs thanked him for the fresh air, and the fog in his head gradually dispersed. He'd drifted away from the cliffs a little, but now that he was on the surface, the swells were already beginning to push him back to them.

Crane lethargically front crawled towards the rocky outcrop, his arms close and weak, swallowing the salty water as he breathed with his mouth open, a constant feeling of needing more air. Just a couple more crawls and he'd be able to reach out his hand and feel the jagged surface. He gave a couple of kicks of his feet just as his body lifted with a powerful swell, and he struggled against it as it propelled him forward and slammed him into the base of the rocky outcrop. He winced as his forearms and knees took the brunt of the impact on the sharp rocks, but he managed to grasp a particularly big rock and quickly clambered out of the water before the next swell could get him. His wet shoes slipped against the wet rocks, and he braced himself for the painful landing, but instead of unforgiving rock, his hands sank into something soft and spongy. He hurriedly pushed himself away and rolled onto the hard and rough rock. He froze as he stared at his brother's body. It didn't go unnoticed that Dylan hadn't flinched or even made a sound.

Crane pushed himself up onto his feet and assessed the damage on himself. Running both hands up and down each leg in turn, then flexing and rotating his shoulders, elbows, and wrists. It was too dark to really see anything properly, but nothing seemed to be broken. He was just grazed and bruised. The skin on his forearms felt as if it were on fire as the seawater seeped into the abrasions.

Crane looked down at Dylan. He was lying facedown and looked as if he hadn't moved since he'd landed. Crane gazed up at the near vertical drop that they had both fallen from; he estimated it to be a good fifty feet, maybe even sixty. It was doubtful anyone could survive a fall like that after landing on solid rocks. Especially not with what he was now sure was blood surrounding Dylan that he'd first mistook for water on the rocks. To make sure, he reached down and pushed his index and middle finger into Dylan's carotid artery. He felt nothing. There was no pulse whatsoever; Dylan was gone. He wondered what he would have done if there had been a pulse. The answer came to him instantly—nothing. Crane had discovered so much tonight, and he wasn't even close to processing it all. But there was one thing he was certain of—he was relieved... no, he was glad Dylan was dead.

Crane crouched down and rolled Dylan's limp lifeless body over the edge of the rocky outcrop, letting it drop into the water, a couple of swells forcing Dylan against the rocky outcrop just as Crane had experienced, although this time there was no fighting to escape, no pain as the rocks tore at Dylan's clothes and skin. Crane stood for a little while and watched as the swells started to calm and his brother gradually drifted a little way into the distance before finally submerging below the inky surface.

As Crane watched the final ripples from Dylan's body, he thought back to his and Beth's wedding day. A day he'd revisited in his head over and over again the past five years. A day he'd been, and he'd believed Beth had been, at their happiest. Now, he wasn't so sure. Everything to do with Beth was question marks and doubts.

He remembered himself standing at the altar, facing towards the back of the room, anxiously waiting for his bride to appear. As a man who often avoided his emotions, he hadn't been able to that day. The guests were all a blur as he focused on the large oak door, shifting his weight from one foot to the other. His breath caught in his throat as the door swung open. There she was. Her long brunette hair was tied back and framed with a rhinestone headband that sparkled with each step she took towards him. But something was different. Beth was wearing a black dress.

He frowned and wiped the sweat from his brow with the back of his hand before turning in confusion to look at the man standing at his left shoulder. His best man. Dylan. Dylan, who was staring back at Crane with the same evil grin he'd had on his face when he was revealing his affair with Beth.

Crane clamped his eyes shut and shook his head, trying to shake the repugnant reminder that the two people he had once been the closest to had betrayed him in the vilest of ways. His cherished memory had turned into a nightmare he wanted to discard. He took a deep breath and turned to the steep but not completely vertical cliff face; now was not the right time to process and grieve.

The cliff face was weather-beaten and extremely coarse—thankfully ideal for climbing. Crane made light work of the initial ascent, but it wasn't long before the gradient was near vertical and he was forced to take his time, checking each hand-hold and foothold before trusting it with his full bodyweight. He soon found a rhythm, driving up with his legs, guiding and stabilising with his arms. When he crossed what he believed to be the halfway point, he noticed his breathing was becoming laboured and his muscles were beginning to burn from the lactic acid buildup. His arms were turning into lead weights and his fingers felt as if they were on fire. He ignored the pain and pushed on. When he was just a few feet shy of the top, he stopped. He could hear something. No, he could hear *someone*. Crane tried to slow his breathing to listen. It sounded like crying. A girl. He immediately knew exactly who it was.

His hands grabbed quicker and his feet raced for secure places to stand and push himself higher as he scrambled to climb the final few feet to reach her. By the time he raised his head over the top of the cliff edge, his energy had depleted to a couple percent over zero and he was breathing incredibly deeply.

The betrayal, the lack of energy, the pain in his body all floated to the back of his mind as his eyes settled on Chloe sitting on the ground just a couple of yards away, hugging her legs tightly, her head down, forehead resting on her knees. He'd spent years obsessing over Beth's death, shutting his family out. He should have been there for his niece, for the brilliant young woman who had shown understanding, care, and forgiveness so easily, who'd added a sense of fun back into his life. He couldn't take the past five years back, but he could write the future.

Crane had just enough energy left to pull himself up and over the cliff edge, although he was struggling to raise himself from his crouched position. "Hey, Chlo Chlo," he said between desperate breaths.

Chloe looked up, peering over her knees through sore, cried-out eyes. "Uncle Tom."

She jumped up and rushed to him just as he was getting to his feet. Chloe wrapped her arms around him and hugged him tighter than he'd ever been hugged before. Crane wasn't usually one for hugs, but this particular hug, at this particular time, melted him. He put his arms around her and squeezed.

"I thought you were dead," she whispered into his chest.

"That makes two of us." Crane lowered his head so that his chin rested on top of her head. "How much did you see and hear?"

The reply came out almost inaudible—"Everything."

Crane closed his eyes and internally winced. He hated the thought of her hearing everything that had been said and, possibly even worse, witnessing everything that had happened. "I'm sorry."

Chloe pulled away and looked at him. "What are *you* sorry for?"

He paused, struggling to process and speak the next words out loud. "For killing your dad." Even in the darkness, Crane could see there was so much going on behind her eyes. He could only imagine the turbulent mixture of emotions churning around inside her.

Chloe moved her mouth to speak, but no sound came out. She blinked and tried again. "You... you had no choice." Her voice sounded weak. She swallowed hard before continuing. "He was going to kill *you*." Her gaze lowered and her brow furrowed. "The things he did." She began to shake her head, more in disbelief than disgust. "He was an evil man."

Crane said nothing and just pulled her back into an embrace. She buried her face into his chest. He knew that Dylan was still her dad irrelevant of what she knew and the fact they hadn't had the best relationship. He knew that she would still be holding on to some fond memories of him, albeit how few and far between they were. He had no doubt a lot of her memories would become tainted by the things she'd seen and heard tonight, but there was no way of going back in time and changing what she'd witnessed.

Eventually, Chloe released her vice-like grip and stepped back. "What happens now?"

Crane shrugged. "I guess I should take you back home to your mum."

Chloe frowned. "But, what are we gonna tell her?"

Crane wasn't prepared to ask her to lie for him. "You can tell her whatever you want to tell her."

"Can I tell her the truth?"

"If that's what you want to do."

Worry lines deepened across her brow. "But... if she calls the police, won't you go to jail?"

Crane hesitated. He felt a little uncomfortable answering the question because it felt as if he was influencing her, but on the other hand, he didn't want to lie to her. So he simply settled on giving her the truth. "Potentially."

Chloe chewed on her bottom lip as she considered this. "I'm going to tell her that Dad went out to buy some beers and didn't come back. He just... disappeared. So I called and asked you to come and get me."

Crane tenderly placed his hands on her shoulders and fixed her gaze. "Look, there's no pressure from me, you need to do whatever feels right for you."

"But I don't want you to go to jail." Her voice was only just audible above the sound of the waves crashing into the cliff face below them.

"That's not on you," asserted Crane, giving her shoulders a gentle squeeze. "I did what I did, and I'll live with the consequences, whatever they may be." He could see a steeliness creeping into her eyes. "You don't need to make a decision now; have a little time to think."

Crane turned Chloe around and draped his left arm across her shoulders. She wrapped her right arm around his waist, and they both took a step forward to start heading back. A step away from Dylan, away from the horrors of tonight, away from... *Shit*.

Crane stopped abruptly and looked at Chloe. "Have you got your phone on you?"

"Yeah, why?"

"Can I borrow the torch on it for a minute?"

Chloe nodded and pulled out her phone from her pocket. She activated the torch and handed it to Crane. He shone the beam on the ground and started scanning the area where he believed the gun had landed. He didn't want it getting into the wrong hands or being found by a child. After a minute or so of carefully sweeping the light back and forth, pausing at every rock and patch of grass, something black eventually caught his eye, stuck in the middle of a clump of grass. It was the revolver. He picked it up and threw it as far as he could off the end of the cliff and into the open water.

"What's this?" Chloe asked from behind him.

Crane turned to look, and his breath caught in his throat as he saw what she was holding.

"It's... it's Beth's phone."

"Oh..." Chloe frowned down at it as if it were now tainted and she didn't know what to do with it.

Crane gave Chloe back her own phone as he took Beth's from her. He pressed a button on the side of the phone, and the screen illuminated brightly. The picture of him and Beth sitting at their table in the restaurant stared up at him. No, that wasn't completely true. A picture of him and a woman he'd never really known stared back at him.

Crane pressed the same button on the side of the phone again, and the screen went black. He'd spent so many years searching for the truth, searching for Beth's phone, and now here it was in his hand, and he couldn't want to be further from it if he tried. A phone he'd thought was full of happy memories was in fact full of deceit and secrets. Despite previously wanting to know everything, he felt no desire to uncover anything further. He already knew the basics, he knew what he needed to know, and he had no urge to further torture himself with the messages. He turned and hurled it off the cliff, in the same direction and probably with a little more force than he'd used to throw the revolver. His brother, the revolver, and the phone could all remain buried at sea.

He turned back to Chloe, and even though it was dark, he could see her eyes were wide and her mouth had dropped open.

"Why did you do that?" she asked.

"Why not?" replied Crane. "What good would it do me to read all of their sordid messages to each other?"

"No," said Chloe. "I mean, why did you throw it in the sea? You're polluting the ocean."

A wry grin crept across her lips, and they both laughed. After what they had both just been through, it should have felt inappropriate, but Crane took comfort in the fact that Chloe was still able to crack a joke and laugh. It was a good sign. It showed him she was going to be okay. And if she ever struggled in the future, he knew about an impressive facility in the Brecon Beacons that could help her.

# Chapter Thirty-Seven

Crane leaned back in the wooden chair with a floral cushioned seat, his stomach rumbling for more after his delicious starter of chargrilled lamb koftas with tzatziki. The slate flooring, broad wooden beams—in the same wood as the chairs—and original log fireplaces gave the pub a cosy and authentic rural feel. He reached for his glass of Chilean merlot, the rest of the bottle in the middle of the candlelit table for two, on the beige tablecloth.

"Cheers to our first date," Crane said, raising his glass.

Ella, looking absolutely breathtaking in a silky black dress that was slightly revealing but in an elegant and classy way, reached for her own glass.

"Cheers to that indeed," she said as they clinked glasses.

Crane had waited a week or so for things to calm down after that night on Giltar Point before calling Ella and asking her out to dinner. He had told her he didn't like the way he'd left things and the least he could do was buy her dinner. He hadn't yet told her that she was right. That there had been a side to Beth nobody had known. That she had hit the nail on the head when she'd said that he must have been looking back through rose-tinted glasses. And the truth was, he probably wouldn't tell her. Certainly not tonight anyway.

Tonight was about Ella. The past was in the past, and that was where it was going to stay.

He looked into Ella's sparkling green eyes and had to confess to himself that he had strong feelings for her, and now there was no guilt associated with those feelings. Where things went after tonight was anyone's guess, but for now he was determined to just enjoy the food, the wine, and the company.

Crane was about to ask Ella if she'd enjoyed her bruschetta when his phone began to vibrate and ring in his pocket. He offered an apologetic look as he pulled it out.

"Sorry, I should have switched this off."

Ella waved off his apology. "It's fine, take it. It might be important."

Crane checked the screen and found himself irritated at the interruption when he found it was a call from a private number. He diverted the call to voicemail and then slipped the phone back into his pocket.

"I never answer private numbers," he said. "They can leave a message if it's important."

Ella took another sip of her merlot. "Oh, I have some good news for you," she announced, practically slamming her glass back down on the table with excitement. "Dylan is responding well to treatment."

*Dylan is... what?* Crane swallowed down his shock, hoping Ella couldn't see the tension behind his eyes. "Wh-what?" Dylan was dead. He had pushed Dylan's lifeless body into the ocean and watched it sink. That was the last anyone had seen of him. His body had been consumed by the ocean. He hadn't even told Ella he was "missing".

"Sorry," Ella said, "I don't think I told you his name. Dylan, the little boy with the rare blood disorder that you funded to go to America for treatment. He's been responding really well to his treatments out there. I don't want to get too far ahead of ourselves because there's still a long way to go, but it's looking really promising."

Crane stealthily exhaled a sigh of relief and smiled. "That's great news."

"It is," Ella said, placing a hand on top of his. "And it's all thanks to you."

Crane felt what could only be described as electricity running through his hand and up his arm. This time, he left his hand where it was and welcomed the feeling, guilt free. "No, it's all thanks to you," he said. "You're the one that organised everything."

"Which I couldn't have done without the money that *you* donated."

"It was a team effort, then."

"It was." Ella smiled. "We make a good team."

Crane's phone beeped and vibrated in his pocket.

"Uh oh, it sounds like someone's got a voicemail," said Ella, giggling. "You have a listen; I need to pop to the ladies' room anyway."

Ella got up and walked away. Crane watched her, unable to take his eyes off her. Just like most of the other men in the restaurant, who were trying to get sneaky glances.

Crane pulled out his phone and pressed the notification to dial his voicemail. A female voice told him he had one new message and instructed him to press one to listen to it. He did.

"Mr Crane," a man's voice began. He sounded older and had a slight cockney twang. "You don't know me, but I certainly know a lot about you. I know that you murdered a very profitable and valued employee of mine, Mr Maddocks." The man paused, allowing Crane to take in his words.

Crane's jaw tightened.

"Now, usually under these circumstances, you would be in the next life by now; however, I've got a feeling that a man with your abilities may be of some use to me in the future. So, I look at it as you owe me one. I don't know when I'll want to cash in on this favour—it may be next week, next month, or maybe even next year—but when I do decide to cash in, it will certainly be in your interest to oblige me. I'm not one to make idle threats, so trust me when I say that you do not want to make an enemy of me.

"All of my employees call me Chief, and even though you are not strictly one of my employees, you will at some point in the near future do some work for me. So, when I do make contact with you, I suggest that you do not ignore me."

The voicemail ended abruptly.

Crane slowly lowered the phone from his ear. *Who the hell is Chief?*

"Is everything okay?"

Crane's eyes darted to Ella, who had already returned and slipped back into her seat. He hadn't even noticed.

"Yeah." He smiled, realising he'd been frowning. He slipped the phone back into his pocket and said, "It was just a message from a potential client."

# Acknowledgements

With special thanks:

To my publisher Cassandra, of Cahill Davis Publishing, for your support and for taking a chance on me.

To my editor, Lauren, for your wisdom and guidance in helping me smooth out all the rough edges.

To my wife, Jo, and daughters, Holly and Summer, for surrounding me with love and being my world.

To all my family and friends for your unwavering support.

And finally to my mother who, when I broke the news to her that I'd written a book and it was being published, told me to - and I quote - "f**k off". True story.

On a serious note, thank you for everything, Mother. You helped mould me into the man I am today.